Wendy Perriam

was expelled from a strict convent boarding-school and escaped to St Anne's College, Oxford, where she read History. After a stint in advertising and a succession of more offbeat jobs, ranging from the bizarre to the banal, she now writes full time.

Her previous novels, which include *Absinthe for Elevenses, Born of Woman, Fifty-Minute Hour, Breaking and Entering* and *Coupling,* have been acclaimed for their provocative mix of the sacred and the profane, and their extraordinary power to disturb, amuse and shock.

She is currently working on a new novel and a collection of short stories.

By the same author

ABSINTHE FOR ELEVENSES
CUCKOO
AFTER PURPLE
BORN OF WOMAN
THE STILLNESS THE DANCING
SIN CITY
DEVILS, FOR A CHANGE
FIFTY-MINUTE HOUR
BIRD INSIDE
MICHAEL, MICHAEL
BREAKING AND ENTERING
COUPLING

WENDY PERRIAM

Second Skin

Flamingo
An Imprint of HarperCollins*Publishers*

Flamingo
An Imprint of HarperCollins*Publishers*
77–85 Fulham Palace Road,
Hammersmith, London W6 8JB

Published by Flamingo 1999
9 8 7 6 5 4 3 2 1

First published in Great Britain by
Flamingo an Imprint of HarperCollins*Publishers* 1998

Author photograph by Jane Bown

The novel is entirely a work of fiction. The names,
characters and incidents portrayed in it are the work
of the author's imagination. Any resemblance to actual
persons, living or dead, events or localities is entirely
coincidental.

Grateful acknowledgement is made for permission to
reproduce lines from *A Little Light Music* by Stephen
Sondheim © 1973 Rilting Music Inc, WB Music Corp, USA
Warner/Chappell Music Publishing Ltd, London W1Y 3FA
Reproduced by permission of International Music
Publications Ltd

ISBN 0 00 649871 X

Printed and bound in Great Britain
by Clays Ltd, St Ives plc

For Sara Stoneham
– my guide in a new world of gigs, clubs,
raves, Doves, flat-shares, fashion, ad-speak.

Heartfelt thanks.

If I could choose
Freely in that great treasure-house
Anything from any shelf,
I would give you back yourself,
And power to discriminate
What you want and want it not too late.

EDWARD THOMAS

I

1

'Keep *still*, Catherine. I'm trying to get your head in.'

Catherine tensed obediently, self-conscious smile in place – she wasn't used to taking centre stage. Her audience had dissolved into a patchwork of colours: dark suits, floral dresses, a sudden splash of crimson or fierce green. Their faces were a blur; only Gerry's well-defined as he gazed into her eyes with a mock-Byronic air, hamming it up for the camera. They were standing at the centre table, about to cut the cake; the damp weight of his hand clamped firmly over hers on the ivory-handled knife.

'Okay,' he whispered. 'Here goes!'

Together they pressed down on the knife. At first the hard white icing resisted, but Gerry's hand tightened on hers, and suddenly the blade slid in, penetrating the moist body of the cake. She wiped the perspiration from her forehead. The marquee was strangely sensual: sultry-dim, and creating its own enclosed and intimate space. Gerry pulled the knife from the cake and held it up triumphantly, again playing to the crowd. For a startled moment she saw him as Macbeth – the first part she had ever watched him in – a lean and shaggy-haired Macbeth, about to murder the king.

A champagne cork exploded, dispelling the wild image, followed by a ricochet of cheers. She was handed a foaming glass and as she took a sip, the whispering bubbles fizzed against her eyes. She swallowed a mouthful of froth, watching her son step forward, immaculate, despite the heat, in a grey suit and crisp white shirt. He cleared his throat; his expression serious, as if he were about to address a business meeting.

'Ladies and gentlemen, please raise your glasses. I'd like to propose a toast to my parents on this very special . . .'

3

Catherine suppressed a smile. Even as a child, Andrew had been solemn; born anxious to please, and briskly mastering each stage of his development – weaned by six months, sitting up at seven months, crawling at eight months, reading *The Times* aged six. It was probably her own fault. She had got pregnant far too young and he must have sensed that his arrival on the scene was highly inconvenient and that he must pull his weight as soon as possible. She forced her mind back to the present. The guests were drinking the toast; eighty-odd champagne glasses glinting in the light. She had a sudden vision of the marquee taking off into the air with all of them on board, and floating high across Carshalton, powered by millions of bubbles.

'Happy Anniversary!'

'Happy Anniversary!'

People had been saying it all day. *Was* it happy, she wondered? Her feet ached really badly and her stomach was grumbling to itself. There hadn't been time to eat; her mouth too full of introductions, chit-chat. She looked hungrily at the cake – *two* cakes, side by side, a figure two and a figure five, tied with silver ribbon, iced with blue rosettes. The '2' was still unscathed, but the gash in the '5' revealed a dark, dense mass of fruit, thatched with yellow marzipan. She could almost taste the marzipan – its rich, damp, cloying sweetness; the tingle of almonds on her teeth. On their wedding day they hadn't had a cake, and certainly no grand marquee in a lush suburban garden. Back in 1968, Gerry had rewritten the script for weddings; directed a modern-dress, low-budget production, attacked by the critics (notably her father).

'Speech!' called Gerry's brother Ian, conspicuous in his party tie with its grinning Mickey Mouse.

Friends, Romans, Countrymen . . .

No, Gerry hadn't acted for more than fifteen years. Now he was playing his role of conventional businessman.

'I want to thank you all for coming today. I know some of you have travelled miles to be here. Well, I only hope it was worth your while!'

Laughter.

'And thank you for all these marvellous presents . . .'

Catherine's eye strayed to the mound of gift-wrapped packages. They had only opened two so far: a set of apostle teaspoons and some ornate silver candlesticks. Secretly, she would have preferred a plastic robot – one which could help her run the business, help her with the chores. Of course, they could always *pawn* the silver – might have to, if their finances didn't improve. They couldn't actually afford this party, especially the marquee: blue-striped, with a ruched blue and silver lining.

'Well, aren't you going to kiss her, Gerry?'

Ian again, red-faced from the wine. Gerry's other two brothers were there as well, plus wives and various offspring. And the whole tribe of aunts, uncles and cousins had made the trek from all parts of the country. Her own family was much thinner on the ground.

Dutifully, she held her face up to Gerry's, expecting a brief kiss, posed just long enough to gratify the guests and to be recorded by the phalanx of prurient cameras. But Gerry was seeking out her tongue, commandeering it, grazing the inside of her lips with his teeth. She could taste smoked salmon on his breath, feel the paunchy heat of his body melting into hers. He had kissed her like that on their wedding day – flagrantly, extravagantly, to the wild cheers of his actor-friends (and the silent disapproval of her father).

She shut her eyes and savoured the kiss, remembering the Gerry she had married: rebellious, thin, intense; the *actor* Gerard Jones, destined to become a star. Her painful feet and empty stomach ceased to matter any more. Gerry was reviving her; arousing her quite shamelessly with the sea-anemone distraction of his mouth. He had punched their secret code into her body and it was responding as it had at seventeen, when they had spent whole days in bed together, shutting out the world.

But today the world was here. She could hear catcalls from the crowd and a voice yelled, 'Break it up, you love-birds!' She pulled away reluctantly, knowing some of their more stuffy guests would regard the kiss as vulgar, and certainly inappropriate for a man who would be fifty next birthday. She blushed as she saw the lipstick stain on Gerry's dark-shadowed chin. Her make-up must be smudged, her hair ruffled, in the heat of the embrace.

She turned from Gerry and slipped into the crowd, wishing more of her own friends were there – her old friends, real friends, most of whom still lived up north.

'Catherine, have some cake.'

Gratefully, she accepted a plate from her daughter-in-law, admiring the elaborate blue rosette on every portion. Antonia had made and iced the cakes, as perfectly and professionally as she did everything in life. And now, with equal efficiency, she had sliced the '5' into dainty fingers and was busy distributing it to the guests.

'It's delicious,' Catherine smiled. 'Though it seems a shame to demolish such a work of art.'

'Well, I've left the second one intact. It'll keep for Christmas if you want.'

Christmas, she thought, with a sudden twinge of panic. Hordes of family and friends again – mostly Gerry's, of course. Not that she didn't like his family – it was the pressure she detested: December exploding into rush and hype as each day became shorter than the last, not just in light – in hours. But it was crazy worrying about Christmas in the middle of July.

She was accosted by a trio of Gerry's aunts before she could finish her cake. She was tempted to cram it into her mouth and guzzle it whole; instead, she sipped politely from her glass, the tart dryness of the champagne cutting through the sweetness of the marzipan. She could still taste Gerry's mouth: whisky and smoked salmon. Maybe tonight she should become the seventeen-year-old virgin for him again. She wondered sometimes if he had married her for her rarity value. Virgins were like unicorns in the so-called swinging sixties.

'How are you, Catherine dear?' Aunt Bridget was asking. 'You look wonderful – so smart.'

'Gosh, thanks. Though I must admit, I don't feel it.' She put an anxious hand up to her hair. She'd had it permed and highlighted, but her usual girl was off sick and the one who'd taken over had made it look unnaturally stiff. And as for her dress, well, Antonia had helped her choose it, steering her away from her favourite pinks and reds to staidly 'classic' beige.

'I see Gerry's on top form,' said Neville, breaking into the cluster of aunts with a wave of his cigar. 'That was some kiss! Real Hollywood style.'

'He's been saving it up for years,' joked Catherine, sipping more champagne to boost her courage. Neville was the most important of their customers.

'It's quite an achievement these days to have lasted twenty-five years,' Aunt Rosalind put in, patting her hand as if in sympathy.

It hadn't been *that* bad, thought Catherine – not all of it, at least. She glanced across at Gerry, who was chatting with his niece Susanna. His boyish figure might have gone, but his hair remained defiantly dark, and he still had such huge energy. She watched him sawing the air with his hands; his whole body involved in the conversation as he hugged himself in delight at something Susanna said, then lunged forward and flung his arm around the girl. It was the same with everything he did – working, eating, talking, even sleeping. Gerry tossed and turned half the night, talked in his sleep as if the days weren't long enough for all he had to say, pushed her almost out of the bed in his unconscious nightly gymnastics. She had grown used to it in time. At first horrified and bleary-eyed, now she could sleep through Gerry as she could sleep through a violent thunderstorm.

She suddenly wished they could be alone, his arm round *her*, not glamorous Susanna. They were so rarely on their own these days. That was the trouble with running a business from home – there were always other people around, and even in the evenings customers must be entertained, or late calls made to stockists.

A customer was approaching now – Francis Fenton-Cox, who owed them a large sum of money, but had to be handled with kid gloves in case he took his business elsewhere. Sometimes she resented *all* the customers. They had killed the man she had married, turned him into a workaholic who talked invoices and orders in his sleep (instead of fantastical gobbledegook). Though today he had been resurrected, become the ardent lover again; proved he could still put on a performance.

'I love your snazzy waistcoat, Francis,' she said, ashamed at stooping to flattery. 'It's so nice when men dress up.'

'My wife says I'm too fat for it, but the pattern helps to camouflage the bulge.'

Catherine laughed. 'Gerry always denies he's got a bulge at all. He calls his muscle!'

Gerry's assistant had sauntered over to join them, and the old couple from next door, and Ian was bearing down on her, a touch unsteady on his feet. She looked enviously at the group of children sprawling on the grass. They had taken off their shoes and socks and were gulping lemonade. She longed to kick off her own shoes, peel down her clammy tights, feel the cool caress of the grass against her naked feet. It was ninety degrees outside, even more in the marquee – extraordinarily un-English weather.

7

'Catherine, hi! I'm sorry to show up so late. But you know what I'm like.'

'I certainly do!' Catherine gave her friend a hug. Maeve was always late. Even on their wedding day she had arrived halfway through the ceremony, despite the fact she was unofficial brides-maid. *Very* unofficial. She had swept in, out of breath, dressed in a black leather jacket and a crotch-skimming red skirt. Today she wore a Chanel-style suit in innocuous baby-blue.

'So, how's Salford these days?' Catherine asked, thrilled to see Maeve in person after so many years of phone calls. They had lived in the same street before she and Gerry migrated south.

'Not the same without you.'

'Are those ghastly people still living in our house?'

'Yes, worse luck. But this incredible guy's just . . .'

'Auntie Catherine, telephone!' Her youngest nephew, Robert, tapped her on the arm. 'It's Kate.'

Catherine murmured her apologies and ran full tilt across the lawn into the house. Phone calls from India cost a fortune, and her daughter earned a pittance.

'Hello! Hello? Kate, can you hear me?'

Nothing but a sort of muffled roar.

'Listen, put the phone down, darling, and I'll phone you straight back, okay? What? Oh, you *are* there. Good. But the line's appallingly bad.' She strained her ears to catch the remnant of a voice.

Kate was saying that the phone call was a present – ten whole minutes, on *her*. She was sorry but she hadn't had a chance to buy them anything else.

'That's okay, we're knee-deep in presents here.'

'How's the party going?'

'Oh, splendidly. I just wish you could be with us.'

Silence. Had she sounded critical, Catherine wondered anxiously, as if she had *expected* Kate to come? She had to be so careful. Kate could be prickly, and anyway, she disapproved of empty shows of wealth. 'How are you, darling?' she asked, to fill the gap.

'Okay.'

Why couldn't Kate say 'fine'? Now she'd worry. She worried enough as it was – dysentery, malaria, no proper sanitation. And Kate's wisp of a voice made her sound as if she had been stricken already by some tropical disease. 'Are they still working you into the ground?'

8

Kate's answer was drowned in static. She ached to cut through all the interference and evasions and to say, 'I miss you, darling, terribly,' but that too might seem a form of disapproval. She had no right to miss a daughter who did worthy work with paupers and untouchables. Kate was based at a centre in Gurgaon, which sounded primitive in the extreme – she washed each morning in a bucket, slept on a thin straw mattress with neither sheets nor pillows, and even travelling the twenty miles into Delhi on the lumbering local bus was apparently quite an experience in itself. It usually entailed being crammed into a seat-for-two with a whole extended Indian family: babies, toddlers, uncles, grandmas, over-flowing shopping bags, plus a few live chickens thrown in for good measure.

'How's Paul?' asked Catherine, seizing on a subject which seemed slightly less remote. Paul was the only other westerner in Gurgaon.

'Busy!'

Kate never opened up about matters of the heart and had given no hint as to whether Paul was 'serious', or just a casual friend. All they knew was that he was writing a new-age travel guide and had an interest in Zen Buddhism.

Catherine glanced over her shoulder. Robert had followed her indoors and was standing in the hall, surrounded by several smaller children. Their inquisitive eyes and ears made the already flagging conversation still more difficult. 'D'you want to speak to Daddy?' she suggested. 'It'll take me a minute to fetch him, but . . .'

'Look, tell you what, Mum – I'll ring again later, okay? And hope we get a better line. Your voice keeps fading away.'

'So does yours.'

'I'll try again at half past ten. I won't have much chance till then. That's six o'clock your time.'

'Lovely, darling. I'll make sure Daddy's standing by.'

'Okay. Happy anniversary and everything.'

'Thanks. And thank you for the call. And, Kate, do take care, for goodness' sake. You know how much I worry. Oh, and by the way, I sent those things you wanted.' She couldn't seem to ring off, wanted to cling to the last vestige of her daughter, however faint or uncommunicative. Sometimes she feared they might never lay eyes on Kate again – she had moved to a different world with a different time-scale and a different set of values. Thank God for

9

Andrew, who lived just down the road and spent every other Sunday with them.

She replaced the receiver slowly, frowning to herself.

'Can we have some ice-cream, Auntie Catherine?' Robert asked. 'We're ever so hot and sticky.'

'Yes, 'course you can.'

The children followed her into the kitchen, where she doled out raspberry ripple, marvelling at their appetite. They had already polished off three giant-size pizzas, several dozen sausages, a regiment of gingerbread men and their own cake in the shape of a video-game, which she had decorated lovingly with Smarties. She had preferred making the children's food to all the fiddly bits and pieces for the grown-ups. Usually she enjoyed cooking, but not in a blistering heat-wave and with one eye on the clock.

She sprinkled each ice-cream dish with nuts. 'Why not take it into the garden?' she suggested. She needed a few moments alone, to get her second wind. The first guests had come at noon and now it was almost four o'clock. A few close friends and family were staying for the evening and she'd be wilting by then unless she grabbed a bite to eat. She picked up the cut-glass trifle dish – very little left but a tablespoon of soggy sponge and a few squashed strawberries bleeding into a swirl of cream. She scooped them up with her fingers, cream and all, then began licking out the bowl. At that moment Antonia walked in. Catherine blushed in confusion. Her daughter-in-law was unfailingly correct and wouldn't dream of gnawing chicken bones or eating fish and chips from the paper, least of all licking out a bowl at a formal luncheon party. She sprang to her feet and dumped the dish in the sink. 'Er, everything all right out there?'

'Yes, fine. I just came to see if you needed any help.'

'It all seems to be under control.' Catherine cast an eye over the worktops piled high with dirty plates. 'I . . . I was just about to stack the dishwasher.'

'Not now, Catherine! You're needed to be hostess. Andrew and I can do the clearing up.'

'No, I wouldn't hear of it. People will be going soon and we can all muck in after that. I'll see you in the garden, okay? I must just dash and have a pee.'

She escaped into the cloakroom, dodging a couple more stray children on the way. She locked the door and stole a quick glance in the mirror. Her cheeks were still flushed and she had kissed off most of her lipstick, but otherwise she'd 'do'. That's what her father always said when she presented herself as a child for his inspection or approval. But he would say it with an air of disappointment, as if he were comparing her unfavourably with the mother she knew only from the photo on the mantelpiece. Even now, when faced with her reflection in the mirror, she felt the same ridiculous hope that her boring grey-blue eyes and fairish 'nothing' hair would be transformed by some instant miracle into the dark dramatic beauty of the lady in the silver frame. Then she wouldn't merely 'do' – she would be beautiful, and loved.

She sat for longer than she needed on the toilet-seat, taking the chance to rest her feet. The shoes were Antonia's choice as well – too high for her, but an exact match for the dress. Thank God her son appeared to be living up to Antonia's ideals. First he had got a good degree from Cambridge, and was now an up-and-coming quantity surveyor at the age of only twenty-four. The pair of them were planning to move house; to find something better suited to Andrew's status and Antonia's aspirations. In another ten years, they'd probably be living in a house like this – detached, four bedrooms, double garage, double glazing.

She stood up and leaned on the windowsill, pushing the net curtain aside and looking out at the front garden. Sometimes she couldn't quite believe that they had finished up in such a conventional suburb, with the things they had once despised: net curtains, crazy paving, leaded lights, even an ornamental pond, for heaven's sake. They had begun their married life in a rented basement in Bolton, moved to a leaky houseboat on the Mersey and upped sticks a dozen times since then. 'Selling out' was a phrase they never used, either to each other or to anybody else. They had tacitly accepted that Gerry could make it as a dealer for office furniture, but not, alas, as Hamlet.

Now she was as rooted in Carshalton as she had been anywhere, though it wasn't exactly friendly. But at least she knew a few people in the road and one or two local shopkeepers, and, as Gerry was fond of telling her, they were lucky that their property had practically doubled in value. (Yet she was still stupid enough to miss the leaky houseboat.)

She started at a tap on the door. Maeve, no doubt. Her friend had never been one for respecting locked doors.

'Darling, it's me. Can I come in?' A conspiratorial whisper from Gerry.

She opened the door with a grin and bolted it quickly behind him before anyone could spot them.

'Antonia said you were in here. I thought I'd sneak away and join you for a moment. I'm melting in this heat.' He splashed his face with cold water, his bulk filling the small room, his hot male smell cutting through the whiff of Floral Bouquet. He kissed her, his face still wet. 'Do you think anyone would notice if we nipped out for a couple of hours? We could drive to the Cobham Hilton and book the honeymoon suite.'

'Oh, *yes*,' she whispered. 'Let's go.' She held him tightly, aware of the fold of flab around his middle. Despite the disappointments, they'd survived. He was still her mate, her rock, her oldest friend.

Suddenly he laughed, and the noise vibrated through her. 'Remember that time your father caught us snogging in the loo and went berserk?'

'It was the only place we could snog. And I still felt terribly guilty, even when he was out. I couldn't imagine Daddy ever kissing anyone.'

'He must have kissed your mother. They did produce *you*, after all!'

She shook her head. 'He probably ordered me from a catalogue.'

'Well, it was a very special catalogue, that's all I can say.'

'Oh, Gerry, I do love you.'

'Still?'

'Mm.'

'Truly?'

'Mm.'

'You sound tired.'

'I am.' They had been up since five that morning; she finishing the cooking; he setting out the drinks and glasses, rearranging furniture, watering the lawn.

'Want me to take you up to bed?'

'Yes, please!'

He picked her up and slung her over his shoulder. 'Okay, off we go. Hold tight!'

'Gerry, *no!*' She struggled in his arms, pummelling his shoulders and laughing helplessly as her elbow bumped against the wall and they all but collapsed in a heap. 'Put me down, you monster! You're messing up my dress. And we ought to go back to the party. People will be wondering where we are.'

'Let them wonder.' He set her on her feet again, held her face gently between his hands. 'Come on, give me a kiss – no, not a peck like that. I want the sort of kiss that used to scandalize your father!'

She stole a glance at the clock. Ten past midnight. Would they ever get to bed? She was operating now on automatic pilot, feet sore, back aching, but smile still fixed in place.

Gerry's father was just coming in from the kitchen and spotted her standing alone. 'Catherine, dear, I've been waiting all evening for a dance. And this nice slow waltz will suit me fine.'

He steered her on to the impromptu dance floor – an area of carpet in the sitting-room clear of furniture and rugs – and pressed her tightly against his chest, elbows out, head held high, as if he were on *Come Dancing*. For a man of eighty-one Jack was surprisingly agile, though his once thick black hair was now a fuzz of thistle-down and his skin was dappled with age-spots like bruises on an apple.

'Where on earth did you find these records?' he asked. 'I'd no idea you had any Victor Sylvester.'

'Oh, you know what Gerry's like! He probably bought them in an auction as part of a job lot. The rhythm's good though, isn't it?'

'Yes, grand! It takes me back to my courting days.'

'I bet you broke a lot of hearts then, Jack.'

'Not half! And I'd be just the same now if it wasn't for my dicey chest. I'm afraid I'd get too short of breath to last the course.'

She laughed. She had always loved Gerry's parents, partly because they loved *her* so much. Right from the beginning they had accepted her and were proud of her. Her own father had been frosty about the wedding. His only child was destined for better things than leaving school early to marry a jumped-up actor. She was surprised he had even given his permission.

'Careful, Jack! We're on a collision course.' She took the lead and guided him out of Gerry's path. Her husband was doing the Charleston – to a waltz – jerking to and fro like a manic puppet on too many strings, all but lifting fragile Susanna off her feet.

She felt tired just watching them. She shut her eyes a moment and the music boomed louder: a roll of drums, a sentimental echo from a soupy violin. Her breasts felt damp beneath the clingy silk, her head spinning from the waltz, the wine. The party had gone well. 'A fantastic day!' the guests had said as they trickled away in twos and threes, hot but clearly happy. Only a few stalwarts remained, but they showed no signs of flagging. Gerry and Susanna were in their element; Maeve had danced with every male except Ian (who was decidedly the worse for wear), and was now twirling round on her own, and even Andrew and Antonia were talking animatedly with another couple – about house prices, no doubt.

'Oh lord!' Jack panted. 'Someone's changed the record. What on earth are they playing now?'

'It's rock-and-roll,' said Catherine. 'And if you'll excuse me, Jack, I'm going to sit this one out.'

'Oh no you're not.' Gerry swooped past at that moment and caught her in his arms. 'Watch this, Susanna. Your Auntie Catherine's quite a little swinger on the quiet!'

'Gerry, no, I *can't*. I'm dead on my feet.'

'Sorry, I insist. Come on, darling – just one dance.'

'Well, let me take my shoes off then.' She eased them off, instantly shrinking to the level of his shoulder. Gerry was six foot.

He seized her hand and threw himself into a manic jive, his arm a powerful spring, pushing her back, pulling her towards him, twirling her round wildly. It was so long since they had danced, even a quickstep, let alone rock-and-roll. Yet it was in her bloodstream, part of Gerry, part of her own youth – Little Richard, Jerry Lee Lewis, Gene Vincent. And the faster Gerry stomped and span, the younger she became, until she was back at Blackpool Palais, with long, long hair and the skimpiest of skirts, on their miraculous two-day honeymoon.

She suddenly realized they were the only ones dancing. Everyone else was standing watching. Gerry put on a show for them, swirling her this way and that, revelling in the limelight, his energy unstoppable. And she was gloriously at one with him, following where he led, his magnetic arm pumping her full of adrenalin like some illicit wonder drug.

All at once he staggered back, clutching his chest with an exaggerated grimace and rolling his eyes up in his head.

'Stop fooling, darling!' she laughed. 'You almost pulled me over then.'

A noise came from his throat – a sort of choking gasp. My God, she thought, he *isn't* fooling. His face had gone a ghastly grey as he keeled over and collapsed against the sofa.

'He's fainted,' said Susanna. 'Quick, someone sit him up.'

Catherine fell to her knees beside him, desperately trying to remember her first aid. She loosened his tight belt, unfastened the top buttons of his shirt. Other people crowded round, voices overlapping in a confusion of suggestions.

'Get some water.'

'No, brandy.'

'Wouldn't he be better lying down?'

She struggled to move him to a more comfortable position, but he seemed almost to be resisting, despite his sluggish state.

'Don't panic,' Andrew said, taking charge with his usual calm authority. 'He needs some air. Keep back, please, everyone.' He took the glass of water Susanna had brought from the kitchen and held it to his father's lips.

'*No.*' Catherine pushed the glass away, trying to make her dead voice work as she cradled the slumped body in her arms. 'Dial 999, for Christ's sake, and get an ambulance.'

2

Catherine lay rigid in the dark. The fear would pass. She mustn't give way to it, mustn't put the light on – that would be cowardly. She was drenched with sweat, but only because of the heat. It was quite normal to sweat in these muggy summer nights.

She reached out her hand and touched the expanse of sheet beside her. She was lying on the very edge of the bed – a habit she couldn't break. Gerry had always needed space.

And yet they had shut him in a coffin, a hateful claustrophobic box, disguised with pompous flowers. All through the cremation she had felt her fury rising: how dare they coop him up like that; no room for him to toss and thresh; no one to hear if he called out in his sleep.

'Gerry,' she mouthed. 'You're all right. I'm here.'

But where was *he*? Not even in his coffin now. If only the vicar was right and there was some peaceful and consoling place, where she could go herself and find him. But she had never believed in an afterlife, not since they had told her (with peculiar forced smiles) that her mother was with Jesus. Even at the age of four, she had known it was a lie. Why should Daddy cry so much if Mummy was safe in heaven? *She* hadn't cried – not then. She hadn't dared. If she wasn't a good girl, Daddy might die too.

The black nothingness was building up, filling the whole room: a thick, black, smothering duvet pressed against her face. She heard her husband's panicked cry in the ambulance – or was it coming from her own mouth? It was the last sound he had ever made. But she had continued talking to *him*, frantically, relentlessly, against the wailing of the siren. 'Gerry, you're going to be all right. We're

16

nearly at the hospital. The doctors will know what to do. Don't leave me, Gerry. I love you, do you hear?'

She plunged out of bed and switched on every light in the room: the central light, the light above the dressing-table, both the bedside lamps. The dark was still there – beyond the curtains, inside her. She hugged her body to stop it shaking. Just breathe, she told herself. Breathe deeply. Morning will come. It always does. Eventually.

Thank God it was summer. It would be light by five o'clock and she could get up and start the day. Daylight always helped. Just the sense of things happening as they should: dawn breaking, sun rising. You took so much for granted – until it wasn't there.

The alarm clock said ten to three. Nights were a new land for her: the different shades of darkness, the different sounds. Or no sounds. Silence could keep you awake. Total numbing stillness. She was so used to Gerry's comforting disturbance.

She ran her hand across the smooth curve of the phone. She couldn't ring Andrew, not at this hour. He and Antonia had been staying since . . . since . . . They'd been marvellous, both of them, but they kept wanting to tidy her up, stop her crying. They had suggested pills, or counselling, and continually looked anxious, which made her feel worse still.

You had to cry. It was a physical necessity, like breathing. She had cried like this just after Kate was born. Post-natal depression, the midwife said. Odd how you cried over birth the same as death. She watched her tears dripping on her nightdress, making blotches on the flimsy pink-sprigged cotton. She ought to be wearing black. There was nothing black in her wardrobe except the new outfit she had bought for the funeral. It had seemed heartless to go shopping for a death, browsing through rails of dresses, posing in front of mirrors.

Kate had worn blue – a respectful blue, drab, like faded ink. She had looked faded altogether and had barely said a word during the whole of her two-week stay.

Perhaps Kate blamed her for the death. And it *was* her fault in some ways. She should have been stricter over his drinking and his diet; made sure he had proper check-ups with the doctor. And they should have talked to each other more, as they never failed to do in public, with friends, reps, stockists, customers. They could put on a show at parties, even kiss each other at parties, but, alone again, they would revert to their fretful busyness. And she was usually too tired for . . .

Sex. Such an insignificant word. Too short for all it meant – like death.

'Stop it,' she said. 'Stop wallowing in misery. Hundreds of people are far worse off.' Children killed; whole families wiped out. Death stained every newspaper; darkened every bulletin on radio and television: carnage, earthquakes, terrible diseases. If she couldn't sleep, she might as well do something useful, rather than cower in the bedroom feeling sorry for herself.

She found her slippers and crept downstairs. It had become second nature to creep, so as not to disturb Andrew and Antonia. They had wanted her to stay with *them*, but she preferred to be here with Gerry. It wasn't just his presence. There were actual tangible bits of him still around the house. She had found his nail-clippings in the waste-bin, and laboriously picked out each tiny fragment from the mess of dirty Kleenex. She had put them in an envelope and locked them in the bureau drawer. And then she'd discovered a few stray hairs in his comb and laid them in there reverently as well. She wished she could preserve his smell – that indefinable smell on his clothes which she was terrified might fade. Last night, she had taken his jacket to bed and held it tight against her, stroking the rough-textured tweed, burying her face in it.

She switched on more lights in the hall, wondering how to keep herself busy. She ought to sort out Gerry's clothes, but she couldn't even bear to look at them. *Or* the stack of theatre programmes he had been collecting since the fifties. Andrew had cleared out all his other stuff, and Philip, John and Graham had already closed the business and found safer jobs elsewhere. She could hardly believe the speed of it. A company Gerry had taken ten years to build, dismantled in a month. The three reps were dead as well, in a sense. She had grown so used to them bustling in and out – Philip with his ginger hair, John invariably smoking, Graham's booming voice. But you could hardly blame them for leaving a sinking ship, especially with the captain gone.

She wandered down the hall to Gerry's offices – once the dining-room and study. How bare the two rooms seemed, drawers empty, files denuded, desks without their usual clutter. Gerry had occupied the larger room while she worked in the smaller one as his assistant and receptionist, screening calls to protect him from time-wasters and doing the bulk of the paperwork. She sat down at her desk again, fiddling with a stray paper-clip. The room was deathly quiet. She was used to the whir of the printer, the judder of the fax machine, Gerry's voice barking down the phone. She would never hear his voice again. The thought was like a stab from a knife. There were so many unbearable 'nevers'. She would never wake in the morning to find him there beside her; never share another meal with him; never see him in her life again.

She made herself get up. Impossible to sit there dwelling on such horrors. Gerry must come back. He *must*.

She mooched into the sitting-room, which looked unnaturally clean and tidy. She had spring-cleaned it yesterday, at two AM – the first night she had been on her own in the house without Andrew and Antonia. The cards, though, she had left. But they couldn't sit there for ever, with their infuriating stunted words. *Sympathy.* You felt sympathy when someone caught a cold or failed their driving test. *Loss.* You lost spectacles, or keys, or games of tennis. Yet it would be callous to throw them out. People had cared enough to send them. A few had added their own embarrassed messages beneath the printed words; promises of help, sometimes followed up with phone calls and visits. She was actually very fortunate.

She opened the top sideboard-drawer. The cards could go in there until she had decided what to do with them. So many decisions, some she'd simply postponed. What to do with his shaving gear, the ancient razor and splayed-out brush which now seemed unbearably precious. Or the cache of old coins she had found in a tobacco tin, including the lucky sixpence given to him by an actor-friend on the first night of *Macbeth*. Lucky. She shuddered at the word.

The drawer was full of tablecloths, so she opened the next one down and found another lot of cards – from the silver wedding. Someone must have stuffed them in there while she was at the hospital. She hadn't even noticed they were gone. How grotesque, she thought, congratulations and condolences arriving within days of each other. She picked up the top one: a silver bow and a huge '25', embossed in silk, looking iced and formal like the anniversary cake. They were going to keep the second cake for Christmas, but she didn't ever want to *see* it again. Two was a mockery now. How could she have been so crass as to have seen those twos as her right: two sets of towels, two toothbrushes, two places at the table, a double bed? Now she was a one.

A widow.

Except widows were other people. And older than her, with grey hair and folded hands. Her hands were never still. She had caught Gerry's restlessness and was constantly seeking things to do.

As she closed the drawer and straightened up, she happened to glance in the mirror. She gasped. Gerry was *there*, behind her own reflection, smiling at her, clear in every detail. She wheeled round, to touch him, hold him, but her arms closed over nothing.

She began to shake. She must be going mad. How on earth could her husband be there when she had seen his death certificate? She hadn't actually read it. Andrew had brought it from the registrar, but she had thrust it back into his hands and stumbled into the kitchen, where she'd been preparing lunch for him. She had poured all her concentration into peeling, chopping, simmering, so that nothing else existed beyond the chopping-board and saucepan.

The panic was returning. She sank down into Gerry's chair, closed her eyes and let the wave break over her; accepting it, submitting, because she had no other choice.

You're all right, she kept repeating. You'll be fine – just give it time.

She gripped the chair's cold leather arm. Gerry's arm had rested there so often, his fingers drumming impatiently as he sat working on some problem.

You're *not* alone, she told herself. You've got lovely children, wonderful in-laws. You're surrounded by kind people.

So why did they all seem dead; the whole street deserted, the world stretching black and barren to infinity?

She dragged herself out of the chair. Stupid to be so melodramatic. She might as well go back to bed for all the good she was doing down here. Yet she knew she would never sleep. She trudged upstairs and drifted into Kate's old room, picking up the koala bear Kate had had since babyhood. 'Poor thing,' she whispered, 'left all on your own.'

Andrew's room was next door – or Andrew and Antonia's now. No shabby ragged bears there, only a magazine of Antonia's lying on the bedside table. She took it into her own room and sat down with it on the stool. There was still no breath of air. The room was stifling and oppressive, as if all the day's heat had accumulated here. The alarm clock said five past three. Time had changed, along with everything else. Widows' time limped and crawled. She leafed through the magazine. Twos again. Everyone in couples: men and women, hand in hand, smiling from advertisements or illustrating stories. Once upon a time . . .

Suddenly she sat bolt upright. There was a spider by the bed. Huge and black, with long hairy legs. She clutched the edge of the stool, not daring to take her eyes off it. Suppose it scuttled towards her, ran across her bare foot?

Gerry had always dealt with spiders. He actually liked the things. Once, at drama school, he'd had to improvise being a spider and had spent hours observing them. The fascination had lasted, developed into a bond of fellow-feeling. 'One of your friends!' she used to joke if she came across a spider in the house, although he knew quite well that she detested them. He would remove them for her, carefully and considerately, with the aid of an inverted jar, and deposit them gently outside. But he wasn't here to do that. And the great thing was advancing towards her – all legs, grotesquely ugly. She couldn't kill it. Gerry would never forgive her. She held her breath in terror, willing it to stop moving. And all at once, uncannily, it did stop. She wondered if spiders had minds; whether they could think, or feel; respond. For all she knew, it too could have lost its mate. Death was so random – a careless foot, a weak heart.

She wiped her sweaty hands on her nightdress, watching the spider all the time. It was alone, like her, sleepless, like her, and perhaps just as scared as she was. After all, however big it looked, she was a giant in comparison – a towering monster which could crush it underfoot, destroy it in an instant. She thought so much about death these days, the millions of deaths throughout history jumbled in her mind: young men like Andrew bleeding in the trenches, medieval peasants dying in the plague, cavemen savaged by wild animals. She had cried for all of them. *And* for the dead bird she'd found in the garden yesterday. Even the dead plant in Gerry's office. It was ridiculous, excessive, but she seemed to feel pain more intensely, especially the pain of weak and tiny things. Like sparrows. Spiders.

She eyed the creature again. It was only inches away, yet she found she could actually look at it without shuddering.

'If . . . if Gerry was here,' she stammered, 'he'd probably talk to you. He used to do that sometimes, you know, just to wind me up. He'd tell you what a handsome chap you are and what fantastic long legs you've got.'

She was using Gerry's intonation, even his teasing voice. And suddenly it dawned on her that Gerry must have sent the spider. He had seen how panicky she was without Andrew and Antonia, so he'd arranged for one of his 'friends' to come instead.

She smiled at the absurd idea, but already she felt better. She might even find the courage to switch off the lights and get back into bed. At least it would be more comfortable than perching on a stool all night.

'Listen,' she told the spider, 'I'm going to get up now, but don't be frightened, will you? I won't hurt you, I promise. I only want to turn the lights off, okay?'

She stood up very cautiously and tiptoed past the spider. She would feel a whole lot safer if she put it under a jar, but it might die without air and she couldn't face another death. Besides, it hadn't moved since she'd spoken to it, so perhaps Gerry was looking after her and would make sure it stayed there motionless, right on through the night.

'Good lad,' she whispered, wondering if it *was* male. Gerry called them all 'good lad', regardless. She climbed wearily into bed and turned off both the bedside lamps.

Even if she didn't sleep, she and Gerry's messenger could keep each other company.

3

'Would you care to take a seat in here, Mrs Jones?'

Catherine followed the receptionist into a small but elegant waiting-room. *Was* she still Mrs Jones? The name – like so much else – was Gerry's more than hers. The family was mostly his, and their circle of acquaintances, and the business, of course, and even the house (in the sense that he had chosen it while she was still up north). She had never really liked Jones as a surname. Gerry Jones had a certain jaunty ring to it, but Catherine Jones was just plain ordinary.

'Mr Ashby won't be long. Can I offer you a cup of coffee?'

'No thank you.' She was anxious to get the meeting over. Accountants made her nervous at the best of times, and Howard Ashby, senior partner at Ashby Storr, had sounded distinctly daunting on the phone. She had never met him before. He had been away for most of August and it was his assistant who had gone through Gerry's papers.

'I'll let you know when Mr Ashby's free.' The receptionist gave her a motherly smile.

Catherine smiled back dutifully. She was already accustomed to the fact that widows were treated like nursery-school children. Or shunned like Kate's untouchables.

She deliberately avoided the sun, which was forcing its way through the window, threatening her with its gloating golden tentacles. Yesterday she had sat for hours in its heat, hoping it might scorch away her grief, transform her pale and vulnerable skin into a tough brown hide which would stop her feeling everything so acutely. But all she had achieved was acutely painful sunburn.

She shrugged at her own stupidity and stood looking at the

magazines and newspapers fanned out meticulously on the table, as if you weren't meant to actually read them, just admire the neat array. She chose the *Daily Telegraph*, merely because it was at the end of the row, and sat down with it in a stiff-backed chair. The centre pages showed pictures of the heat-wave: office-workers sun-bathing in Hyde Park; half-naked tourists queuing for ice-cream. People shouldn't die in the summer. It was supposed to be happy – holiday time. She scanned the statistics in the text: the hottest summer since . . . The driest August for . . .

The coldest, saddest August for quarter of a century.

She laid the *Telegraph* aside and stared down at the carpet: grey squiggles on maroon. The furniture was expensive repro – something Gerry loathed. 'If you can't afford antiques,' he would say, 'then buy honest junk till you can.' They owned some of each: bargains they'd picked up in the early days and kept for sentimental reasons, and some really nice Victorian stuff, bought more recently. Their house was bursting at the seams, but *this* room seemed bare and dead. And the flower arrangement on the table reminded her of the funeral: regimented waxen blooms with no smell to them, no character.

She picked up the paper again, determined not to think about that terrible occasion. The long delay had upset her more than anything – 'fully booked' sounded more like a restaurant or hair-dresser's than a crematorium: desperate corpses queuing at the door for a blow-dry or a meal.

'Mr Ashby will see you now, Mrs Jones.'

Instinctively she smoothed her skirt; put an embarrassed hand up to her sore, sun-reddened face. She was ushered into an oppressive-looking office, with tobacco-coloured walls and heavy curtains shrouding both the windows. No chance of the sun gaining entry here.

'Ah, Mrs Jones. How good of you to come at such short notice.'

The voice was plummy, the handshake firm. And Mr Ashby was thin: a tall and angular man, with sparse grey hair and a finely sculpted face. Mrs Ashby probably kept him on a rigid diet, as Antonia did with Andrew – a low-fat diet to reduce the risk of heart attacks.

'Do sit down – that's it. I'm so sorry I was away at the time of Mr Jones's death, but may I take this chance to express my deepest sympathy.'

'Thank you.'

He pulled his chair closer to the desk and opened the folder in front of him. 'Well, I'm glad to see there are no problems with the will and that probate has been sorted out.'

She nodded. She and Gerry had made their wills a few years back. They had treated it as something of a joke, feeling they were far too young to take the matter seriously. They had each bequeathed everything to the other, which seemed the simplest solution and dispensed with the need for lawyers.

Mr Ashby cleared his throat and removed a sheaf of papers from the folder. 'Now, as you know, Mr Lloyd has been going through your late husband's affairs . . .'

Late husband. Gerry was *still* her husband. She glanced at the photo on Mr Ashby's desk, showing a wife and two daughters with peachy complexions and perfect teeth. She suddenly ached to be Mrs Ashby – her skin not red and sore, her husband lying close to her each night.

'. . . So you see, Mrs Jones, things aren't as straightforward as we might have hoped.'

Lord! What had he been saying? She hadn't heard a word. Her mind wandered so, these days. She spent too much time with Gerry, even now, six weeks after . . . 'I'm sorry, Mr Ashby, I didn't quite catch what you said.'

'Well, you remember the second mortgage your late husband took out in 1986?'

She fixed her eyes on the expanse of mahogany desk, forcing herself to concentrate. 'Yes. Sixty thousand pounds. It was for a special pension plan.'

Mr Ashby picked up a paperclip, studied it a moment, then put it down again. 'Mm, I'm afraid it *wasn't* a pension plan.'

'What d'you mean? Gerry and I discussed it. I remember it distinctly. Things were going well then, and we felt we could afford to make . . .' Her voice faltered to a stop. Mr Ashby was looking slightly awkward, deliberately avoiding her eyes. He had placed the tips of his fingers together and was frowning down at them.

'No, Mrs Jones, the money was actually invested in a theatre company.'

'A what?'

'A small fringe company. It was run by one of Mr Jones's old friends – someone he'd known at drama school, apparently.'

'But I don't understand. Are you *sure*? I mean, he told me . . .'
Gerry wouldn't lie to her. They had always shared the important
decisions, been open about everything. 'Anyway, it seems such a
crazy thing to do. D . . . do you know more about it? Where was
it based? And what sort of company was it?'

Mr Ashby slowly unlatched his fingers. 'Well, they appear to
have set it up in Manchester, in a room above a pub. And as far
as I can gather, it was rather avant garde. They planned to do
modern-dress Shakespeare, interspersed with contemporary plays,
and take the productions on tour throughout the Pennines.'

She stared at him incredulously – he must have got it wrong.

'It's true such projects can, of course, be precarious,' he continued in a maddeningly unhurried tone. 'But this proposition
seemed relatively sound. Several experienced actors were involved,
who'd agreed to work for next to nothing in order to keep the
costs down. And there were one or two other backers – solid local
people who felt there was an educational need for such an enter-
prise. And Mr Jones obviously thought he'd get a return on his
investment.'

'That's madness!' she burst out. 'I can't believe he'd be so
gullible.'

'Yes, unfortunately, the venture folded.' Mr Ashby leaned back
in his chair, as if to put more distance between them. 'And I'm
afraid that means that when you come to sell the house, the proceeds will be much less than you expected. I mean with such a
substantial amount outstanding on the second mortgage.'

'But I'm not going to sell the house,' she retorted, angry with
him as much as with Gerry. 'I've decided to hand it over to my
son. He's looking for a new place, so it seems an ideal solution.'

She had broached the idea yesterday, when the three of them
were sitting in the garden having tea. (She had cursed herself for
getting out four cups.) Antonia had jumped at the offer – she had
always liked the house and hadn't seen anything else remotely
suitable. And Andrew was delighted at the prospect of living in a
fair-sized place without the financial strain, not to mention cutting
out the hassle of estate agents. She had already thought of how
she'd divide the house: she would have the top floor – the cosy
attic floor, which could easily be made self-contained. The last
thing she wanted was to get in their way, or be any sort of burden.
But with them living below, she wouldn't feel so frighteningly

alone. And she would be there on hand to babysit, once they decided to have children.

'But Mrs Jones, will your son be able to meet such heavy mortgage repayments? I understand he's only twenty-four.'

'Well, if he can't, *I'll* pay them.'

'I'm afraid that might prove rather difficult – with the business gone and your husband's other debts.'

'Wh . . . what other debts?' Catherine closed her eyes. She felt faint and sick, and not just from the sunburn. How could Gerry have deceived her like this, left such a ghastly mess? Mr Ashby was droning on about unpaid bills, income tax overdue . . .

'Why didn't Gerry *tell* me?' she cut in. 'He always told me everything.'

Mr Ashby shook his head, as if uncertain how to answer. 'I expect he didn't want to worry you, my dear. And remember, the business was in profit then, doing remarkably well. He probably thought he couldn't lose.'

'Well, he must have taken leave of his senses, that's all I can say. He worked in fringe theatre himself, so he knew how insecure it was. Experimental companies were the first to go to the wall. We saw it happen often – directors bursting with ideals, but without the business nous to make it work.' She brushed her tears away. Once she had *shared* those ideals; supported Gerry (emotionally and financially) when he had joined a tiny impoverished company who charged peanuts at the box office in the belief that theatre should be accessible to everyone, not just the well-heeled.

'I do realize what a shock it must be, Mrs Jones. But let's try to be positive and see what we can do to make the most of your assets. If you put the house on the market, that will release *some* money – yes, even with the second mortgage. And of course, there's your late husband's life insurance, which amounts to quite a tidy sum.'

Catherine fumbled for her hankie. Such stupid meaningless words. Nothing was tidy, not now.

'And I understand you have some fine pieces of antique furniture . . . ?'

She scrunched the hankie tightly in her hand. Not just Gerry gone, but the very bricks and mortar, the chairs they'd reupholstered, the Victorian table they had restored so lovingly. And, worst of all, her basic trust in Gerry gone; great gaping holes opening up in their marriage.

27

'Look, I'm sorry you're distressed, Mrs Jones, but . . .'

'I'm *not* distressed. At least, not about the house. *Or* the bloody furniture.' She was startled by her own words – she never swore. 'I'm upset because my husband bloody lied to me.' She slumped back in her chair, embarrassed by her outburst, tears still sliding down her face.

'Yes, but I'm sure he did it with the best of intentions, to spare you any worry, my dear. I see it very often in this business. Many husbands mean well, but, alas, they get themselves into financial tangles and are then reluctant to admit it, even to their nearest and dearest. Look, what I suggest is that we have a second meeting when you've had time to digest the news. And meanwhile, here's a detailed breakdown of . . .'

She took the folder from him. She didn't give a damn about the figures – tax returns, outstanding debts. What mattered was her marriage. Had Gerry deceived her from the start, or only in the last few years?

'I'll phone you in a day or two, Mrs Jones, and we can make another appointment.'

'Thank you.' In a daze she let him lead her to the door, aware that he was supporting her with a kindly, condescending arm. And then she was handed over to the receptionist – the bewildered child who must be guided to the exit, dismissed with a pat on the head.

She stumbled out into the clamour of the High Street, flinching at the slap of the sun. She looked around in confusion – the place seemed utterly alien. The shop-signs and hoardings might as well have been in Urdu for all the sense she could make of them. But she was causing an obstruction, standing like a dummy in the middle of the pavement. A woman with a pushchair was trying to get past, her baby whimpering fretfully and another child dragging at her arm.

She made herself walk on, blinded by the display of fruit outside a greengrocer's: vicious greens, stinging yellows, a lurid pile of blood-red plums. Other people lived in 3-D Technicolor, but her world had become dark and flat, like an old black and white television set with blurred pictures, fuzzy sound. Gerry too was receding into shadow. Had she ever really known him? What hurt the most was the fact that he hadn't confided in her. Investing in a theatre company would be a long and complex process – negotiations, phone-calls, maybe trips to Manchester, back to their old haunts. But she hadn't known a thing about it. And when the project folded, he must have felt an appalling sense of shock. Yet he had still concealed the whole disaster. To spare her, Mr Ashby said. But how much worse to find out now and feel so bitterly betrayed.

She trudged on along the street, unsure where she was going, but too despondent to drive home. She ought to be thinking about practical matters: when to put the house on the market, how to pay off the debts, but she couldn't think about anything except Gerry, her late husband. Her legs felt weak and shaky. She hadn't eaten since last night, and then only a mug of instant soup, which she'd somehow managed to force down, gagging on the slimy noodles. Gerry liked decent home-made soup, with bone-stock and fresh vegetables. She hadn't realized how much time it took, cooking for him, shopping. She avoided all those shops now – they held such painful memories: the baguettes she'd bought him from Upper Crust, his favourite fish from Webster's, the butcher's spiced game sausages. Anyway, there was no point in cooking for one.

Yet all around, people were bustling in and out of shops or carrying loaded bags. Life went on – other people's life. A young couple just in front of her were strolling along the pavement arm in arm, dressed in matching tee-shirts. And a woman with three children was sharing out a bag of sweets between them; a man planting rows of pansies in the flower-bed by the war memorial.

She sat down on the bench and watched him, affronted by the richness of the purple velvet petals. Nature was so callous: flowers riotously in bloom, weeds sprouting on the path, everything lush and fulfilled but her. Yet even her own body was resilient – her fringe was growing out, her nails needed cutting, and she had noticed this morning that the hair on her legs was beginning to show through. Surely such processes ought to have stopped, in deference to Gerry.

Gerry. The actor. The man who could be a spider, or Macbeth. And who'd had such a marvellous gift for improvisation, such an electrifying voice. She remembered him as Kent in *King Lear*: dropping his voice to a whisper as he accepted banishment – a shellburst of a whisper which could be heard up in the gods.

It must have been a terrible wrench for him, giving up the theatre, like ripping out some part of himself or sacrificing a limb. He had often told her how satisfying it was to be part of a company and connected to an audience. A troupe of actors was almost like a family, intimate, supportive. It made one feel less alone; provided a sense of purpose and community. She could understand that better now when *she* was alone and purposeless. Yet at the time, she had let herself be influenced by trivial worries about how they'd make ends meet. If only he were here, beside her, she could apologize, explain. His sudden death had left so much unsaid. 'It wasn't easy, Gerry,' she said desperately, 'being married to an actor. You were always out, or away, or busy learning lines. And it was a constant struggle to pay the bills, especially as we had the children so early . . .'

She got up from the bench and walked slowly round the flower-bed, remembering the many times they had been behind with the rent, or even short of food. It was easy to look back with nostalgia at leaky houseboats and a bohemian youth, but the reality was chronic fatigue, since she was often working full-time as well as looking after the children. That was no excuse, though. Gerry must have resented her profoundly for suggesting he took on that dreary sales job with Salford Office Supplies.

'It was just to tide us over,' she pleaded in her defence. 'It never even crossed my mind that you wouldn't act again. Or that we'd move down south, and that eventually you'd *own* a business . . .'

The gardener straightened up and rubbed his back. Then he packed away his seed-trays and walked past her without a word. It was as if he hadn't seen her; as if she didn't exist. She was alone now with the sun, which fixed her with its insolent stare. Wherever she went, it seemed to seek her out, accuse her.

'You didn't kill his passion for the theatre, you simply drove it underground. Can't you see? – that's why he stockpiled all those theatre programmes and kept every single copy of *Plays and Players*. And why he put money into a fringe company connected with his drama-school days.'

Angrily she looked round for some shade. There was a tiny patch of shadow by the war memorial, but even there she couldn't escape the hectoring voice.

'No wonder he didn't tell you. You'd only have been boringly practical and nagged him about the risks. But it's obvious why he did it. It was the only way he had of keeping in touch with his profession, resurrecting the dead actor.'

It was the actor she had fallen in love with – the wild, Byronic rebel who was such a thrilling contrast to her prudent, industrious father. Yet she had played her part in changing him into a prudent, industrious businessman.

She searched vainly for a tissue. Her handkerchief was damp already, ridiculously small. She had better buy some Kleenex from the chemist – man-size, marriage-size.

She crossed the road, wheeling round as someone called her name. Hastily she wiped her eyes on her sleeve, forced a semblance of a smile. It was Stella Watts from the dress shop, a woman she detested.

'How *are* you, dear? I'm so sorry about your husband. I heard the news from Mrs Cunningham.'

Catherine mumbled an inaudible reply. To them Gerry's death was just another juicy item of gossip.

'I have to say you don't look well at all, dear. It must have been an awful shock.'

Catherine backed away. Stella was standing uncomfortably close, peering into her face; her perfume cloyingly sweet, her body hot and overbearing.

'It's a dreadful business, isn't it?' Stella shook her head. 'D'you know, I heard on the news the other day that someone, somewhere, drops dead of a heart attack every half-hour.'

'Really?' Catherine muttered, as the statistic expanded into a hideous image: parents, spouses, lovers, collapsing with that strangled gasp, in every household across the globe.

'Ah, well, duty calls! I'd better get back to my customers. But do pop in, dear, won't you, and we can have a little natter. Oh, and by the way, I've got some lovely new autumn stock . . .'

Catherine watched in relief as Stella strode off towards her shop. At least the wretched woman hadn't talked about Gerry 'passing away' – the loathsome phrase her next-door neighbour used. It made him sound so flimsy, as if his reassuring bulk had crumbled and dissolved.

But that's exactly how it *is*, she thought with a shudder. He's no more than a few ashes now, scattered in a rose garden.

She made herself walk into Boots, her face a rigid mask. Gerry must have dissembled like that, presenting her with a cheerful façade when he had just lost thousands of pounds. What sort of inadequate wife had she been if he hadn't dared to tell her? And shouldn't she have *sensed* that something was wrong? He had often been quite irritable, now she came to think about it – snapping at her for nothing, or complaining of tension headaches – but she had simply put it down to overwork.

She wandered desolately along the aisles, trying to remember why she had come in here. Tissues, that was it. Row upon row of useless products seemed to be shouting for her attention – everything but tissues.

She stopped abruptly as she caught sight of herself in a mirror on the make-up counter. She looked absolutely terrible: her cheeks blotchy and inflamed, her hair hanging limply around her face. If Gerry were to see her now, he would barely recognize her. She moved closer to the mirror, shocked at the tiny lines around her eyes – she hadn't even noticed them before. Had Gerry found her plain these last few years? Middle-aged and overweight? Undesirable?

'Can I help you, madam?'

The salesgirl was about seventeen, with long black hair and dark lustrous eyes. 'No thanks,' she said tersely, resenting the girl's complacent bloom of youth. What if Gerry had been unfaithful: a liaison kept secret, like his investment in the fringe theatre? All those nights he'd been out late – visiting a stockist, having a drink with a customer – he might actually have been seeing some woman. That would explain the debts: expensive presents, hotel rooms.

She stared at the array of cosmetics: lipstick, blushers, eye-gloss. It was true she had let herself go. She dressed up for special occasions, but not at home, for Gerry. It was too late now, too late to keep her husband. Too late to ask him outright if he had ever had a mistress, and why he'd deceived her over the pension plan. For all she knew, the two might be connected. Suppose he had only backed the venture because the woman running it was one of his old flames? Or some stunning actress he had known since drama school? They would have had so much in common: the language they spoke, their training, their ambitions and ideals. What did she and Gerry have in common? Not much these last few years – except a failing business and an over-mortgaged house.

She crashed her basket to the floor. She didn't want beauty products, or tissues for that matter. Why the hell should she cry for a man who'd betrayed her? She was *furious* with him – furious with him for dying. Furious with the lot of them: registrars, accountants, those clumsy bungling ambulancemen who could have saved him if they'd tried. And the witless cardiologist who could only bleat, 'I'm sorry, it's too late, Mrs Jones.'

She turned on her heel and blundered to the door, tears streaming down her cheeks. Someone caught her arm, tried to steady her. 'What's wrong?'

She shook her head, pulled her arm away. She had lost her husband twice over – *that* was what was wrong. One Gerry had died six weeks ago, and another just today – the man she thought she knew.

II

4

Catherine sloshed a glassful of brandy into the melted chocolate mixture, grinning to herself. It was the first time she'd rebelled. She was tired of being the perfect mother-in-law in Antonia's immaculate house, tired of eating healthily. She wondered sometimes why Andrew didn't object to all the self-righteous salads and weight-watchers' this and that, especially as he had never been fat in his life. But *she*, at least, had decided to take a stand, and so was making her most wicked chocolate mousse (defying Antonia's request for a low-calorie dessert).

She set the saucepan aside while she whipped a pint of double cream, showering in caster sugar. Then she blended the cream with the chocolate, and poured the mixture into a large glass bowl. Actually, she wasn't looking forward to tonight. Antonia's dinner parties were something of an ordeal. It was kind of them to include her, but she always felt the odd one out. Everyone else was glowingly young – and in couples – and she certainly wasn't clever enough to compete with Antonia's fellow solicitors or Andrew's Cambridge friends.

She covered the mousse with clingfilm and put it in the fridge, then did the washing-up. She had promised Antonia she would tidy the whole house before the guests arrived. It shouldn't take longer than ten minutes, since nothing was ever out of place. Once a show-house, always a show-house – that was number one Manor Close. Andrew and Antonia had snapped it up the minute they had seen it in the so-called executive development in Stoneleigh; enchanted by the champagne-coloured carpets, the Laura Ashley curtains, and stylish printed blinds. Although the house was small ('compact' in estate-agent-speak), they had achieved their longed-for third bedroom and a well-tended mini-lawn.

She drifted into the sitting-room, straightened a couple of cushions, repositioned one out-of-line carnation in the vase of flowers on the table. Frankly, she didn't feel at home here. She missed the comfortable clutter of her own house; the sense of space and freedom. But her own house had been finally sold, after being on the market for well over a year. She kept wondering if she had made the right decision in moving in with Andrew and Antonia. At the time she'd been so inert, she had let Andrew sort things out, and though she suspected he had offered her a home chiefly out of duty, she had accepted with relief. The prospect of living on her own had seemed too terrifying, after a lifetime of safe coupledom. She had moved directly from her father's care to Gerry's, hardly realizing how dependent she had been. But part of her still clung to that dependency.

Besides, as Andrew pointed out with his usual practicality, living here saved money – she had no rent or mortgage to pay. In fact, her finances weren't as dire as she had expected. After settling her various debts, including the solicitors' and accountants' bills, and paying for the funeral, she was left with a small capital sum. Mr Ashby had worked wonders to 'maximize her assets' and, although (infuriatingly) she was just too young to qualify for a widow's pension, she could manage reasonably well. Indeed, she wished Andrew would let her make a bigger contribution. She was continually offering to pay for things – food, petrol, the major household bills – but he seemed loth to accept her money, treating her as a helpless child who must be taken in and fed, rather than his once capable mother. She tried to earn her keep in other ways, by doing most of the chores, but then she worried that they'd see her as interfering, or that her standards were less meticulous than theirs. Whatever happened, she didn't want to be a nuisance.

She picked up Antonia's graduation photograph, resplendent in its silver frame. There were photos of her daughter-in-law in almost every room – in riding gear, a ballgown, even in her pram. Although she would never dream of admitting it, she wished Andrew had a photo of *her* somewhere in the house, or, better still, of her and Gerry. But perhaps they weren't quite suitable for a show-house – too worn around the edges.

She sat down on the elegant cream sofa to watch *Morning Magazine*. Normally it helped to pass the time. But today she began to feel irritated by the relentlessly jolly presenter and the stream of commercials for January sales; besides, if she wasn't careful she'd turn into a couch potato. She switched off a Colgate toothpaste ad – yet another lovey-dovey couple, relishing a minty kiss – and went upstairs to do a quick tour of inspection. The bathroom was impeccable, as always. Champagne carpet even here, and fixtures and fittings perfectly co-ordinated: towels, flannels, toothbrushes and soap all harmonized with the bath and basin in a shade called 'New Gardenia'. The only jarring colour was the Blue Flush in the toilet-bowl, but presumably they didn't yet make lavatory cleaners to tone with bathroom suites.

She tried to imagine Gerry here – slopping water all over the place and leaving a tidemark round the bath. Yet the well-trained Andrew managed to shave without depositing a speck of foam on the spotless oval basin, or smearing the shiny taps.

Next she looked in at the main bedroom – the duvet virginal white and reflected in the bank of mirrored cupboards. The sight of a double bed was still stupidly upsetting, even after all this time. *Her* room here had a single, but she simply couldn't adapt to sleeping on her own; sometimes felt like a Siamese twin brutally severed from its other half. And the room could be claustrophobic when she was marooned upstairs in the evenings, pretending she wanted to read or had opted for an early night (but really trying not to intrude on Andrew and Antonia's privacy).

Still, in many ways she had reason to be grateful. At least she hadn't landed up in some poky little flat. And she had certainly made progress since the frozen desolation of the months following the death. She no longer lay awake all night, and she had survived a second Christmas on her own. Of course, she hadn't been alone – they had driven all the way to Devon and spent the week at Antonia's parents' house, but although her face had ached with the strain of being cheerful, she hadn't disgraced herself in public by breaking down and crying.

The clock in the hall chimed ten. It must be later, surely? Perhaps she'd go out for a walk – that would kill half an hour. She put on her coat and fur-lined boots, locked the house carefully and emerged into the frosty air. The road was deserted, as usual – not so much as the twitch of a net curtain. Sometimes, during the day, it seemed as if no one else actually lived here; the whole place just a cardboard cut-out.

She walked briskly to the recreation ground. There might be

one or two young mothers there, pushing their children on the swings. It would be nice to talk to someone, perhaps make a local friend.

No, not a soul, unfortunately. It was probably too miserable for people to venture out – a dank and foggy day, with a great weight of pewter-coloured sky pressing down on the dripping trees. The swings and slides looked uninviting, wet with condensation and chilly to the touch. She wished she had a dog for company. She and Kate had always wanted one, but Andrew had been asthmatic as a child (and was still allergic to fur and feathers) so pets were out of the question.

'Fido!' she called suddenly, breaking into a run and hearing her imaginary dog racing along behind her – a Dalmatian maybe, all lollopy and spotty. Or a puppy would be even better: an inducement for people to stop and talk.

She continued running, out of the gate and up Tregunter Road, astonished at her energy. Her normal mood was lethargic, if not downright weary, and it seemed almost an affront to Gerry to feel so invigorated. She was also starving hungry. Breakfast had been Special K with delicate slices of peach. And they always had it early, so that Andrew and Antonia could catch the 7.42. (That was togetherness on a grand scale: catching the same train. But then Andrew and Antonia did everything together.)

'Come on, Fido,' she panted. 'Let's get back for our Pedigree Chum.' An image flashed into her mind of Antonia serving Spiller's Shapes instead of coq au vin; the sophisticated guests wagging their tails in excitement as they crunched their way through the biscuits and then begged for marrowbones.

'Sorry, old chap, I'm afraid you'll have to disappear. Muddy paws are definitely *verboten*.'

She sat on the front step to remove her boots, thinking of her daughter, as she did so often nowadays. Would Kate ever get her dog, ever settle down? She hadn't been home since the funeral, and phone conversations were always too short and often rather self-conscious. Occasionally they talked about Gerry and she could tell from the tightness in her voice that Kate was still grieving. Yet how could she help her, halfway across the world? Perhaps they'd be reunited *next* Christmas.

She let herself in, remembering to put her coat in the cupboard, rather than draping it over the banisters. Then she went into the kitchen to find something to eat. The fridge was full of food, but it was mostly for this evening's dinner. She and Antonia had prepared the salmon pâté and coq au vin last night, Antonia watching surreptitiously in case she smuggled in any illicit substances, like butter.

Which reminded her – she'd better have a look at the mousse and make sure that it was setting. She put it on the table and peeled the clingfilm back. Damn! It was still runny – too much brandy, no doubt. She tried a teaspoonful. Yes, runny but delicious. Using a clean spoon, a tablespoon this time, she swirled a dollop of the mixture into her mouth. It tasted wonderful: rich and dark and chocolatey, with a distinct kickback from the brandy. She scooped a portion into a dish and ate it quickly, standing up, like a thief. Not that she was stealing – there was plenty left for the others. After years of cooking for Gerry's healthy appetite, she still tended to over-cater.

She filled her dish to the top. This was Gerry's favourite pudding and she was eating it for *him*. It slipped down so easily; its texture velvety smooth. She pulled a chair up to the table – if she was going to eat, she might as well do the thing in comfort. She moved the big glass bowl towards her and began dipping into that, one spoonful after another. After another. After another. There was a satisfying rhythm to the process, a sense of consolation. She hadn't realized how empty she was. Since Gerry's death she had lost two stone – the initial shock had put her off her food completely, and she had gradually got into the habit of missing meals, or grabbing a quick snack. Even here, with Andrew and Antonia, she rarely bothered to eat lunch, except sometimes at the weekends when the two of them weren't playing golf. But today her appetite had come roaring back, along with a crazy sort of urge to indulge herself, break out.

She continued eating almost hypnotically, mesmerized by the movement of the spoon. It seemed to dip into the bowl without any assistance from her, then glide towards her mouth, then down again and in again. She was remembering the many times she had made this mousse for Gerry: birthdays, anniversaries, dinners for his business friends. He seemed almost to be *there*, sitting right beside her and tucking in with his usual gusto, not giving a damn about calories or cholesterol.

Her spoon scraped the bottom of the bowl. She stared, appalled

41

– it was empty. She had gobbled the lot – a rich, fattening chocolate mousse, intended for eight people. What a disgusting greedy pig she was! She giggled suddenly. Well, Antonia had her low-calorie dessert: a big bowl full of nothing.

She wiped her mouth, hardly believing what she had done. Hastily she washed the bowl and mopped a drool of chocolate from the table. That got rid of the evidence, but she still had to produce some sort of pudding for tonight – a light fruit sorbet, perhaps. It would mean another trip to the shops, another bout of cooking.

She fetched her coat and car keys and was on her way out of the kitchen when she remembered the chocolate wrapper and cream carton – more incriminating evidence. She bundled them into a plastic bag to be disposed of in a litter-bin far from Manor Close. Good thieves covered their tracks.

She was still laughing as she started the car. Okay, she was a glutton, but no one need ever know. And, amazingly, she didn't feel the slightest bit sick. She also had the marvellous feeling that Gerry was still with her, laughing too, enjoying her rebellion.

Having bought mangoes and lemons for the sorbet (and a potted plant for Antonia as atonement for her crime), she drove on to Carshalton. The Williamsons were moving in on Monday, so it was her last chance to collect the mail. She hadn't been to the house for a fortnight – she found it too depressing to see it stripped of its furniture.

Nervously she let herself in and stood shivering in the hall. An empty house was so unwelcoming, so cold. There were dark patches on the parquet where the furniture had stood; ghost-shapes on the walls where the pictures used to be. Losing the family home was like another death. All the things she and Gerry had bought together had been cleared out by the auctioneers as so much filler for their catalogue. Yet she had to admit it was a huge relief to be rid of the hordes of prospective purchasers. For fifteen solid months she had shown them round, repeating the same selling points like some fatuous estate agent; a smile clamped to her face, while inside she was screaming with frustration. No one seemed inclined to buy, as if they sensed instinctively that the house had been witness to a death, or could feel the weight of her past grief still hanging in the air. It had enraged her to think that a stream of thoughtless strangers were trampling over Gerry; sitting in his chair; criticizing his taste.

'It's a bit dark, this room, isn't it? We'll have to change the colour scheme.'

'We can always tear that fireplace out. It's terribly old-fashioned.'

'Good riddance!' she shouted at their departing shades, hearing her voice echo dully through the hall.

She collected up the letters from the mat – several addressed to Gerry. How could they not realize he was dead? For her, it was the first numbing fact she woke to every morning; her last despondent thought each night.

She took the letters into the sitting-room and perched on the window-seat, wishing she could light a fire and warm her chilly hands. Most of the stuff was junk mail – circulars and catalogues – and there was a letter from an old customer enquiring about the business. Peculiar how she missed it. Although she had never really liked the work, at least it had kept her fully occupied. There hadn't been time to wonder whether she was happy or fulfilled, with the phone ringing every minute and all the bills to pay and deliveries to chase and customers to keep sweet. And of course it was such a help to Gerry if *she* dealt with the admin, leaving him free to do the selling. Not that he ever thanked her – he simply took her role as general factotum for granted. But then she had taken *him* for granted; never thought to tell him how grateful she was that he was simply there – alive. And as for the business with the fringe theatre company, well, having tried (and failed) to find out more about it, she had finally managed to convince herself that it was simply an example of Gerry's famous generosity – albeit on a reckless scale. And then she had done her best to put it out of her mind.

Frowning, she picked up the last envelope, which was addressed to them both and contained an invitation. *The Directors of Shaw Hilliard request the pleasure of your company to celebrate the publication of* From Rep to Riches – An Actor's Life *by Jonathan Monroe.*

Jonathan! They hadn't seen him for an age, not since they'd moved south. They had followed his progress at a distance, of course, and she recalled Gerry snorting once when he read of some new triumph. 'He's sold out to television, but then he never had much talent in the first place.' Poor Gerry – he was clearly jealous. The once impecunious Jonathan had now become a house-

43

hold name, the current star of a new sit-com and regularly featured in the gossip columns. And here he was publishing his memoirs and celebrating with a launch party in Mayfair!

Well, good for him, that's all she could say. She must send him a brief note and break the news about Gerry. Not immediately, though – no point in being the spectre at the feast. It seemed odd he hadn't heard already, but then for the last few years they'd moved in completely different circles. And though Andrew had put a notice in *The Times*, not many people read death notices for fun. She peered at the date on the embossed white card – the launch was tonight, seven-thirty. So, while she was steaming the mangetout for Antonia, velvet-voiced Jonathan would be greeting his celebrity guests.

She stuffed the invitation back into its envelope and dragged herself upstairs. There was one remaining thing to be done: clear out Gerry's clothes. Everything else had gone – either sold or moved to Stoneleigh, but she had refused to disturb the clothes, or let anyone else so much as lay a finger on them. They were still hanging in the built-in wardrobe, exactly as he'd left them. Last time she was here she had brought her largest suitcase, determined to pack them up and dispose of them. But she had lost her nerve and left the case empty on the bedroom floor. Now she flung the lid open and began yanking the suits off their hangers, ruthlessly bundling them in. It was no good weeping over every one, as she had done so many times already; smelling them and fondling them, conjuring up sad memories. If she mummified her grief for ever, she would turn out like her father, who had made her childhood home a shrine to his Great Loss, wearing black, metaphorically, for his remaining thirty years. He had died at sixty-two, but *she* might live until her eighties, like Gerry's hardy parents. Which meant she was only half-way through her life.

It was such a sobering thought, she stopped what she was doing and stood staring into space. What had she achieved since Gerry's death? Admittedly, selling the house had kept her really busy, but that chapter in her life had closed two months ago. Yet she had made no move to get a job, and was behaving as if she'd retired – not just from work, from life. Gerry would be horrified. He had always assumed she could juggle several jobs at once – children, housework, the business – and still have time to ice party-cakes or run up home-made clothes. Yet because he had died she was living in a sort of purdah, battening on her son and frittering away the time watching mindless soaps. She had thought herself lucky that she could scrape by without working – just about. But why the hell should she *choose* to live like that? She had all the necessary skills to get another job, for heaven's sake. The thought of toiling in some soulless office wasn't exactly inspiring, but better that than spending the next forty years stagnating on the sidelines, and forced to deny herself luxuries like holidays and decent clothes.

She returned to the wardrobe and folded the last suit – one of Gerry's favourites: charcoal-grey and flatteringly cut. She clicked the suitcase shut and carried it down the stairs. The clothes could go to a charity shop, then she'd find a good employment agency and put herself on the market – like the house.

The British Heart Foundation shop was squeezed between a Chinese restaurant and Croydon Camera-Mart. She had driven all this way to avoid meeting anyone she knew; it also seemed appropriate, since Gerry had died of a heart attack. Carshalton had only Age Concern, and it was right opposite Stella Watts's boutique.

She heaved the suitcase out of the boot and lugged it to the doorway. Should she simply dump it and flee, or take it in and unpack the clothes (which might upset her all over again)?

'Excuse me, are you going in? If not, do be an angel and let me past, would you? I'm fearfully late for an appointment.'

Catherine was startled by the voice, which sounded vaguely familiar – commanding yet melodious. She turned to see a striking woman with auburn hair swept up on top, and wearing a scarlet fun fur and long black shiny boots. She too was carrying a case, a distinctive-looking one in olive-coloured leather.

Catherine stood back to let her pass, wondering what so dazzling a creature was doing in this dreary place. Then, hesitantly, she followed her inside and watched her dart towards the young girl at the till and kiss her on both cheeks.

'I'm back! Did you have a lovely Christmas, Janet? Mine was utterly loathsome!' She gave a dramatic throaty laugh, then lifted the case on to the counter and began tossing garments to left and right – exotic items in brilliant colours, quite unlike the rejects hanging forlornly round the shop. 'I decided it was high time for another clear-out,' she continued in her ringing voice. 'I'm such a dreadful hoarder, you know!'

45

'Gosh, thank you,' said the girl, picking up a shimmering sequined dress and inspecting it admiringly. 'They're absolutely beautiful. The last lot sold like hot cakes.'

'Splendid! Glad to be of help. Must dash, though – I'm atrociously behind schedule.'

Catherine stood immobile, watching the grand exit as the woman seized the empty case and swept out of the door. She saw her dash across the street and zoom away in a low-slung sports car, the same red as her coat.

Back at the counter, a second, older, assistant had joined the younger one and they were examining the clothes together, jabbering excitedly.

'You know who *that* was, don't you, Peg?'

'Well, I'm sure I've seen her somewhere, but I just can't place her at the moment.'

'It's Marsha Booth. You know – from *EastEnders*. Apparently she lives up near the golf club, in one of those big swanky houses. She's ever so friendly, though. I've only met her twice and she treats me like I'm family or something.'

'Yes, I noticed! I have to say I warm to that. I mean, you'd think she'd be a bit of a snob, wouldn't you? Most well-known people wouldn't dream of coming to a shop like this.'

Catherine listened in surprise. She had seen Marsha Booth just yesterday – on screen – but had failed to recognize her in the flesh. And it seemed odd that she should live in plodding Croydon, rather than upmarket Hampstead or Belgravia.

She cleared her throat, feeling distinctly drab. 'I've, er, brought these clothes,' she murmured, pointing to the case.

'Oh thanks, dear. If you'd like to take them out and pop them on the counter here. I'm afraid there's not much room. Let's see if we can clear some space.'

Catherine moved aside a long jersey-knit dress in a vibrant pattern of purples, with an ostrich-feather trim. It looked barely worn and incredibly expensive. On a sudden impulse, she held it up against herself, discovering it wasn't a dress but a jumpsuit with a deep V-neck and wide flowing silky trousers.

The woman nodded encouragingly. 'It's just your size, dear, isn't it? You're lovely and slim, like Marsha.' Her voice became a confidential whisper. 'Why don't you try it on?'

'Oh, no, honestly – I couldn't. It's not my sort of thing at all.'

'But the colour suits you, it really does. Don't you think so, Janet?'

'Yeah. It's great. And I bet it's an original. The label says Missoni. Does that mean anything to you, Peg?'

The older woman shook her head.

It meant nothing to Catherine either, but then she didn't usually stray beyond the safe confines of Marks & Spencer, with the occasional foray to Adèle's Boutique in Cheam. She put the suit back on the counter with a shrug, but Peg immediately scooped it up again, looking at it wistfully as if it were an orphan desperate for a home.

'Are you *sure* you won't try it on, dear?'

Catherine shuffled from foot to foot. This was worse than Stella Watts. Hard-sell made her nervous, even in a charity shop. Yet she had to admit it would be rather fun to buy something donated by a television star. Even if she didn't wear it, she could keep it as a sort of trophy. 'Okay,' she said. 'Where's the fitting room?'

'Just behind that curtain, dear. There's a full-length mirror and all.'

Catherine went through into the cubicle and took off her grey skirt and navy sweater. Since Gerry's death, she hadn't had the heart to wear her usual cheerful colours. She wriggled into the jumpsuit and steeled herself to look in the mirror. The transformation was astonishing: smiling back at her was a genuinely glamorous woman. And the suit fitted so well, it might have been made to measure. The fabric was daringly clingy; emphasizing the curve of her breasts, rippling over her thighs, but the effect was sensuous rather than blatant. Of course, it was quite impractical. Ostrich feathers were out of the question for a suburban office job, and the neck was too low for Antonia's starchy dinner.

Suddenly, she had a brilliant idea – why not skip the dinner and go to Jonathan's launch party instead? This was just the outfit for an arty Mayfair club, awash with theatre people. In fact, Marsha Booth and Jonathan must move in the same world. She *ought* to go, for Gerry's sake. Dressed in Marsha's clothes, she could become the sort of woman he had probably always wanted: artistic, outrageous even.

She put her head round the curtain. 'You wouldn't have shoes, by any chance? Something to go with this?'

'What size?'

'Five and a half.'

'That's Marsha's size. You're in luck again! She brought in this pair of fantastic purple platform boots.'

'Platform?'

'Well, only little platforms. And they're the same purple as the suit. She must have bought them to match.' The girl handed them over reverently. They too looked practically new: knee-length with a chunky heel, and superbly made in the softest, most luxurious suede.

Catherine unzipped the right boot and stroked the calfskin lining. She *couldn't* wear platforms, even tiny ones – not a widow in her forties. It was ridiculous.

She pulled them on almost guiltily, keeping well behind the curtain. They felt strange at first, uncomfortable, but they certainly made the outfit come together. Her legs seemed longer and slimmer, and the rich bloom of the suede, peeping out beneath the sheen of the silk jersey, looked wonderfully opulent. She had shed ten years at least, just by changing out of widow's weeds. Her hair, though, let her down. It was not only dry and frizzy but boringly middle-aged. Frankly, she wasn't keen on perms, but what else could she do with hair as straight as hers? It had been different when she was young, or before Gerry took over the business. *Then* it had been all right to drift around with long, flowing locks, but once she'd become the linchpin of a busy office she had felt obliged to look more conventional.

'How are you getting on in there, dear?' the older woman called.

'Okay, I think. The boots fit.'

'Go on, then – give us a peek!'

Embarrassed, Catherine emerged from the cubicle, to be greeted with delighted exclamations.

'Wow, look at that! Amazing, isn't it, Peg?'

'My goodness, yes! You're a different person, dear, if you don't mind me saying so. That colour really makes you come alive. And the boots give you a bit more height. I think you should snap it up quickly before anyone else gets their hands on it.'

'I *am* tempted,' Catherine said. 'But I'm . . . er, wondering how much it'll all cost.'

'Well, we haven't priced any of Marsha's stuff yet. What do you reckon, Janet? Would a tenner sound right for the suit?'

48

Janet looked dubious. 'A bit on the high side, isn't it? *I*'d say seven-fifty.'

'And the boots?' asked Catherine anxiously.

'Well, they're hand-made, you know. Italian. And really good quality suede. I couldn't let them go for less than twelve.'

'There's a mark on one of the heels, though,' Janet pointed out. 'I noticed when I unpacked them.'

'Okay, how about seventeen-fifty for the boots and suit together? D'you think you could manage that, dear?'

'Yes, that's fine.' Catherine stifled a grin. They must think she was some down-and-out, without the price of a cup of tea. She dived back behind the curtain. Two other customers had come in and she didn't want them digging in their pockets and tossing her their loose change. She glanced in the mirror again, wishing she could keep the outfit on. Her own clothes looked so dreary in comparison. But she was going on from here to make enquiries about a job and could hardly turn up in such style. Actually, she ought to get a move on – there was the sorbet still to make and the vegetables to prepare, and by the time she'd changed and done her make-up . . .

She left the shop with a new spring in her step, clutching a crumpled Sainsbury's carrier bag – her booty.

She strode along, scanning the nearby shop-fronts for an employment agency. Just because she'd decided to have a fling tonight, it didn't mean she could neglect her future. She would give herself a fortnight to find a suitable job: by the end of January she would be a committed working woman again.

About a hundred yards on, she stopped dead in her tracks, struck by a poster in a hairdresser's window. It showed a girl with startlingly short hair, shorn to a couple of inches all over – no crimped curls or lifeless frizz, just a smoothly gleaming skull-cap with a dark purplish tinge to it.

'DARE TO BE DIFFERENT!' urged the caption. 'TURN HEADS WITH OUR SENSATIONAL SPICED PLUM!'

She hesitated, but only for a moment. Damn the job! Damn the sorbet! This was the only possible hairstyle – and colour – to set off that stupendous outfit.

5

'Mother, you don't intend to go out like *that*, do you?' Andrew's usually pale cheeks were flushed, his distress – distaste – apparent on his face.

Catherine fought the urge to laugh. 'And why not, my darling?'

'Well, that . . . that thing looks downright vulgar. And I'm sure it's meant for someone half your age.'

'Marsha Booth is forty-eight.'

'What?'

'Oh, never mind.' She hadn't told him about the charity shop. He would strongly disapprove of 'germy' clothes.

'And your hair, for heaven's sake – what on earth have you done to it?'

'Had it all cut off.'

'But the colour. It's . . . it's . . .'

'Spiced Plum. Unusual, isn't it?'

'Listen, Mother, Antonia and I do realize you're . . . I mean, these things take time to . . .' He sat stiffly on the sofa, fiddling with his wedding ring. He was never happy talking about emotions. 'Look, *I* still find it upsetting sometimes when I see Dad's watch on my wrist, or his photo on my desk at work. But it must be a lot worse for you. Oh, don't think I'm criticizing. You've been wonderful – everybody says so. But bottling everything up isn't supposed to be a good thing, you know. We've said all along that you really ought to talk to someone. A counsellor, or . . .'

'So I need to see a counsellor because I've dyed my hair?'

'Don't be silly, you know what I mean. All I'm trying to say is . . .' Suddenly he sneezed: an urgent honking sneeze, closely followed by another.

Oh lord, she thought – the ostrich feathers. Poor Andrew. He would probably be sneezing the whole evening now; struggling to be the perfect host with inflamed sinuses and streaming eyes. 'It's these feathers, darling – you're obviously allergic to me. Anyway, if I don't get off now I'll be late. I'll just say goodbye to Antonia.'

She found her in the kitchen, pureeing the mangoes with a somewhat martyred expression. But Catherine refused to feel the slightest twinge of guilt, either about the sorbet, *or* the exorbitant cost of her hair and matching Spiced Plum nails. It was the first professional manicure of her life and she'd enjoyed every minute of it. Antonia must spend as much each month on vitamins alone. Besides, when *she* was twenty-six, she had been living in a squalid basement with two young children to feed – and on beans and chips, not exotic fruit.

'Don't worry, Antonia, if the sorbet doesn't freeze in time. It'll taste just as good, even if it's mushy.'

Antonia slowed the mixer and spoke above the whirr. 'Catherine, I don't like to interfere, but about this do you're going to tonight . . . Well, Andrew thinks . . .'

'I *know* what Andrew thinks. But I'm afraid it's too late. I've already phoned Shaw Hilliard and told them I'll be there.' She was interrupted by a succession of muffled sneezes from the sitting-room. 'Anyway, the sooner I get out of his way the better.'

Her coat was waiting in the hall. She hadn't worn it since the winter before Gerry died, but red was Marsha's colour and it clashed gloriously with the jumpsuit.

'Have a lovely dinner!' she called, as Andrew emerged from the sitting-room, his face shrouded in a handkerchief. 'Oh, and don't wait up, my darlings. I may be a bit late.'

She dithered in the shadows a few yards away from the club. The place looked formal, even forbidding, rather than convivially bohemian. A doorman was standing to attention beneath a sombre grey-green awning, flanked by two clipped bay trees; the three stiff shapes uniting to convey the message: 'Only nobs allowed in here. Keep out!' The street itself was oppressively dark – no other clubs or restaurants in the vicinity, just offices and mansion blocks, rising tall and impersonal above her.

She crossed the road and clopped down to the corner, having not yet fully mastered the knack of walking on platform soles. Even these relatively low ones seemed to throw her slightly off balance, and she felt the more conspicuous because of being alone. Always in the past Gerry had been with her at functions of this sort – not that there had been many in the last six or seven years. Slogging away at the business, they had gradually lost touch with the gregarious acting crowd, and often felt too tired even to go out on their own.

She stopped under a lamp-post and looked at her watch again. Nearly ten to nine. Her train had been late, to start with, then there'd been a hold-up on the tube, both of which had sapped her buoyant mood. If she didn't pluck up courage soon, the party would be over. Alternatively she could stay out here and freeze to death. The raw night air seemed to be pressing icy hands against her face, running rude fingers inside the collar of her coat. For the last half-hour she had been hanging around, watching people stride into the club. As far as she could tell, most of them were quite casually dressed. She began to regret her impulse buying in the charity shop – Marsha's outfit would look absurdly out of place. How could she ever have imagined it was elegant? Tarty, more like. Andrew and Antonia were right after all. Perhaps she ought to go back to Stoneleigh, sneak up to her bedroom and change into something demure, then join them for coffee and After Eights. Except she was stuck with the hair, of course – the colour wouldn't grow out for weeks. They would be ashamed to introduce her to their friends, whose mothers were bound to be twinset-and-pearls types. So where else could she go? A pity this was Mayfair, otherwise she might have found a friendly tramp and shared his patch of pavement for the night.

Cars kept flashing past – faceless drivers, yet at least they knew where they were going. She was tempted to flag one down and hitch a lift, to make her feel less rootless. Though in fact she wasn't rootless – she had always had someone to lean on: first her strict guardian of a father, then confident, outgoing Gerry, and even now, as a widow, she was protected and cocooned. Easy to criticize Andrew and Antonia, but they were *there* for her – shields against the void.

She walked slowly back towards the club. The boots were beginning to pinch her toes now; the toes themselves almost numb. 'Stop whingeing,' she told herself. 'Thousands of people are truly on their own, without kind sons to go home to. Anyway, you're *not* going home. You're going to count to five and then walk in through that entrance.'

'. . . three . . . four . . . five . . .'

She blinked in the glare of headlights. A taxi was approaching and drew up with a jolt outside the club. The passenger door opened and a pair of long, black-stockinged legs swung out. Above them was a svelte black skirt and coat, belonging to a woman of about thirty-five with bright fuchsia-pink lipstick and startlingly blond hair. Well, *here* was someone who had bothered to dress up. Seizing her chance, Catherine quickly fell into step with her.

'Excuse me, is this the Jonathan Monroe party?' she asked, feigning innocence. If she struck up a conversation, at least they could go in together.

'Yeah, that's right.' The girl gave a friendly laugh. 'I'm glad to see I'm not the last! I was kept at work – again.'

Catherine smiled sympathetically. They had sailed past the doorman and were now safely inside. 'What sort of work do you do?'

'Well, at the moment I'm trying to write a commercial for some revolting orange drink. But let's not talk about it. It serves me right for going into advertising. My name's Nicky, by the way, Nicky Maitland.'

'I'm Catherine Jones.'

'Great to meet you. God, it's hot in here!'

They had moved from the marble-columned foyer to a large reception area, with silk-weave wallpaper and a massive crystal chandelier. Two huge bowls of out-of-season flowers stood on marble pedestals, braving the sub-tropical heat.

Nicky swept up to the desk and scrawled her name in the leather-bound visitors' book. 'Hi!' she said to the porter. 'Where's the action? I'm gasping for a drink.'

'Shouldn't we leave our coats first?' Catherine murmured.

'Yeah, and I must go for a pee. There's not even time for *that* at work.'

'The cloakroom's to your right, madam, just along the passage.' The porter's snooty tone implied a reproof to Nicky's bluntness. 'And the party's in the Hardwick Room upstairs.'

'Mm, I can hear it now.' Nicky moved to the foot of the staircase, which curved upwards in a graceful spiral. 'Sounds like feeding-time at the zoo. Right – loo first, then champagne. After you, Catherine.'

She held the door and Catherine stepped into a cloakroom almost as elegant as the reception hall, though more intimate in scale. There was another impressive flower display opposite the row of marble basins. An attendant hovered, waiting to take their coats. Catherine unbuttoned hers reluctantly, Andrew's word 'vulgar' nagging in her head.

'God, I love your outfit! That slinky retro-shape is just brilliant. I've been looking all over for something like that. Where on earth did you find it?'

Catherine hesitated. 'In . . . in a charity shop.'

'You're joking! I thought it was a Missoni.'

'Well actually it is.'

Nicky looked incredulous. 'A Missoni in a charity shop?'

Catherine nodded, wishing (for the second time) she knew who Missoni was. A fashion designer obviously, but male or female, classic, trendy . . . ?

'Wow! – it's probably an original seventies design then. Where do you live, for heaven's sake? Hollywood?'

'No, Stoneleigh.'

'Where's Stoneleigh?'

Catherine laughed, already feeling better. 'About as far as you can get from Hollywood. It's a rather nothing sort of place near Worcester Park, in Surrey.' She gave a sidelong glance in the mirror. 'You don't think it's a bit . . . over the top?'

'Christ, no! I'd die for an outfit like that. How much did it cost?'

'Seven pounds fifty.'

'I don't believe it! Pity we're not the same size, or we could do a swop. I'm tired of this old black thing.'

'It looks great.' The dress was beautifully cut, with daring side-slits revealing a formidable expanse of leg. Nicky was a good head taller than her and almost boyishly slim. Although not pretty in a conventional way, everything about her merited a second glance: her well-defined cheekbones and healthy winter tan; surprisingly dark eyes contrasting with the ash-blond hair (which couldn't be natural, surely). And even her accessories had been chosen with panache: brutally modernist earrings made of scraps of twisted steel; a natty black suede pouch to hold her mobile phone, and marvellously strappy shoes, which wouldn't be seen dead in any boring high-street shop.

Catherine surveyed her own purple boots with a glow of satisfaction. For once, she too felt special.

'So how do you know Jonathan?' Nicky asked, barging into a cubicle and banging the door behind her. She continued talking unabashed. 'Are you an actress too?'

'Er, no.' A pity Marsha Booth's identity didn't come with the clothes. She had no wish to mention Gerry; least of all bring death into a party. It would be bad enough breaking the news to Jonathan. 'I . . . met him years ago, when he was living up near Manchester. I presume he must have moved since then.'

'Yes, he's got a place in Chelsea. Very swish – near Cheyne Walk.' Nicky erupted from the cubicle, flicked some water over her hands and gave a quick pat to her hair. 'Actually, he'll be wondering where the hell I am. I did promise to get here early, you see. We'd better get a move on.'

She propelled Catherine to the door and took the stairs two at a time, despite her spindly heels. 'I hope they've laid on some decent eats. I'm starving. All I had for lunch was a packet of crisps.'

Catherine said nothing about her own indulgent chocolate lunch. She too was starving, though with far less cause than Nicky.

The bray of voices grew louder as they approached the Hardwick Room. Nicky led the way into a rumbustious press of people, Catherine tailing her closely, resisting the temptation to flee. She was used to Gerry taking charge, greeting friends, fetching drinks, making her feel part of a relaxed and happy circle.

'Angus, great to see you!' Nicky rushed over to embrace a satanic-looking character in a black shirt and long black sideburns, who hugged her enthusiastically. 'Where's the booze? I'm parched!'

'Calm down! I'll fetch you some.'

'Make it two, will you? This is Catherine. We met on the way in.'

'Hi,' said Angus, flashing her a smile. 'I like the feathers. They don't *bite*, do they?' He brushed his hand against the ostrich trim and immediately snatched it away in mock alarm. 'Oh God, they're lethal!'

Catherine laughed, relieved that the ice was broken. And while Angus went in search of drinks, Nicky introduced her to several other people: a television producer whose name she didn't catch, a girl in publishing called Ruth, and a foreign-looking couple – he with a long straggly beard, she in a weird caftan-thing.

55

'Where's Jonathan?' asked Nicky, her eyes sweeping round the room. 'I can't see him anywhere. Ah, Angus – thanks. That was quick.' She took both glasses and handed one to Catherine. 'Cheers!' She winked. 'Here's to Stoneleigh and its amazing shops.'

'Cheers!' said Catherine, forcing a smile. The fizzing bubbles had suddenly reminded her of the silver wedding – the last time she'd had champagne. She fought a wave of panic, seeing Gerry's face: a grinning skull-face looming into close-up as they drank the celebration toast. It was impossible to concentrate on what the television chap was saying.

'Of course, we couldn't get the backing for the series. It's always the same damned thing – no bankable names, no track record . . .'

'Ah, there's Jonathan!' said Nicky, and began pushing her way to the far end of the room.

Catherine followed, leaving the producer railing against the strictures of his budget. She was surprised how youthful Jonathan looked – his hair neither thinner nor greying, his face remarkably unlined. Perhaps he'd had a little help – a few tucks and pleats over the years, or maybe the odd hair-weave. He greeted Nicky exuberantly, then turned to her with a vague and slightly puzzled smile. Good lord, she thought, he doesn't recognize me.

'Catherine Jones,' she said, putting out her hand. 'From Salford. I hope you haven't forgotten me after all this time?'

'Catherine!' He ignored the hand and kissed her on both cheeks. 'I *was* confused for a moment. The hairstyle threw me, that's all. It's fabulous! You look absolutely stunning.'

'Thank you.'

'And where's the old man?'

She swallowed. A succession of images suddenly flashed into her mind like stills from a forgotten film: Jonathan and Gerry side by side in *Waiting for Godot*; downing pints of Guinness after the performance; laughing in her tiny kitchen as they rehearsed their lines for the *next* play. Her cheeks were burning, yet the chill of death hung in the air, threatening to descend on her; on the whole happy carefree party. 'I'm . . . er . . . afraid he couldn't come.'

'Oh, I *am* sorry. What a shame.' He looked downcast for a moment, then raised his eyebrows quizzically. 'But hold on a minute – you're blushing. This all seems rather suspicious, I must say. I mean, Gerry not here and you looking like a million dollars. Don't tell me you've chucked him over for a toy boy!'

'Something like that.' The laugh lacerated her throat. 'But how are *you*, Jon? Oh, and congratulations on the book.'

'Thanks. If you want a copy, do nick one with my compliments. They're stacked up on that table over there. It'll save you fifteen quid.'

'And lose you precious royalties! Don't worry, I'll buy my own from Waterstone's. It's the least I can do for a friend.'

'Actually, I've just remembered – Gerry's *in* the book. Only a brief reference, but he's immortalized in print.'

How sad, she thought, that he would never see it. She was about to ask why and where he was mentioned, but some instinct made her stop. What if it was something to do with that ill-fated theatre company? For all she knew, Jonathan might have been involved in it as well, as an actor or fellow-investor. Now that she had more or less succeeded in putting it behind her, why dredge the whole thing up again?

As luck would have it, she spotted a waiter gliding towards them – one of the many circulating with champagne bottles. She held her glass out thankfully, leaving Jonathan to talk to Nicky.

She took a few deep calming breaths. The champagne would help her relax. Indeed, the other guests already seemed less daunting – just a friendly crowd enjoying themselves. Of course she wasn't out of place, or vulgar and overdressed. Jonathan had told her she looked absolutely stunning. Flattery, no doubt, but he had seemed genuinely struck by her appearance. Secretly she had always rather fancied him, and was gratified that he had noticed her at last, as someone other than Gerry's capable but rather ordinary wife.

A waitress stopped in front of her with a tray of canapés – miniature works of art: asparagus tartlets jewelled with caviar; elf-size eclairs oozing salmon pâté; tiny mushroom footstools topped with cushions of cream cheese. She took one, and then another – the fishy tang of caviar succeeded by the rich saltiness of Roquefort. All her senses seemed sharpened: piquant tastes zinging in her mouth; the sounds and colours in the room amplified to a brilliant clashing cacophony.

'Have you tried the chicken satay?' asked a well-modulated voice. A man had appeared at her side: pale-skinned and rather willowy. He wore a conventional grey suit, but his long fair hair and smooth complexion made him look more the boyish student than the hardened executive.

'Er, no,' she said, noticing his ring: a silver snake's head, swallowing its tail.

'Well, do! It's hot, and quite sublime.' He beckoned another waitress over and Catherine helped herself to a morsel of hot chicken and dipped it in the sauce.

'Oh, one's not enough,' he said, picking up four pieces and polishing them off in quick succession. Finishing his last mouthful, he introduced himself. 'Simon Wallace – Jonathan's TV agent. I adore your purple feathers!'

She smiled her thanks. Marsha's outfit was certainly a great success, prompting compliments, not sneezes. Three different men had admired it: a heady new experience. Always before, she had been in Gerry's shadow – *he* the centre of attention, the one receiving applause. She drained her glass, beginning to feel light-headed, and not just from the champagne. It was as if she was thawing into life again after a protracted hibernation; realizing there *was* a world beyond loneliness and grief and early nights. Simon had moved a little closer and gave the ostrich-feather trim a mischievous tweak.

'You haven't told me *your* name.'

'Oh, sorry. Catherine. Catherine Jones.'

'Katherine with a K?'

'No, a C. You know, it's funny you should ask that. As a child, I always wished it was spelt with a K. It seemed more glamorous somehow. I was rather a plain child, you see, and . . .'

'Oh, come on! You don't expect me to believe that, do you? And even if it was true, it's certainly a case of ugly duckling turning into swan – in fact, a quite sensational swan!'

She blushed. Simon was a good deal younger than she was, and attractive in an arty sort of way, yet he was flattering her outrageously. She banished the plain motherless child with another draught of champagne. If Jonathan's TV agent told her she was sensational, she damned well would be – and enjoy it.

'You won't believe this, Simon,' she said, lolling back in her chair as she swallowed the last spoonful of crème brûlée, 'but earlier today I ate a whole chocolate mousse – I mean enough for eight or ten. I simply wolfed the lot.'

'You didn't!' He opened his eyes wide; unusual eyes, green, with long fair lashes.

'Yes. Wasn't that wicked of me?' She giggled. It seemed hilariously funny. She was laughing a lot. And drinking a lot. The wine just kept coming and coming. There had been Muscadet with the sole, claret with the duck, and some unpronounceable sweet wine with dessert. Not to mention all the champagne beforehand. Well, never mind, they'd be bringing coffee soon, and she would have hers strong and black. It wouldn't do to sit giggling on the train all the way to Stoneleigh. She should have gone home hours ago, but Jonathan had asked her to stay on for the dinner hosted by Shaw Hilliard for a select few party guests. At first she'd said no, but Jonathan insisted. Apparently someone had dropped out minutes before they were due to leave for the restaurant, and he declared it a heaven-sent opportunity – she absolutely *must* come. Simon had added his own inducements and then bagged the seat beside her, gradually edging closer and closer throughout the course of the meal until now his thigh was squeezed tightly against hers. It felt really rather nice; warm and sort of tantalizing.

There was a minor commotion as Jonathan lurched to his feet. He looked distinctly the worse for wear and had spilt red wine down his shirt. 'I'd like to propose a toast,' he said, seizing his glass and slopping more wine on the tablecloth. 'To my fantastic editor, who's not only beautiful but a bloody genius.' He bowed to the fragile-looking woman on his right. She had been drinking only Perrier all evening, Catherine had observed. In fact, most of the Shaw Hilliard contingent had remained sober, in all senses, while the author and his friends subsided into various degrees of drunkenness. Nicky had taken off her earrings and her shoes, and was draped across an actor called Sebastian. Angus and his neighbour were duelling with their cheese-knives, and a brash woman in television whose name she'd completely forgotten was using her untouched pudding as an ashtray.

'Without Margery,' Jon continued, swaying slightly on his feet, 'this book would never have been written.'

He had evidently forgotten that he had already proposed a toast to her when they'd first sat down to dinner, and used almost the same words (though minus the 'bloody'). And everyone had toasted *him*: drunk to the success of his book and the success of his new TV series.

'And while I'm on my feet . . .'

'You won't be for much longer, by the looks of it!' Kevin called jeeringly from the far end of the table.

'Shut up and stop barracking,' Jonathan snorted. 'As I was saying . . . What *was* I saying? Now you've put me off my stroke.' His eyes flicked from face to face, as if seeking inspiration, then came to rest on Catherine. 'Ah, yes!' – his face brightened – 'I want to drink to absent friends. And especially my old friend Gerry Jones. I haven't seen him for ages, but we were very close at one time. Catherine here is his wife.' He gestured to her grandly. 'And a very wonderful woman. But unfortunately Gerry couldn't come himself.'

Aghast, Catherine tried to stop him. 'Listen, Jon . . . I . . . he . . .' It was useless – he couldn't hear. He was still rambling on about his old friend from the north. Her cheeks were on fire and she was aware of Simon looking at her oddly, perhaps worrying about a jealous husband's wrath.

At last Jonathan sat down, and Catherine somehow managed to stumble to her feet. 'I'm terribly sorry, but I . . . I'm afraid I'll have to go.'

'Can I order you a taxi?' asked the Shaw Hilliard sales director, who was sitting opposite.

'Thank you, but I can get the tube to Waterloo.'

'At this hour?'

'Why? What *is* the time?'

'Ten to one.'

'It can't be!' The last train to Stoneleigh was 11.51.

'I'm afraid it is. But don't worry, let me phone a cab.'

A cab, she thought – all the way to Stoneleigh, *and* after midnight. That would cost a fortune.

'I'm sorry I can't offer you a lift,' said Simon, also getting up. 'But I never drink and drive – well, not since my brother got done last year.'

Nicky uncoiled her long body sinuously from Sebastian's lap. 'Why not stay the night with me, Catherine? I'm just about to leave.'

'No, honestly, I . . .'

'It's no trouble, really. We've got a room free at the top of the house.'

'But are you sure? I mean, it's very kind of you, but I don't like to impose.'

'Don't be silly, I'd be pleased to help out. And if Jonathan speaks so highly of you, you must be okay! Isn't that right, Jon?'

'Absolutely. And Catherine's a marvellous cook. She can make you breakfast in the morning.'

'Don't mention food, please, Jon.' Nicky put a hand on her stomach and rolled her eyes dramatically. 'I'm *stuffed*!' She turned to Sebastian and kissed him on the cheek. 'Goodbye, Sebbie darling, and thanks for all your help. Give me a buzz tomorrow and we'll arrange a drink or something. Oh, and talking of phones, I've got my mobile here, Catherine. D'you want to ring your husband and tell him where you are?'

'He's . . . away,' she blurted out, feeling more and more embarrassed. 'But I really ought to phone my son, if you don't mind. He'll be getting rather worried.' She looked down at her jumpsuit, almost surprised to see that her finery hadn't turned to rags. Midnight had struck (unnoticed) and the glamorous freewheeling actress had changed back into a suburban wife and mother.

6

Catherine opened her eyes, squinting against the glare of the sun. The window was in the wrong place; the blue curtains not drawn – not *there*. She sat up in bed, shivering despite the sun, and puzzled that her neck should feel so cold. Her hand encountered a smoothly shaven nape and hair cropped short all over. She remembered the Polish novelist last night who had told her, in his charming broken English, how much he loved the style. And of course, it was that marvellous colour, though not quite the deep mulberry of these walls. She looked around the room, which had sloping eaves and a quaint old wooden balcony just outside the window. The furniture was sparse – little more than the lumpy bed she was sleeping on, a rudimentary desk and a battered wardrobe (containing a tripod and a camera-case, as well as a cache of trendy clothes). Three multi-coloured rag-rugs covered the bare floor-boards, though with uneven gaps between them.

She groped for her watch on the upturned cardboard box which served as a bedside table. Nearly half past ten. How on earth could she have slept so long? And woken without a hangover? She pushed the bedclothes back, revealing the eccentric nightclothes Nicky had dug out for her: tracksuit bottoms, woolly socks (one black, one salmon-pink) and a tee-shirt with RICH BITCH emblazoned across the front. Looking up, she caught the eye of a flagrantly nude man gazing from a poster on the wall; his genitals on full display, his expression combining the sardonic with the sensuous. Damned cheek! – he must have been watching her all night. Her bedroom walls at Stoneleigh were adorned with dainty flower-prints, the furniture was pristine white; the bed a brand new Slumberland. She could just imagine Antonia's horror at these pock-marked walls (where other – perhaps even more erotic – posters had been removed, presumably), not to mention the dire state of the rugs.

She stretched luxuriously. Never mind Antonia – she *liked* the room. It had real character, and was wonderfully high up. The house was tall and narrow and occupied four storeys in a terraced street in Camden Town, and she was right at the top. She got out of bed to inspect the view: a jumble of grey roofs, an exhilarating expanse of sky and, immediately below, a strip of garden overgrown with spindly shrubs. The sun was pressing against the glass, as if determined to come in. It was a summer's day in January: gauzy clouds, strong shadows, and North London stretching away in a shimmering blue haze.

Wrapping herself in a rug from the bed, she crept down to the bathroom, which was on the floor below, next to Nicky's room. Judging by the silence, everyone else was still asleep, despite the lateness of the hour – well, late for *her* (and Stoneleigh). Nicky had said little about her living arrangements, remarking only as they got out of the taxi that 'the others' would have probably gone to bed.

Her brief visit to the bathroom last night, dazed by wine and euphoria, had left her with a vague impression of a dark and almost sinister place. In daylight it was extraordinary: black walls and royal blue ceiling, a jungle of tropical plants erupting at one end, and treasures everywhere: a clown puppet dangling overhead, an old apothecary jar full of glittering coloured marbles, a weird African mask glowering above the mirror. The bathtub was a monster – ancient, badly chipped and mounted on claw feet; a yellowy-green stain-line snailing down from beneath each tap. Clearly, little time was wasted here on cleaning. There was grime on every surface, the towels were crumpled in a damp heap on the floor, and a bewildering assortment of jars, bottles and potions sat collecting dust on two shelves above the bath.

She flushed the toilet, wincing at the noise. The washbasin was full of underclothes soaking in scummy water, so she tried the bath-tap marked HOT, but although she ran the water for several minutes, it remained obstinately cold. She wiped her hands on her tee-shirt, hitched the rug around her shoulders again, and set off down the next flight of stairs. There were two bedrooms on the first floor, but no sign of life from either.

Reaching the ground floor, she peered in at the sitting-room, again torn between delight and distaste. The room actually *smelt* – of stale wine, stale curry, cat's pee – and it was incredibly untidy. Magazines and papers were littered all over the floor; a cluster of dirty mugs stood on top of the rickety piano, while the remains of someone's supper occupied the sofa. Each chair was from a different era – tubular steel, thirties chintz, and a couple of genuine antiques. None the less, the room had definite charm and wherever you looked there was something to engage the eye. Every inch of wall space was covered with photographs and pictures – old prints in ornate frames rubbing shoulders with starkly modern paintings – and more canvases were stacked against one wall. Books jammed the shelves and were piled up on the floor: glossy tomes on art and film and fashion, as well as lurid-covered paperbacks. And other intriguing objects jostled for attention: an ancient mandolin leaning against a chair, an animal skull with great grinning teeth sitting high up on a shelf and looking down at a sort of abstract sculpture made of steel and string.

She stifled a fleeting impulse to whisk away the dirty mugs, and remove the egg-stained plates from the sofa. She was a stranger here, a guest. However, Nicky had urged her to help herself to tea in the morning, so she walked through into the kitchen, which was painted mustard-yellow and (inevitably) a shambles. A tabby cat was curled up on the windowsill, a bedraggled creature with scurfy-looking fur. She put out a hand to stroke it, but it shrank away, scratching fretfully at its ear.

'Poor puss,' she said. 'D'you want some milk?' Ditching her rug, she opened the fridge, which contained a dozen cans of beer, a thick coating of ice, and little else. There was an empty milk carton on the table and two torn biscuit-wrappings. Well, it would have to be milkless tea and an imaginary digestive. She turned on the kettle and hunted through the cupboards for the tea bags, which she eventually found in a stone jar labelled SUGAR. The sugar itself was still in its bag – and damp. There appeared to be nothing substantial to eat; no eggs or bacon, no cereals or bread; just a tin of catfood and an impressive array of spices: coriander, turmeric, fenugreek, cardamom, and dozens more, unlabelled.

'I'm afraid it's curried Whiskas for breakfast,' she informed the cat, but it had gone back to sleep again. There was still no sound from the rest of the household. At home, she would have been up for at least a couple of hours, helping Andrew and Antonia with their Saturday-morning schedule: hoovering and cleaning, washing the cars, sweeping the garden path – a whirlwind of activity. She made her tea and sat sipping it in deliciously decadent idleness, stretching her legs towards the boiler, which miraculously was hot. Last night had been a milestone: the first time since Gerry's death that she had enjoyed herself wholeheartedly, without an undercurrent of either guilt or grief. She cupped her hands around the mug, feeling a glow of warmth inside her.

'God, it's perishing down here!'

Nicky was standing in the doorway, dressed in luridly-striped leggings and a faded navy sweatshirt. 'Hi, Catherine,' she said with a yawn. 'Did you sleep okay?'

'Yes, thanks – amazingly well.'

'Good. More than I did! I've got a splitting headache.'

'Oh, dear. Poor you. Would you like a cup of tea? The kettle's just boiled.'

'Coffee, please.' Nicky flopped into a chair. 'It's in that right-hand cupboard, next to the hob. Do excuse the mess. Sharing a house seems to make everyone sink to the lowest common denominator. Slob's law, I suppose you'd call it. Darren's the worst, I have to say. But I don't like to make a fuss when he was the one who invited me here.' Nicky lapsed into silence, looking suddenly downcast.

Catherine washed up another mug, feeling slightly nervous. 'Is . . . *he* in advertising?' she asked, keen to keep the conversation going.

'Yeah, my partner.'

'You mean your . . . boyfriend?'

Nicky's eyebrows shot up. 'No way! He's only twenty-seven. We *are* great friends, though, which takes some doing, actually, when we see so much of each other. No – partners is the term we use at work. Every copywriter is teamed with an art director and the two of you share an office and work on ideas together. I suppose it *is* confusing. I remember one of the girls at the agency saying she'd told her next-door neighbour that her partner was expecting a baby. The poor woman was terribly embarrassed – she assumed they must be lesbians who'd gone in for artificial insemination.'

Catherine laughed and passed Nicky her coffee. 'I'm afraid there isn't any milk.'

'Shit! I bet that's Jo. She eats us out of house and home. Well, she can bloody well go and buy some more.' Nicky banged her mug down, slopping coffee on the table.

'And what does Jo do?' Catherine asked, hoping to sort out Nicky's house-mates before they put in an appearance.

'She's a journalist. She works two days a week for that new glossy mag *Elite*. She does a sort of book column – not so much reviews, more gossip from the literary world. You know, who's sleeping with their publisher – all that sort of stuff. And the rest of the time she works freelance.' Nicky took a sip of coffee and pulled a face. 'Pass the sugar, could you, Catherine. Thanks.' She took three spoonfuls, stirring vigorously. 'Believe it or not, Jo and Darren went to school together. They come from the same Hampshire village, and when they both got jobs in London, they decided to share a flat. Then Fiona arrived a few months later – you're sleeping in her room. She's a photographer and, luckily for us, she's got a share of a tiny studio in Islington. Otherwise there'd be cameras all over the place, or she'd be trying to turn the kitchen into a darkroom or something. Still, who am I to complain? I'm the new girl here. Well, maybe not so new. I moved in almost a year ago.' Nicky's voice had become despondent. 'I never really meant to stay that long. It was just a sort of . . . stopgap thing.'

'So where were you living before?'

'Battersea. In a super flat near the river.' Nicky kicked her foot against the chair-rung. 'That was with my *real* partner. But once we had a place together, the whole thing fell apart. So in the end we gave up the flat and both of us moved out. That's how I landed up here. You could say Darren took pity on me. You see, I'd more or less hit rock bottom and just didn't have the heart to find my own place. It was decent of him, really, because I was pretty useless at work and he covered for me there as well. Sean and I had been together eight years, so I was shattered when it all broke up.'

'Gosh, I'm sorry. It must have been quite awful.'

'Well, I suppose I should have seen the warning signs. I mean, he was getting really heavy, wanting kids – which I'm not ready for – and expecting me to settle down.' Nicky scrunched up the biscuit-paper and tossed it in the bin. 'I think it may have been jealousy on his part. You see, I was earning more than him and he couldn't handle it. And he hated me being late home. It was like living with a nagging wife. Mind you, I miss him terribly. In other ways we had a lot in common.'

'I'm sorry,' Catherine repeated, touched that Nicky should confide in her so freely when they had known each other less than twenty-four hours.

'Well, I should have got over it by now. In fact, I've been meaning to look for somewhere on my own. I'm much too old for this lark. I had enough of flat-shares in my twenties.'

'How old *are* you?' Catherine asked, hoping it didn't sound rude.

'Ancient. Thirty-five.'

'I'm *forty*-five next birthday.'

'Well, you don't look it, that's all I can say. And anyway, it's different for you – you're married.'

Catherine kept her eyes fixed on the table, studying the bare wood. 'Actually, I'm . . . I'm *not* married.'

Nicky looked bewildered. 'But I thought Jon said . . .'

Catherine put her mug down. 'That was my fault. It was all extremely awkward, I must admit. You see, my husband . . . died. But Jonathan didn't know, and I just couldn't bring myself to tell him at a party.'

'*Died?* God, Catherine, I . . . don't know what to say. Was it . . . recent?'

'Well, no. Eighteen months ago. But we'd rather lost touch with Jonathan and . . .'

'Hell.' Nicky looked embarrassed. 'Forgive me, Catherine. I've been rambling on about me and Sean, and *we* weren't even married.'

'Well, that makes it worse in some ways. I mean, people don't tend to sympathize like they do with a bereavement. Yet it can be every bit as painful. My friend Maeve broke up with *her* partner and she said it was a bit like a death.'

'Yeah, it did feel like that, especially the first month. D'you know' – Nicky looked up, smiling, from her cup – 'it's really nice to talk to you about it. The others don't understand. They're much younger, for one thing, and they've never had a serious relationship. They just don't realize what a wrench it is to lose your home and the whole way of life you've built with someone. But you don't need me to tell you that. My situation's nothing compared with what you've been through.'

'Mm.' Catherine nodded. 'Gerry and I were married twenty-five years.'

'Good God, you must have been a child bride! Sorry, that sounds awfully flippant, but . . .' She broke off with a curse as the ear-splitting bray of a trumpet reverberated through the ceiling. 'That's Darren, I'm afraid. He's into Wynton Marsalis. Christ! He and I may share a house and an office, but we bloody well don't share a taste in music. Oh, well' – she grinned – 'at least the din will wake Jo and she can go and get some milk. I loathe my coffee black. It's funny, you know,' she continued, rocking back in her chair. 'Jo can spend all day quite happily, fussing over half a measly paragraph, yet she's bone idle when it comes to shopping and stuff.'

At that moment a small, dark-haired girl bounced into the kitchen. 'Ah, Jo, right on cue! I was just having a go at you. This is Catherine. We met last night.'

'Hi,' said Jo. 'And if it's the milk you're slagging me off about, what can I say? I'm sorry. I forgot.'

'That's okay,' Catherine smiled, warming to the girl, who was pretty and petite, with dark curly hair and hazel eyes. The rough donkey jacket she wore looked incongruous with her stylish velvet hat. Though who was she to talk, in mismatched socks and baggy tracksuit bottoms? Actually, she found it rather refreshing that it didn't seem to matter in this house how weird or even dishevelled you looked. Nicky's hair was sticking up on end and there was a rent in the sleeve of Jo's jacket.

'Jo, can you get the papers while you're out?' Nicky asked, returning to her chair. 'And some more digestive biscuits. I see you've finished those as well.'

'That was Darren, if you *don't* mind. He went out drinking last night and said he had to line his stomach. Okay, I'm off. And don't talk about me while I'm gone.'

'Don't worry, we've got better things to do.'

'What's the matter, Nicky?' Jo demanded. 'If it was Darren being so shitty, I'd say he was pre-menstrual.'

Nicky smiled, despite herself. 'Sorry. I've got this terrible head-ache and I can't find the sodding aspirin.'

'Well why didn't you *ask*? I've got a whole bottleful upstairs. I bought them in case I couldn't make the deadline on that piece for *Harper's and Queen* and decided to top myself. I'll go and get them.'

'Wait a minute. Are you working today?'

Jo shook her head. 'No, why?'

'I thought we could all go out for brunch. They've opened this new place in Camden High Street and I want an excuse to try it.'

'Mm, sounds a good idea.'

'Is that okay with you, Catherine? I mean, you're not planning to rush back home?'

'Well, I . . . I hadn't really thought.'

'Stay, then. It's quite fun here on a Saturday, with the market and everything. And it's such a super day, we could go up to Primrose Hill. Darren's got a kite he made himself – and it actually flies!'

'Are you sure I won't be in the way?'

'No, 'course not. In fact, I'm dying to find out more about the gorgeous Jonathan. I only met him recently and I'm intrigued to think you knew him in his youth.'

'He and Gerry were at drama school together.'

'Oh, you were married to an actor. How exciting!'

Catherine was saved from replying by Darren's bleary-eyed arrival. At least, she assumed it was Darren, since only one man lived here and Darren looked fiercely male, despite his ponytail. He was wearing an almost indecently short dressing-gown, and very little else. His long legs were furred with thick black hair and more tufts of hair sprouted exuberantly on his chest. His stubble, though, was the well-tended designer kind, and his ponytail was tied neatly with a ribbon. Catherine tried to keep her eyes from his legs. He had only to bend over and all would be revealed.

'Hello,' she said shyly, after Nicky made the introductions.

Darren grunted in acknowledgement, then asked her if she smoked.

'Sorry, no,' she said. Noxious fumes were forbidden in salubrious Manor Close.

'Pity. I'm out of fags.'

'Darren, you are foul. You've only just met Catherine and already you're bumming fags off her.'

'I'll get you some,' said Jo, who had returned with Nicky's aspirin. 'I'm going out anyway. But it's strictly cash up front. Last time you didn't pay me back for weeks.'

'That's libel.'

'You mean slander, actually, but never mind. It's neither – just the truth.'

'Oh, don't be so pedantic, Jo. I'm not in the mood. I feel really shitty.'

'What's wrong with everyone this morning?' Jo herself looked smugly healthy. 'Here, have some aspirin too, Darren. And if you want your fags, I'm leaving in two minutes and I need money on the table.'

'He's not as bad as he sounds,' Nicky whispered once Darren had shambled out of the kitchen. 'But he takes for ever to wake up. He's at his best around midnight.'

'That's libel too,' groused Darren, reappearing with a five-pound note in his hand.

'*Slander.*' Jo grabbed the note and slammed out of the front door.

'Ah, blessed peace,' said Nicky, shaking three aspirins from the bottle.

'What's the matter with the cat?' asked Catherine anxiously. She had noticed it scratching its ear again and whimpering.

Nicky shrugged. 'Emotional deprivation. It's Fiona's cat and Fiona's away. Her mother's ill, so she's had to go back home and hold the fort. She thought she'd be back in a couple of weeks, but it's been well over a month now, and poor William's pining for her.'

'William?'

'Yeah. She named him after Wordsworth, though he's a most *un*poetic beast. William the Conqueror would be more appropriate – at least before he started moping.'

'Maybe it's something physical, though? I mean, his ear seems to be bothering him.'

'He'll survive,' said Darren. 'Fiona should be back next week. They're taking her mother into hospital, which lets her off the hook. *And* us,' he added, extracting a dirty glass from the sink and filling it with water. 'It's a bloody nuisance looking after Will.'

'Oh, he's okay,' said Nicky. 'And it's *William.* I have to warn you, Catherine, Darren insists on shortening names. He calls Fiona Fee and it drives her up the wall. I'm Nick, of course, and you'll be Cath, no doubt.'

'My father would go mad!' said Catherine. 'He even used to object if people pronounced it Cath-rine. I had this friend at school called Maggie, but *he* called her Marg-*ar*-ret, much to her annoyance.'

'Well, I'm Nic-o-la,' said Nicky, enunciating absurdly. 'And I live with Jo-se-phine Ro-sann-a.'

Darren put his glass down. '*I* didn't know her second name was Rosanna. God, what a bloody mouthful!'

'Well, don't let on I told you. She'll be furious – she hates it.'

'Ros,' said Darren reflectively.

'Ssh, she's coming.' The front door had just slammed again, and footsteps were approaching.

'Which means she can't have done much shopping.'

'Jo never does much shopping.'

'So is anyone cooking today?' asked Darren, fiddling with the box of matches, as if impatient to light up.

'We're eating out – all of us.'

'Oh, really? Thanks for telling me.'

'I'm telling you now. We're going to Alfredo's.'

'Who's Alfredo – Alf, I mean, of course!'

'It's that new place Carol recommended. She went there last weekend.'

'Oh, yeah. She liked the decor.'

'We'll hardly be eating the decor.'

Jo plonked the shopping on the table: milk, biscuits, the *Independent, Guardian* and *Sun*, a couple of glossy magazines, twenty Camels and a tin of Kit-E-Kat.

Nicky picked the tin up. 'William's off his food.'

'What, still?'

'Yeah. Catherine thinks there might be something wrong with him – an ear infection, maybe.'

'Well, I could take him to the vet on Monday. I'm not that busy at the moment.'

'Christ! It'll cost a bomb,' Darren said from behind the *Sun*.

'No more than a week's supply of your bloody cigarettes.'

'Lay off, will you, Jo? Just because you've given up . . .'

'Reformed smokers are the worst,' agreed Nicky. 'Once, Sean and I had some friends to dinner and one of them asked him not to smoke. Can you imagine – in his own flat! Of course, it turned out she'd just kicked a forty-a-day habit and was positively oozing virtue.'

'Have *you* ever smoked?' Jo asked Catherine, making an obvious effort to include her in the conversation.

'No, never.' She almost wished she had. Her life seemed suddenly so mundane – no vices, no affairs, no way-out music or high-powered job. 'Look, let me make the tea,' she offered. The role of Mum seemed all that she was good for.

'Thanks,' said Nicky, reaching for the *Guardian*. 'There's a teapot in that cupboard over the sink.'

Catherine refilled the kettle, then collected up the dirty mugs and washed them. The water was running warm now, so she began working through the whole pile of washing-up – it was the least she could do in return for her free bed. A comfortable silence had descended on the kitchen. The other three were leafing through the papers; Darren smoking, Nicky munching biscuits. It must be getting on for midday, yet no one seemed in any rush to go anywhere or do anything. It felt a bit like being a student – not that she'd experienced college life first-hand. She had gone straight from school to marriage and had her first child at eighteen. How odd, she thought, for Nicky to say she 'wasn't ready for kids'. Surely she was leaving it rather late? When *she* was thirty-five, Andrew was practically grown up, sitting his Cambridge entrance exam, and Kate was doing GCSEs. She'd had four pregnancies altogether, two, alas, ending in miscarriage. She and Gerry had always wanted more children, though looking back she wondered how they would have managed. As it was, pregnancy seemed to have taken up a huge chunk of her youth (morning sickness, swollen ankles, backache), or recovering from a labour or miscarriage. And she had always been an adjunct to the rest of them – Gerry's wife, or the children's mother, or the receptacle for a baby – not a person in her own right. At Andrew's playschool, they had even referred to the parents by the children's Christian names, so she'd been 'Mrs Andrew'; yet another suppression of identity. Of course, at the time she hadn't seen it in those terms – only now, faced with three single independent people, was she beginning to reflect on what she had missed. Or *gained*, perhaps. Did she envy them or pity them? Their freedom was certainly enviable: freedom not to cook or clean, freedom to put off having kids until they'd enjoyed a life of their own. And yet . . .

'Cath, leave the washing-up.' Darren exhaled a lazy plume of smoke. 'It's Saturday. Come and read the papers.'

'Okay, I . . . I'll just make the tea.' Andrew and Antonia never read the papers till the evening. Work came first, or chores. But she wasn't Mrs Andrew any more; she was Cath – a party girl, a single. She left the bowl half full of greasy dishes, then made the tea *their* way: no sugar basin or milk jug, no matching cups and saucers.

'Tea up,' she said, putting the pot on the table with four assorted mugs, two of them still badly stained inside.

'Great!' said Jo. 'Here, have a pew.'

Catherine poured the tea and sat back contentedly on a battered kitchen chair, with two chocolate biscuits and *The Face*. She had never read *The Face* before. There was a man on the cover with a dozen silver spikes through his tongue, and the blurb for an article on drugs. She turned to the drugs feature straight away – it was time she broadened her outlook.

Can you feel the rush? she read, sucking the chocolate off her biscuit. *You're on the elevator, going up. Think big. Go wild. No compromise. You're off your head. You've arrived!*

I'm not sure about that, she thought, but I'm jolly well going to be a hedonist for once, and enjoy a day of utter self-indulgence.

7

'Hi, Nicky! How're you doing?' A curvaceous girl in frayed jeans and
a tatty sheepskin jacket came bouncing up to their table, almost falling over Darren's kite, propped precariously against his chair.

'I'm fine, Liz. How about you?'

'So-so.'

'Want to join us?'

'Love to, but I can't. I'm meeting Greg and I'm late.'

''Bye, then.'

''Bye.' Once she had gone, Nicky turned to Catherine. 'That
was Elizabeth O'Neil. She's only thirty-one and she's just set up
her own production company. Two years ago she was still a runner,
would you believe.'

Catherine hoped she didn't look too blank. Much of the discussion over brunch had needed an interpreter. Apart from the
advertising jargon, there were names she'd never heard of, and
strings of initials – HHCL, GGT and so on – which she found
terribly confusing. And wasn't it odd that a girl who owned her
own company should look so down at heel? Nicky, in contrast, was
dressed to kill, in a leopard-print micro-skirt and clumpy patent
shoes with silver buckles. And Darren had changed from his shabby
dressing-gown into black leather trousers (wickedly expensive,
judging by the cut) and an oversized black sweatshirt with
DESTROY printed down one sleeve in bold white letters. Yet Jo –
like many others in the café – was dressed, workman-style, in old
jeans and heavy boots. *She* came somewhere in between, in a denim
skirt of Jo's, shorter than she had worn in years, and Nicky's angora
jersey – pistachio, striped with pink and white, and apparently
known as her 'ice-cream top'. She felt a childish pleasure in wearing

fancy dress – she was a multi-coloured cassata melting gloriously in the heat. And in borrowed clothes she could be someone else; slam the door on the last dark depressing months.

'Another drink, Cath?' Darren asked, moving the kite to safety under the table.

'Do you think I ought?' she laughed, draining the last inch of neon-red liquid in her glass – a concoction called Blast-Off, which she had chosen on the strength of its name (although Saturday Siren and Love Byte had also sounded tempting). It tasted innocent enough – lemony and fizzy – but it had gone straight to her head. The others were drinking lager, which seemed, frankly, unadventurous in a setting like this. Alfredo's looked more space-age than Italian, with its magenta-coloured walls, spangled 3-D mirrors and silver metal chairs. The place was heaving with people and noise – an excited buzz of conversation rising above the thump-thump-thump of the music; its insistent beat pulsating through her body like an electrical charge.

Darren glanced around for their waiter – a young Armenian with one large silver earring and a sleekly shaven head. Like most of the staff, he had only a smattering of English, yet somehow the right order always arrived at the right table, *and* in record time. Catherine watched in fascination as the waiters sped in and out of the kitchen at an almost dangerous pace, while the barman juggled glasses and bottles with nonchalant skill. Darren, on the other hand, was indolence personified. He had abandoned his blinis after only a few mouthfuls, evidently preferring to smoke, and was lolling in his chair, his legs stretched out in front of him and a lazy arm draped along the back of Jo's chair. He spotted the waiter and ordered more drinks by sign-language, holding up his glass, then pointing to the other three. The Armenian nodded and pranced off.

Nicky took the last bite of her bagel and cream cheese and looked longingly out of the window. 'You know, on a day like this, we should be down at the coast.'

Jo had just forked in a frill of designer lettuce, but she shook her head vigorously before swallowing it. 'Let me warn you, Catherine – steer clear of Nicky's trips to the coast! She's a windsurfing fanatic. And I *mean* fanatic. She's got certificates and things to prove it. I'm hardly the world's best swimmer, but she talked me into going last September, and God, I practically drowned.'

'Rubbish. You were brilliant. You should take it up, I told you.'

'No way! I like keeping warm and dry – *and* staying upright.'

The waiter was back already with their drinks. Darren helped him clear a space on the table, then took a gulp from his brimming glass. 'Cath, have *you* ever tried it?'

'What?'

'Windsurfing.'

'Er, no, I haven't.' There were so many things she hadn't tried which *they* had: Ecstasy, flotation tanks, playing in a rock band, trekking in Kashmir. Never mind Kashmir – she hadn't even crossed the Channel, although she wouldn't dream of admitting it in such cosmopolitan company. They'd be shocked, if not incredulous, to hear she'd never been abroad.

'You don't know what you're missing, Catherine. It's the nearest thing to heaven.'

'Bar sex,' grinned Darren.

'No, *not* bar sex. How could any mere man compare with a cross-shore force five and peeling waves?'

'I don't know what the hell you're talking about, but you've met the wrong men, obviously.'

'Yeah, you're probably right. Anyway, I'm going to the Virgin Islands at Easter, to put in some serious practice. I decided last night. Sebastian's just come back from Virgin Gorda and he said the conditions were ideal.'

'It's okay for some,' groused Darren. 'Leave me stuck in the office, slaving over a layout pad, while you're lotus-eating on some tropical island.'

'Windsurfing's bloody hard work, I'll have you know.'

'You're telling me,' said Jo. 'My idea of a good holiday is lying in the sun doing bugger all.'

'Talking of sun, let's drink up and go. It's a crime to waste this weather.' Nicky waved to the waiter and made a scribbling movement. The bill arrived in seconds, but provoked a heated discussion about who owed what and how big a tip they should leave. Catherine sat in silence, embarrassed by the arguments and alarmed that a few drinks and snacks should amount to such an exorbitant sum.

'Let *me* do this,' she offered, in a burst of guilty gratitude. She could always economize next week – next month.

'Certainly not,' said Nicky. 'We all pay our own way. And take no notice of the bickering. We wouldn't enjoy going out together if we didn't have a good bitch about the bill.'

'D'you realize,' Darren said, extracting a twenty-pound note from his wallet and laying it on the table with a flourish, 'we haven't *been* out for at least a month – not all of us. What with Christmas and New Year and then that hassle with Kendall's Krisps. You won't believe this, Cath, but Nick and I had to go into the office every single Saturday in December, including Christmas Eve. We were working for this nightmare of a client who rejected six campaigns on the trot, then sodded off to another agency.'

'I suppose we were lucky not to get the chop,' Nicky murmured. 'I mean, Rebecca was fired from BML after they lost that big car account.'

'At least she was given three months' money and allowed to stay in the office for a few weeks.' Darren turned to Catherine with a wave of his cigarette. 'Often you're out the same day. This friend of mine who worked in computers had a really gruesome experience. They invited him and a dozen others to breakfast at a swanky hotel – silver teapot, starched white napkins, the lot. Then when they'd finished noshing and were expecting some sort of promotion, or at least a pat on the back, the company solicitor waltzed in and gave them this spiel about "downsizing" and "restructuring" . . .'

' "Delayering's" my favourite,' Jo put in. 'It sounds like a post-modernist haircut.'

'Anyway,' said Darren, 'the bottom line was they weren't allowed back into their offices – not even to fetch their things. It was tea and toast, then out into the cold.'

'*Don't.*' Nicky gave a dramatic shudder. 'You're spoiling the weekend.'

'Let's go and see Greta,' Jo suggested. 'She'll cheer us up. And anyway I want to buy a hat.'

'You've *got* a hat,' said Darren. 'In fact, you've got hundreds of hats.'

'Yeah, but she's making these fake-fur ones and she said they'd be ready today.'

'Great!' said Nicky. 'Perhaps she'll have one to match my skirt. Catherine, fancy a leopardskin hat?'

'Mm, maybe.' Catherine struggled with another pang of conscience about the state of her bank account. Hedonism certainly didn't come cheap. Well, never mind. Tomorrow it would be back to Stoneleigh in all its Sabbath lethargy: empty streets and no noise beyond the occasional dutiful purring of a hedge-trimmer and *The Archers* in the background.

A far cry from Camden Town. They had stepped out of Alfredo's into a blast of sound, a shriek of smells; the High Street exuberantly alive. Swarthy-skinned men were frying sausages and onions on makeshift pavement stalls, or making sizzling crêpes. Music throbbed and pounded on all sides: lush-stringed ballads, haunting blues, and more aggressive types of music she couldn't put a name to. The whole world seemed to be concentrated in this one area of London – all ages, types and skin-colours; Jamaicans jostling Japanese, Arabs cheek by jowl with turbaned Asians. Catherine gazed around. She couldn't remember seeing a non-white face in Manor Close and its environs – well, apart from the black labrador's, at number twenty-eight. It was as if she'd gone abroad at last and touched down in some exotic bazaar: a maze of bustling stalls selling everything from rugs to incense, beneath a dazzling sun. This surely wasn't England – or midwinter.

She stopped at a candle stall, entranced by the array of styles and colours – an army of tall phallic towers, a squad of smaller cones, and ingenious novelty shapes: half-peeled bananas with curled-back yellow skins; shiny black hob-nailed boots. The stallholder had a ring through his nose and a row of studs along one bushy eyebrow. Her eyes were drawn to the nose-ring as she imagined him at one of Antonia's formal candlelit dinners, lighting a fat wax phallus in place of her non-drip Easi-flow. She dismissed the thought hastily. What was wrong with her today and why did she keep criticizing Antonia? She was a perfectly good daughter-in-law. Yet occasionally and secretly she wished her son had married someone else. Both the children had grown up to be so *serious* – Andrew committed to his career, Kate to high ideals. Sometimes they had made her feel quite frivolous, even when she was working for Gerry and had been the soul of conventional virtue.

'This is mostly tat,' said Nicky as they fought their way through the crowds. 'But up at the Lock you get a lot of craft stalls – people like Greta who sell their own stuff. She was at art school and she's talented. We're nearly there now. See that bridge – well, that's the canal.'

'Oh, it's gorgeous!' Catherine exclaimed as they turned off the tacky High Street and on to cobblestones. Her magical mystery tour had transported her from Eastern bazaar to quaint rural English scene. Water was foaming through the lock-gate and, beyond, graceful willows cascaded in green fountains over the bank.

'The residents don't think it's so gorgeous,' Darren said, tossing his cigarette-end into the water. 'They're always bitching about the noise and the drug-pushers and the danger to their precious kids. The local papers are full of it. Apparently someone's twelve-year-old daughter was sold crack on her way to school last week.'

'Well, that *is* awful,' Nicky said. 'Suppose it was *your* child?'

'I don't intend to have any, thanks. Besides, I doubt if it was true – grass, perhaps, but not crack.'

'Come off it, Darren, *you*'ve been offered stuff enough times.'

'Yeah, but I'm not twelve.'

'Stop arguing, you two. I'm going to say hello to Greta.' Jo disappeared into the mêlée of stalls which stretched beyond the canal. Catherine followed at a more leisurely pace. She was still wearing her purple suede boots, which tended to slow her down a bit. Anyway, what was the point of rushing when there was so much to see and enjoy? Having gorged herself at Alfredo's, she was now feasting on colours: sherbet-lemon yellow fizzing on her tongue, claret-red exploding in her stomach. Her eye moved from stained-glass plaques to glittering mosaic tiles, brightly painted wooden toys and, finally, to Greta's stall, where Jo was already trying on hats. And what hats! Every type of fake fur from ponyskin to zebra, and other styles in coloured felt, adorned with plastic grapes or huge silk flowers. She was introduced to Greta, who wore a sunflower-trimmed black stetson above her ancient duffel coat and tracksuit-bottoms below.

'Hello, you people,' she called, rubbing her mittened hands and shivering extravagantly. 'I'm absolutely frozen.'

'But the sun's quite warm,' said Nicky. 'Especially for mid-January.'

'I'm not *in* the sun. And anyway, you're walking about. I'm just sitting here, and honestly, I can hardly feel my feet.'

'Shall I fetch you a coffee?' Jo offered.

'I'd rather you kept an eye on the stall. Would you mind – just for a few minutes? So I can go and get a sandwich.'

'Sure. No problem. It'll be practice for next Saturday.'

Once Greta was out of earshot, Jo grabbed Darren's arm. 'She's asked me to run the stall again! She's branching out into waistcoats. She says she's made dozens already and wants to see how they go in Portobello Road, while I hold the fort for her here.'

'I can't think why you're so excited. She only pays you peanuts.'

'That's okay – it's all she can afford. Besides, it's not the money, stupid. I want to write a piece about it – you know, Camden Market from the stallholder's angle. I should have done it the first time, but I was too busy working out people's change and making sure the stock wasn't nicked.'

'We'll come and give you moral support.' Nicky tried on a zebra beret and inspected herself in the mirror.

'If we're not working,' Darren said morosely. 'We can't expect two weekends off in a row.'

'God, you're gloomy today.' Nicky turned her back on him. 'Found anything you like yet, Jo?'

'Yeah, this one.'

'Mm, it suits you.' Nicky unpinned a leopardskin hat from the back of the stall and held it against her skirt. 'How much are they, by the way?'

'Only ten quid.'

'I'll have a couple then – the zebra and this leopardskin. Catherine, how about you?'

'No, I don't think . . .'

'Let me buy you one – I'd like to.'

'Oh, no, honestly. I wouldn't hear of it.'

'Why not? I'm flush today. I haven't spent my Christmas bonus yet.'

'But you've already put me up for the night and . . .'

'Oh, come on! It was only a grotty bedroom that wasn't being used. Jo, what do you think for Catherine? Fur or flowers?'

Catherine stood there, grinning like a kid, while Jo and Nicky picked out half a dozen hats, debating which would be best for her. It was like having sisters, or being part of a big family – something she'd missed out on. Her childhood had been solitary and her father always distant, emotionally at least.

Her 'sisters' had finally agreed on a wide-brimmed black creation, decorated with a bunch of purple grapes. 'It's perfect with your hair, Catherine,' Nicky said, holding up the mirror for her. 'What do you think?'

'Yes, it does look rather good. But *I'll* buy it.' She got out her purse, praying there'd be enough money left.

'No you won't! It's *my* treat.'

'But . . .'

'Ah, Greta, thank God you're back!' said Darren, rescuing his kite from the clutches of an inquisitive child. 'Do stop these women fighting.'

'What are they fighting about?'

'Ignore him,' Nicky said, producing a sheaf of five-pound notes. 'I'll have these three, please.'

'And this one for me,' said Jo.

'Fantastic! I could do with a few more customers like you. Business is really slow today.' She put the hats in pink-striped plastic bags. 'I suppose most people are cleaned out after Christmas.'

'Actually, I'd like to wear mine now,' said Catherine. 'It seems a shame not to show it off.'

'Good idea.' Greta took it out of the bag again. 'And if anyone asks where you got it, be sure to direct them to me. The more publicity the better!'

'Of course we will, Greta,' Nicky laughed, 'but we'll expect a discount next time.'

Catherine put her hat on, tilting it to a rakish angle. She had never bothered much with hats, disillusioned early on by her blue school felt with its stupid badge and limp elastic. But this was in a different league: original, flamboyant.

Greta nodded in approval, her mouth full of bacon sandwich. Everyone around seemed to be eating on the hoof – munching pitta bread or burgers, or dipping into steaming cartons with plastic spoons and forks.

'Let's go to West Yard,' Jo suggested, 'and get some hot spiced wine. Greta's right – it *is* cold once you stop moving.'

She led the way through a covered market area, down some twisty stairs and into a cobbled courtyard, again swarming with people and rich in smells, predominantly (and fiercely) curry. Catherine smiled to herself. Her whirlwind tour had now plunged her into several different continents at once. In the space of a few square yards, a host of rival stalls were dishing out their various wares: Chinese noodles, tandoori chicken, spicy tortillas, doner kebabs, even Sammy's Fish Stall. It was deliciously absurd – her nose assailed by Eastern spices and English fish and chips, her head adorned with a bunch of purple grapes, and the last red rush of the Blast Off still skittering through her bloodstream. She *deserved* a day abroad. For so many years, holidays had been practically nonexistent. Her family had travelled: Gerry the actor on occasional foreign tours (always on the cheap, of course), Andrew and Antonia enjoying weekend breaks in Amiens or Bruges or wherever, and Kate backpacking intrepidly round India before taking a job in Delhi. But *she*, the wife and mother, had stayed put. Oh, she had often dreamed of holidays, even planned them sometimes, but they never quite materialized. And once Gerry bought the business, they had become slaves to it in effect; never able to get away together. So if a European supplier needed visiting, it was Gerry who would go, leaving *her* at home to deal with irate VAT inspectors or temperamental fax machines.

Even London was largely unknown territory, although they lived so near. When they'd first moved south, so many prospects beckoned – theatres, galleries, cinemas, museums – but all they ever seemed to manage was a film at the local Odeon or the odd Chinese meal in Worcester Park. They had turned into a pair of boring workaholics, trapped behind their desks; reading reviews of new exhibitions and plays, but invariably deciding that there wasn't time to go this week (or next week, or next month).

Well, today she was making up for it. So to hell with tedious money worries. The mulled wine would be on *her* (and if she didn't have enough cash, she would just have to pay by cheque). After all, any self-respecting holiday was supposed to clean you out.

'If I eat or drink another thing, I'll burst!' Catherine wiped away her whipped-cream moustache. 'Chocalissimo' had proved more a meal than a drink – marshmallows melting in the giant-sized cup, and an avalanche of cream on top, sprinkled liberally with chocolate flake.

'Shall we go back after this?' said Jo. 'I'm knackered after our walk.'

Nicky spooned chocolate debris from her cup. 'It's your fault, Darren – you and your wretched kite! I didn't realize we'd have to run with it.'

'Don't blame *me*. We needed a bit more wind, that's all.'

'My daughter used to have a kite,' said Catherine. 'And we were flying it in the park one day, when . . .' She broke off in shock, staring at the door. Gerry had just walked in with his arm round another woman. She sprang to her feet to confront him, only to realize it wasn't Gerry, but someone uncannily like him, with the same colouring and build, the same engaging smile.

'What's wrong?' asked Jo, seeing her stricken face.

'Er, nothing. I . . . just need the loo.'

She stopped on the way to the toilet, watching Gerry's double sit down at a table in the corner. His girlfriend looked much younger than him, but they were obviously in love – gazing into each other's eyes, their fingers intertwined.

How *dare* you, she muttered under her breath. How dare you die and leave me on my own. She stood rooted to the spot, with a feeling of desperate loneliness. She didn't belong with this trendy crowd. She had never smoked a joint in her life, and had never even heard of GHB, which Darren had mentioned earlier and was apparently some other type of drug. And the music that was playing now – what *was* it, for heaven's sake? She dared not ask, for fear of revealing her yawning ignorance. Techno, garage, jungle, hiphop, were just words to her – and foreign words at that – but the others had been discussing them with enviable expertise. Some parents learned from their offspring, but Andrew was more likely to listen to Haydn, and Kate had never really progressed beyond Joan Baez. Even the photos on the walls here were of people who meant nothing to her; all young people, of course. She pulled off her hat and stuffed it in her bag – mutton dressed as lamb.

She stumbled downstairs to the cloakroom, wondering where she did belong. Her own house had gone and she was living like a parasite, without the guts to be herself. In an hour or two she would be back at Manor Close, sitting in her spotless room, waiting for Andrew and Antonia to return from a Rotary dinner. And tomorrow Jack and Maureen were coming to lunch. How unfair it was that Gerry's parents should live into their eighties while Gerry had failed to make it even to fifty. But she couldn't change the facts; deny a death with crazy clothes and exotic drinks. She was a middle-aged widow, whether she liked it or not, and the sooner she got back to reality, the better. In any case, the others were probably sick of her tagging along, pretending to be one of them, when she was old enough to be Jo and Darren's mother.

She splashed her face with cold water and washed London's grime off her hands. When she got back to the table, Darren was doing his Maggie Thatcher impersonation, to the amusement of those in earshot.

Jo stopped laughing and looked at her in concern. 'Are you okay?' she asked. 'We were getting a bit worried.'

'Yes, I . . . I'm fine. But I really should be going. Can I get the tube from here?'

'There isn't one at Primrose Hill. But we'll walk you up to Chalk Farm. It's only a few minutes.'

'Hold on, Catherine,' Nicky said. 'Your clothes are still at the house. Wouldn't it be easier to stay another night? It's Jonathan's do tomorrow, don't forget.'

'What do? I thought he'd had it?'

'No, the private lunch at his flat.'

'I don't remember him mentioning lunch.'

'I'm not surprised. You were so involved with Simon . . . And by the way, Simon's bound to be there. And I imagine you want to see *him* again!'

Catherine paused. It would be rather exciting, but was it worth the risk? In the cold light of day, he'd realize how old she was. She should never have flirted with him so shamelessly in the first place. She didn't belong with a man of thirty-two, any more than with Nicky and the rest of them.

'Anyway,' Nicky persisted, 'Jon made me promise to bring you. He said he wants to catch up with your news.'

'Well, in that case, I'm not sure I . . .'

'Oh *please* come. It'll be great. We can have a good old gossip on the way.'

'What Nick means,' Darren interrupted, grinning sardonically at Catherine, 'is that she's planning on shagging Jon and wants you to help things along.'

'That's absolute rubbish!' Nicky retorted, blushing.

'Well, we've heard nothing else but Jonathan this and Jonathan that since you first laid eyes on him.'

'Okay. So what? I don't meet famous actors all that often.'

'Mm, especially *handsome* famous actors – conveniently divorced and on the prowl.'

'Oh, piss off, Darren.' Nicky slammed her cup down on its saucer. 'Catherine, if you'd like to stay, you'll be more than welcome. I'll even drive you to the party, if that'll change your mind. In fact, it probably wouldn't hurt me to lay off the drink for a day.'

'Well, it's sweet of you, but I'm afraid my in-laws are coming to lunch tomorrow and I ought to help entertain them.'

'Okay, it doesn't matter. But let's keep in touch anyway. Scribble down your phone number and I'll give you a ring in a week or two.'

Catherine wrote her number on a paper serviette and passed it to Nicky with her last remaining five-pound note, to cover her share of the bill. Then, buttoning up her coat, she followed the others out into the street.

'God, it really is cold now,' Nicky said.

'And so dark,' Jo added, with a shiver.

Dark. And cold. The words echoed in Catherine's head as she walked along the now littered pavement; empty cartons underfoot, smashed bottles in the gutter. Cold in her Stoneleigh bedroom, despite the efficient central heating. Dark in the empty house, for all its blaze of lights. Did she really need to be there tomorrow? Jack and Maureen came to lunch at least once a month and invariably talked about Gerry – heavy, black-edged talk which left a pall on the whole ensuing week.

She could see the tube ahead, only a few yards away. Dark down there, too. And lonely. Travelling back on her own, letting herself into a house which wasn't home. Two beggars sat hunched by the entrance; one of them, a girl of roughly Kate's age, had neither coat nor sweater, only a tee-shirt saying SHARE NEEDLES. Her eyes were open, but she stared vacantly at the passers-by, inhabiting a dark world of her own.

Dark. And cold.

'Listen,' Catherine said, suddenly jerking to a halt. 'I've changed my mind. If you're sure it's no trouble and nobody objects, I'd *love* to stay another night.'

8

Catherine peered at herself in the steamed-up bathroom mirror, running a finger along the outline of her lips and almost surprised to see no trace of Simon's kiss. Shouldn't it have marked her mouth indelibly? She was still tingling from that kiss, dazed by it, triumphant. He had seen her in the cold light of day and it *hadn't* put him off. Far from it – he had asked her out to dinner tomorrow evening.

She turned off the taps and stepped into the bath, hoping the hot water would help her to relax. So far, sleep had proved impossible. Every time she closed her eyes, Simon slid beneath her lids, his come-to-bed smile enticing her. She had never been to bed with anyone but Gerry, so no wonder she felt nervous – a gauche and awkward teenager embarking on her first date, and with a TV agent at that.

She looked critically at her body, trying to see it through Simon's eyes. Her breasts were still passable, full and reasonably firm, but she had tiny silvery stretch marks on her stomach. They were so faint they barely showed; all the same, she wished she could wave her magic wand and erase them, *and* her appendicitis scar. Naked bodies were unkind – mercilessly exposed their owners' history and vices: operations, pregnancies, greed, intemperance. She stroked her pubic hair – at least that was nice and thick, but an uninspiring brown. If she'd been truly daring, she would have had Spiced Plum top and bottom.

She lay back in the water and willed herself to relax, but a shoal of new anxieties instantly swam into her head. Had she seemed too eager in agreeing to tomorrow's dinner? She ought to have made a show of consulting her (blank) diary, juggled dates, pretended men were queuing up to see her. And whatever should she wear? Missoni or no, the purple jumpsuit wouldn't do a third time; besides, the boots had begun to hurt so much it was agony to walk. She was going back to Stoneleigh first thing in the morning to search out something suitable – her turquoise dress perhaps, except she hadn't worn it for an age and it probably needed cleaning. She would have to go to Sketchley's and pay extra for the same-day service. And also buy some decent tights. And wash her hair. And shave her legs. And she had promised to drive to Walton and call in on Jack and Maureen, to make up for not seeing them today. She would be really pushed for time, especially as Simon had suggested she meet him straight from work. She had to admit he had seemed eager, too, now that he knew she wasn't married. She had arrived at Jonathan's early, so she could break the news of Gerry's death. He had been shocked, of course, and they had arranged to meet again when they could talk more fully and freely. But at least she had surmounted the first hurdle, and Jon had tactfully told Simon.

She reached out for the soap – or what was left of it; a slimy shell-pink stump. She must get to bed and catch up on her beauty sleep, not wallow in the bath all night. Having sponged herself hastily, she stepped dripping on to the lino. Bathmats were a refinement unknown in Gosforth Road. She dried herself as best she could on the damp and grubby towels, before donning her eccentric nightclothes and Jo's long chunky cardigan, which she was using as a dressing-gown. Pausing outside Nicky's door, she wished they could continue the lively conversation they'd had driving back from Jonathan's. But Nicky had plumped for an early night and, judging by the silence, was already fast asleep.

She set off up the next flight of stairs, then changed her mind and turned back again. A milky drink might help her sleep. There wasn't very much milk left, so it would have to be a small one.

The kitchen was still warm and, due to her blitz this morning, far less grease-encrusted. She had cleaned up partly for William's sake. The poor cat seemed so miserable and if he did have an infection, dirt and grime would only make it worse. Jo was supposed to be taking him to the vet in the morning, though she had gone to see her parents in Brockenhurst and still wasn't back.

She shared the warm milk between them – half a cup for her and a saucerful for William, but he merely sniffed it and turned away. 'You need some tender loving care, Puss,' she murmured, gently fondling his head. He winced at her touch and slunk into the sitting-room. She followed him and sat down on the sofa with her drink, trying to work out what to say to Andrew and Antonia about tomorrow evening's engagement. She hated the thought of lying to them, but she certainly didn't intend to reveal that she was going out with a man only five years older than *they* were.

Suddenly she was distracted by a noise from above – the rhythmic creaking of a bed. She listened, both embarrassed and intrigued. Darren's girlfriend had come round earlier on and he had taken her upstairs, ostensibly to listen to his new CD. The music had been short-lived, and the only sounds now were the continued shuddering of the bedsprings and a gasping cry from Sarah.

Hurriedly she turned on the television to drown the noise. *Snooker Special* was on BBC1 and full of long tense silences, so she switched to ITV. Two faces zoomed into close-up – open mouths meeting in a torrid kiss. She couldn't escape from sex: not only was it smouldering on screen and banging away overhead, but she was beginning to feel it stirring through her own body; the raw passion of the screen kiss rekindling the excitement of Simon's mouth on hers. She was astonished at the change in herself. For the last eighteen months her sexual feelings had been in cold storage, but since that party on Friday night they had come frothing up inside her like some potent bubbly yeast.

She lolled back on the sofa, watching the lovers in the film slowly peel off their clothes. They were lying on warm golden sand beneath a tropical sky, their bodies bronzed and gleaming and dappled by the shadow of feathery green palms. The soundtrack was unashamedly erotic: swooping glissandos from the strings and a feverish mounting drumbeat. Darren and Sarah were adding their own sound-effects: long drawn-out moans and a subtle change in the rhythm of the rocking bed. Catherine unbuttoned her woolly cardigan. She was not only flushed but sweating. Simon was in that bed with her – naked and dishevelled, his green eyes gazing into hers, his small slender hands cupped around her breasts.

She glanced back at the screen. She had left the lovers way behind. They were still languidly fondling each other, whereas Simon was insatiable. He rolled on to his back and pulled her on top of him, his tongue flicking across her nipples. The bedsprings juddered still more violently as he responded to her urgent rhythm.

They were so ecstatically in tune with each other, she had lost her separate boundaries; her breathing, heartbeat, body, synchronized with his. And from overhead came Sarah's high-pitched cries; the final frenzied cry echoed by her own.

She closed her eyes and slumped against Simon's chest, relishing the warmth of his slim and sated body. Then, all at once, the front door slammed and she heard footsteps in the hall. She sat up in confusion. Blue sky and sparkling water vanished; exotic date-palms shrivelled. Dazed, she looked around for her clothes, then realized she was fully dressed.

'Hi,' said Jo, tossing her coat on to a chair. She sounded irritable and exhausted.

'I . . . I'm sorry,' Catherine stammered, aware of her flaming cheeks. 'You must think I'm a permanent fixture here. Nicky persuaded me to stay another night. We didn't get back till nearly nine, you see. But I'm off first thing in the morning . . .'

'It doesn't matter to me – stay as long as you like.' Jo plonked herself down in a chair, her voice still querulous. 'I'm just livid after a fucking awful journey. Forgive my language, but British bloody Rail really surpassed themselves today. Of course, it's Sunday isn't it, so they do these sodding engineering works. They turfed us out at Eastleigh and made us catch this potty little bus. It meandered all over the countryside, stopping at every godforsaken station it could find. And even when we were back on the train, there were more delays at Woking. You won't believe this, Catherine, but I've been travelling seven hours altogether.'

'Gosh, it sounds horrendous. You must be absolutely whacked.'

'Too right! I need a stiff drink. Or maybe camomile tea would be safer. I'm in a frightful state. And it's not just the bloody trains. I've been given this commission. I've got to go to Sicily. Tomorrow.'

'Sicily?'

'Yeah. And if I don't buck up I'll never be ready in time.' Jo laughed suddenly unwinding her long scarf and draping it across her knees. 'I shouldn't be complaining. I'm lucky to have the chance. It's only because the girl they asked originally went down with some weird bug today. So *Elite* phoned me at my parents' and begged me to drop everything and fly out to Palermo. Imagine – it's seventy degrees there. I'll need a bikini and some sun-screen. Actually, I don't know *what* to take – or what to expect. I'm meant to be covering a writing course run by David Davine-King.'

'Wow,' said Catherine. 'You're brave!' David Davine-King had been splashed across the papers last week. Not only had he abandoned his fourth wife for what must have been his fortieth mistress (tempestuously Italian and famous in her own right), he was also conducting a highly public quarrel with his publishers.

'Oh, he's nothing like as bad as he's made out to be. But the set-up's rather odd, I must admit. He's running the thing in his girlfriend's villa and it sounds more like a palace. I mean, most creative writing courses are held in dilapidated farmhouses, and you sleep in spartan dormitories and take turns with the cooking – and it's shepherd's pie and veggie-burgers or starve. But *he*'s hired a professional chef for the week. And apparently the rooms are really sumptuous. I can't decide whether to turn up in jeans or a tiara.'

Catherine laughed. 'Both, by the sound of it.' Maybe that's what *she* should wear tomorrow evening. With nothing in between. 'How long are you going for?' she asked, trying to keep her mind from leaping back to Simon.

'Till Friday. They want me to stay for the whole course and keep an eye out for any extracurricular activities. David's in particular. He's got such a reputation, they're sure he'll try it on with one of the young students as soon as Francesca's back's turned. Look, I mustn't stay here rabbiting – I'll go and put the kettle on.'

'*I*'ll do it,' Catherine offered, 'if you want to start packing.'

'Oh, five more minutes won't hurt. And anyway, I'm starving. Look, you do the tea and I'll make some cheese on toast.' She led the way into the kitchen, stopping short when she saw William. 'Oh hell!' she said. 'The cat. I'd forgotten all about him. I'll never make that vet's appointment *and* get to Heathrow in time. Catherine, you couldn't be an angel and . . .'

No, said Catherine silently. Don't ask me.

'The vet's not far – Prince of Wales Road. I'm afraid Nicky's car's not insured for anyone else, but you can always take a taxi.'

I've no money for a taxi, Catherine said under her breath. I've got to do that too – find a cash dispenser and then go on to . . .

'You'll need a cardboard box to put him in. There's a nice strong one out by the dustbin. We haven't got a cat-basket, needless to say.'

Catherine found her voice at last. 'Listen, Jo, I'm terribly sorry but I don't think I can manage it. I've got an awful lot to do tomorrow.'

'It won't take long, I promise – an hour at the very most.'

'Yes, but I'd planned to get off sharp, you see. I've arranged to have coffee with my in-laws and I have to go home first to get the car. I've let them down once already, so I don't like to change the plans again.'

'Okay, forget it.' Jo hacked a piece of bread off the loaf and stared at it dejectedly. 'I'll phone the vet first thing and cancel the appointment. I'll take him *next* Monday – if I haven't been sent somewhere else.'

'But that's another week. And he's hardly eating anything. Don't you think he ought to go a bit sooner?'

'Well, yes he should, ideally. But if there's no one free to take him . . .'

Catherine glanced from Jo to William, feeling guilty on both counts. Jo and the others had been generous with everything: food, clothes, friendship, time. And, as for the cat, he looked the picture of misery, huddled in the corner with half-closed eyes. 'Okay,' she said, abruptly. 'I'll take him. No, honestly, it's no trouble. It's just that' – she gave an embarrassed smile – 'I haven't any money left. I mean literally not a penny. But if you could let me have, say, a tenner, I'll write you out a cheque.'

'Of course. Make it twenty if you want. Is there anything else you need?'

'Well, I'd love to borrow some shoes – size five and a half. Any old thing'll do. Those purple boots are crippling me. And Nicky's are all too big.'

'And mine would be too small.' Jo put her tiny foot beside Catherine's to illustrate the point. 'You could always try Fiona's. I'm not sure what size she takes, but she's roughly your height so you might be lucky.'

'But won't she mind?'

'We'll phone her. I want to speak to her anyway, and find out when she's coming back.'

Catherine glanced at her watch. 'You don't think it's rather late?'

'Oh, no. She never goes to bed before midnight, not even at her mother's. She'll probably be glad of a chat. It's so dreary for her there, looking after an invalid in the wilds of Herefordshire.'

Jo unwrapped a hunk of Cheddar and broke off a piece to taste. 'Do you want some cheese on toast, Catherine?'

'No thanks. I've been eating all day. We had marvellous food at Jonathan's and then we went on to this tapas bar. In fact, if you don't mind, I think I'll take my drink upstairs.' It would be more tactful to leave Jo to make the call in private. The mysterious Fiona might object to her room being occupied, her possessions commandeered.

'Right, I'll come up and see you as soon as I've spoken to Fee. And I'll bring the money and draw you a map for the vet. Oh, and you'll need a front door key. Gosh, you *are* an angel, Catherine. I just can't thank you enough.'

'No wings yet,' Catherine laughed, pretending to feel for them on her shoulders. 'See you in a while, then.' She walked slowly upstairs, rearranging Monday in her mind. The vet's appointment was at ten, so she should be back with the cat by eleven at the latest. If she left straight after that, she would be home by half past twelve, and could drive to Jack and Maureen's for a brief lunchtime snack instead of coffee. She'd still have most of the afternoon free. Jo and Nicky and Darren had full-time jobs, for heaven's sake, yet *they* managed to fit in a social life without all this stupid fuss.

She closed the bedroom door and put her cup down on the desk, suddenly catching the eye of the model in the poster. He was as blatantly naked as Simon had been just now, with the same seductive expression. She walked over and stroked her finger slowly down his body – down, and further down.

'Oh, lord!' she said, looking him straight in the eye. 'How the hell will I sleep with *you* here?'

9

William weighed a ton. Catherine shifted the box from one arm to the other. The cat was struggling violently inside his cardboard prison and the string cut into her fingers, leaving painful red marks. She kept glancing around for a taxi, but hadn't seen a single free one since she left the surgery. And anyway, she was worried about the expense. She had £10 to her name, and the only cash dispenser she'd found had spat her card back rudely. So much for magical Camden Town. It did indeed look sadly changed from its Sunday carnival. Gone were the cheerful crowds, the bouncy music and colourful stalls; replaced by clusters of black dustbin-bags and mounds of stinking rubbish being noisily devoured by the scrunching jaws of a dustcart. On top of everything else it had just begun to rain, but there was no way she could cope with an umbrella.

She allowed herself a brief rest, rubbing her sore fingers. William scrabbled at the sides of the box, letting out frustrated howls. It was a good thing the streets were so empty, otherwise she might have been accosted by an indignant member of the animal-rights brigade. She squatted down and peered in through the air holes, reminded of two-year-old Kate in a tantrum.

'It's all right, William,' she murmured in the same soothing voice she had used when the children were small. 'We're almost home. Then we'll make you comfortable and give you your nice medicine.'

As she straightened up she caught sight of her reflection in a shop window and immediately felt better. The last traces of the suburban widow had vanished; in her place stood a dashing young photographer in black leather jacket, skin-tight Levis and black kid ankle-boots (size five and a half exactly and wonderfully comfortable). Heartened, she picked up her pee-stained cardboard box, transforming it into a £5,000 Leica as she jetted off to direct a shoot in Bangkok; her minions rushing around with light-meters and props, and a bevy of male models striking suggestive poses against a moody city backdrop. There was something intensely freeing about stepping out of her own role and into someone else's, and Fiona's clothes gave her a sense of power; even changed the way she moved. She had never worn Levis in her life. Gerry hated women in jeans and always told her she was too fat for them, but she had gone down a whole two sizes since his death. Anyway, who cared? Fat or no, why shouldn't she dress as she pleased?

She turned into Crosswell Road – only two more streets to go. And William seemed to have quietened at last, thank heavens. Perhaps the antibiotic injection had also contained a sedative. She shuddered, recalling his cowed form as the vet inserted the needle – William the Conqueror pathetically subdued.

As soon as they got in, she released him from the box. He shook himself, enraged, and darted under the dresser, his tail swishing menacingly. She left him to recover while she put the kettle on. The vet had diagnosed an abscess, but said it hadn't yet come to a head and would need bathing in warm salt water several times a day. Meanwhile he had given her some pills to reduce his temperature, and told her to bring him back on Wednesday. That would be a problem. She was loth to leave the poor creature alone, but could she really stay here another two days, living like a nomad, with a borrowed toothbrush and no clean underclothes? Whatever else, she must ring Jack and Maureen. She would never make it in time for lunch – it was already ten to twelve.

Jack answered, sounding low. Since Gerry's death all the sparkle had gone out of him and his dispirited voice had its usual effect on her: prompting sympathy and sadness (and also a flicker of resentment that he should continue to parade his grief). She had to admit she felt profoundly thankful the visit was postponed, and *that* in turn induced a surge of guilt. But it was such an awful strain sitting in their small front room and mouthing platitudes; having to suppress the irrational anger she still sometimes felt towards Gerry: anger with him for dying, for losing all their money.

She took off her jacket (*Fiona*'s jacket – she mustn't get too possessive), and prepared the things she needed for treating

William's ear. The vet had instructed her to stand the cat on a table and wrap him in a bath-towel, so she could hold him down securely without getting scratched. Unfortunately William hadn't been instructed to co-operate. She managed to prise him from under the dresser and get him up on the table, but when she tried to bundle the towel round his legs, he thrashed around violently, yowling in indignation.

'William, keep *still*! I know this isn't much fun. I'm not enjoying it either, but it's going to make you better in the end.'

After several abortive attempts she succeeded in restraining him with the towel, though not before her arms were beaded with blood. He stopped struggling for a moment and she seized the chance to dab at his ear with the dampened cotton wool. The reaction was instantaneous. William burst free of the towel and sprang off the table, sending bowl and water flying, and hurtled out to the hall.

Having mopped up the spilt water, she went in search of him. He was cowering under a chair, eyeing her with suspicion and obviously ready to bolt again at the slightest provocation. She felt torn between duty and compassion. Perhaps she'd better leave him to calm down. She could do with a break herself, and a restorative cup of coffee.

Back in the kitchen she washed a mug, deliberately ignoring the other dirty dishes which had accumulated since last night. Already she was learning from Nicky and the others that there was a lot to be said for lounging about enjoying a leisurely chat, rather than fretting about the state of the house. She made the coffee, helped herself to a couple of biscuits and sat down in the most comfortable chair. She *wouldn't* go haring off to Stoneleigh – it was too much of a rush and she didn't like to leave the cat. Besides, there were more glamorous clothes upstairs than her tired old turquoise dress. Fiona had been so grateful for her promised help with William, she had offered her the run of her wardrobe. Also, she was sending a cheque to cover the vet's bill, and would be back on Friday anyway, as her mother was going into hospital that morning.

She dipped a biscuit in her coffee. Dunking biscuits was not done in Manor Close; nor in her childhood home, come to that. Her father had been a stickler for good manners, and had set great store by cleanliness and tidiness and stoical English reserve – all the virtues Andrew seemed to have inherited (from the grandfather he'd rarely seen). Strange how she had never rebelled, either as a child, or later. Well, of course her marriage to Gerry had been a rebellion in itself, but, that aside, she had continued to be tidy, clean and industrious; to be 'good', in short – the 'good girl' expected by a poor struggling widowed father. Goodness had become a habit, so that once she was married, she did her best to be a good wife and mother: devoted to her children, loyal to Gerry, patiently making allowances for the temperamental actor or stressed-out businessman. And after moving to Stoneleigh, she still felt a need to toe the line; not to let her son down, or put a foot wrong with Antonia, or untidy a show-house. She found herself concealing things – the fact that she bought lottery tickets (which she knew Andrew would regard as a total waste of money); her visit to a psychic. ('Your husband is happy and peaceful and sends greetings from the spirit-world.' Okay, perhaps it *was* a load of rubbish; none the less it had given her great comfort.)

One of the problems with Stoneleigh was that she always seemed to be waiting – waiting for Andrew and Antonia to come home in the evenings, or back from golf, or functions; waiting to eat until *they* were ready; waiting for *them* to suggest an outing; or waiting for the morning if she was stuck up in her room. Waiting to live, in effect. And the extraordinary thing was, she hadn't even realized the full extent of her imprisonment there. Of course, it wasn't their fault – or Gerry's, for that matter. She had been her own gaoler. Yet here at Gosforth Road, she had no set persona and nothing was expected of her, so she could re-invent herself. In fact, if only William hadn't been ill, she could have had a blissful time today, with Camden to explore and an attentive man to take her out this evening.

The thought of the cat reminded her that she ought to be bathing his ear. She went to seek him out, astonished to find him curled up on the sofa, fast asleep. The shot he'd had *must* have contained a tranquillizer. It seemed a shame to disturb him, so she decided to nip out while she had the chance – not to explore Camden but to find a functioning cash-dispenser and buy some basics, like clean pants.

'William,' she whispered, 'don't move a whisker till I'm back. I won't be long.'

*   *   *

Nearly two hours later she returned breathless to the house, imagining the worst. He might be feverish, delirious, miaowing pitifully for help. Fiona would never forgive her. And it *was* her fault, entirely. She had got distracted by the shops – so intriguingly different from the ones in Worcester Park, and selling things like dried African scorpion, sunglasses with windscreen-wipers, pasta in the shape of breasts, with exaggerated nipples, and even fetish footwear and ball-gowns for transvestites. And she'd wasted more time in the chemist's, picking out the right nail varnish for her toes, trying to choose between Midnight Blue and Bilberry.

She unlocked the front door and rushed to find the patient. He was still lying on the sofa – not asleep, but certainly nowhere near expiring. He fixed her with a baleful stare; his green eyes evoking thoughts of Simon. Green eyes were rare in men. She had only come across them in bad romantic novels, where they were usually combined with sensuous mouths, broad shoulders and masterful temperaments. Simon had narrow shoulders and seemed laid-back rather than masterful, but his mouth was more than merely sensuous – it was electrifying, voracious.

Oh lord, I'm nervous, she thought, as she dumped her shopping on the kitchen table. She decided to leave William for the moment; first she'd treat herself to her Camden-Town-style lunch. The main course was a carton of curried beans from a Burmese take-away. Take-aways were extravagant, but today she was on holiday, and at least she had resisted the temptations of spicy wild-boar sausages, brazil-nut bread, even mind-expanding Whizzard Tea. Pudding was a Mr Men yoghurt – Mr Lazy, of course.

Tucking into her beans, she deliberated on the choice of numbers for next Saturday's lottery. Something connected with Simon, perhaps. Yes, thirty-one for his age, and maybe eighteen for his birthday (which was 18 May, he'd told her), and then the last four digits of his phone number. That particular combination might be lucky. It *wasn't* such a senseless waste of money. Three people she knew had won quite useful sums. She imagined seven million pounds arriving at the door: not a flimsy cheque, but sacks and sacks of shining solid coins. She'd book a flight to Delhi, where she would shower largesse on Kate and all her Indians, then trek through the Himalayas, tour Nepal by camel, while away an indolent month in Tibet. She filled in the lottery ticket and, reluctantly returning to earth, washed her hands and went in search of the patient.

It was three o'clock before the treatment was completed. The vet had failed to tell her that several pairs of scratchproof hands were required – to hold the cat down and ward off attack, quite apart from the actual bathing. Mission achieved, the two of them retired to lick their wounds; she eventually going upstairs to begin her preparations for the evening. She had already decided what to wear: a slinky two-piece in goldy-coloured satin and a pair of smart black patent shoes.

She enjoyed a leisurely bath, shaved her legs, washed her hair, then began applying the Bilberry nail varnish to her toes. Halfway through, she broke off. What on earth did she think she was doing? Why should Simon see her *toes*? Or her breasts, or pubic hair, which she had been scrutinizing earlier? However frustrated she might feel, she had no intention of going to bed with him tonight – if at all. She called to mind those anguished letters to agony aunts written by teenage girls: 'I went the whole way on my first date and now my boyfriend thinks I'm a slag. Please tell me what I should do.'

What you should do, she told herself, is play hard to get – be the elusive older woman; charming but reticent. Which meant, of course, she could have saved herself the expense of buying that ludicrous wisp of lace, masquerading as a pair of pants.

She watched with growing unease as Simon unbuttoned his shirt. In his clothes he'd been *safe*, but he was becoming more of a stranger with each garment he took off. His chest was naked now and disconcertingly pale and smooth. And he was the wrong build altogether: not just slender – scraggy. She noticed an angry red spot on his back, which reminded her how young he was. Gerry hadn't had a spot in twenty years.

He leaned towards her and fondled the back of her neck, his fingers feeling for the zip on her dress.

'Look, Simon,' she stammered, pulling away. 'W . . . we're going a bit too fast.'

'Too *fast?*'

They had, admittedly, been sitting on the sofa for well over an hour. That was probably the trouble – the effects of the wine had worn off. She had been relaxed and even expansive in the restaurant, and when he'd invited her back for coffee, she had accepted with barely a qualm. Now, however, she felt ridiculously afraid, and also rather dizzy.

'Let's just . . . cuddle for a bit longer. That was nice.'

'Okay.' He gave a nervous laugh. 'But it's difficult to get close to you in that dress.'

She let him ease the zip down, wishing she could *feel* something – something other than fear. But she couldn't seem to get it out of her head. Her body might as well not have been there, for all the good it was doing her – or him. And the chaperone crouching in her skull kept up a constant barrage: 'How can you be so cheap? You hardly know the man. And you're betraying Gerry, aren't you?'

He pulled the dress over her head and for a moment she was blinded by folds of clingy satin. As she struggled free, he unhooked her bra and kissed her breasts, almost violently. She tried to enjoy it, but it was actually more painful than arousing and anyway, the voice in her head was commanding her to stop.

'Simon, I know you'll think I'm stupid, but I . . . I need a bit more time.'

'But what's the matter? You were perfectly okay before.'

It was true – she had led him on. While they were waiting for the coffee to brew, she had let him kiss her passionately, his tongue exploring her mouth. It wasn't fair to change her mind, mess him about like this.

She put her arms around him, thinking back to her fantasy last night. She had gone all the way with him then, completely unabashed. Of course it was one thing dreaming of Romance on Paradise Island, but here in the flat there was no tropical sun or gentle lapping waves – only a one-bar fire and the noise of traffic thundering through Shepherd's Bush. And she found the place coldly impersonal: no trinkets on the mantelpiece, no pictures on the walls. It made Simon seem still more a stranger – faceless and one-dimensional. She had assumed that a television agent would live in relative style, surrounded by photos of celebrities, and with designer furniture and the odd tigerskin rug. In fact, the rug was sisal and the furniture so characterless it could have come as a job lot from a second-rate hotel.

'Why don't we make ourselves comfortable next door,' he suggested, as if he had read her mind. He coaxed her up from the sofa and steered her towards the bedroom. She knew she ought to refuse, to stop the whole thing here and now, but she had become the awkward teenager again, and the state of her undress (breasts exposed but tights still on) seemed to symbolize her conflict: part resisting, part compliant.

As the bedroom door clicked shut, she felt a wave of panic. Despite his modest build he seemed to fill the room; his body looming over hers; his skin sweating slightly, as if he could barely contain his eagerness. Yet how could she avoid him when there was nowhere to sit except the bed? It was a narrow single bed which looked distinctly uninviting. She was used to sex in nice surroundings: a large centrally-heated room with a decent-sized bed and clean sheets. But wasn't that dreadfully suburban? And unfair again, in any case. Agent or no, Simon couldn't afford a mansion – not at thirty-one. He'd been extremely generous as it was, treating her to a lavish dinner. However apprehensive she might be, she owed him something in return.

She started to remove her tights, peeling them down slowly, only to realize that he found her reluctance exciting. He was gazing enthralled at her bare legs, evidently turned on by her performance.

'Mm,' he murmured, slipping his hand between her thighs. 'What sexy pants!'

She forced a smile, trying not to tense up at his touch. She'd *bought* them for him, so she must let him take them off. Now that she was completely naked, he hurried to catch up, unzipping his trousers and tossing them on the floor. Underneath he was wearing baggy boxer shorts patterned with prissy little bows. Gerry wore tight Y-fronts, stark black or blatant red. And once he'd wriggled out of the shorts, the contrast with Gerry was still more glaring. His naked body was pale, thin, hairless, almost girlish. No, hardly girlish with that . . . that . . . She struggled for the word. Most of the names for the male organ sounded either downright crude or coldly clinical. Gerry's had been christened on their wedding night – Malvolio, the part he was currently playing. And Malvolio was large, thick and usually self-important (though given to sulks and droops in the latter years of their marriage). Simon's was a different species entirely: long and sort of tapering, and his pubic hair was mousy brown, not Gerry's exuberant black.

God! She shouldn't be thinking of Gerry – she shouldn't be thinking at all. Yet that nagging voice in her head refused to let up. 'You'll regret this later, won't you? Tell him you've got to leave and get out while you can.'

'You're beautiful,' said Simon, thrusting his hand between her legs again. He seemed so rough compared with Gerry, and in too much of a hurry. Urgently he pushed her back on the bed and reached for something in the bedside drawer.

She watched in fascination and distaste. She had never seen a condom, except in packets at the chemist's. Gerry had left the matter of contraception to her. And thank God, she thought, as Simon extracted the flabby yellow teat. Far from reassuring her, it prompted still more fears. What if it split and she got pregnant, or caught AIDS? Simon was bound to have a girlfriend, maybe more than one. After all, he hadn't wasted much time in inviting her back to bed. Who else, she wondered, had lain between these crumpled sheets? Yet the rubber penis was moving purposefully towards her; only inches from her groin now. She pushed him away and sprang up.

'I . . . I'm terribly sorry. I, er, need the bathroom.'

'Bloody hell,' he muttered, slumping back on the bed.

Shivering, she locked the bathroom door. What if he turned nasty? He had sounded really irritable, and no wonder. Normal women wouldn't bolt at the sight of a condom. There must be something wrong with her. Perhaps she had always been unresponsive, but Gerry was too kind to say. That would explain his droops. Easy to blame *him* – or Simon – when actually she was the one at fault.

She sat on the edge of the bath, shoulders hunched, arms huddled across her breasts. 'Go for it,' Nicky had said breezily. 'Give it a whirl, and see what he's like.' Instead, she was skulking in an unheated bathroom, unable to drag her thoughts from Gerry. She would never make it as an independent woman if she clung to her husband's corpse for the rest of her life. Besides, she had an ominous feeling that if she didn't go through with it this time she would never dare to try again, with anyone. Rather like that thing about falling off a horse – you had to get straight back on again or you'd lose your nerve for good. Simon was doing her a favour, if she could only see it in that light: helping her make the transition from cosy marital sex to the freedom of affairs. She needed that freedom to survive in Nicky's easy-going world.

She splashed her face with cold water and returned to the bedroom. Simon was lying almost as she'd left him, spread-eagled on his back and looking utterly dejected. The difference was, he had lost his erection, though he hadn't removed the condom, which hung limp and shrunken like a punctured balloon. His miserable expression made her feel so guilty that she eased herself on top of him and began kissing his throat and chest. She let her lips slide slowly down to his stomach, flicking her tongue across his navel, determined to make some recompense. Instantly the condom re-inflated and bobbed towards her mouth. It was obvious what he wanted, and whatever her misgivings, she must gratify him this time.

She took a deep breath in and closed her eyes. The rubber tasted foul. She had always vaguely thought that condoms came in fruit flavours, like yoghurts: strawberry, banana, cherry. Alas, no. But what mattered at the moment was *his* pleasure, not hers, and at least he was responding – with excited little moans. She tried to open her throat and stop herself from gagging. The problem was she hadn't done it for so long. In the years before Gerry's death, sex had become a rather perfunctory experience.

She moved her mouth upwards, trying to squeeze with her lips and swirl with her tongue. The whole complicated process felt like an exam – an arduous A-level in Sex After Widowhood, which she was failing ignominiously. Her knowledge was rusty and she had neglected her homework. In desperation, she used her hands as well, in the hope of doing *some*thing right, and was rewarded by a wild cry from Simon. Then suddenly the phone rang.

'Leave it,' he muttered urgently.

Leave what? she thought, confused. He would hardly expect her to answer his phone, so he must mean stop what she was doing. She sat up uncertainly.

'No, go on,' he begged, guiding her head back down again.

Silently she complied, still hating the taste of the rubber, its unpleasant slimy texture.

'Go *on*,' he repeated in a choked, imploring voice. 'Don't stop now, for Christ's sake!'

How could she go on with that horrendous phone shrilling in the background? At this time of night it must be something urgent: bad news, an accident. Or perhaps it was for *her*. William was worse – dying.

She was aware of Simon dwindling in her mouth, but she had

become hopelessly distracted now that her thoughts had turned to the cat. She should never have left him with Nicky and Darren. They wouldn't have the patience to give him his pills, or go through that whole rigmarole with the towel. 'Answer it!' she prayed.

As if in response, Simon pulled away and rolled off the bed. 'Shit!' he muttered through clenched teeth, blundering out to the hallway. 'If that's Anthony, I'll kill him.'

She strained her ears to listen, ready to bundle her clothes back on if necessary. Simon's voice sounded terse and impatient, but she couldn't make out any words. Then the receiver was slammed down and he reappeared at the door.

'Sorry about that,' he said abruptly. 'I'll be back in a moment, okay?'

'Y . . . yes. Of course.'

What had happened, and where was he going? Simply to the bathroom, or to help out in an emergency? Perhaps it was another woman, a jealous girlfriend who had seen them in the restaurant together and rung to make a scene. And who was Anthony? His boss? A flatmate? Some actor with a problem?

She pulled the covers up, shivering in the feeble heat of the fire. With Simon gone, her worries had more space to swarm – not just William, but AIDS again, and pregnancy, and Andrew and Antonia. They'd be disgusted if they could see her now. She stared up at the plain white wall, envying them their closeness; the fact they were in bed together. Sex was so *secure* in marriage – being at ease with a familiar cherished partner, when making love did mean love. But it was hardly fair to keep wishing Simon was Gerry. She must have unnerved him, dashing out to the bathroom like that; injured his male pride. Perhaps her normal sexual feelings had died with Gerry, and she was frigid now, a dried-up spinster, condemned to spend the next forty years loveless and alone – unless she steeled herself to go through with tonight as a sort of baptism of fire.

She peered at the alarm clock: 10.45 already. What was Simon *doing*? She could hardly go through any regenerative experience with him if he had grabbed his clothes and run. There wasn't a sound in the flat, apart from the low purring of the fire; no movement from the other room.

She swallowed. Her throat felt dry and she was longing for a drink, but if she went out to the kitchen, he might think she was

103

checking up on him. On the other hand, if he *had* left, what was she meant to do – simply lie here till dawn and wait for him? She put a tentative leg out of bed, hastily withdrawing it as the door-handle turned.

Simon shambled into the room, a sweater draped across his shoulders and a towel tied round his waist. She felt a certain relief that he hadn't actually abandoned her (tempered with weary resignation at the prospect of having to arouse him all over again).

'That was, er, my mother,' he mumbled, avoiding her eyes. 'Stupid cow, to ring this late.'

She suspected he was lying. Even if he wasn't, it didn't make it any better. She felt an instant affinity with mothers, especially those called stupid cows by rude, unloving sons.

Neither of them spoke. Three floors below, the ceaseless flow of the honking, speeding traffic seemed to mock their own inertia.

'So, what do you want to do?' Simon asked at last, perching on the edge of the bed.

'Er, *do*?'

'Well, I mean, Ma's killed it, hasn't she?'

'No,' she lied, 'of course not. Here, come in and get warm.' She lifted the covers and made room for him beside her, praying the phone wouldn't ring again. This time it must work, for the sake of Simon's pride (and her own future).

She sat astride him, taking the initiative. In fact, *she* would put the condom on – he'd probably expected all along that she would play the role of experienced older woman, not bashful virgin.

She tore the end off the foil wrapper, struggling with the fiddly rubber teat, and wishing condoms weren't so unappealing. Then she guided him straight in, afraid to delay any longer. He felt much smaller than Gerry, and somehow feebler altogether, and although his body was moving with hers, he kept his eyes shut and made no noise at all. She was so used to Gerry's sound effects, his silence seemed an affront. And despite the fact that he was actually inside her, she felt dead down there, and yes, frigid. He might as well have remained in the other room for all the effect he was having. She could only think of Gerry – his smell, the feel of his skin. It would never work with Simon, or any other man, unless she kicked her husband out, and violently if need be.

She slammed against him, working herself into a storm of anger as her body flailed and pummelled. Why did he have to die so young, annihilate her future, kill her as a woman? Yet *he* was just as angry; fighting back defiantly, his breathing hoarse and laboured, his voice returning, startling her. Then suddenly he was coming – coming noisily and extravagantly, the way she loved. Tears streamed down her cheeks and she broke into wild sobs, calling for him desperately as he slumped, a pale corpse, beneath her.

'Oh Gerry, Gerry, Gerry, Gerry, *Gerry*!'

10

'Look, it wasn't your fault,' Nicky said, kicking off her shoes and flopping back on the bed. 'In fact, I feel guilty about it myself. I should never have encouraged you.'

'No, honestly, it was *me*, Nicky.'

'Stop blaming yourself – okay? Life's too short. Christ, I've had enough fiascos of my own. And since things broke up with Sean I've been practically on the shelf.'

Catherine took a sip of wine. 'Yes, but that was only a year ago. It takes time to get over . . .'

'I haven't *got* time, unfortunately. Judging by Jonathan's total lack of interest, it's obvious I've lost whatever pulling power I had. It's like work. Thirty-five's really old in advertising. If I haven't made it by now, I probably never will.'

Catherine looked at her in surprise. Nicky *had* made it, surely. Her room was far less of a hotchpotch than the rest of the house, and conspicuously less shabby. The furniture was modern in style and looked new, and her many possessions seemed further proof of success: a laptop computer sitting on the desk next to a state-of-the-art CD system; a wardrobeful of smart clothes, a portable TV and, parked outside, her VW Golf, a mere two years old and filled with all her windsurfing equipment. Even the wine they were drinking was classy.

Nicky topped up both glasses and tucked her feet underneath her. She was wearing a miniskirt in a wild shade of blood-orange and matching patent shoes. There was always an air of brilliance about her – not just her clothes, her dazzling blond hair and brightly coloured lipstick. Outside it might be dark and cold, but Nicky set the room alight. Yet her voice was wistful, subdued.

'I feel so sort of . . . rootless, Catherine. I mean, I've grown away from my parents, and I'm not sure that I want a family of my own. But I'm fed up with getting pissed each night with the kids at work. And the future's so uncertain in this job. You're always worrying about whether you'll get the chop, where you'll be when you're forty, all that sort of thing. Besides, when you're older it's a hell of a challenge keeping in touch with the under-twenties. There's nothing more pathetic than thinking you're on their wavelength but actually missing by a mile. The youth market's so media-wise these days, they reject half the stuff that's aimed at them. They expect something new and buzzy all the time, but' – she grimaced – 'it's not that easy to come up with it when they're so damned cynical. I'm just coasting at work at the moment, yet I can't seem to get my act together. I suppose I could move to a smaller agency and maybe win more awards and stuff. But I've done all that already. I used to be over the moon if I won something, but now I just think "So what?" You kill yourself thinking up a fabulous TV ad half the population never sees because they're busy putting the kettle on or going to the loo. Or if they *do* see it, they couldn't give a toss. Sorry!' She smiled sheepishly. 'I'm being a dreadful bore.'

'No you're not. I can understand. When you're in a high-powered job you've got so many choices – what's important, what to give up, what your values are. It was much easier for me. I just got married very young and that was that.'

'Yes, but don't you ever feel you missed out?'

Catherine laughed suddenly. 'Well, I did on Monday night. I couldn't sleep a wink when I got back. I just lay in bed going hot and cold all over and praying I'd never set eyes on Simon again. Even now, I feel terrible about it.'

'Well don't. He's not worth it. Just put it down to experience.'

Catherine stifled a yawn. 'Excuse me – I feel whacked. If this is what men do to you, I think I'll settle for celibacy! And I really must get to bed. The vet promised to fit William in before surgery tomorrow, so I have to be there first thing.'

'You *are* decent to keep taking him. I hope Fiona's grateful.'

'Oh, yes. I phoned her last night. Anyway, with any luck it should be his last appointment. I know I'll miss him when I'm back home, though. I've become quite attached to him.'

Nicky grinned. 'Well, there you have it, Catherine – cats are

107

obviously the answer. Less trouble than blokes, whatever else.'

'Yes, on balance, I think I'd rather have William than Simon.' Catherine studied the golden liquid in her glass. 'D'you know, I realized last night that part of the trouble with Simon was that I didn't actually like him. I was just so flattered to be asked out by a *man*, especially one whose life seemed exciting. I mean, he works with famous actors, and he's learning to parachute and . . .'

'Big deal! I've heard it said that men who take up parachuting often have problems in bed. It must be a form of compensation, I suppose. Aren't parachutes meant to be the ultimate phallic symbol? Sean stuck to golf, thank God.'

'My son plays golf. He . . .' Catherine broke off, suddenly jolted by the thought that Andrew was the same age as Jo and Darren. Yet he and Antonia might belong to a different generation entirely – so conventional and settled. She couldn't imagine talking to them as intimately as she was doing to Nicky. In fact, she had vowed not to breathe a word to anyone about her disastrous evening with Simon, and had been astonished to hear herself pouring out the whole story. Now that she'd confessed, though, she felt nothing but relief. Nicky had listened sympathetically, waved away her self-reproaches and told her of course she wasn't frigid or hysterical – the reaction was perfectly understandable when she had never slept with anyone but Gerry. And, after two glasses of wine, she was beginning to believe it. It was marvellous having Nicky to confide in. Since moving south she had never really found a close friend like Maeve in Salford. People in Carshalton tended to keep themselves to themselves, and Stoneleigh was even worse.

Nicky tugged off her earrings and sat fiddling with the large gold hoops. 'D'you know, I can really relate to what you said about not *feeling* anything with Simon. It's happened to me, too. Sometimes I've been in bed with a bloke and while he's pumping away and telling me it's great, I'm lying there trying to dream up a slogan for Kendall's Krisps! Mind you, that says more about my job than about my sex life. Is there ever a minute when I'm *not* thinking about some bloody product or other? It's a sort of slavery of the mind, Catherine. Whatever I'm doing, I can't get away from it – crispy, crunchy, munchy, fucking Kendall's. Which are full of fat and additives and probably cause heart attacks. Not that I let my scruples intrude – not since I refused to work on a cigarette account and was told if I took that line, I wouldn't be working on *any*thing.'

Catherine stretched her legs out in front of her, admiring Fiona's Levis, which felt practically like hers now, after four days' 'ownership'. 'Forgive me for asking, but why did you go into advertising if you're so opposed to it?'

'Well, of course, at the time I wasn't. I just accepted the general consensus that it was glamorous and trendy and the sort of well-paid job women were meant to want. I assumed I'd make a pile and be seen to be successful, and that was the be-all and end-all. The trouble is, the more you get, the more you want. There's always something bigger, brighter, better, you feel you've got to have.' She slipped an earring over her finger and twirled it round and round. 'Bloody hell, Catherine, I always seem to be moaning! I'm jolly lucky really. I've got a lot of things other women would kill for.'

'Well, so have I,' said Catherine. 'And I've been moaning too. I know I'm very lucky to have two healthy children. But don't you think it's more about being allowed to be your*self*?' She put her glass down and sat staring at it reflectively. 'Since Gerry died, I've thought about it a lot. I mean, so many people get sucked in to a way of life they didn't really choose, whether it's marriage, or a job like yours, or keeping up with the neighbours, or doing what your parents want, or what society expects. It struck me recently that I've never actually chosen any of the various jobs I've done. I just took what was on offer at the time, either because it fitted in with the children, or was close to home, or whatever. Then, later, I worked for Gerry because he needed an assistant and couldn't afford to pay one. And that became my whole existence. I never asked "What do *I* want?" or "Who *am* I?" I just got sort of . . . annexed. That probably sounds self-pitying, but it's not intended to be – it was a good life in many ways. No, it's more a feeling of surprise that it took me so long to realize. It seems extraordinary that in all those years I didn't stop to wonder what I was actually cut out to do or be. I'm sure I'm not unusual, though. There must be hundreds of people stuck in jobs they hate, or married to the wrong partner, or struggling to be someone they're not. It's such an awful waste.'

'I say, Catherine, that sounded as if it came from the heart!'

'Sorry. I did get a bit carried away.'

'No, you're absolutely right. In fact, now I come to think of it, I was probably only trying to compete with my elder brother, Tom. *He*'d made it, so I had to. But, like you, I never asked "Make what?" I just swallowed what I was told – sex is great, fast cars are great, success is eighty grand a year and a gold credit card in your wallet.'

Catherine laughed. 'My daughter-in-law's just got one of those – at twenty-six, would you believe! It's funny, my own daughter's completely different. She lives in one room, with nothing but a makeshift bed, a rickety table and a row of hooks for her clothes. Yet *she*'s the one I envy. I felt quite a pang when I saw her off at the airport. I knew I'd miss her terribly, of course, but it was more than that. She seemed so . . . *free*, setting off to travel the world, going wherever the fancy took her, with just a rucksack on her back and wearing an old pair of jeans. I couldn't help thinking that when *I* was her age, the only trips I made were short bus-rides to my in-laws, encumbered with two children and all their paraphernalia.'

'It must be odd when your kids sort of . . . overtake you.'

'Very odd! Actually, Kate's often done things I've envied. She used to play rugby at school and that seemed incredibly emancipated to me. My father hated tomboys and made me do ballet, or sit at home with a book. I had to wear pretty dresses and even bows in my hair, when I would have given anything for a Davy Crockett outfit.'

'*My* father was never there. He preferred his mistress to his wife, I'm afraid. But let's not go into that.' Nicky picked up the bottle and waved it in her direction. 'Do you want to finish the wine?'

'No, I'd better not. I had an awful lot last night.'

'Well, if you will go out with Darren . . .'

'How could I refuse an invitation to one of his gigs? Anyway, I enjoyed it.'

'Rather you than me! The band's so rackety. In fact, I have to say it's delightfully peaceful this evening, with Darren out and Jo away. Perhaps we should get our own place, Catherine – just you and me and no raucous music.'

Catherine looked up, startled. Could she be serious?

'That's another thing, of course – where one decides to live. Except mostly we *don't* decide. I'm fed to the teeth with London, but I can hardly work in Mayfair and still expect to . . . Hey, is that the phone?' She sprang up from the bed and dashed to the door. 'Pray it's Jonathan. This is his last chance!'

Catherine glanced from Nicky's departing form to the double bed with its luxurious fur coverlet. How sad that none of Nicky's relationships had worked, when here was the perfect set-up for romance. Yet the room was full of men: faded sepia photographs in silver frames of imposing types like commissars and colonels, and more informal snapshots of presumably the real men in her life – past lovers, perhaps, or her absent father, or her successful brother Tom. And there were two large modern paintings on the wall, rather unsettling ones, to be honest, but again depicting men.

She continued gazing round, intrigued by the mix of the exotic and the homely. This was the first time she'd seen the room. The last two nights Nicky had been out and only now had they found a chance to talk.

'Catherine!' Nicky was calling from the bottom of the stairs. 'You're needed on the phone.'

She froze. It must be Simon! No, surely he wouldn't ring. But . . .

'Get a move on!' Nicky shouted. 'It's Jo.'

What on earth could Jo want, she wondered, as she hurried down the stairs. Nicky passed her the receiver, lowering her voice to a whisper. 'Quick! It's long-distance. And she's in a bit of a state. She wants to know if you can run Greta's stall on Saturday.'

'*What?*'

'Well, she was going to ask Darren, but he and I are working this weekend.'

'But isn't she due back tomorrow?'

'No. There's been a change of plan. Look, talk to her yourself.'

'Hello,' said Catherine nervously, and was immediately bombarded with explanations and entreaties. Jo had to stay on in Palermo for another three days, but she couldn't let Greta down at such short notice, so it would be great if . . .

'But, Jo, I wouldn't know where to begin! I've never run a stall in my life.'

'There's nothing to it, honestly. Greta will help you set up and all you have to do is stand there and take the money. It's fun. You'll enjoy it.'

Catherine hesitated, a spark of excitement flickering through her fear.

'So you *will?*' Jo prompted.

'Well, I . . .'

'Oh, Catherine, you're an absolute saint! I just can't thank you enough. I'll phone Greta right away and tell her.'

'But suppose she objects? I mean, she might not want me to do it.'

''Course she will. I'll give you a glowing character reference. And I'll get her to ring *you*, so you can make all the arrangements. Which number should I give her? This one or your home number?'

Catherine tried to think. Every time she planned to go back to Andrew's, something seemed to crop up. It was like being granted constant extensions of a holiday – a rather haphazard one, where she was living out of suitcases and never quite sure of the next move. Tomorrow was Friday, so there was little point in returning to Stoneleigh for just one afternoon. 'Tell her to phone me here,' she said. 'I should be back from the vet about ten.'

'God, I'd forgotten all about the vet. Honestly, Catherine, how did we manage without you? How is the wretched cat?'

'Much better. The abscess burst yesterday. But how are things your end? Are you enjoying the course?'

'Yes and no. But I'll tell you all about it when I'm back. Must dash now. And thanks a million.'

'Jo is a shit,' said Nicky, as Catherine replaced the receiver. 'I wouldn't be surprised if she's just decided to take a few days' holiday. Yet she expects us all to rally round and bail her out. It's okay for *her*, doing damn all in the sun, while you shiver in the snow at Camden Lock.'

Catherine laughed. 'Hardly snow.'

'Well, they have forecast a cold snap for the weekend. You'll have to wrap up well. I'll lend you my old sheepskin coat, and Darren's got a weird leather hat with ear-flaps.'

'Lord, I'll frighten all the customers away! If there *are* any, that is. What will Greta say if I don't sell a single thing?'

'It'll be okay, don't worry. I'd come and buy a hat myself if I didn't have to work. I know' – she poured the last inch of wine into her glass – 'we'll get Fiona to rustle up a few friends.'

'Gosh, I'd forgotten she was coming back. She'll want her room.'

'She can sleep in Jo's and lump it. You've done enough for William, for heaven's sake. Jo's room is nicer anyway. I'm afraid you've got the worst room in the house.'

'I like it.'

'Catherine, you're so *polite*!'

'I'm not being polite. There's a fantastic view from up there.'

'Yeah, a lot of dreary grey roofs.'

'Actually, they're not dreary. I was looking out at the chimney-pots this morning, and they're really rather interesting – all different shapes and sizes. Some are twisted and gnarled and obviously very old, and they're every sort of colour – yellow, brown, sooty-black . . .'

'You're easily pleased.'

Yes, she thought, it's true. She did enjoy sleeping in a photographer's room in such a fascinating part of London, and having a new friend to talk to and a big tabby cat to pretend was hers. And it was fun eating exotic foods straight out of the carton whenever the fancy took her, instead of sitting down to late formal meals with Andrew and Antonia. And today's trip to Hampstead had been an unqualified success: front seat on the top of a red bus, a brisk walk on the Heath; hot chocolate in the village, and then a tour of the chic boutiques. Also, she liked the sense of being needed – someone who could lend a hand with cats or market stalls. It had been easy as a wife and mother to feel useful, indispensable, but at Stoneleigh she often wondered if she was, frankly, in the way. And it was even quite a treat going to bed whenever she pleased, instead of feeling guiltily unsociable if she disappeared too early, or worrying about disturbing Andrew and Antonia if she stayed up later than them. In *this* house no one cared: you did what you liked when you liked, and to hell with any guilt.

'Thanks, Nicky,' she said, draining her wine. 'That was lovely. But I think I'll go up to bed now.'

'Okay, see you in the morning. And listen, Catherine . . .'

'What?'

'Promise me you won't worry about Simon?'

'All right, I'll try.'

'And you're not nervous about running the stall?'

'Well, yes, I'm terrified! But who knows, it might turn out to be fun.'

11

Catherine climbed on to the trestle table, hampered by her bulky sheepskin coat. Snowflakes were spiralling down into her eyes, stinging on her lashes, smarting on her lips. The table felt dangerously rickety and she only hoped it wouldn't give way as she reached up to screw a light-bulb into its fiddly metal socket.

'Okay?' Greta asked, her voice muffled by a black balaclava. She struggled to tether the flapping tarpaulin, the wind whining in shrill protest as it tugged the other way. 'Shit!' she muttered. 'This weather's a real pig. It'll keep everyone at home. I sometimes wonder why I bother.'

Catherine grunted in sympathy. She fixed the last light-bulb in place, licking snowflakes from her lips, then clambered down from the table, avoiding a large puddle. Her feet were soaked as it was. Fur-lined waterproof boots would have been ideal today, but Fiona's footwear was stronger on fashion than on boring practicality.

Cautiously she followed Greta across the slippery pavement into the covered market hall, relishing the warmth and light after the dank grey cold outside. The hall was buzzing with activity, as crates and boxes were carted down the stairs and cumbersome rails of clothes manoeuvred through the door. She envied those who had their stalls inside and could stay in this haven, protected from the elements. She stood watching a girl unpack a case of hand-painted bottles, glowing like stained glass, and arrange them on tiered shelving, the tallest at the back, going down step by step to squat but brilliant miniatures. This attention to detail had struck her already – the care and artistry lavished by the traders on displaying their various goods.

She tore herself away from the jewel colours of the glass and hurried to find Greta, who was talking to a small wiry man carrying a load of rolled-up rugs. They broke off when they saw her.

'Derek, this is Catherine,' Greta said. 'She's minding the stall for me today.'

'Hi.' Derek gave her a brief and almost suspicious glance. He looked cold in his old jeans and thin green anorak, his straggly hair escaping from a woolly pom-pom hat.

She returned his greeting, then stood in silence, wondering what to say. He seemed equally ill at ease, and with a terse nod in her direction, shambled off with his rugs.

'He's always a bit of a misery,' Greta whispered. 'Take no notice. He's okay really, and his pitch is next to mine, so you can ask him if you need any help.'

Catherine nodded, her attention now diverted to a young girl in her teens, staggering under the weight of a tower of earthenware pots stacked two feet high. She hadn't realized how much sheer physical labour was involved in setting up, nor how long it took. They'd been at it for an hour and a half and were nowhere near finished yet. She had arrived to find a picture-postcard scene: white seagulls and white snowflakes whirling over the dark water of the canal. The market, though, had looked ghostly, and utterly changed from the bright and cheerful bustle of last weekend. The stalls themselves were nothing but gaunt skeletons: metal frames awaiting their tarpaulins and their wares. She had lurked in a corner, watching shadowy figures loom out of the darkness, lugging heavy suitcases and boxes and all absorbed in what they were doing. It had been a relief to see Greta – a familiar face in this alien world.

Now she followed her across the hall and outdoors once again, bowing her head against the slap of the wind and picking her way through the slush. Fortunately, Greta's stall was only a few yards away, and at least they had some shelter with the tarpaulin up in place.

'We need to make a bit of a display,' Greta said, unpacking the first box of hats and pulling them into shape. 'I usually group them together – the fur ones go in front here, and these plain felts at the back. Then I pin some to the sides, like this. And by the way, do encourage people to try them on. There's a mirror at each end – see? And can you keep a record of everything you sell?

Write it in this notebook. We'll run through all the prices in a tick. I'm going to leave you some waistcoats, too. I want to see how they go here and compare it with Portobello. Mind you, in this weather, we'll be lucky to sell anything, either of us.'

She lifted a suitcase on to the table and opened it to reveal the waistcoats: some in velvet, some in silk.

'They're beautiful,' said Catherine, admiring the dazzling colours.

Greta took out half a dozen and hung them at the side of the stall. 'Well, the punters may not think so! I'd better warn you, Catherine, some people can be bloody rude. But don't let it upset you. They're plain ignorant, that's all. And you've got to watch the stuff like a hawk. Only last week, someone walked off with a hat. Luckily, I saw the bloke nick it and I raced after him and got it back. He tried to tell me he'd bought it from another stall. Bloody nerve! I'd made those hats from an old astrakhan coat of my mother's, so I'd know them anywhere. Anyway, if you need a pee or a cup of coffee, get Derek to keep an eye on things, then you'll be okay.' She stood back to survey the waistcoats, blowing on her mittened hands. 'Look after Catherine, won't you, Derek?' she called to him. 'She's new to this, so she might need a bit of a hand.'

He nodded – a man of few words, evidently.

Another man bounced up to them: an eccentric-looking character whose muscly bulk and cheerful grin were in marked contrast to Derek's scrawny surliness. 'Derek, do us a favour and give us a fag.'

'Fuck off and buy your own. I've only got two left.'

'Oh, don't be like that.' The man thrust out a hand adorned with silver rings, one on every finger. 'Come on, mate. It's worth a half in the Stag's Head.'

'I'm not going to the Stag's Head. I've got to be off sharp.'

'Brad, this is Catherine,' Greta interrupted. 'She's looking after things for me today, so be sure you're nice to her.'

'I'm always nice, ain't I? Pleased to meet you, darlin'.'

He fixed Catherine with his fiercely blue eyes – a startling blue, as if speedwells, sapphires, gentians had been boiled together in a cauldron until their essence was distilled. Yet for all the magnetism of his gaze, she felt distinctly apprehensive. He had taken off his cap to reveal a shaven head, which looked somehow sinister. And that long raised scar running down his cheek – had he got it in some drunken brawl? She couldn't tell his age, nor whether he was gay or straight. He wore a butch black leather jacket over effeminate cotton trousers in a swirly snakeskin print. In addition to the array of rings on his fingers, he sported both an earring and a nose-ring.

'Catherine, you don't smoke, do you, babe?'

'No, I'm sorry.'

'Shit! I'll have to go and *buy* some bleedin' fags. Want anythin', you lot?'

'Yeah, a coffee,' Derek mumbled. 'Two sugars.'

'Do *you* want a coffee, Catherine?' Greta asked. 'It'll warm you up.'

'Yes, that would be nice.' Catherine was aware how prissily middle-class she must sound, compared with Brad's brash Cockney and Derek's flat South Londonese. They'd probably regard her as a snob. She fought a temptation to bolt, to turn on her heel and vanish into the gloom. The lowering sky made it feel more like night than daytime, as if morning was suffering from a hangover and was reluctant to get out of bed.

'I must be off soon,' Greta said, stowing the empty cases under the stall. 'We'll just run over the prices before I go. And here's a money-bag for you. Tie it round your waist, under your coat. That's it! Sure you'll be all right?'

'Yes, fine,' said Catherine with more conviction than she felt. Appalling weather, rude pigs and thieves as customers (or no customers at all), and two intimidating men to 'help' her. What in God's name was she *doing* here?

'Well, I can let you have it for ten, but . . .'

'Nine.'

'No, sorry, ten's my limit,' Catherine said firmly. 'It's still a bargain. Those zebra hats cost more than that to make.' Already she had learned the art of creative exaggeration.

'Nine-fifty.'

'No, honestly. I can't go any lower.' Greta had told her to haggle only with obstinate cusses, and even then to fix a limit.

The woman studied herself in the mirror from various angles. A fraction more encouragement might do the trick, Catherine felt. 'It really does look good on you,' she said with her most persuasive smile.

'You think so?'

'Mm. It sets off your hair so well.'

The woman thrust a crumpled £10 note into her hand. 'Okay, I'll take it.'

Catherine held the note up to the light: Greta had warned her to look out for fakes. But so far no one had tried to cheat her, or insult her, or nick the stock, or any of the other hazards she'd been dreading. In fact, she was doing surprisingly well. Those years she had spent being nice to Gerry's customers were paying dividends. And of course the change in the weather had helped enormously. In place of driving snow, a wan winter sun had broken through and was continuing to shine heroically, banishing the murky gloom.

Derek wandered over again. He had kept his promise to Greta and come up every so often to see how she was getting on. 'You're doing bloody well,' he said, watching the woman walk off with her purchase. 'I've hardly shifted a thing all day.'

'Gosh, I'm sorry.'

He shrugged. 'Some days are like that. And January's a lousy month. It's always bloody slow.'

Slow? She watched the crowds jostling between the rows of stalls. The sun had brought them out – the invigorating air and almost tangible excitement at the first snow of the winter. It must be something like a ski resort, she imagined: the exhilaration, the glittery light of sun on snow, the brightly coloured clothing and holiday atmosphere. Or perhaps not so much a ski resort as a street carnival, since many people looked as if they were wearing fancy dress. A man strolled past in baggy crimson harem trousers and a huge wool poncho in psychedelic stripes. His girlfriend had green hair, sticking up in long greased spikes, and a highly impractical full-length satin skirt in matching emerald green. Both were eating slabs of pitta bread stuffed with beans and salad – a late lunch, presumably, although she had lost all track of time and meals. She suddenly thought of Antonia, cooking for another formal dinner party tonight. And Andrew, the well-trained husband, helping with the preparations: laying the table, hoovering the immaculate house.

Talking to them on the phone last night, she had felt a sense of dislocation – cut adrift from their ordered sphere, but without a proper role of her own. Here in Camden people had such different priorities, and seemed quite happy to ignore the chores and troop out in search of diversion. Yet she was very much a novice in this foreign world of the market: a whole complex society with its own rules and values, maybe its own enmities and feuds. She was seeing only the surface, learning a few names and mere scraps of people's histories, without understanding what made them tick. Brad was the only one who had opened up, describing his traumatic childhood in Hackney as one of seven children, always in trouble with the police and not sure who his own father was. Surprisingly, he was only twenty-nine. He seemed far older somehow and had endured so many knocks in life, he made her feel naïve and over-privileged.

She stood watching him at work, amazed at his sheer energy. He appeared never to be still: stamping his feet in the cold, or jogging on the spot, or sweet-talking the customers with his lively banter and extravagant gestures. He was like one of the battery-operated toys Rosie was selling opposite; programmed to prance around and divert the passers-by until the power-supply ran down – if it ever did. She would never have met a man like Brad in Stoneleigh. Her life there was so narrow, and her few suburban friends (mere acquaintances, in fact) were all middle-aged and middle-class: 'safe' and 'suitable' people who had barely lived, compared with Brad.

He saw her looking at him and raised his eyebrows comically, then a minute later he was bounding over. 'Fancy a beer?' he asked.

'No thanks, Brad. It's kind of you, but . . .' He had already bought her a mug of tea, and she was afraid of drinking too much and having to keep dashing to the loo. Okay, Derek might watch the stall for her, but he had customers of his own to attend to, and she was alarmed to think that Greta had had a hat pinched when she was actually *there*. She was determined the day should go well, not just for Greta's sake, but for Jo's and even Nicky's. Nicky had sent a couple of friends along, with instructions to buy hats. They had bought two each (*and* the most expensive ones), so she felt doubly grateful to Nicky, who would be slaving away at this moment on the hated Orange-O account – tangy, zingy, nervous-breakdown-inducing Orange-O.

Brad was still hovering by her stall. 'I like your rings,' she said, in an attempt at conversation. So far he had done most of the talking and she didn't want to seem stuck-up.

'Yeah, unusual, aren't they? I make 'em all myself.' He took one off and laid it on her palm. The chunky stone was tiger-striped in black and tan, and mounted in an intricate silver setting. She was impressed by the workmanship, especially in view of the bad start he'd had in life. Apparently he had played truant so much from school he could hardly remember his teachers' names, let alone pass exams.

'This mate of mine called Gary – 'e taught me all I know. 'E started off with debts up to 'ere' – he held his hand level with his eyebrows – 'and now 'e's rakin' it in. Oh, sorry, darlin' – gotta dash!'

He had spotted a customer and dived back to his stall. Admiringly, she watched him go through his repertoire, realizing what a lot she had to learn. Besides his engaging energy, he possessed a genuine warmth and friendliness and seemed able to relate to every type of person. He could make them laugh, break down their defences; above all convince them that his jewellery was the best bargain in the market. If only she could do the same with the waistcoats, which hadn't sold at all, largely, she suspected, because she was being undercut by a rival – an Indian guy a few yards along, who was selling waistcoats for a mere £9.99. But his were crudely made from cheap fabric, whereas Greta's were works of art.

She put her gloves back on, wishing she had some fingerless mittens, like Derek's, and had worn a few more pairs of socks. However, apart from her hands and feet, she was reasonably warm, cocooned in several layers of clothes, with Nicky's thick-pile coat on top. The main requirements to work in the market seemed to be a capacious bladder, endless patience, a hardy constitution, and no objection to looking like Michelin Man.

'Do these waistcoats come in different sizes?'

A man had stopped in front of the stall – wild black curly hair, stocky build, grey eyes. His voice, though, was his distinguishing feature – the first pukka accent she had heard all day.

'Oh, yes.' She held one up to show him. 'Small, medium and large. And they're adjustable here at the back. This is a medium. I should think it's about right for you.'

He fingered the silky fabric with hands strangely at variance with his voice: a labourer's rough hands, the nails bitten short and none too clean. 'They're new, aren't they? I bought a hat here for a

friend a couple of weeks ago, but I didn't know Greta made waistcoats too. Where is she, by the way?'

'At Portobello Road. Selling more waistcoats! Every one's different, as you see, so you're getting something unique. And if you
prefer a warmer material, there are just a couple left in the velvet.
Is it for you, or . . . ?'

'Yes, 'fraid so. I've never worn a waistcoat before, but I'm doing
an important gig next week and I thought I ought to look the
part.'

He seemed inclined to chat, so she had better show some interest. Greta had said there were three kinds of 'talkers': the time-
wasters (often lonely and occasionally deranged), the smart-arses
(rude, aggressive and unlikely to buy) and the genuinely friendly
(to be encouraged).

'What instrument do you play?' she asked, glad she'd had the
experience of Darren's gig and so wouldn't seem a complete
ignoramus.

He laughed. 'Oh, I'm not a musician, only a humble poet. And
I usually give readings on my own, or with just another couple of
writers – you know, fairly low-key affairs. But a friend of mine's
arranging this big do on the South Bank, and seems to have roped
in every performer she knows – actors, poets, jugglers, jazz bands
. . . You name it.'

Catherine had never met a poet in her life, but she certainly
hadn't imagined they would have work-worn hands and a weather-
beaten complexion, nor wear faded denims and an ancient donkey
jacket. Surely the purple velvet waistcoat he was examining would
be more appropriate, though frankly, she couldn't picture him in
it. Still, her job was to sell, not to dispense unbiased advice. 'It'll
look really good on you,' she said encouragingly.

'You don't think it's a bit . . . sissy?'

'Oh no. Everybody's wearing them. And the purple suits your
dark hair.' She was astonished at her own boldness. For some time
after Greta left she had cowered behind the stall, hardly daring to
open her mouth, let alone shower compliments about. But as the
day wore on she had become more confident. After all, the customers were harmless (even the grouchy or peculiar ones), and
since she wasn't likely to meet any of them again, she could be as
brazen as she liked. 'They're a bargain price today,' she went on.
'Only thirty pounds. Greta says they'll be thirty-five next week.'

'Well, in that case . . .' He pulled two £20 notes from his wallet and held them out. 'Wish me luck for Friday. It'll be the biggest audience I've ever had and I must admit I'm nervous.'

'I'm sure you'll be fine,' she assured him. 'And you'll look wonderful in this.' She could relate to nervous people, who always roused her sympathy. 'Purple's a good colour.' Grinning, she removed her hat to show him her Spiced Plum hair. 'See? It's brought *me* luck so far.' Well, except for Simon, she thought, although she had forgotten Simon until now. One of the advantages of running a stall was that you hadn't time to worry about much else. She put the waistcoat in a stripy bag and gave it to him with his change. 'Good luck for Friday. I'll think of you.'

'*Will* you?'

She blushed. She was supposed to chat with people, not chat them up.

''Bye, then.'

''Bye.'

She was almost sad to see him go. There was a certain vulnerability about him which she had to admit she found appealing: the grey eyes anxious, the untidy hair in need of a trim, a button off his coat. It must be satisfying to get to know people's names and something of their lives, to gradually build up relationships with the regulars. Gerry's customers had been so much less diverse: businessmen, invariably, and all roughly the same type and class. Today she was meeting the world in microcosm.

Derek mooched over, looking as morose as ever. 'I've just got shot of this real slimeball. He put his filthy mitts all over the rugs, then told me they were crap.' He lit a cigarette, crooking his fingers protectively round the match-flame. '*You've* been coining it in all day, I see.'

'It . . . it must be just beginner's luck,' she stammered, relieved to see Brad waltzing up again, this time clutching a bottle of scotch and three polystyrene cups.

'Thought it would keep out the cold,' he said, sloshing a hefty measure into the first cup and handing it to her.

She hated whisky, but it would be churlish to refuse. 'Thanks,' she said, watching him fill the other two cups and praying he wouldn't spill any on Greta's precious hats.

'Cheers!' he said, knocking it back.

'Cheers.' Catherine took a tentative sip. Almost at once she was aware of a warm glow in her veins; her body a hot water bottle slowly filling up. Heartened, she drank a little more, wondering what she could offer in return. Spirits were expensive, but she had seen a man selling hot roast chestnuts. *They* would be warming, and she could also take the chance to have a pee.

'Could you mind the stall for a moment?' she asked Derek, who had pulled a magazine from his pocket and was busy ogling the pin-ups with Brad.

It was Brad who answered, giving her a friendly punch on the arm. 'Yeah, 'course – off you go. And don't look so worried, darlin'! Nothin' terrible's goin' to 'appen just because you turn your back for five minutes.'

'Thanks,' she grinned, draining the whisky too fast and gasping as it burned her throat. Still, it provided good central heating and a few minutes later even her hands were warm. She had taken Greta's tip and thawed them under the hand-dryer in the toilet.

Outside again, she bought three bags of chestnuts and crammed them in her pockets, keeping her hands cupped over them as another form of heating. The crowds were beginning to dwindle with the light, but there were still enough people around to give the market a buzz. She stared in fascination at a gruesome black spider's web tattooed across the neck of a man of roughly Andrew's age. His girlfriend's hairstyle was equally dramatic: the front of her scalp was cropped to a fuzz, but at the back her hair was long, reaching almost to her waist. The traders were as varied as the customers – sharply dressed, fast-talking spivs; frail young Japanese girls; blowsy women in moth-eaten furs; Rastafarians; ageing hippies; earnest bearded Asians. Why should she feel an outsider amidst such a wealth of different types? Surely there was room for her as well. After all, she had proved herself today, learned the ropes in record time and sold a lot of hats. And far from being tired, she felt energized by her achievement – not just the sales, but the heady sense of entering a community so unlike anything she knew.

She stopped to smile at a baby lying in a milk-crate at the back of a cassette stall. It was wrapped in what looked like an old curtain and surrounded by boxes of tapes, and seemed completely unperturbed by the raucous music blasting from the speakers overhead. She felt a sudden bond with its mother: a skinny waif with dark circles under her eyes and bare skin showing through the holes in her blue jeans. *She* must have looked as young as that when Andrew was an infant, and he had slept just as soundly not in a plastic milk-crate but in a battered wooden drawer. (They didn't have a proper cot till Kate was born.)

On impulse, she decided to buy a cassette. She wished she could afford the lot, to finance some warm new clothes for the girl and a decent shawl for the baby. She chose a rock band Darren liked, although she'd never heard of them till this week. Never mind – it would be a challenge, another way of broadening her horizons. She might have left school early, but that didn't mean she couldn't catch up now, though in rather different subjects from reading, writing and arithmetic.

'Enjoy it!' the girl said, handing over the tape.

'Thanks, I will,' said Catherine. That was the key – enjoyment. It had never figured high on her agenda, but she had a chance to change that, to break with her dutiful past.

She strode towards the canal, her feet picking up the catchy rhythm still booming from the stall. Several other kinds of music were playing, which added to the general festive air. Christmas might be a fading memory for the rest of sombre London, but Camden Lock retained some vestige of it, if only in the brilliant colours, the strings of twinkling lights.

She stood leaning on the stone parapet, gazing down at the canal. Litter floated on the surface of the water – empty cans and cartons, fag-ends, paper cups – yet far from looking sordid, it had a strangely magical glitter in the fiery light of the sunset. The sky was a deep golden-red; nature eclipsing the traders' displays with its own magnificence.

She checked her watch: four-thirty. She had been away longer than five minutes, yet she wasn't even worried. It might be the effect of the whisky, or maybe just relief at having survived the bulk of the day without mishap. Whatever the reason, she felt remarkably at ease, even – dare she say it? – happy.

'No, this round's on me,' Greta insisted, picking up the empty glasses. 'You did bloody well today.'

'Thanks,' said Catherine, flushed from the wine and the compliment. Although she had taken off her coat and thick wool cardigan, she was still perspiring in Fiona's mohair sweater. Despite its tatty decor, the pub exuded a cheerful glow, partly from the coal fire crackling in the grate and partly from the scores of bodies jammed into too small a space – laughing, talking, smoking, drinking, and generating their own heat. Many of them were Greta's friends; fellow traders unwinding after their long day in the market, who appeared to have accepted her quite happily as one of the crowd. In fact she felt more at home in the Stag's Head than in Andrew and Antonia's local, the chi-chi Rose and Crown. That was all bronze warming-pans and frilled cretonne at the windows, whereas here the drab brown curtains had uneven saggy hems and looked as if they might disintegrate if you were unwise enough to pull them. But the very shabbiness was endearing in a way, displaying a heroic disregard for normal commercial considerations such as cleanliness and modernity. The plain wooden floor was stained and scuffed, the Bisto-brown wallpaper peeling off in places, and little pools of sawdust had leaked from the torn covers of the bar-stools. From the outside, indeed, the place looked almost derelict, as if thumbing its nose at the public with a defiant 'Take me or leave me' air.

Yet more new arrivals were streaming in, many of them Irish, attracted by the music – a fiddler and an accordionist playing jaunty reels. They all seemed to know each other, calling out greetings to their friends and joking with the Irish landlord, Mick, and his flame-haired daughter behind the bar.

'This is Lynne,' said Greta, returning with a tray of glasses and a small fair girl in tow. 'She's been helping me make the waistcoats. I'll miss her. She's starting a new job on Monday.'

'Nice to meet you,' Catherine smiled, hoping she'd remember all the names. Both Brad and Greta had introduced her to various people, but after a couple of glasses of wine everything was blurring slightly. Brad had moved to the next table now and was talking to a tall black guy with dreadlocks. Lester, *he* was called, and the stunning girl beside them (also black but with straightened hair dyed blue) was Bina? Bita? – some name she hadn't quite caught. Sitting at her own table were Rosie, Stan and Gareth. Rosie was a single parent whose husband had walked out two days before their baby was due; Stan sold fifties clothes (and looked a fifties relic), and Gareth was studying photography at Brighton University and eking out his grant by selling his own framed photos at the weekends.

She squeezed up to make room for Lynne on the ancient

wooden bench. It was quite a squash already, what with Gareth's thigh pressing into hers and Rosie's cigarette smoke drifting across her face. Still, all part of the family . . .

'What sort of work do you do?' she asked Lynne, who was now armed with a pint of Guinness and licking a foam moustache from her top lip.

'Well, they've just taken me on as a wardrobe-mistress at Sadler's Wells. I can't believe my luck! I've never worked in a theatre before.'

'Not very lucky for me, though,' Greta wailed. 'I'll never find anyone who can sew as well as you, Lynne.'

'Don't be silly. 'Course you will. And those waistcoats are dead simple. No sleeves, or fitting, or complicated patterns.'

'Come off it, they're not *that* easy. The buttonholes are awfully fiddly and it's a bugger getting the lining right. Anyway, time's my main problem at the moment.' Greta turned from Lynne to Catherine. 'I haven't told you yet,' she said, 'but I had a special order today. This American girl fell in love with the waistcoats. She's getting married in June – a big fancy do in Oregon – and she wants the bridegroom and her father and the half-dozen little pageboys all to wear them for the wedding. She's obviously got pots of money, so it's too good a chance to miss.'

'Oh, I say,' said Catherine. 'That's wonderful.'

'Yeah. The thing is, though, she's going back to the States on Monday week and I haven't even bought the fabric yet. She wants a special brocade to match the bridesmaids' dresses and it may take a while to track it down. Then I've got the actual sewing and all the buttons to cover and . . .'

'Maybe *I* could help?' Catherine suggested, emboldened by her third glass of wine. 'I'm afraid I'm not quite in the wardrobe-mistress class, but I used to make the children's clothes and even some of my husband's. And I've got a machine at home with a buttonhole attachment and all that sort of thing.'

'You're mad!' grinned Rosie. 'Greta's a frightful slave-driver. She'll have you working all night.'

'Shut up, Rosie,' Greta said, opening a bag of peanuts and offering them around. 'If you *could* help, Catherine, that would be fantastic. I've been wondering how on earth I'd cope. You see, I run a stall here four days a week, which doesn't leave much time for sewing. And on top of everything else, my mother's broken her wrist, so I'm having to flog to Greenwich and back every other day.'

'Well, I'm free at the moment, luckily,' Catherine said. 'I've got to find a proper job, but another week won't hurt. And anyway I'm not exactly panting to get back to office work.'

'Are you a secretary?' Stan asked.

'No.' She hesitated. 'I'm, er, well . . . nothing really. I used to work for my husband, but . . .'

'Pissed off, did he?' Rosie said in a bitter tone. 'D'you know, I'd never trust a bloke again – not after Pete and Jim.'

'Thanks very much,' said Gareth. 'Just because you married a couple of bummers, there's no need to damn the entire male sex.'

'Oh, *you*'re all right, Gareth,' Rosie said, patting his arm maternally. 'I don't mind the under-twenty-ones.'

Stan bristled. 'And what about the over-fifties?'

'Dodgy!'

'When you've all quite finished,' Greta said, 'I'm trying to talk to Catherine.'

'Watch it, Catherine,' Rosie said in a stage-whisper. 'She's notorious for her starvation wages.'

'Lynne, did I pay you well, or not?' Greta demanded indignantly.

'Yes, love. I'm so flush, I'm off to Barbados for the winter.'

'Hey, look,' said Stan, pointing at the television mounted on the wall. 'The lottery's about to start. Maybe you *will* be off to Barbados, Lynne.'

'No chance. I've given up. I mean, what's the bloody point? All these weeks and I haven't won a thing.'

'It's all right for them with full-time jobs at poncy Sadler's Wells,' Stan said in a hoity-toity voice.

'Anyway, that's not the spirit,' Brad remarked, returning to their table. '*Life*'s a gamble, innit? You gotta get in there and 'ave a go, otherwise you'll never change your luck.'

'So how many lines did *you* do?' Gareth asked him.

'Me usual – fifteen quid's worth.'

'Well, I've got no chance then,' Catherine moaned, getting out her ticket. 'I only did a pound's worth.'

'That's all it takes, love,' Brad insisted, leaning over to see what she had marked. 'Six little numbers to turn your life around. This mate of mine won two grand last week, and that was just for a quid. And the very same day 'e backed a six-to-one winner at Aintree.'

'Quick! Give me his phone number,' Rosie said. 'I can't wait to meet him.'

'I thought you was *off* men, Rosie?' Stan put in.

'Not blokes with luck like that. The trouble with me is I always fall for losers.'

'That's negative though, innit?' said Brad. 'It's like if you tell yourself you never win, you don't. You gotta *will* those balls to come up, do a Mystic Meg on 'em.'

Stan snorted in derision. 'You can't do worse than her. She's bleeding useless!'

'Well trust yourself, then. But you gotta really really concentrate.' Brad closed his eyes melodramatically and spread his hands out in front of him, as if groping for an invisible force. 'Put the *'fluence* on them balls.'

Catherine hid a smile, imagining how Andrew would scoff. Neither he nor Antonia had gambled in their lives, beyond buying a few safe blue-chip shares. Yet she was attracted by Brad's optimism, his cocksure confidence. Maybe it was irrational, but willing things could work. The power of the mind was gaining respect even in scientific circles. There was that extraordinary piece in the *Guardian* about a group of cancer patients who had successfully willed their malignant cells to dissolve, and another recent study which seemed to prove the power of prayer.

She closed her eyes, like Brad, and fixed her full attention on her numbers. It wasn't so much the money she wanted as the achievement of winning in itself, which would be a hopeful sign. As Brad had said, she had to turn her life around, especially at this crossroads, poised as she was between a past of missed opportunities and a future still uncertain.

Eyes still closed, she was vaguely conscious of the wave of sound swirling through the pub – manic cheers and drum-rolls from the television as the pre-lottery hype exploded to a climax; shouts and laughter from the Irish contingent clapping along to the band, and Brad's strident voice continuing to extol the force of willpower.

'Let me choose right,' she whispered, without the faintest notion as to who or what she was addressing. 'So I can become the person I was born to be.' God! she thought, I sound worse than Mystic Meg. Yet that choice seemed really vital. Did she settle for continued stagnation, or commit herself to something new, where *she* decided what to do with her life?

'Ssh!' Gareth ordered Brad. 'They're starting.'

A hush fell over their table as the first ball rolled down the chute, followed by a shout of triumph from Rosie. Catherine let out a despairing wail, remembering only now that she had chosen her numbers around Simon. How could she even expect to win after that disastrous Monday evening?

'Don't give up yet,' Brad urged her. 'You're still in with the shout. Hey, look, you got the next one.' He seized her ticket and jabbed number 23. 'Come on, come on! Psych 'em up! Five and a bonus and you're away. Yeah, seventeen! You got two now. It's workin', babe! Keep willin'. There you are – what'd I say? Three's a definite tenner.'

Catherine stared at her ticket in disbelief. She had never had three numbers up before. Coincidence? Or could Brad's system actually work? She concentrated hard, determined to win again.

'Shit!' Brad groaned, as 42 rolled into the slot. 'Never mind. A tenner's better than nothin'. ''Old on – 'ere's the last. Gor blimey!' he shouted. 'Would you believe it? You got that one, too. Bloody 'ell!' He shook his head. 'Four numbers on one fuckin' line. And I've got sod all on fifteen. Well, that's the way it goes, babe. Mind you, I probably lost because I was 'elpin' *you*. All me brain cells was goin' in the wrong direction.'

Catherine sat in stunned silence, embarrassed to be the centre of attention as a crowd of envious faces tried to get a glimpse of her card. No one else had any winning numbers except Rosie, who had got the first but nothing subsequently. 'Oh, B . . . Brad,' she stammered finally, 'I've done it – *we*'ve done it. I feel I owe you a share.'

'Don't be daft. Enjoy it! It'll only be about forty quid, in any case. Mind you, it all helps, dunnit? And I got a feelin' it's the start of a lucky break for you. I 'ad these vibes just now and they was comin' through really good and strong.'

'Well, I'd better stick around with you,' she laughed.

'Yeah, stick with me any time. *I*'ll change your luck – you wait and see.'

She clasped the ticket in her hand. Her luck was changing already. Not just the forty pounds, but the sewing job for Greta, which meant she could keep in touch with these new friends. Their informality appealed to her; their capacity for enjoyment. She thought of Andrew and Antonia's guests, who would be discussing heavy issues like human rights abuses or the British penal system. And the ones with children would be deploring the lack of nursery schools, or comparing their offspring's progress in cutting their first milk teeth or passing Grade 3 clarinet. Okay, such things were important, but she sometimes felt she'd been serious her whole life, from the time of her mother's early death and her father's almost monastic regime. Some secret part of her was longing to rebel; not to care a fig whether she was a credit to her family; not to feel ashamed of her lustful thoughts about Brad. She glanced at him now, his legs splayed wide apart, the clingy cotton fabric of his trousers leaving little to the imagination. Though, in fact, her imagination had been working overtime. They had already been to bed together; she tentative at first, stroking his shaved head, flicking an exploratory tongue across his silver nose-ring, then gradually working herself up, roused by his sheer noisy thrusting energy.

Her eyes moved surreptitiously to Lester. *He* was in bed with her now; his dramatic dreadlocks a black cascade on the pillow; his long muscular legs twined around her own. Never before had she been so aware of men as males. The pub was overflowing with them – men in dirty work-clothes she was mentally undressing; total strangers slipping warm sly hands beneath her jersey; tangled hairs on brawny arms, stubble-roughened chins, broad shoulders, deep bass voices. Seeing Simon naked had made her realize how pathetically inexperienced she was. And although the affair had been a fiasco, it had aroused her curiosity; left her eager to see other men – do more than simply see them. Her recent talks with Nicky had influenced her too. Nicky and the others were so frank, so matter-of-fact. Sex for them wasn't tied to holy matrimony or hedged about with restrictions and anxieties. Not that *she* could be so free – not while she lived at Stoneleigh. Andrew and Antonia wouldn't dream of mentioning sex, and she never heard them making love, or caught them staggering from the bedroom looking well-shagged (as Nicky put it graphically). Besides, in Manor Close she was still the virtuous mother, the conventional mother-in-law – a profoundly inhibiting role, which put an outright ban on steamy fantasies.

But at least such fantasies were proof she wasn't frigid, as she had feared on Monday evening. She grinned to herself. She was behaving like an adolescent, lurching from one extreme to the other: a vestal virgin on Monday and practically a nymphomaniac tonight.

'What's the joke?' asked Greta.

'She's plannin' 'er new life,' said Brad. 'Dreamin' of a bloody great 'ouse with a sauna and a swimmin' pool and a private plane parked in the drive.'

No, not a private plane, she thought, but a new life – certainly. And the first decision in that new life was to join them here next Saturday again. After all, she would have the finished waistcoats to deliver, and if her work came up to standard, Greta might give her more.

She put the winning ticket in her pocket and stood up. 'Okay, everybody, drinks on me this time. And if I win the jackpot next week, we'll *all* go to Barbados!'

'Where *have* you been?' Nicky let Catherine in, shivering in the blast of cold night air. 'We were getting really worried. Darren thought you might have gone off with a drugs baron.'

Catherine followed her into the sitting-room, laughing as she unbuttoned her coat. 'Well, I almost went off with a man called Brad. He wanted to take me to a rave.'

'Good God, you're living dangerously!' Nicky curled up in her chair again, reaching for her glass. 'Hey, look at William. With devotion like that, you don't need men.'

The cat had trotted up to greet her and was rubbing himself against her legs, purring ecstatically. 'It's only cupboard love, isn't it, William?' she said, picking him up and settling him on her lap. 'I've been cooking him steamed fish and things, and I think he expects it every time he sees me now. Oh, and I bought him a box of Milky Drops from the pet shop and something called a cat chew.'

'Lucky William,' Darren muttered. '*We* don't get cat chews or Milky Drops.' He was lying on the sofa smoking a joint – a piney, slightly sickly smell she was learning to recognize.

'Shut up, Darren.' Nicky chucked a cushion at him. 'I want to hear how Catherine got on. Well?' she asked. 'Did you manage to sell any hats?'

'Yes, quite a lot. Greta was really pleased. She said I sold more than *she* usually does.'

'Great! Did Sue and Laura buy any?'

'Two each. You are a darling to send them along. Fiona didn't come, though.'

'Don't mention Fee.' Darren placed the cushion over his face and gave a histrionic groan.

'Why, what's wrong?'

Another groan issued from the cushion.

'You'll have to forgive us, Catherine,' Nicky said. 'We've had an absolutely shitty day and we've decided to get pissed. Do join us if you want. There's plenty of gin and stuff.'

'No, I'd better not. I've had rather a lot of wine already.'

'So you *have* been out on the tiles,' Nicky grinned. 'What happened to – who was it – Brad?'

'I left him in the Stag's Head.'

'Oh, Darren, we're leading Catherine astray. She was the soul of respectability before she came here.'

'Speak for yourself,' Darren mumbled.

'Actually, Catherine, I'm jolly glad to see you. I want you to get me back on the straight and narrow. I really shouldn't get pissed, whatever I've just said. Stop me drinking this poisonous stuff, I beg you, and pack me off to bed. I'm going windsurfing tomorrow – I've got to work on my gybes before I go on holiday, and the last thing I need's a hangover.'

'Bloody hell,' Darren grumbled. 'You might at least have told me you'd be out.'

'Well, it doesn't affect you, does it?'

''Course it does. We're meant to be going to those galleries tomorrow and if you're pissing off to Brighton or wherever . . .'

'Oh, sod the galleries! Anyway, I'm not going to the coast. It's too damned cold. I'll just content myself with a couple of hours at the reservoir. Catherine, I can give you a lift to Stoneleigh, if you want. It's not far out of my way and it'll save you hanging about for Sunday trains.'

'Gosh, thanks,' said Catherine, disconcerted by the thought that she would be returning to normality tomorrow. Andrew and Antonia had invited her to Sunday lunch at the golf club, and since there was no more reason to stay longer here in Camden, she would be back in suburban seclusion from then on.

'You are a pain, Nick,' Darren bleated. 'I was counting on you to be here, so we could go to the Hayward together.'

'Can't we go *next* Sunday?'

'No, it finishes tomorrow. And you know what Wayne said about going out and getting fresh ideas.'

'Bugger Wayne!'

'Who's Wayne?' asked Catherine.

'Our Creative Director, Wayne MacDonald.'

'Any bloke called Wayne's bound to be bad news.' Darren raised his head languidly, dislodging the cushion.

'He can't help his name, Darren. Anyway, yours is just as naff. Still, I must admit he is vile.' Nicky turned to Catherine, her voice rising in exasperation. 'He struts around the office like the great I Am, and the awful thing is he's *younger* than me. He was lecturing us yesterday about being stale and uninspired. Apparently we need more stimulation. Which means finding time to see all the latest films and exhibitions. Though God knows how we're supposed to fit it in.'

'Well, you give up windsurfing for a start.' Darren inhaled deeply. His eyes were closed and a seraphic smile settled over his features.

'Are you mad?'

'And sex.'

'That's non-existent at the moment, so . . .'

'Well, men then . . . Parties . . . Meals out . . . Flying kites.'

'Then I'd be more stale than ever. For heaven's sake, I'm even beginning to *dream* about work. Last night it was Orange-O. I was imprisoned in a tiny cell, writing in this syrupy orange ink. But when I tried to read it, the words were in a sort of foreign script and didn't mean a thing. I woke up drenched with sweat.'

Darren started to laugh. 'Better than drenched in Orange-O. Hey, I've just had an idea – free dreams with Orange-O. Fill in the handy coupon. Or better still, free orgasms. Orange-flavoured, of course. Two for the price of one.'

'Ignore him, Catherine,' Nicky said. 'Once he gets giggly, he's impossible. *I* feel more like crying. Today was the pits – just the two of us in that great morgue of a building, with a lone security guard pacing up and down. And what really bugs me is that Wayne's quite likely to shoot the whole thing down again on Monday and we'll be back where we started. It's incredibly frustrating. The deadlines are tight enough as it is, without *him* putting his oar in. I'm sure I'll have an ulcer by the time I'm forty. Mind you, they'll have sacked me long before then for not seeing the latest Quentin Tarantino.'

'*I* haven't seen a film for months.'

'Why not, Cath?' asked Darren. '*You*'ve got loads of time.'

'Well, I suppose it seems sort of . . . indulgent, going on my own.'

'Indulgent?' Nicky raised her eyebrows. 'You'd better come with us then. It's our homework, after all, so we can make it grim and dutiful.'

'Okay, you're on,' she laughed.

'Actually, I was going to ask you something . . .' Nicky looked slightly embarrassed. 'I mean, it's probably out of the question, or you'll loathe the whole idea, or think it's an awful cheek, or . . .'

'What? Something to do with William?' She fondled his ears, glad he looked so much better. The Milky Drops contained vitamins, and they must be doing him good.

'Oh, no. Well, yes, I suppose it does involve him in a way, though I hadn't even thought of that. No, it's Fiona. She's not coming back – not for ages, anyway. Her mother's got cancer. They've only just found out. Fiona's absolutely devastated.' Nicky ran a distracted hand through her hair. 'And it puts *us* in a bit of a spot. You see, she can't leave Hereford, so she's suggested that a friend of hers moves into her room here, to help out with the rent. He's another photographer, actually, called Melvyn. We met him once, and once was enough, I can tell you. He's an utter pseud, and our ever-tactful friend here went and told him so.'

'Well, someone had to,' said Darren, still smiling beatifically.

'But of course we didn't like to say anything when Fiona was so upset about her mother. And anyway, it rather threw us. We told her we needed time to discuss it.' Nicky took a final sip from her glass, then screwed the cap on the gin bottle and put it out of reach. 'Well, we talked for ages last night, but we didn't really get anywhere. The only thing that's certain is we have to let the room as soon as possible, otherwise we're simply throwing money down the drain. Darren's got a friend who's looking for a place. He plays guitar with Pink Treacle, but frankly, two musicians under one roof is pushing it a bit.'

'Mm, Bill's a great guy,' said Darren, 'but he's not what I'd call house-trained.'

Nicky shuddered. 'And there's a girl at work who wants a pad, but she's just bought one of those snappy little terriers, and I draw the line at dogs. William's bad enough.'

Catherine continued stroking the cat, trying to hide her growing unease. She knew exactly what was coming and didn't want to hear it. How could she say yes? It was one thing staying here a week on just a casual basis, but to move in permanently . . .

'And then we thought of *you*, Catherine. I know you're living with your son and it would mean an enormous upheaval, but – well, you're seeing him tomorrow, aren't you, so maybe you could talk it over. And you did say you found the suburbs rather boring.' Nicky paused, still frowning. 'You needn't commit yourself to longer than, say, six months. But then we could tell Fiona you're desperate to stay on, and that would keep the dreaded Melvyn at bay. I know it's terribly selfish of us, but you do fit in so well. Besides, Fiona's mother might be better by the summer. They're starting chemotherapy right away.'

'Or she may be dead,' Darren put in lugubriously.

'Darren, *don't*. She's only fifty-five.'

'Keats died at twenty-five.'

'What's that got to do with it?'

'And Kurt Cobain at twenty-seven.'

'You're a comfort in a crisis, I must say,' Nicky retorted. 'Well, Catherine, what do you think?'

She could hardly think at all. Her head was still floaty from the wine. But warning lights had begun to flash. To afford rent each week, she would need a proper job. Running up a few waistcoats wouldn't bring in enough. But wasn't it ridiculous to burden herself with rent when she could live free at Manor Close? She might criticize Andrew and Antonia – as she'd done disloyally all the week – but they were her bedrock, her security, and the prospect of giving up her only real home filled her with alarm. Besides, it could be another wrong decision: doing something to help someone else out (a repeat of the old pattern) rather than doing what *she* wanted. Even Greta's sewing job no longer sounded quite as appealing as it had done in the pub. Starvation wages, Rosie had said, and it would mean working on her own again, cut off from other people. She could look for a different job, though – an office job in Camden, for instance. The rates of pay were higher in London than the suburbs; besides, the last few days had shown her how stuffy and conformist life in the suburbs was, and how much she longed for change. Well, here was a chance to prove she meant it. She had felt happier today than she'd felt for a long time, mixing with people who were lively and free-spirited and also extraordinarily creative: making toys or jewellery, weaving rugs, producing arty photographs (often despite being branded failures at school, or by society at large). She found it heartening, somehow, that there was so much talent about. Even if they were only scraping a living, at least they were *using* their talent and their selves. It had even occurred to her this afternoon that maybe she could run a stall of her own; be equally creative and sell children's clothes, or cakes, or jams and chutneys. She no longer felt such an outsider in their world. In fact, in some respects she had quite a lot in common with the traders. Most of them seemed to be single or divorced, with no supportive partner or regular job, let alone a large bank balance, so she would fit in rather well.

But explaining the idea to her ultra-respectable son was a different matter entirely. Even if she found herself a conventional job, he would be against her moving to Camden. He already thought it odd that she had stayed so long with what he saw as a bunch of strangers, and if he discovered they smoked dope and consumed large quantities of alcohol he would be genuinely shocked. And then there was Jo to consider. She had almost forgotten the fourth inmate of the house, who might well object to her staying. 'Won't Jo mind?' she asked, suddenly realizing that Nicky was looking at her expectantly, still waiting for an answer.

'No, Jo's okay. We've rung her.'

Darren gave an extravagant yawn. 'Actually, she was so involved with some Italian guy, I don't think she'd care if we let the bloody room to Jack the Ripper.'

'Darren, that's not exactly flattering to Catherine.'

'Sorry, Cath. Nothing personal.' Darren lumbered to his feet, tripping over his glass. 'God, I'm flaked! I'm going up to bed.'

'Well, if you *will* smoke that junk,' said Nicky.

'Sorry, Mum.' He shambled out of the room and they heard him giggling to himself as he clump-clumped up the stairs.

Lord, thought Catherine, if Darren regarded Nicky as Mum, what did that make *her*? Grandma, probably. She was far too old to be part of this household. The others were bound to feel she cramped their style – Jo and Darren, certainly. Besides, she might offend Andrew and Antonia if she moved out of Manor Close, when they had been kind enough to offer her a home there (and gone to so much trouble over her room). Or would they be secretly relieved, perhaps? It was so difficult to know. The three of them rarely talked about their feelings. But maybe she could put a few antennae out before the golf club lunch, try to discover how they felt. 'Look, Nicky,' she said uncertainly, 'it's sweet of you to ask me, but it's not an easy decision. Can I phone you tomorrow evening, when I've had a chance to talk to Andrew about it, and let you know definitely then?'

'Well, it had *better* be yes,' grinned Nicky, listening to William's loud contented purr, 'or you'll do grave emotional damage to that cat. He's lost one mistress as it is . . .'

'Can't Fiona have him with her in Hereford?'

'No, she's already looking after her mother's dog, who happens to have a strong aversion to cats.'

'Poor William.' Catherine put her arms round him protectively.

'Yes, poor William,' Nicky echoed.

Catherine glanced at the scar from his abscess. It would be a wrench to leave him when they had built up such a bond, but she was equally loth to upset Andrew. God, what a dilemma, she thought – torn between her loyal supportive son and a great soppy tabby cat. She eased him gently off her lap and reached out for the gin bottle. She was sick and tired of dilemmas. 'Nicky, I've got an idea. Why don't we change places? You go up to bed with a nice healthy cup of Ovaltine and I'll stay down here and get pickled on the gin!'

12

'Not far now,' said Catherine. 'Just turn right at this crossroads, then it's the second road on the left.'

'Pretty round here, isn't it?' Nicky remarked as they passed an early-flowering cherry struggling into bloom.

'Mm.' Catherine was noncommittal. Far from being pretty, the neighbourhood seemed barren, devoid of life and colour. Anyway she wasn't really in the mood to appreciate her surroundings. Last night's gin had left her with a vicious headache. Also, the nearer they got to Manor Close, the more apprehensive she became about turning up with Nicky, Darren and Darren's bizarre friend Scott, and was praying they wouldn't come in.

Scott had shambled round to Gosforth Road at breakfast-time this morning, clearly at a loose end and looking for a way to spend his Sunday. Darren, pleading a hangover, had refused all his suggestions, until finally an exasperated Nicky invited them both to the reservoir: the new leisure centre there had pool tables, video games and a sauna and jacuzzi. So the four of them had piled into the car and driven out to Surrey. Scott, who seemed manic in the extreme, had talked the whole of the journey, telling puerile jokes, reading snippets out of the papers and giving his opinion on them (and also airing his views on life, death, drugs and sex). It was just as well no one else could get a word in edgeways, since the rest of them weren't feeling at their best. Now, however, even Scott fell silent as they turned into Manor Close.

'It's just here on the corner,' she said nervously. 'Number one.'

The house looked even more self-satisfied than usual; the neatly paved front garden a far cry from the Gosforth Road jungle of dustbin bags and weeds. The door-knocker was freshly Brasso'd, the net curtains smugly Persilled, and the paintwork was so pristine-white it was hard to believe it hadn't been touched up in the last half-hour.

'Cor!' drawled Scott. 'Posh.'

Catherine blushed. 'Thanks for the lift,' she said to Nicky. 'And thanks for a marvellous week. I've really enjoyed it.'

'And we enjoyed having you. Just make sure you're back soon – like tomorrow!'

Catherine smiled. 'I'll phone this evening, I promise. And whatever happens, let's keep in touch.'

'Yes, we must. We will.' Nicky leaned over and gave her an affectionate hug. It seemed to express the closeness they had achieved in so short a time. Catherine realized with a pang how much she would miss her new friend.

'Break it up, you two,' jeered Scott, prodding her in the back.

Catherine twisted round in her seat and blew him and Darren a kiss. 'Goodbye,' she said. 'Have a good sweat in the sauna! And thank you, Darren, for everything.'

'Hang on a sec, Cath, I'm dying for a slash. Would it be okay if I came in?'

'Y . . . yes, of course.'

'Me too,' said Scott, clutching his groin. 'That coffee's gone straight through me.'

Nicky shook her head in despair. 'Honestly, you lot, you're worse than a kindergarten class.' She switched off the engine and briefly checked her hair in the driving mirror. 'Actually, I think I'll come in too, if you've no objection, Catherine? I'd love to meet your son. And I'm not in any rush. A couple of hours' windsurfing is more than enough on a day like this. The wind's so strong, it'll be damned hard work.'

Catherine opened the car door, wishing she had the gall to tell Scott and Darren to use the public toilet at the recreation ground. But they had already clambered out and were advancing on the front gate. She stole a quick glance at her watch: twenty-five past twelve. Nicky might not be in a rush, but *she* was awfully late. Antonia, a stickler for punctuality, had specified twelve sharp for drinks. Jack and Maureen were also invited and she could see their grey-green Volvo parked a few yards on. Well, Nicky would get to meet more than just her son.

As she rang the doorbell, she heard Scott behind her, imitating its ding-dong chime and jigging about, impatient for his pee. Andrew came to the door, wearing smart grey flannels, a navy blazer, a spruce white shirt and his golf club tie. His initial sense of shock was quickly disguised by a politely welcoming smile.

'H . . . hello,' he said, riveted by Scott's hair, which was shoulder-length and spectacularly matted; a reddish-brown version of dreadlocks. His own hair was as tightly clipped as the privet hedge next door. His eyes moved to Darren, then Nicky, then her. Judging by his uneasy expression, no one's hairstyle passed muster – although at least her Spiced Plum crew-cut wouldn't seem so shocking alongside Darren's ponytail or Scott's flamboyant mane. And Scott's *clothes* were now subjected to his scrutiny: two shaggy jerseys with the elbows out, crumpled army fatigues and hulking great Doc Martens.

He finally dragged his eyes from Scott and gave her a nervous kiss. 'How are you, mother?'

'Fine, darling.' She made the introductions, explaining that her friends weren't staying and just needed to use the loo.

'Yes, of course. Come in.'

''Scuse me, where's the bog?' Scott asked, barging past him into the house. 'I'm desperate.'

'Just along here.' Andrew rushed him through the hall.

Scott's dishevelled figure vanished into the cloakroom, but he didn't bother to close the door and soon a fierce torrent could be heard spattering on to porcelain, accompanied by a groan of relief.

Antonia chose that moment to appear, elegant in an oyster-grey two-piece, with her hair swept up in a chignon. Catherine was embarrassingly aware of her own tightly clinging tube-dress. She had searched Fiona's wardrobe this morning for a reasonably conventional outfit, but this was the best she could find. It was straining over every curve (as well as revealing the line of her bra and pants), and seemed to be getting tighter by the minute.

Antonia, however, gave no hint of disapproval, either of her or of the others. 'It's very nice to meet you,' she smiled, shaking hands with Nicky and Darren. 'Will you join us for a drink?'

Say no, Catherine implored.

'Yes, that would be lovely,' Nicky replied, 'so long as we're not intruding. I know you've got a lunch appointment.'

'No, we don't need to go just yet.'

'Well, thanks,' said Nicky, unbuttoning her coat. 'It's very nice to meet you, too. I've heard such a lot about you.'

Thank God you don't know *what* she's heard, Catherine thought with a twinge of conscience, as she followed them into the sitting-room. (Darren remained outside, patrolling the cloakroom door and urging Scott to get a move on.)

Catherine kissed Jack and Maureen, dismayed to see how stiffly they got up. With each visit they seemed slower and more worn, as if Gerry's death had speeded up their ageing process. Maureen's arthritis was clearly worse, her fingers twisted and the knuckles red and enlarged. Catherine longed to find out how they were, but etiquette demanded another round of introductions.

Jack shook hands with Nicky, his eyes straying to her crotch-length skirt. Then he turned to Catherine and ruffled the nape of her neck. 'Well, this famous hair's not as bad as Andrew made out. In fact, I rather like it.'

'Thanks, Jack. You're a sweetie.'

'Well frankly, I don't,' Maureen put in, with rather a strained smile. 'You know I'm not one for mincing words, and I have to say I think it's far too short.'

'It'll grow,' said Nicky tactfully.

'Do sit down,' Antonia plumped up a cushion. 'And what can I get you to drink?'

'Alka-Seltzer for *that* lot.' Scott strode into the room, still doing up his flies. 'They've all got lousy hangovers.' He threw himself in a chair. 'Christ, it's hot in here!' He struggled out of his jerseys, revealing a dirty tee-shirt underneath, with JESUS HATES ME printed on the front.

Oh no, thought Catherine, trying to shield him from Maureen's line of sight. As a committed Christian she might well take offence. Fortunately Darren stumbled in at that moment, still wearing his black sunglasses (a necessity, he'd insisted, after last night's dope and drink). She saw a flicker of apprehension on Jack and Maureen's faces. He did look rather menacing, dressed, as usual, all in black, and with his face half hidden by the shades. Still, at least he was relatively presentable and, unlike Scott, he did believe in washing his hair.

'Nicky's going windsurfing,' she said brightly, partly to distract attention from Scott and Darren and partly to remind Nicky that she ought to be leaving soon.

141

'Oh, that sounds fun,' said Maureen, 'but isn't it rather cold this time of year?'

'Yeah,' said Scott, 'but Nicky's a fanatic. In fact she's a bloody masochist.' He grabbed a handful of nuts from the dainty glass dish, scattering some on the floor.

Antonia was hovering with the sherry decanter, filling Nicky's glass.

'Beer for me,' said Scott.

'You weren't asked,' said Maureen tartly.

'No, it's quite all right – I'll get it.' Andrew jumped up, looking glad of a chance to escape.

'And can I have an ashtray, mate?' Scott extracted a packet of Gauloises from his back trouser-pocket and offered them around. Everyone but Darren refused.

'Beer for you, Darren, or sherry?' Andrew had already appeared at the door again, armed with several cans of lager.

'Just water, thanks. I'm not feeling too brilliant today.'

'Well then, you shouldn't smoke,' said Maureen.

'Darren and me believe in smokers' rights,' Scott interjected, snapping his lighter on and off. 'All this anti-smoking lark's a load of crap, if you ask me. I mean, why stop at fags? You have no-smoking carriages on trains, right? And no-smoking bars and restaurants. Well, why not no-ugly-people restaurants, or no-fat-people bus seats?'

'Because fat people don't give *other* people cancer,' Maureen retorted, herself on the tubby side.

'Yeah, but it's still not healthy, is it? And they take up just as many hospital beds as smokers.'

'Do you *all* live in Camden Town?' Jack enquired, diplomatically changing the subject.

'Yeah,' said Scott, 'though God knows why. It's a real shit-hole. The sickest place in London, so they say, with more AIDS cases and schizos than anywhere else in the country. And of course everyone's on drugs – pushers all over the show. Any sign of the fuzz, though, and they just chuck their gear in the canal.'

'Come off it, Scott,' said Nicky. 'It's nothing like that bad.'

'It's a Third World hell,' Scott insisted obstinately.

Catherine rubbed her aching head. Scott was extremely immature and said things for their shock-effect, as she had realized in the car, but her relations weren't to know that. His words would frighten them so much they'd never want her to set foot in Camden Town again, let alone move there permanently. And they would doubtless assume that Scott was part of the Gosforth Road household, which would prejudice them against it even more. The very room seemed to shrink from his presence; the spotless carpet cringing under his none-too-clean Doc Martens; the coffee table mortified when he carelessly flicked ash on to its highly polished surface. If only Nicky or Darren would help her out. Nicky *had* made a few stabs at conversation, first with Antonia, then with Jack and Maureen, and was looking as embarrassed as *she* was by Scott's atrocious manners and loud, attention-getting voice. But far from trying to silence him, she sat uncharacteristically subdued, evidently still affected by her hangover. Darren, too, was slumped in an armchair, smoking moodily, and had exchanged little more than a few trite remarks with Andrew.

Scott, however, continued to regale Jack and Maureen with Camden Town horror stories – knifings two a penny; eight-year-olds on crack cocaine; mutilated corpses fished out of the canal.

'So why do you live in such a terrible place?' Maureen asked, aghast.

'Because I can't afford to move, that's why. My brother owns a flat there and he lets me have a room dirt cheap.'

'What sort of work do you do?'

Scott blew out a plume of smoke. 'I'm an artist,' he said grandly.

Catherine glanced at Nicky, willing her to remove Scott bodily before they started on that controversial subject. Scott had been discussing his 'art' in the car. Apparently he sculpted nudes from butter, soap and chocolate, in order to make the point that human life was short, insubstantial and messy.

But Maureen's face had brightened. She dabbled in art herself – gentle, pastel watercolours of the River Wey or Richmond Park. And Art for Jack (always with a capital A) meant Leonardo da Vinci or Van Gogh.

'The trouble is,' said Scott, 'I'm way ahead of my time. People are such philistines they don't appreciate my stuff. So,' he shrugged, flicking ash into the nut dish, 'I've been on the dole for years.'

In the tense silence which followed, Catherine could guess what Maureen was thinking: why on earth should a young, able-bodied man accept hand-outs from the state? And even Andrew seemed uneasy. She was well aware of his feelings about the vast amount of benefit fraud being a drain on the country's economy.

It was Jack who spoke, though, not Andrew. 'I'll tell you something, my lad,' he said, leaning forward in his chair. 'I got my first job at fifteen and I've never taken a penny from anyone, or missed more than the odd day's work until I retired at seventy-five.'

'Brilliant,' said Scott. 'If you *like* work.'

'Liking it's not the point, Scott.'

'But what *is* the point? You tell me. I mean, why kill yourself slaving from nine to five every day, when we'll all die soon enough in any case?'

There was another awkward silence, followed by a sudden protracted rumble from Scott's stomach. 'Shit!' he said, tipping the remainder of the nuts from the dish into his mouth. 'I'm famished. All I had for breakfast was coffee and fags.'

Nicky was galvanized into action at last, clearly appalled by Scott's behaviour. 'I think we'd better be going,' she murmured, rising to her feet with a 'drop-dead' look at him before turning to Antonia. 'Thank you so much for the drink,' she said, making a belated effort to be gracious. 'It was a great pleasure to meet you.' She shook hands with Jack and Maureen, then propelled Scott and Darren firmly towards the door.

There was a general sense of relief as the trio trooped out to the car, Scott kicking the front gate open with his boot and leaving a mark on the paint.

'Do forgive the invasion,' Catherine blurted out, once the front door was safely shut. 'When I told you I was coming by car, I thought it would be just me and Nicky.'

'Mm, Nicky's an attractive girl,' Jack mused.

'But where *does* she find her boyfriends?' Maureen wiped ash off the coffee table with her lace-edged handkerchief.

'Oh, they're not her boyfriends,' Catherine laughed. 'Darren's the chap she works with and Scott's just an odd acquaintance.'

'*Very* odd,' said Maureen acidly.

'Have I got time to change?' Catherine asked, before Maureen could expand on the theme. 'I've had to borrow clothes all week and this dress is far too tight.'

Antonia consulted her watch. 'Well, we've booked a table for half past one, so if we leave in fifteen minutes . . .'

Catherine ran upstairs to her room. She stopped at the doorway, gazing in at the virginal white sanctum – strangely unfamiliar after a mere eight days away. She had grown used to crimson walls, to Fiona's cheerful clutter and a seductive male nude looking down on her each night. This room seemed more suited to a nun.

She opened the fitted cupboard and hunted through her clothes, which also seemed drearily sedate. Who *am* I? she wondered, staring in the mirror with a sudden surge of panic. And where do I belong?

The mirror reflected a background of chaste white walls and a demure flower-sprigged counterpane, with her shorn wild-purple head a brash intruder in the foreground. With a sigh of resignation she took out a plain beige dress, tied a bandeau round her hair to hide the worst of the purple, and put on some shell-pink lipstick.

It was only five past one, so she picked up the letters which Antonia had left in a neat pile on the dressing-table. The top two were addressed to Gerry, forwarded from Carshalton. Seeing his name on the envelope always hit her like a blow. It seemed so crassly insensitive, assuming he was still alive; still interested in office supplies or book clubs or insurance schemes. She shoved them in a drawer and sorted quickly through the rest, consoled by the sight of an airmail envelope with colourful Indian stamps. She treasured Kate's rare letters, which, apart from anything else, were a marvellous form of armchair travelling. Reading the vivid descriptions she could almost smell and taste the Gurgaon streets: buzzing mopeds overtaking ox-carts; push-bikes wobbling dangerously under loads of green bananas; patient fruit-sellers dwarfed by piles of water-melons. She propped the letter against the mirror – a treat for later on. She would read it and re-read it, to bring her daughter closer.

One other item caught her eye: an official-looking envelope, which she tore open right away.

'WITH LOVE ALL THINGS ARE POSSIBLE' was printed in capitals across the top of a sheet of paper. Intrigued, she read on.

This letter has been sent to you for good luck. It has already been around the world nine times, and if you send it on to twenty other people, you will receive good luck in your turn.

Do not send money – fate has no price – and do not throw it away. For some unknown reason it works, *as you will find to your own advantage remarkably soon.*

She stared at the words. She mistrusted chain-letters and normally *would* have thrown it away without a second thought. But it did seem rather extraordinary that such a thing should arrive at the very moment in her life when she was faced with a big decision – a time when she needed luck. And it seemed to tie in with her lottery win, as if luck were favouring her already.

Pure coincidence, Andrew would say scornfully. Chuck it in the waste-bin, Mother. Chain-letters can be dangerous.

The problem was, everything was dangerous – Camden Town and its low life, gin and sex, even Nicky's windsurfing, and certainly new starts. But if she continually avoided danger, she would end up as a hermit. Most of her life she had been waiting for some vague and unspecified future; it was always 'when', never 'now': *when* she grew up and could leave her father's gloomy house; *when* Gerry made more money as an actor (or worked less punishing hours as a businessman); *when* the children were older; *when* she wasn't needed any more . . .

She walked slowly to the window, looking out at the grey and sullen sky. The New Year was already three weeks old, but *would* it be new for her, or would she simply scuttle back to hibernation? Gerry was dead, and the children off her hands, but she was still shying away from the future. Crazy as the idea might sound, could this letter be a sort of . . . call, to go out and seek her own luck, make the future happen?

Her thoughts were interrupted by a real call: a summons from Andrew, downstairs.

'Are you ready, Mother? We ought to be leaving.'

Oughts and shoulds again. Would she ever escape them? She hid the letter under her pillow and hurried obediently downstairs. Andrew and Antonia had already washed the glasses and restored the sitting-room to rights. She had a sudden bizarre vision of them scouring away every trace of Scott and Darren: sterilizing ashtrays, disinfecting the furniture, sending the carpet to be fumigated.

'I love that dress,' said Andrew, obviously relieved that the golf club would be spared the sight of Fiona's whorish clothes.

Impulsively she gave him a hug. 'And I love *you,* my darling.' She felt him tense with embarrassment. Mothers shouldn't say such things; naked emotion was dangerous.

'Er, we ought to make a move,' he said, frowning down at his feet.

She let go of him, feeling a deep sadness that Nicky, whom she had known a week, could embrace her with such simple natural affection, whereas her own son felt so threatened by her touch.

'Beef for you, or lamb, Mother?' Andrew picked up the menu: a pretentious-looking affair hand-written in italic script and bound in tooled green leather. 'Or there's salmon trout, if you prefer. And of course, the chef's speciality – steak and oyster pie.'

'No, the lamb, please,' Catherine said. She must be a good little lamb herself and not touch a drop more alcohol, not after last night. Her headache was still hammering away.

'I love oysters,' Maureen remarked, unfolding her starched white napkin, 'but unfortunately they don't like me. I think I'd better have the trout.'

'And for you, Grandpa?'

'Oh, good red beef. There's nothing finer, in my opinion. And never mind mad cow disease! It's just a lot of scaremongering, if you ask me.'

Catherine squeezed his hand. Like father, like son. Gerry had always chosen the beef when they'd come here for lunch with Andrew, and showed the same contempt for health warnings. He would eat his way blithely through the menu, starting with a huge plate of hors d'oeuvres and finishing up with double cream *and* ice-cream on his apple pie or cheesecake. If only she had been stricter about his diet, he might be here today.

She gave Jack a sympathetic smile. For all his years of hard work, he too was something of a rebel, and he, if anyone, might sympathize with her own desire to break free. Though she had decided not to broach the subject of becoming part of a house-share, at least not until they were back home. Scott's portrayal of Camden Town as a drug-infested hellhole was probably still ringing in their ears – hardly the best inducement for a move there. Besides, she found the golf club ambience inhibitingly formal. The dining-room seemed stranded in a time warp, with its dark-oak panelling and heavy velour curtains, and gilt-framed portraits on the walls of past bewhiskered captains. And most of the diners looked so old and staid; men in plus-fours or regimental ties, their bald heads gleaming beneath the soft pink-shaded lamps; ladies (never 'women' here) in Jaeger suits and pearls, with corrugated perms.

The waitress glided up to take their order, smartly turned out in her black and white livery, with a black bow on her hair. A wonder she wasn't wearing starched white gloves, Catherine thought, breaking off a piece of bread roll. She knew from past experience that the service was incredibly slow and they might not finish lunch until half past three or four. It was all part of the formality; an attempt to ape the gracious lifestyle of earlier, less harassed decades. Such a contrast with the market – traders burning their mouths on scalding mugs of coffee, or dashing off between customers to snatch a bite to eat. She wished she could talk about her day's work in the market, but Andrew and Antonia would probably be shocked. And there were other subjects she couldn't talk about: the night with Simon, her lottery win yesterday, and the long session in the pub, followed by her communing with the gin bottle. She had never felt the need to hide things from her family before. It made her feel a black sheep.

'Now, my dear.' Maureen turned to her, as if she'd read her mind. 'Tell us what you've been doing with yourself.'

'Oh, this and that. I . . . I went to a gig with Darren the other night.'

'A what?'

'A sort of . . . concert. Darren plays bass guitar in a rock band.'

'So *that* explains his appearance,' Maureen said, shaking her head. 'I can never understand why young people do themselves up in all that dreary black. You see these pretty young girls, barely out of school, looking as if they're going to their own funerals.'

'And how's the cat?' asked Jack, sipping his wine appreciatively.

'Oh, he's miles better now, thanks. I've been dosing him with vitamins. I got them from this amazing pet shop near Nicky's. It looks a bit of a dump, but it's one of the oldest in the whole of Europe and they sell all sorts of weird creatures – things I'd never even heard of, like plumed basilisks and poison-arrow frogs. And a fantastic range of snakes. I almost came home with a boa constrictor.'

Antonia gave a delicate shudder.

'It's all right – I'm only joking. I was there for the vitamins, that's all, and cat food. *That* was exotic, too. They had Kit-e-Kat and stuff, of course, but also designer meals – salmon in cream sauce or breast of guinea-fowl, which you defrost in the microwave. Terribly expensive, of course.'

'Would you believe it?' Maureen tutted. 'And to think of all the poor old souls trying to exist on bread and dripping.'

'Ah, look,' said Jack, as the hors d'oeuvres trolley was trundled up to their table. 'We're saved from bread and dripping!'

The waiter hovered beside Maureen with his spoon poised over a selection of some twenty dishes.

'Oh, dear. They all look rather rich,' she said. 'Well, just a little of the avocado. Oh, and some grated carrot and tomato. And a tiny piece of pâté. Thank you. Nothing else.'

Antonia took less still: a dab of cottage cheese and a few fronds of crinkly lettuce. She was so slim already, Catherine thought, she would have put a greyhound to shame. Gerry had often teased his daughter-in-law about her constant dieting, and would even lean across and help himself to the food she'd left, saying better in his stomach than the waste-bin.

God, she missed him still so much, especially here. Maureen had Jack, Andrew had Antonia, but she was the odd one out, a single. It had seemed so different in London. Singles were practically the norm in Nicky and Darren's crowd, and in the market and the Stag's Head, whereas here she felt conspicuous, spare. At almost every other table sat man and woman, husband and wife; two by two, two by two. Gerry's name hadn't even been mentioned, which somehow she resented. Of course, the others were probably trying to spare her feelings (especially if Andrew had told them that her butchered hair might be a sign of deep emotional disturbance). Yet it actually made things worse *not* to talk about him, to swamp his death in a tide of empty chit-chat.

The waiter approached her with the trolley. As he indicated each dish in turn, she gave an emphatic nod. She would have a little of every one – no, a *lot* of every one – as a way of bringing Gerry back, making him real and substantial. It was also a tiny way of rebelling. So often at Manor Close she ate far less than she wanted, for fear of seeming greedy compared with her health-conscious son and abstemious daughter-in-law. But her real self *was* greedy, and it was time she acknowledged the fact.

Her plate was piled with seafood and stuffed mushrooms, ratatouille and artichoke hearts, feta cheese and pâté, plus various sorts of salad. Even so, she asked for another spoonful of risotto, a second hard-boiled egg. She saw Andrew and Antonia exchanging surreptitious glances, but knew they were too polite to comment.

Jack, though, was more forthcoming. 'Well,' he said, with a laugh. 'You'd better change your mind about the wine. You'll need something to wash that lot down.'

She let him fill her glass – might as well be hung for a sheep as for a lamb. She winced at the appalling pun, on a par with Scott's. Not that anyone like Scott would be allowed within a mile of this place. Gentlemen were expected to be 'correctly attired', which meant wearing a jacket and tie. She remembered lunching here one Sunday when the vice-president of American Ford was escorted swiftly from the dining-room because he had an open-necked shirt beneath his cashmere jacket. Ponytails and dreadlocks would be totally beyond the pale. And as for nose-rings . . .

She imagined the po-faced steward ejecting a whole stream of market traders – Derek out, Greta out, Brad and Lester most definitely out. She looked around at the members and their guests: all so privileged and well-spoken. No blacks, of course; no working class. Yet what right had they to ban people on account of their accent or skin-colour, or label brave souls like Brad as uncouth, or 'not our type'? There were so many footling rules – no women in the men's bar, no guests in the private lounge, no mobile phones or Walkmans anywhere on the premises, no shouting, swearing, singing, no *living*, for God's sake.

'Do you remember the Boothbys, Catherine?'

She forced her attention back to Maureen. 'Er, no.'

'Tom and Lorraine – that couple who lived next door to us. I think you met them once. He was something to do with the Water Board, or whatever you call it now. And she bred pedigree dogs. They were a lovely couple, weren't they, Jack?'

Jack nodded, busy with his hors d'oeuvres. 'Though I'm not sure I'd say the same about the dogs!'

'Well, anyway, they've moved to Aberdeen. Lorraine's half-Scots, apparently. But it does seem a big upheaval, don't you think? I mean, Tom's not exactly a spring chicken, and it's so cold in Scotland, isn't it?'

'Mm.' Catherine had no interest in the Boothbys, and they'd intruded into her fantasy. She had been imagining this hallowed room full of market traders – all her personal guests. She had assumed the role of steward and turfed out the upper crust to make room for people down on their luck, or those struggling to survive without the luxury of investment plans or two cars in the garage. It would be nice to treat them to a slap-up Sunday lunch, *and* the time to enjoy it. Sunday was the busiest day at the market – 'customers-from-hell day', Derek had called it glumly.

'Which wine for you, Derek?' she asked him, 'the claret or the Chardonnay? No, don't worry about a thing. Today's a market holiday – with pay. I've just declared it official.'

She giggled to herself. The wine must have affected her already – or the sherry before lunch. Yet her headache had completely vanished, which seemed miraculous in itself. Not only had she lost her earlier lethargy, she felt almost on a high, as if she'd been smoking Darren's dope. She was beginning to suspect that one of the reasons she had always been a 'good girl' was her fear of going way over the top if she did ever dare rebel. She certainly felt peculiar right now: scatty, childish, angry and elated at once, and increasingly at odds with her surroundings. Not to mention ravenous. She crammed a piece of cheese into her mouth. Her guests all needed feeding, especially skinny Derek and the waif-thin girl with the baby in the milk-crate. Babies weren't permitted in the golf club (no children under ten, in fact), but *she* was in charge today, so she could invite a whole nurseryful of infants – and Brad's six siblings, while she was about it, including the brother in borstal. And what about his alcoholic mother? Didn't *she* deserve to indulge herself after bringing up that huge brood single-handed?

'Of course, we do find it quieter without the dogs. And the new people seem very pleasant, don't they, Jack? Well, Jack's not too keen on his lawn-mower, are you, dear? It's one of those dreadful motor things.'

'Surely he's not mowing the lawn this time of year,' Antonia remarked.

'Well, no,' said Jack, putting down his fork. 'I think he's only tuning and repairing it. But it still makes a hell of a noise.'

The conversation turned to gardening in general; Andrew and Antonia's plans to train a few dwarf fruit trees against the south-facing wall. Catherine's attention drifted away again – back to Mrs Brad. She snapped her fingers at the waiter and ordered a double gin for her; told him to leave the bottle on the table. Brad himself was sitting on her right, Stan and Gareth opposite, Lester on her left; Bina, Lynne, Rosie and her ten-year-old still to be squashed in. But why should anyone be squashed? All the other tables were free, now that the *beau monde* had departed. She *would* go way over the top and invite the crowd from the Stag's Head; the fiddler and accordionist could provide an Irish sing-song. And that man she'd seen last night playing his guitar in Camden High Street, dressed in jeans and shirtsleeves despite the sub-zero temperature, and singing to an audience of full moon and brilliant stars.

'Yes, come in,' she told him. 'It's nice and warm in here.' And 'Welcome!' she said to Darren's band and the long-haired rock fans she'd met at the gig. Not a jacket or tie among them, but who cared?

The chef would have to work overtime to feed so many mouths. And she must do her bit as well. She chewed three garlicky prawns, forked in half an egg, then helped herself to a second bread roll and spread it thickly with butter.

'Eat all you like,' she told her guests. 'It's free today, with the compliments of the Captain, Sir Edward Digby-Soames.'

'I'm looking forward to the spring,' said Maureen. 'The daffodils make such a lovely show.'

Catherine's mouth was too gloriously full to respond. And there was still dessert to come. Brad had a sweet tooth, so she intended to pig out on the puddings for him: apple pie with double cream *and* ice-cream, a big chunk of treacle tart, and as much fruit salad as she could cram into the bowl. Gerry would approve. He had never been a snob, and she knew he found the golf club starchy, although he kept his feelings to himself, as *she* did. They adored their son and wouldn't want to hurt him, but Andrew had different values, partly because he had married into such a fastidious, snooty family.

She glanced at Antonia's glass: mineral water, as usual, and the still kind, not the sparkling. Even bubbles were probably dangerous in Antonia's quiescent world. But not for *her*, not today. However crazy it might sound, she somehow felt protected today – by fate, by her new luck.

'A magnum of champagne, please,' she told the waiter silently. 'No, can you make that a crate?'

She had just made a big decision (without even having to agonize about it) and she wanted to celebrate the start of the future – *now.*

III

13

'Fancy a coffee?' Rosie asked. 'I'm just getting one for me and Brad.'

'Yes, please!' said Catherine. 'I'm frozen. Here, take this.' Hands clumsy with cold, she extracted a pound coin from her money-belt.

'No, it's on me today,' said Rosie.

Catherine watched her stride off, head ducked against the pelting rain, her long black mac flapping around her ankles. The weather had been atrocious all day and the market was comparatively empty – especially for a Sunday – not only fewer people buying but fewer selling, too. According to Brad, some traders took other work during the slack months after Christmas, then came back again in March or April. And some travelled to exotic lands in search of stock to sell: wooden carvings from Bali, fringed shawls from Katmandu.

Derek's stall next door was just a bare metal frame, like a gap in a row of teeth. *He* wasn't in Katmandu, but in bed with tonsillitis, and Trevor, further along, had decided to pack it in altogether. His jewellery had hardly sold at all – too much competition from Brad and others. But among those still left there was an increased sense of camaraderie, a fighting spirit almost, especially on a day like this when they were battling against bad weather as well as dwindling trade.

Catherine made a thumbs-up sign to Colin, who was sweeping away the worst of a pool of water right in front of his stall. The pavement was uneven in places and large puddles would form, which were offputting to the customers. Colin had once owned a chain of shoe shops, but lost everything in the recession. She had been chatting to him about the strain of running a business; the headaches over deliveries or staff. She felt more at home in the market now that she'd got to know people on her own wavelength. In fact, she and Rosie had developed quite a bond, having discovered they had certain things in common, including mothers who'd died young. Also, Rosie had shown her the ropes, introduced her to the market manager, advised her where to go for the cheapest food and drinks – acted as her guide, in short.

The market community was something like a village, or a big obstreperous family, complete with feuds and quarrels. And despite the hand-to-mouth existence (and the present bitter weather), she felt a sense of triumph that she was managing to survive here, and had already made a friend.

She could see Rosie now returning with the coffee, stumping along in her moon-boots, her long brown hair bundled under a hat.

Diving under the shelter of the tarpaulin, she handed Catherine a cup. 'I've bought some flapjacks, too – Jean's home-made. They're lovely and gooey inside.' She took two clingfilm-wrapped squares from her pocket and passed the larger one to Catherine.

'Let me pay you for that, at least, Rosie.'

'No – my treat. I've hardly seen you today. Every time I was going to come over for a chat, you were busy with a customer.'

'Oh, most of them weren't customers, just friends of friends. Remember I told you about the people I live with? Well, they keep sending their mates along to say hello. It's great to have the company, but I've sold very little today.'

'Same here. Mind you, I can't complain – I did brilliantly over Christmas.'

'And *I'm* all right,' said Catherine, 'since Greta pays me anyway. Though she probably *won't* when she sees how badly I've done.'

'Oh, I don't think she'll kick you out just yet! She needs you, after all.'

Catherine prised the lid off her coffee and took a warming sip. It was true that Greta had hit a lucky streak: the American bride-to-be had been so delighted with the waistcoats, she had ordered a dozen more for friends back home, to be dispatched to Oregon as soon as they were ready. And Greta's luck had spilled over to *her*, in providing plenty of work: minding the stall three days a week and helping with the glut of sewing. And that, in turn, meant she could pay her way in the house – rent and food and so forth.

Last but not least, she was enjoying her new life; had already seen three films with Nicky, been to another gig with Darren, and was putting her individual stamp on Fiona's room. She sometimes wondered, secretly, if her good fortune was connected with that mysterious chain-letter. Almost as a joke, she had sent out twenty copies (anonymously, of course) to stuffy people in Stoneleigh and Carshalton. She had no idea whether *they* had had good luck. Stoneleigh and Carshalton felt like distant planets now. And she hadn't seen the family since the disastrous golf club lunch. She had packed her things that same evening, including her sewing machine, and been back in Gosforth Road in time for a nightcap with Nicky.

Brad dived across, dripping wet without his coat. 'Quick, Rosie, you got a customer. Some nutter, by the sounds of it, who wants to know if you sell wind-up dinosaurs – wait for it – life-size.'

'That's all I need!' said Rosie. 'Cheerio, Catherine. See you in a while.'

Brad remained, leaning against her stall. 'How's it goin', babe?'

'Not bad.' It wasn't done to moan – though Derek made it an art form (and would be even more doom-laden today, nursing his sore throat). On the whole you were expected to take the bad days with the good, and if *you*'d done well and your neighbour hadn't, then you bought him a consolatory pint or even lent him a tenner.

'I like them jeans. New, ain't they?'

She nodded. 'I bought them from Slippery Spike. He let me have them cheap.' She stroked the denim lovingly. Her own Levis at last, 501s like Fiona's, and probably a quarter the price. She had also found a real bargain of a jacket, second-hand but wonderfully shaggy fake fur in a brilliant shade of red. Again, Rosie had helped her out, taking her to Slippery Spike's and wangling her good prices. It was exciting buying new clothes, the sort of clothes *she* wanted, to suit her new emerging self. Unfortunately the jacket was concealed under a boring plastic mac today, but at least she was reasonably dry.

Which was more than could be said for Brad. 'You're drenched,' she said. 'What happened?'

'Lent me bleedin' coat to Lester, didn't I. Five minutes, 'e said, and I ain't seen 'im since.'

'He's probably sold it,' she laughed, 'and run off with the proceeds.'

'I'm packin' up soon, anyways,' he said. 'I'm fed up with gettin' pissed on.'

Catherine consulted her watch: not quite half past four. Unlike Brad, she wasn't her own boss – Greta paid her for the whole day, so she must stick it out for another hour at least. Still, working for Greta did have its advantages. She got a flat fee, regardless of the takings (which were dispiritingly low today), and there were no overheads to worry about. Stall rents were pretty hefty at weekends. In fact, Derek had complained last Sunday that he might as well have stayed in bed, since he had taken less than what he'd shelled out to the manager. All the same, she didn't have much security. When Greta no longer needed her, she would be summarily laid off. And setting up on her own was quite a daunting step. She'd need plenty of stock – something she was sure would sell, but which wouldn't encroach on other people's lines. That created ill will, as she had seen for herself last week when a newcomer set up a toy stall only yards from Rosie's. Still, whatever happened, she was determined to hang on as long as possible before accepting a dreary office job and spending her days tapping keys and staring at a computer screen. Why go back to work she'd never liked?

'Ta-ta for now, Plum,' Brad said, returning to his stall. She grinned at the nickname. It made her feel accepted. Nicknames were quite a feature of the market. As well as Slippery Spike there were characters called Sunflower Sal and Hawk-Eye, and even a Karl Marx. She watched Brad packing up, admiring his practised speed. It took *her* much longer to set up and take down, but at least she could do it on her own now, without Greta needing to be there.

There were still no customers for the hats, so she finished her coffee at a leisurely pace, taking small bites of her flapjack to eke it out. She found herself thinking of Gerry, recalling how he had told her once that theatre companies worked best when the actors had no set ideas but simply discovered things in the moment, by doing, being, exploring. They could find out what a role required by letting go, he'd said, freeing themselves from '*how* can we do it' to 'let's just see what happens'. She wondered now if, in some strange way, his words had influenced her own decision to venture out and start afresh (though she hadn't thought of them consciously for fifteen years or more).

She bent down to put the paper cup in the rubbish-bag, and

when she straightened up, a man was standing in front of the stall. He looked vaguely familiar with his stocky build and thick dark curly hair, the sort of exuberant hair which went its own way regardless. His broad chest and shoulders were emphasized by the bulky jacket and the Aran sweater he was wearing underneath. And though he must be thirty-five or forty, he had a student's scarf, black and yellow striped, thrown carelessly around his neck.

'Hello,' he said, smiling. 'I hoped you'd be here.'

The instant he spoke she recognized him – that distinguished accent, which made her own voice seem almost common. For the past three weeks she had been toning it down (more or less unconsciously), so as to sound less middle-class.

'H . . . hello,' she mumbled, hastily swallowing the last mouthful of flapjack.

'I wanted to thank you for bringing me luck. You probably don't remember me, but . . .'

'Oh, I do. You're the poet – you bought a waistcoat for a special gig.'

'That's right. And you told me purple was a lucky colour, and that you'd think of me on the night. Believe it or not, it worked. The evening was terrific. It probably sounds big-headed, but I had the audience eating out of my hand.'

She tried surreptitiously to suck the crumbs off her teeth, registering that word luck again. In fact she *hadn't* thought about him the evening of the gig. On that particular Friday there had been a row with Jo, who was annoyed about her running the stall for Greta. (Not that Jo could have done it anyway, with the amount of writing work she had on, but it was obvious she felt piqued.) It had all got very awkward – the first bad feeling in the house, and perhaps a sign that Jo resented her staying there.

'Actually, it brought me luck twice over.' The man huddled in front of the stall, shaking rain from his hair. 'You see, the waistcoat inspired a poem – no big deal, but it practically wrote itself, which is unusual for me, I can tell you. Normally it's weeks and weeks of writing and rewriting, but this one just seemed to flow. Anyway, it's being published in the *London Magazine* next week. *And* I'm getting a decent fee. So I'm doubly grateful. Thank you.'

'Well, it was nice of you to come back, especially in this weather.'

'It's worse for you, stuck there all day. I know from past experience. I've worked in a market myself.'

'Oh, really? Where was that?'

'A hell of a way from here. Totnes, in Devon.'

'What did you sell?'

'Antiques. Well, junk, to be honest.'

She laughed. There was something rather appealing about him. He was obviously keen to chat, yet there was a wariness about his face, as if he was afraid of being rebuffed. His hands were still ingrained with dirt, she noticed – another paradox: the sensitive poet combined with the manual labourer.

'I've still got quite a bit of it at home – things that didn't sell. As a matter of fact, I've been thinking of setting up here. A friend of mine sells antiques in West Yard and he said I could try to flog some of my own stuff in return for minding the stall when he's out buying.'

'That sounds a good idea.'

'Well, at least it would be a toehold in the place. And I can see what business is like before I commit myself. Anyway,' he shrugged, 'whatever else, it's better than being a waiter. I've been doing a stint at the Camden Brasserie and I must admit I've found it rather a trial.'

'Oh, so you live round here,' she said.

'Just up the road in Kentish Town. I used to live in Torquay. And before that Sacriston, in Durham.'

'You certainly get about! I'm from the north myself.'

'Oh, are you? Whereabouts?'

'Well, not as far north as Durham. I was born and bred in Cheshire. And then I moved to Salford. I liked it there, although I've heard people say it's a dump.'

He nodded. 'I know what you mean. It's like Blackpool being vulgar or Milton Keynes soulless. You can actually enjoy the vulgarity or the soullessness, so long as you enter into the spirit of the thing. And of course ... *Ow!*' He ducked as a gout of water suddenly sluiced off the tarpaulin on to his head.

'What happened? Are you all right?'

'Just a bit wetter, that's all.' He tossed his head like a skittish horse, spattering her with raindrops. 'My name's William, by the way.'

'Oh no!'

'What's wrong?'

'Sorry, that must have sounded rude. It's just that William's the name of my cat.' She enjoyed saying 'my' even if it wasn't strictly true: *my* cat, *my* room, *my* stall.

'And your William's a monster, I take it.'

'Well no, not really. He is big, and he does have an aggressive streak, but he's actually quite a softie underneath.'

'Just like me,' grinned William. 'Except I'm usually called Will.'

She was aware of the conversation subtly changing. He had adopted a more intimate tone and was standing so close she could smell curry on his breath. She backed away a little. It wasn't that she objected to curry (with so many tandoori stalls in the market, it was simply part of the ambience); it was his *eyes* she found disconcerting. He was looking at her intently, deliberately holding her gaze until she was forced to glance away.

Rosie, too, was watching her, clearly intrigued by the proceedings, although too far away to overhear. Of course Rosie would probably assume that Will was another of her house-mates' stream of friends. Just as well, since she wasn't too sure of the etiquette regarding over-familiar customers.

The grey eyes were still fixed on her. 'Aren't you going to tell me *your* name?'

'Er, Catherine.' Thank God no one else was looking at the hats. There were a few bedraggled tourists about – Colin was busy with a couple now – but generally they seemed more concerned with dodging each other's umbrellas (or the puddles) than actually buying anything. Greta would be annoyed if she lost sales for the sake of an idle chat-up.

'Catherine,' he repeated. 'That's nice. It means pure, you know, in Greek. I'm afraid I'm a mine of useless information.'

Pure, she thought, blushing as she remembered Simon. 'Tell me about your poetry,' she said, quickly changing the subject. 'What sort of things do you write?'

'Tricky question. It varies so much, you see, depending on my mood. The waistcoat poem was definitely light-hearted, almost comic, you could say. Then the one I wrote next was about a tiny piece of stalk I found in a packet of frozen peas. That started off comic as well, but developed into something much more serious. I felt it symbolized human error – the stalk I mean, not the poem – all that technology directed at weeding stalks *out*, so that there's nothing but the peas, pure and unadulterated. But a fragment gets in all the same.' He yanked at his scarf, which was slipping off his shoulder. 'Of course, you could call it reality, or even a rather precious imperfection in an over-standardized world. God, that does sound pretentious, doesn't it, like something out of Pseuds' Corner.'

'No, it's interesting.' Catherine straightened the mirror at one end of the stall, surprised to see how flushed she looked. 'I hardly ever read poetry, I'm ashamed to say, but I thought it would be more about . . . you know, life-and-death issues.'

'Well, it is – very often. But sometimes it's easier to get there via frozen peas or waistcoats.'

'Did you read your stalk poem at the gig?' she asked.

'No. I hadn't even written it then. I told you, the waistcoat brought me luck. And part of a poet's luck is things just coming out of the blue. I won't call it inspiration – that's a corny word – but it's a sort of energy or aliveness, like a tuning fork striking the right note.'

His eyes looked very bright, reflecting the lights on the stall. Dusk was falling around them; the surroundings blurring into shadow. More people had appeared from nowhere – a few late customers and a gang of Asian youths – but they remained vague shapes in the background. Only Will seemed in focus: standing there tangible and solid, yet making her unaccountably nervous.

She wasn't sure what else to say – poetry wasn't her forte. He, too, had lapsed into silence, as if affected by her own unease. He picked up one of Greta's hats, and put it down again. 'I . . . was, er, wondering if you were busy after this?' he said finally.

She hesitated. Neither Brad nor Rosie was going to the pub tonight, so she had planned to go straight home.

'I'd like to buy you a drink, you see, to thank you properly – if you can spare the time, that is.'

'Well . . . I won't be finished here for an hour or so.' Did that sound brusque, standoffish? Secretly she was flattered that a second man should take an interest in her, even ask her out. But there must be no repeat of Simon.

'I can come back at six,' Will suggested. 'I'll help you pack up, if you like.'

'No, honestly, I . . .' The last thing she wanted was Rosie trying to eavesdrop or Colin's beady eyes on her. Already he was watching them with interest, now that his customers had gone. That was the trouble with the market – it was a highly public arena and the 'family' loved gossip. Any hint of romance and she'd be teased.

'Well, if you'd rather not . . .' Will looked crestfallen and was fiddling dejectedly with the end of his scarf.

She played for time, repositioning a couple of the hats, torn between caution and excitement. 'Yes, okay,' she said slowly. 'It would be nice. But why don't I meet you somewhere? Then you can keep dry if I'm delayed.'

'Fine. How about the Crown and Goose? D'you know it?'

'Yes. It's in Arlington Road, isn't it? I've never actually been there, but . . .'

'It's quite civilized. And not too noisy.'

And not too near here, she thought with relief. Out of the corner of her eye she could see Colin still observing them.

'Would seven o'clock be all right?'

'Well, it might be nearer ten past.'

'That's okay. See you there. I'll keep a seat warm for you.'

She waved him goodbye, feeling warm already. Despite the persistent rain and the sub-zero temperature, he had left her with a definite glow.

Be careful, she told herself. It's just a friendly drink, that's all. No leg-shaving nonsense this time, or sexy wisps of pants.

She stood at the door of the crowded pub, looking anxiously around. She hated walking into pubs alone, and she couldn't see Will anywhere. Still, at least it was warm and she was out of the rain. She ventured in a bit further, scanning every face at every table, but there was no sign of him at all. The Crown and Goose wasn't large – there seemed to be only this one room, and it was more like a genteel club. The walls were olive green, with an elegant white frieze and gilt-framed pictures and mirrors. True, there was a certain element of shabbiness – no carpet on the wooden floor and the tables rather battered – but it was a sort of classy shabbiness, quite unlike the Stag's Head. The clientele, too, were a world apart; no noisy Irish or market traders, and not a punk hairstyle to be seen (except for hers, of course). Most of the customers were young and casually dressed, but they seemed solidly middle class. And instead of frenzied Irish jigs, soothing classical music floated discreetly in the background.

She sat at an empty table where she could keep an eye on the door. Perhaps Will had been held up. She was late herself, delayed by a maddening woman who had started trying on a dozen different hats just as she was packing them away. She checked the time: 7.31. Perhaps he'd arrived early and got tired of waiting – they could have missed each other by seconds. Or perhaps he'd had an accident: been mugged, or knocked unconscious, or was being held at gunpoint by a group of Middle Eastern suicide bombers. No, that scenario didn't sound convincing – he had probably simply changed his mind and decided not to come at all. Weren't poets supposed to be unreliable, subject to strange moods? It was stupid to panic. If he didn't show up, so what? She would put it down to experience and go back to Gosforth Road for beans on toast with Nicky.

And she really must stop looking at her watch; 7.32 it said now. Surely more than a minute had passed? She felt ridiculously apprehensive – the way she had with Simon – like a teenager stood up on a date. If things went wrong a second time she would lose her nerve completely. She was also uncomfortably hot in the plastic mac, but she didn't want to take it off and reveal her conspicuous jacket. It was bad enough being the only woman sitting on her own.

She gave the watch a shake. It must have stopped – how else could it still be 7.32? But no, as she watched, the figure two dissolved into a three in its maddeningly unhurried way. She decided to wait till 7.40, then leave. Any longer and she'd be a gibbering wreck.

She scanned the bar again, catching the eye of a fair-haired man in a trench coat who gave her a suggestive smile. Hastily she looked down and studied the book of matches in the ashtray. There was a goose on the front with a crown slung round its neck. She traced the outline of its body, then opened the flap and started counting the matches – anything to distract herself.

One, two, three, four . . . one, two, three, four.

Lord! She must be in a state if she couldn't get beyond four. She did her best to concentrate. One, two, three, four, five, six, seven . . .

'*Catherine!* Thank goodness.'

She jumped. Will was standing on the bottom step of a narrow staircase she hadn't noticed before. He all but swooped on her, scarf flying. 'I was looking for you upstairs. There's a snug up there, but it's full of lager-swilling kids. I . . . I thought you must have changed your mind and decided not to come.'

Exactly what she'd thought about *him*. She stumbled to her feet, half-amused to realize he was nervous too. His words had spilled out in a rush and he was looking almost stricken. 'I'm terribly sorry,' she said. 'I was delayed by a customer.'

He took her arm and steered her further away from the door, as if afraid she might escape. 'I've saved us a table by the mirror.' He indicated an impressive antique mirror mounted on the side wall. 'That way I can see two of you at once – back and front.' He picked up his coat, which was draped across two seats, and bundled it under his chair. 'Let me take your mac,' he offered. 'It's soaking wet.'

As she peeled it off, he watched in delight. 'You've *hatched*,' he said. 'Out of a black egg. A fluffy red phoenix. Amazing!'

She blushed. He sounded so . . . so extravagant, and the people nearby were listening.

He reached out to touch the fur. 'Is it real?' he asked.

'No, completely and utterly fake.'

He shook his head. 'It's too brilliant to be fake. Perhaps it's red yak.'

'Red what?'

'Yak – roaming the mountains of Tibet. The greater scarlet yak, an extraordinarily rare species.'

She wondered if he'd been drinking, or whether this was standard fare for poets. The latter, she assumed, since there was no empty glass on the table. She sat down gingerly, rather intimidated by his fanciful depiction of her and hoping he wouldn't be too disappointed by the reality.

'What can I get you to drink?'

A double brandy, she thought, to steady the nerves. But brandy was expensive and he must be short of money if he had to take waitering jobs. 'Half of bitter please, Will.' Drinking bitter made her feel somehow liberated, one of the lads. She had only acquired the habit since moving into Gosforth Road, influenced by Nicky and Jo. In fact, she was drinking more altogether – not worryingly so, but as part of the process of opening up, letting go some of the controls.

She watched Will at the bar: well-mannered, waiting his turn, exchanging pleasantries with other customers. He looked slimmer without his jacket, although the cream sweater was none too clean. Her own jersey was one of Nicky's, an ancient thing, but bright candyfloss pink. She unbuttoned the jacket to show it off, enjoying the clash of colours.

He returned with the drinks and sat down. 'Cheers!' he said. 'To yaks.'

'Cheers!'

He subsided into silence, the fingers of one hand drumming on the table. She found it disconcerting that one minute he was disgorging words in shoals, and the next he seemed to dry up.

She cast around for something to say. Everyone else appeared to be deep in conversation; bursts of laughter from the adjoining table surfacing above the general hubbub. Even the espresso machine on the bar was merrily hissing and frothing, and the music had changed to a louder and more lively piece. 'It's nice in here,' she said lamely, wishing she were a piping flute or soaring violin, so she would sound a bit more sparkling.

'Yes, it's one of my favourite pubs. And they do marvellous food. D'you *like* food?'

'Oh, yes,' she said, surprised. Did anyone *not* like it?

'Good. I'm quite concerned about the future of eating. It seems to be going out of fashion, with many women, anyway. D'you know, I did a reading once with an American poet and nearly all her work was based on anorexia – titles like "Starvation" or "Force-Feeding". She looked like a Belsen victim herself and somehow it put me off my stroke. I just dried up completely. That's never happened before and I felt an utter fool. The silence seemed to last for ever, with people coughing and shuffling their chairs.'

'But don't you *read* your poems?'

'Yes, but you're meant to give a little spiel first. You know – what you've chosen and why, and how you came to write them. Normally it's no problem. I make a few jokes to get the audience on my side, or tell them some personal anecdote. But this time I was really shit-scared.'

'Well, I know how nerve-racking performing can be. My husband was an actor.'

'Husband? You mean you're married?' He sounded shocked, indignant almost.

'No, widowed.' Even after all this time, it was still difficult to say, and invariably it made other people awkward. They didn't know how to react and would mumble vague apologies or clichés, as Will was doing now.

'It's okay,' she said. 'It was quite some time ago.' Immediately she felt disloyal to Gerry. Would he be upset to see her with another man? She took a long draught of beer, trying to put him out of her mind. She couldn't let him intrude on every date.

'I'm sorry, Catherine. I've been banging on about myself and I haven't asked a thing about *you*. Poets are such self-centred bastards. I suppose because our work comes from our innermost experience, we continually focus on ourselves. For all I know, you may be a poet too. Or a philosopher. Or a striptease artist. Or an authority on the hammerhead shark.'

'No, none of those,' she laughed.

'What do you do, then? Well, I know you work at the market, but is that full time?'

'Practically, at the moment, if you include the sewing work.'

'Oh, you make the waistcoats, do you? No wonder mine brought me such good luck.'

His flirtatious smile made her nervous again. 'I'm afraid I didn't make yours. That's one of Greta's, fortunately for you! She's more professional than I am. Actually, I'm only working for her on a temporary basis and I'm not sure what I'll be doing after that. To tell the truth, my life's a bit of a muddle at the moment. You see, I'm trying to find out what I *want* to do, and who I am, and all those adolescent sorts of things I should have discovered years ago. Forgive me, Will, but I'd really rather not talk about it. It sounds so . . . pseud, to use your word.'

He put his glass down and sat back with a triumphant air. '*I* know what you are,' he announced. 'You're a work in progress.'

'A what?'

'You know, like an embryo poem. Not sure where you're going or whether you'll end up as an epic or a haiku. But with lots of potential, whichever – confusion raging, creative chaos. And of course you don't want to talk about it – no writer ever does. After all, you may stop the process in its tracks if you pin it down too soon. You need to grope and fumble a bit, explore dead ends, maybe. In spite of their name, they can often be very enlivening. Then suddenly, one day – whoosh! – you've arrived. You're on paper, with a form and structure. You've worked yourself out. You're completed and complete.' Abruptly he broke off. 'God! I'm getting dreadfully pretentious again. And talking too much, as usual.' He leaned forward, edged his hand towards hers on the table. 'It's your fault, Catherine. You inspire me.'

'I . . . I thought you said inspiration was a corny word.'

'Not where you're concerned. In fact, if you're looking for a role in life, you'd make an excellent muse. They're very thin on the ground these days. I fear they're going the way of butlers and carbon-paper salesmen.'

Their hands weren't touching – not quite; his large and tanned and grubby; hers small and clean and pale. She felt unbearably hot (from nerves as much as anything), but if she took her jacket off, it would mean moving her hand from the table, which he might interpret as a rebuff. Yet if their fingers did make contact, they would have crossed an invisible boundary, and she wasn't sure she was ready for that.

He too seemed diffident, moving his hand a fraction, but only to trace a fissure in the wood. 'This table's cracking up,' he said, forcing a laugh. 'Like me.'

'It looks old but sort of . . . dignified.' Her voice was equally strained. 'Is it an antique?'

'Not really. It's sort of Arts and Crafts style.' He stroked the wood affectionately. 'Nice, though.'

'Do you know a lot about furniture?' she asked, relieved to be on safer ground.

'I'm learning. I love renovating things, you see, and you learn a lot that way. I tour all the local skips in my old van and scavenge anything worth saving. Then I mend it, stain it, tart it up and sell it at a profit if I'm lucky. It's a bit like poetry, if you'll forgive me for returning to that subject yet again – making something out of nothing.'

While he spoke, she watched his fingers caress the table-top. Of course, she thought, furniture-restoring would explain the state of his hands.

'And you never know what you might find. That's another thing I love – the element of chance. I rescued an old Hoover once, just because it looked slightly better than the clapped-out thing I had at home. And – you'll never believe this, Catherine – I saw something glinting inside the dust bag: a gold bracelet. Which turned out to be Victorian. Eighteen-carat. It was like a fairy tale – you know, the diamond ring in the belly of the fish.'

'Good gracious! What did you do with it?'

'Well, after quite a battle with my conscience, I decided I had to trace the owner. Which was easier said than done. I succeeded in the end, though, and was confronted with this eccentric artist who looked about a hundred and three. She gave me one of her paintings as a reward – an absolutely hideous thing. But of course I had to be duly grateful. A few years later I managed to get rid of it, thank God. I sold it to an American, who paid way over the odds. He saw it on my stall and thought it was a Frank Auerbach.'

'So virtue received its reward,' she smiled.

'On that occasion, yes. Though it's not my usual experience.'

She noted the bitterness in his voice and quickly steered him back to the subject of furniture, glad to see his expression brighten. His face was a barometer, registering his every change of mood. He seemed incapable of dissembling, or even of concealing his emotions.

'I must admit I find junk fascinating. And it always annoys me that it's *called* junk. I mean, who decides what's valuable or not? Junk often has as much history as antiques. It's the same with weeds. If dandelions were on display at the Chelsea Flower Show, gardeners would pay a fortune for them, and experts would write learned papers on their tap roots or their wonderful clocks.' He held up an imaginary dandelion clock, pursed his lips and blew. She could almost see the gossamer shreds floating above his head.

'When I was a little boy, I used to think . . .' He broke off as the waitress (a young girl in jeans and trainers, with shiny hennaed hair) squeezed behind his chair, carrying a tray of food for the people at the next table. A tantalizing smell of garlic wafted from the plates. He sat sniffing it appreciatively, forgetting to finish his sentence.

She wondered whether to prompt him to continue – it would be nice to hear what he had thought as a small boy. She knew little enough about him as an adult – not even his age or whether he was married, single or divorced – but she didn't want to appear intrusive by asking personal questions.

'I suppose I just love *things*,' he reflected, returning to the earlier conversation. 'More than people, frankly. When I worked in Totnes, it was the buying trips I enjoyed, rather than the actual selling.'

'Well, for someone who doesn't like people, you're very brave to invite me for a drink.' *She* felt brave for saying such a thing. It must be the beer – her glass was empty, although she didn't remember finishing it.

'You're different,' he said, looking at her intently.

'Different? Why?'

'I don't know. I like your face. Your eyes especially. They're a very interesting blue.'

She looked away, not sure if he was serious. She had always regarded her eyes as an extremely *ordinary* blue. If she thanked him for the compliment it might sound rather smug (especially if he hadn't meant it anyway). But the silence was getting awkward again, going on too long. She half stood up, to take her jacket off – a move she regretted as his glance strayed to her breasts. Nicky's sweater was tight, embarrassingly so. She had chosen her clothes this morning mainly for warmth and colour, not imagining for a moment that they would be subjected to such scrutiny.

'That's a fabulous sweater,' he said. 'The colour looks great on you, especially with your hair.'

This time she managed to blurt out an acknowledgement, although she could feel herself blushing like a schoolgirl. How pathetically gauche she must seem – a novice when it came to men. It had been so easy with Gerry, so safe. He had more or less grown up with her and knew her through and through, whereas now she had to start from scratch, with strangers.

'People who wear bright colours should receive good-citizenship awards,' he said. 'For cheering the rest of us up. Most clothes are so drab, especially men's.'

'You should see Nicky's!'

'Who's Nicky?'

'One of the girls I live with.' She could tell his curiosity was aroused, but she wasn't sure how much to tell him. Of course, she was a stranger, too, as far as he was concerned, but maybe better that way for the moment – at least until she had worked out what she felt about him. She was certainly intrigued (and flattered by his attentions), but also somehow wary. 'Look, let me get you a drink,' she offered. His glass was still half-full, but she needed a breathing space.

'No, the drinks are on me this evening – I insist. Would you like another half? Or shall we order something to eat and have some wine with it? I must admit these smells are making my mouth water, especially the garlic butter. I'm mad on garlic – pity it's so anti-social. I'll fetch a menu, shall I?'

'No, I'm sorry, Will. I can't. I . . . I've arranged to have supper with someone.'

'You didn't say.' He sounded hurt, his expression plunging into despondency again.

'Well, it's only a very casual thing – with Nicky. We decided we'd . . .' The sentence petered out. She hated lying and would only tie herself in knots.

'But surely she wouldn't mind? I mean, if you see her all the time. Couldn't you phone her and ask?'

'No, I'd better not.' Someone else seemed to be speaking through her voice; no longer her new self but a mistrustful killjoy, reminding her of the meal with Simon – and look what had happened then.

'Well, let me buy you another drink, at least. Have you got time for that?'

'Yes, of course. We don't eat till fairly late.' That was true anyway. It had been after ten last night before they got round to raiding the fridge.

He jumped to his feet and was half-way to the bar when suddenly he came back. 'Promise me one thing,' he said, putting his hand lightly on her shoulder.

'What is it?'

'Don't ask. Please. Just say "Yes, I promise".'

She said nothing. The gentle pressure of his hand seemed to be spreading from her shoulder through the whole of her body.

'Go on,' he urged. 'It's nothing too terrible.'

'It's a risk, though, isn't it?' she laughed.

'Oh yes. But risk is what it's all about – life, death, birth, love – and even quite a lot of poetry, the sort that teeters between brilliance and banality. Anyway, the most exciting people tend to take big risks.'

'Well, in that case, yes, I promise.'

'Thank you.' He let out a sigh, as if he'd been holding his breath in anticipation.

'Right, tell me the worst! What have I risked?'

'Dinner with me *another* evening. If that's okay?' he added anxiously.

She nodded. His hand hadn't moved from her shoulder, as if he were laying claim to her; keeping her gently captive.

'How about tomorrow?'

'No, I'm afraid I can't make that.' Tomorrow was Maureen's birthday and she had promised to take her in-laws to the new Italian restaurant in Walton. She wasn't looking forward to it, but some duties were inescapable.

'Well, Tuesday, then. Yes – let's try and make it Tuesday. It's St Valentine's Day.'

She didn't answer. He was going too fast: red roses, hearts entwined.

'Though you're probably booked already,' he said forlornly.

'Actually I am going out, for a drink with Nicky.'

'Who *is* this Nicky? You seem very close.'

'Well, it's not just her, it's a group of her friends. She works in advertising and they're meeting in a wine bar after work.' She didn't tell him the whole story: Nicky had suggested a consolatory drink for those of her friends without partners, who wouldn't be getting cards, flowers, chocolates, or romantic candlelit dinners. The idea was to prove they were quite capable of enjoying Valentine's Day without recourse to men, or schmaltz.

'Well, perhaps we could meet afterwards,' he suggested. 'How long will it go on?'

'Oh, probably all night, knowing Nicky. But I ... I could get away earlier, if you like.'

'I *do* like. What time have you planned to meet?'

'Between half past five and six, Nicky said, depending how busy they are on the day.'

'Well, suppose *we* met at half past eight. Would that be rushing you?'

'No, that's ... fine.'

'And shall I come and pick you up?'

'Oh, no,' she said more vehemently. It would contravene the whole spirit of Nicky's party for a man to barge in and whisk her away. In fact, she was beginning to wonder if she had any right to be there at all. Wasn't it rather devious to masquerade as 'manless', only to creep out two hours later for a dinner-date?

'Well, where would you like to meet?'

'How about here again?' It was a long way from the Mayfair wine bar, but she could tell the others (truly) that she had to go back to Camden to see someone connected with the market.

'Okay,' he said. 'But let's eat somewhere else. Somewhere quieter and more intimate.'

His hungry gaze gave the word still greater charge. His eyes were devouring her so greedily she felt herself consumed, digested.

Oh lord, she thought, quickly looking down – what on earth am I letting myself in for?

14

Catherine let the glass door close behind her, gazing around the impressive foyer of Hobson Huntley Armitage. Nicky's frequent complaints about the place had led her to expect something on the lines of a prison or a slave-ship, whereas HHA in reality looked more like a modern art gallery fused with a stylish hotel. The carpet was a subtle oyster-grey and dominated by an enormous L-shaped sofa, starkly black. Three abstract sculptures were mounted on white pedestals, and opposite hung a dramatic unframed canvas daubed in red and orange. Reproductions of past advertising campaigns covered another wall, though they were so cleverly displayed, one got the impression that they were works of art themselves.

Nervously she approached the desk – a white marble affair framed by a jungle of exotic plants, including a couple of palm trees, more Marrakesh than Mayfair.

'Yes, can I help you?' The receptionist was a daunting female with scarlet talons and jet-black hair cut in a harshly geometric style.

'I'm, er, meeting Nicky Maitland. Should I wait for her here, or . . . ?'

'I'll buzz her for you. Name, please.'

'Catherine Jones.'

The woman pressed a button on the switchboard, then sat inspecting her perfect nails, her haughty expression unchanged. 'She'll be down as soon as she can. Would you like to take a seat?'

'Thank you.' Catherine trekked back across the expanse of carpet and perched on one end of the sofa, thinking of the grotty dives *she'd* worked in when the children were young: offices with scraps of dirty lino on the floor, where the only 'art' was the odd tattered poster from Torremolinos or the boss's girlie calendar. It must give employees a sense of importance to be part of a place like this, knowing there were David Hockneys (genuine) in the boardroom and a pair of flamingoes (ditto) strutting around the roof-garden.

She watched people emerge from the lifts, presumably on their way home. A group of impeccably suited executives was followed by a lad in army fatigues, then a rangy black girl with a shaven head and huge earrings, wearing a crotch-high satin skirt. Camden Market meets the City, she thought, glancing at her own plain black skirt – one she'd brought from Stoneleigh and brightened with a silver shirt (courtesy of Nicky) and her scarlet 'yak' on top. She hadn't really known *what* to wear. Nicky and her friends were dressing up, to make the St Valentine's Day party more of an occasion and to show they didn't take trouble solely to please men. But if she followed their example, she would look overdressed for Will, who might well turn up in old corduroys and a sweater. Every time she thought of Will she felt a twinge of apprehension – made worse because she had no one to confide in. It had seemed insensitive to mention him to Nicky, who was feeling depressed about men in general and Jonathan in particular, or to Jo for that matter, who had been dumped by her Italian *inamorato* after one brief but glorious week.

She sorted through the magazines on the oversized glass coffeetable – *Media Week, Marketing, Creative Review, Campaign* – titles unfamiliar to her. She picked one up to study in more detail, startled by the images, so clever yet so blatant, and the photos of directors who looked barely out of school, yet who, according to the articles, were earning six-figure salaries. The advertising business seemed a curious mixture of avarice and art; High Seriousness lavished on trivia; ideals served by hype.

She was engrossed in a piece on 'Has Television Had Its Day?' when she heard someone call her name. She looked up to see Nicky coming towards her from the lift, her hair dishevelled, her red dress creased.

'Catherine, I'm sorry! It's panic stations upstairs – I thought I ought to warn you.'

'Why, what's happened?'

'It's Laura – you know, that girl I mentioned who came back

175

from maternity leave last month. I'm doing *her* work now. I've finished my own, thank God, and anyway she's in no state to do it herself. She's in floods of tears at the moment. Look, do you want to go on to the wine-bar without me? It's only round the corner, and quite a few people will be there already. I've invited some friends from Saatchis and BBH, as well. You could introduce yourself and . . .'

'No, honestly. I'd rather wait for you, Nicky.'

'Okay. But I don't like leaving you stuck down here on your own. Why not come up to the office and have a cup of coffee while I try to sort things out? Quick! Let's catch the lift.'

They both squeezed in just as the doors were closing, Nicky continuing to explain the crisis whilst they were gliding swiftly up. 'Laura's been doing these press ads for a new range of face-creams called Vigilant. But the client's shot the whole thing down. He says he wants more science and less poetry. *Last* time he briefed her, it was more poetry and less science.' Nicky snorted impatiently as she ushered Catherine out of the lift, which had stopped at the third floor. 'She's got to come up with something tonight, but the trouble is she's left Ben with Nina – that's the baby-minder – and when she rang to say she'd be late, the girl went mad. She's supposed to be going out, you see, and she told Laura in no uncertain terms that if she wasn't back within the hour, she'd refuse to look after Ben any more. Well, Laura just went to pieces. She can't afford a proper nanny, and anyway, she *likes* Nina, and Ben seems happy there.'

Catherine found it hard to concentrate. She was striding after Nicky along a wide grey-carpeted corridor past a series of open office doors – though offices seemed hardly the right word for these colourful chaotic rooms, furnished not just with desks and filing cabinets, but with televisions, stereos, sofas and armchairs. She stopped to peer in at a couple, distracted by a plush giraffe sitting earnestly at a desk, or a giant red nose she recognized from a recent cold-cure commercial. The walls were a brilliant jumble of posters and bulletin boards, with postcards, cuttings and photographs pinned up. And as for the workers, there wasn't a grey suit to be seen, not here in the Creative Department – nor indeed much sign of any work. She watched in astonishment as two lads in faded denims kicked a football up and down the corridor. Another boy lay fast asleep on his office floor, while a girl in a tartan micro-skirt and glittery platform shoes was lounging on a window-seat, smoking a cheroot.

'Hi, Sharon,' Nicky called. 'How's it going?'

'Don't ask!' said Sharon, with a shudder, returning languidly to her desk.

'This is Catherine, by the way,' said Nicky. 'She's coming to the party with us.'

'Hi, Catherine,' Sharon smiled, flicking ash on her layout-pad. 'See you about midnight, if I'm lucky!'

Catherine stole a glance at her watch, already worrying about her date with Will. There wouldn't *be* a date with Will if the party was so dramatically delayed.

Nicky stopped at the last office on the right. 'This is mine and Darren's,' she said. 'Darren's left already. He said face-cream wasn't his thing, though actually, he's rather good with women's products. He did this brilliant tampon campaign last year. People still ask him when his period's due! Anyway, let me introduce you to Laura.'

Catherine followed her into the office, where an attractive girl in her twenties with chestnut hair and a curvaceous figure was sitting at one of the desks, her eyes puffy and inflamed. She seemed embarrassed to see a stranger, and hastily dabbed her face with a tissue.

Nicky made the introductions, then drew up a chair at the other desk, frowning at her computer. 'I'm going to be a while yet, Catherine. Could you be an angel and make coffee for us all? The kettle's on the side there. Nice and strong for me, please. And Laura likes two sugars but no milk.'

'I'll do it,' Laura offered wanly.

'No, it's quite all right. Let me.' Catherine switched the kettle on, spooned coffee into three clean mugs, and eventually found the sugar in an enamel tin marked 'TEA'.

'Does anyone object to some music?' Nicky asked, plugging in her CD player. 'It might help me concentrate. In fact, why don't you two go and sit in Bruce's office? He and Phil have gone, so you'll have the place to yourselves, and you can have a good old natter.'

'And get out of your way, you mean.' Laura managed a half-hearted grin.

'Frankly, yes. Speed's the essence at the moment and I can work much faster on my own.'

'I'm still worried about you doing it, Nicky. Are you really sure you can manage? And you won't forget what I told you about . . . ?'

Nicky sighed in exasperation. 'Look, just leave me in peace and let me have a bash at it, okay? If I need you, I'll shout. The kettle's boiling, by the way.'

Catherine made the coffee, passed Nicky and Laura their mugs, then followed Laura to an office down the corridor.

'Come and sit here,' said Laura, patting the cushions on a squashy vinyl sofa. 'We might as well be comfortable. And look, I am sorry to delay you like this. It's great of Nicky to bail me out, but not much fun for you.'

'Don't worry. She told me about the problem with your baby-minder, and I sympathize entirely. It takes me back to the days when *I* had two young children and was trying to work full-time. Sometimes I felt close to cracking up. And my job was pretty routine – nothing like as demanding as this.'

'Yeah, I suppose that's the trouble really. I feel permanently frazzled. When I finish here, I pick Ben up and dash round Sainsbury's with him wailing in the trolley. Then it's off home to throw a meal together and catch up with the washing and ironing. My figure's gone to pot, so I should work out in the gym, but when, for heaven's sake? Ricky – that's my husband – plays squash three times a week, but there's something I've noticed recently – working mothers *don't* play – not games, not sport, not anything. They simply haven't time. Mind you, I'm not knocking Ricky – his job is frightfully pressured, too, and it's worse for men in some ways. They can't even have a good cry! One of the guys in his office says he's given up life for work. Apparently he's too exhausted even to have a proper relationship.' She pulled a tissue out of her bag and sat shredding it in her fingers. 'I'm sorry, Catherine, you don't want to hear all this. I'm afraid you caught me at the worst possible time. Usually I can just about manage to juggle everything, but when Nina threatened to stop looking after Ben, I just felt . . .' Tears slid down her face, leaving black streaks from her mascara. 'I . . . I'm sorry,' she repeated, struggling for control. 'I didn't mean to burden you with . . .'

'It's okay – really.' Catherine squeezed her hand. 'I understand. I've been through it myself. And it sometimes helps to cry.'

'Yes, but I feel so . . . so *guilty*. Not just about being a lousy mother, but . . . Hold on a minute.' She went to the door and closed it, then stood awkwardly by the sofa. After a moment's silence she suddenly burst out, 'There's this girl who works here – Jonty – and last month she got herself sterilized. She's only twenty-eight, but she knew she didn't ever want children. She was terrified of getting pregnant and being tied down with a kid for twenty-odd years. Most of the others were rather disapproving, even if they didn't say so outright, but *I* felt . . . almost envious.' She returned abruptly to the sofa and slumped down, looking wretched. 'I've shocked you, Catherine, haven't I? I mean, it's wicked to feel like that. And terribly unfair to Ben. I *do* love him, but . . .'

'Of course you do. And it's not wicked. It's perfectly understandable. You're tired, that's all – shattered, by the sounds of it. Look, I know it's probably easier said than done, but couldn't you take a few days off and simply rest – sleep when the baby sleeps, grab every chance you can?'

'Well, yes, I suppose so, but it wouldn't look too good. They'll probably think I'm slacking. It's bad enough Nicky doing my work. That's never happened before and it makes me feel awfully guilty. Your work's like your baby, you see – another sodding baby – which needs just as much attention.'

'Well, I still think you need a break from at least one of the babies.'

'Yeah, but if I did take time off, I'd still have to return to the treadmill. And it might feel worse than ever, after a taste of freedom.'

'But Laura, if it's as bad as that, perhaps you'd be better off without the treadmill. Do you *have* to work – for financial reasons, I mean?'

'Well, I suppose we'd manage if we did without holidays and things. But it's not just money, is it? It's self-respect and status – the idea of having it all, I suppose – to use that ghastly phrase.'

'But we can't have it all. It's impossible.'

'Loads of people try, though.'

'Well, maybe they're wrong. You could make out a good case for us being supersluts, not superwomen.'

Laura gave a hollow laugh.

'No, I'm serious. I've become rather sluttish myself, to tell the truth – about twenty years too late, unfortunately! And I find I'm questioning lots of things I used to take for granted. Like do I need to read a paper every day? Or watch the news on television? Or accept the general consensus that you aren't truly civilized unless you keep up with the latest detail of every crisis in the world. And I've stopped bothering about "proper meals" – whatever *they're* supposed to be. Oh, I know it's much easier for me – I'm on my own with no ties, but maybe you could do the same in a small way. Start with, say, the gym. You said you ought to go, but why? They didn't *have* aerobics and stuff when I was young. Now it's all the rage, but if you're not careful, it becomes just another pressure, something else to be fitted in.' She stopped, realizing how bossy she must sound. 'Oh dear, I hope you don't think I'm interfering, Laura? We've only just met and here I am telling you what to do with your life!'

'You're not telling me – you're suggesting things. And actually, it's great. Just talking to you helps. The others don't really under-stand – not even Nicky. She's an angel, and incredibly loyal, but until you've had a kid of your own . . .'

Catherine nodded, wondering for a traitorous second how dif-ferent her own life might have been if she'd never had Andrew and Kate. She didn't regret it – of course not – yet she had to admit they had brought her and Gerry years of worry and expense.

'I do remind myself I have choices. But I always seem to end up doing what I ought to do. Or trying to behave like a successful woman – whatever that is! In fact, the thought of doing what I *want* makes me feel quite . . . scared. I'm not sure I even know what it is.'

'I feel just the same, Laura, and *I'*m in my forties. But I'm doing my best to find out.'

'It's not that easy, though, is it? I mean, so many other people seem to put their oar in – parents, for example. I sometimes suspect I only had a baby because my mother was so keen to be a grandma. She pressured me all through school to be top of the class and get a good job, but when I'd actually done that, she changed her tune entirely and . . .'

'Laura, I need you!' Nicky burst in at that moment, a far less soignée figure than the one who'd left Gosforth Road this morning. She had taken off her earrings and her shoes, and there was a smudge of Biro down one cheek. 'I've rejigged a couple of your headlines to fit their comments, but I'm stuck on the night cream. What do they want to say about it now?'

'The new brief's on my desk. I'll get it.'

The pair of them disappeared down the corridor, leaving Catherine alone, still brooding on Laura's predicament, and wondering if Antonia planned to give up her job when she and Andrew eventually had children. If not, she might become another Laura. The choices seemed so difficult these days and there were certainly far more of them. But was it worse to *have* no choices than to make the wrong decisions?

She prowled around the room, trying to avoid the cold stare of the clock, and totally unable to relax. It was already twenty-five to seven and Nicky might be ages yet. She didn't like the thought of leaving the wine-bar almost as soon as they'd arrived. Nicky might be upset; the other girls offended.

Suddenly a phone rang, one of a battery on the desk. Her instinct was to pick it up, the correct formula coming instantly to mind: 'Hello, Universal Office Supplies. Can I help you?' Even after a gap of eighteen months, old habits were hard to break. It seemed appalling now, all those years working in a soulless job. But Gerry had sacrificed so much more than *she* had, exchanging Macbeth's dagger for a briefcase.

At last the phone stopped shrilling, giving way to other noises: snatches of music from Nicky's office, men's voices in the corridor, the thud of the football being kicked against the wall. These people were so lucky in their ultra-glamorous workplace, with their inflated salaries and tremendous freedom to express themselves – yet it all came at a price. Once you were locked in the nine-to-five routine (or nine-to-seven, worse), you became defined as a person solely by your job, and grew into it, like ivy bound inextricably to a tree. It made her more determined not to return to office-life herself and become an obedient robot.

Laura reappeared and flopped down on the sofa. 'I've just rung Nina and told her I'm leaving any moment. If only it was true.'

Catherine's eyes strayed to the clock again. Being late for dinner was nothing compared with Laura's dilemma, yet she still felt very tense, and annoyed with herself for over-reacting. Her date with Will might prove to be a one-off, so why make it so important?

Laura looked equally on edge as she sat fiddling with her hair. 'Oh God, Catherine!' she said. 'Now I'm beginning to worry about the *next* campaign. It's for a new brand of cereal, and they want it to be a cult product. As if you could produce a cult as easily as that! All you can do is come up with something a bit off-the-wall, but it could just as well turn out to be naff. It's a knife-edge situation.' She gave an apologetic smile. 'I'm sorry, Catherine, that sounds a bit over the top. But you get like that in this job. A box of fucking bran flakes becomes a matter of life and death. We've already had a meeting about it, and the client waffled on about how they wanted psychedelic visuals. Honestly, it's so old hat, but try telling them that! They've only just cottoned on to the fact that we're living in a drug culture. Actually, I find it rather pathetic, all those trippy commercials suggesting Pot Noodles will get you high, or Rice Crispies give you a rush. Anyway, I'm the last person to know. I've never been stoned in my life.'

'Same here,' said Catherine, laughing. 'The only drugs I've ever taken are the odd aspirins for a headache.'

'Here, have a look at this.' Nicky padded in again and thrust a sheet of paper into Laura's hands. 'I reckon we're almost there now. The pun in your old headline works better with this new visual, don't you think? I can't draw, I'm afraid, but it's supposed to be a woman's face looking like an alabaster statue. How does it grab you?'

Laura scanned it briefly, her expression brightening. 'Yeah, it's great. Miles better than mine. The only thing I'd suggest is that we add the word "eternal", to give a sort of promise of a beautiful skin for ever and ever, amen. If they believe that, they'll believe anything!'

'Perfect! I'll go and scribble the layout.'

'Then I'll nip down to Wayne with it.' Laura rooted in her handbag and took out a make-up case. 'Pray he's not in a meeting.'

'He shouldn't be. It's nearly quarter past seven.'

Oh no, thought Catherine. She would have to leave for Camden in three-quarters of an hour. If Wayne *was* in a meeting, she'd miss the party altogether.

Laura tissued off the mascara streaks and applied fresh blusher and lipstick. 'Wayne mustn't see I've been crying,' she explained to Catherine. 'He's anti-women anyway, especially those who produce babies. If we have to have the beastly things, I think he'd rather we bought them from a supermarket – you know, ready-delivered and washed. Actually, he's probably got a point there. I'd have saved myself forty hours of labour! Right, let's go. Nicky should be finished now.' She held the door for Catherine, then dashed ahead into Nicky's office, whisked the corrected sheet of paper from the printer and flew off down the corridor. 'Keep your fingers crossed,' she called.

'*She*'s cheered up,' said Nicky, switching off the computer. 'How on earth did you manage it?'

Catherine shrugged. 'I just told her to stop trying to be superwoman.'

'Christ! I can't imagine that. You should have seen her when she was pregnant. As if she hadn't enough to do, she got it into her head that she had to have the perfect pregnancy, right down to really crazy things like stimulating the baby in the womb. She played it Mozart, would you believe, to make sure it had good vibes. And she dragged Ricky to antenatal classes to do his father's bit. You see, she planned to have the perfect birth, as well – natural childbirth at home, with Ricky there, and no drugs or fuss or anything. Of course, it all went horribly wrong. The labour lasted two whole days and she was finally rushed into hospital with complications and given every drug there was. But she was back to work in six weeks, still sore from the stitches and absolutely whacked. Anyway, enough of all that. You must think we're terrible wimps here. If it's not *me* moaning, it's Laura falling apart. No wonder they don't take on many female staff.' She picked up her briefcase and stuffed a sheaf of papers inside. 'Come on, let's go and join our women-only contingent round the corner. They'll be well away by now. We'll just wait to hear what Wayne says, and if everything's okay we can make up for lost time!'

'Is, er, Jo coming?'

'No. I did invite her, but she's been asked to do a piece on some Valentine's do at Groucho's.'

Catherine hoped her relief wasn't too apparent.

'Catherine, you're not still worrying about Jo, are you?' Nicky put her shoes back on and ran a comb through her hair.

'Not really.'

'What's that supposed to mean?'

'Well, she . . . she still seems annoyed about the market. And I get the feeling she's not too happy about me being in the house at all.'

'You mustn't take it so seriously. She's moody, that's all, especially now, when she's been ditched by that Italian creep. Besides, house-shares do have their down side. You're bound to get bad feeling sometimes, with four people living together. I get narked with *her*, for instance, because she never pays her whack when it comes to buying basics. You're great in that respect, Catherine. And yet you earn less than any of us. You put us all to shame.'

'Yes, but I suspect that's part of the problem. She got quite stroppy when I suggested buying toilet rolls in bulk, and told me I was boring and would I kindly not interfere.' Catherine rebuttoned her coat, frowning. Having run her own household for twenty-five years, it was sometimes difficult *not* to interfere. It had become almost second nature to switch off lights, or make shopping lists, or pick up dirty washing. But that sort of thing could be a source of irritation to someone so much younger. 'Nicky, d'you think Jo feels I'm . . . ?'

She was interrupted by the phone. She held her breath as Nicky picked it up. Another delay? Another urgent job? Laura's and Nicky's tension was beginning to affect her, as if she too had spent a hectic day battling against deadlines. Listening in, she tried to work out if this was some new crisis, but Nicky was saying little more than 'Yes', 'No', and 'I see'.

She occupied herself by looking at the bulletin board. Amongst the stills from the Orange-O commercial and the visuals for Kendall's Krisps were a couple of old photographs, one of which she recognized as Nicky as a child. The face looked sad: eyes solemn, small mouth puckered, as if on the verge of tears. She glanced back at the real Nicky – eyes dramatically enhanced now with eye-gloss and mascara, but still troubled, none the less. She wished she could wave a magic wand and sweep away the pressures – *and* conjure up a devoted man to replace the feckless Jonathan.

Nicky put down the receiver at last. 'I'm sorry, Catherine,' she said, scribbling a note on her jotter.

'What's wrong?'

'Oh, it's just tomorrow's problem – another campaign bites the dust! But I refuse to let it spoil this evening. Hey, that sounds like Laura. Her footsteps are double the speed of anybody else's.'

'We're saved! Wayne says it'll do.' Laura flung open the door with a triumphant smile. 'Oh, Nicky, I could *kiss* you!' She proceeded to do so, gave Catherine a hug for good measure, then rushed off again, calling out goodbye.

Nicky shook her head. 'I only hope there isn't a hold-up on the tube. Right, let's go.'

'Nicky, you ... er ... do know I can't stay that long? I'm meeting...'

'Yeah, you said. Someone from the market. Pity though. You couldn't phone and put them off, I suppose?'

'No, I haven't got the number.' That was true at least. She and Will had discussed so many things, yet failed to exchange phone numbers. If he couldn't make it for some reason, he'd have no way of letting her know. She would have left the party early, only to sit all evening on her own.

'Well, you can be a bit late, can't you? From what you told me about the market crowd, they're not exactly punctual. Anyway, let's not waste precious time.' She grabbed her jacket from the coat-stand and held the door for Catherine. 'St Valentine, here we come!'

The wine-bar was crowded with bodies and thick with cigarette smoke. Nicky pushed her way in, to be greeted by shouts and cat-calls from a group of women occupying a long pine table.

'Hang on a minute, girls. Where's Catherine?'

'Here,' said Catherine, hurrying to catch up. 'Sorry, I got waylaid by a man.'

'Dangerous creatures!' called a dark-haired girl in a beret, sitting at one end of the table. 'We've given them up tonight.'

'That's a good one,' her neighbour retorted. 'We all know you're going home to darling Robert.'

'He's *not* darling. He didn't send me so much as a card. Hey, did you hear about Shirley on reception? She got the works, apparently – red roses, Belgian choccies, a heart-shaped card in a padded satin box ...'

'Ugh! Pass the sick-bag. Anyway, I wouldn't want a bloke like hers if he was the last one left on earth, Belgian choccies or no Belgian choccies.'

'When you've all quite finished,' Nicky said, shepherding Catherine to a seat. 'This is Catherine, who shares our house. She didn't get Belgian choccies and she doesn't work in advertising, so will you please be nice to her.' She started reeling off her friends' names: Julie, Sarah, Stella, Rachel, Lisa ...

Catherine wondered how many she'd manage to remember and was relieved when someone (Lisa?) poured her a glass of wine from one of the numerous bottles on the table.

'To women without men,' grinned Rachel, clinking her glass to Catherine's. 'Happier, healthier, and definitely much calmer.'

'And bloody celibate!' wailed Julie.

'Who cares?' demanded a fair-haired girl in a low-necked velvet top. 'I've hardly ever met a bloke who could get it together in bed. They either come too soon and call you frigid if you expect a bit of foreplay, or they go on for ever and half-choke you with their willies. I simply can't be bothered any more, and I'm far too busy anyway.'

'How are you finding your new job?' another woman asked her – a butch type with cropped hair.

'Not bad. It's a bit laddish, I suppose, but with only three women out of forty-one in the Creative Department, what can you expect?'

Catherine sipped her wine in silence, feeling rather out of it. Manless or no, these females seemed so self-assured, speaking in loudly confident voices and knocking back the wine. She daren't look at her watch again, but she had a nasty feeling it was getting on for eight. If she had the courage of her convictions, she would excuse herself right now, not sit here for another half-hour, becoming more and more uptight.

'Do you know a girl called Camilla at BBH?' Rachel asked the fair-haired woman. 'She's a planner, I think.'

'Oh, yeah. Tall and rather glamorous.'

'Well, she may be glamorous, but her boyfriend ditched her at Christmas and she started doing Dateline. She said it was a nightmare. The men she met were unspeakable – you know, jumped-up salesmen calling themselves company directors, or balding wrinklies who'd obviously lied about their age on the form.'

'Yeah, she must be pretty desperate. She even went to one of those Asda singles nights. Imagine, romance over the shopping-trolley.'

'*I* wouldn't mind. At least it would mean the bloke was reasonably house-trained.'

'I doubt it. After the first few weeks, I bet you'd be doing the shopping on your own again.'

Catherine wondered if their bitterness sprang merely from frustration. It was evidently hard work trying to find and keep a man. There were men in droves, here in this very wine-bar – crowding the tables, clustered by the door – but as Nicky had complained so often, half the men in London were married, gay or otherwise unavailable, and the other half were depressingly unappealing. Jo too had bewailed her string of brief relationships, none of which ever seemed to work out. When you were married, she now realized, it was all too easy to take companionship and sex for granted, rather than having to go out and hunt for them. She had been lucky in a way, marrying into a large and friendly family; unlike poor Nicky, who, still partnerless at thirty-five, felt very much alone in the world.

'Has anyone tried love on the Net?' Julie asked, dipping into a bowl of salted almonds. 'Well, *don't* – that's my advice. You get these absolute nerds boasting about their pecs.'

'Oh, for God's sake,' said the dark girl in the beret. 'There must be something better to talk about than men.'

'Like what?'

'Well, religion, politics, the Common Agricultural Policy . . .'

'No thanks!'

'What do *you* do, Catherine?' Rachel asked.

She flushed as they turned to look at her. Her eyes were smarting from the smoke and it was difficult to make herself heard with so many people talking at once and waiters shouting orders against a background of thumping music. Besides, it would be rather hypocritical to adopt the general tone of anti-male world-weariness when she was so anxious about being late for Will. To her relief, though, she had no sooner mentioned Camden Market when someone else butted in.

'D'you know the joke about what women do after sex with the average man?'

'No,' said Julie, lighting a cigarette. 'What *do* women do after sex with the average man?'

'They *come!*'

There were a few half-hearted titters and an impatient groan from Lisa. 'Look, we're back to bloody men again. Can't we change the subject?'

Nicky took the initiative, refilling Catherine's glass and giving her a sympathetic smile. 'Hey, listen to this,' she told the group. 'Catherine's won on the lottery *twice* in the last three weeks.'

Again, all eyes turned to her. She appreciated Nicky's attempt to include her in the conversation; none the less she didn't feel at ease here. Apart from anything else, she was still wondering how to leave discreetly without being regarded as a party-pooper.

'So how many millions did you make?' Julie asked her with a laugh.

'Hardly millions, I'm afraid.'

'Enough to buy a Porsche?'

'One wheel, just about!'

'You did well to win at all,' said Rachel. 'I've never won a bean, and I've been doing it since it started. What's your secret?'

'Oh, it was just a matter of luck.' Though rather amazing luck, she thought. Her second win had been £87. Maybe not enough to buy a Porsche, but £87 for doing nothing more than fill in a few numbers. In fact, it meant she had funds enough tonight to treat herself to a cab to Camden Town, instead of taking the tube, which involved hanging around for trains, changing at Euston and a long, cold trek each end.

She stood up decisively, no longer cowed by the fear of seeming rude. Why the hell should she care what these girls thought? Okay, Nicky was a friend, but the rest were virtual strangers. In any case, she was free to do what she liked. The trouble was, that had never quite been true, or perhaps she'd never quite believed it. But it was time she asserted herself. And if she trusted in her luck (as she had with the lottery), not only would she manage a cool, collected exit, she would also find an empty taxi waiting right outside, the traffic would be minimal, and – most important of all – the evening with Will would be something rather special.

15

Catherine gave the taxi-driver a generous tip for getting her to the Crown and Goose in under a quarter of an hour. 'Thanks,' she said. 'You've saved my bacon!'

She put her purse back in her bag and was about to walk into the pub when a familiar figure rushed towards her.

'Catherine! At last!'

'Oh, Will ... hello.' What did he mean – at last? It was only 8.35, so she was hardly late at all. 'Didn't we say eight-thirty?'

'No, eight o'clock.'

She didn't like to contradict him; besides, he sounded so certain, perhaps *she* had got it wrong. 'Gosh, I'm sorry. I felt sure it was half past.'

'No, I wrote it in my diary.'

So had she, but there didn't seem much point in arguing the toss. 'Well, at least we're both here now,' she said brightly.

He held the door for her, still looking rather disgruntled. 'I've been waiting outside for half an hour. I'm frozen.'

'But Will, we did say *in*side.'

'Yes, I know. I'm sorry.' He turned to face her, his expression switching from annoyance to contrition. 'It's just that – well, I ... I thought you might have changed your mind.'

He had said that last time, she remembered, wondering why he should be so insecure. Only now, in the bright lights of the pub, was she able to see him clearly. He was wearing the ancient donkey jacket with another of its buttons missing. Well, fair enough – he probably had no other coat – but his hair looked, frankly, a mess: too long and in need of a wash. Couldn't he have made more effort, as *she* had?

Swallowing her resentment, she offered to buy him a drink. 'As compensation,' she smiled, 'for keeping you hanging about.'

'No, tonight's my treat.'

'Well, dinner maybe, but not everything.'

'Yes, everything. I insist. In fact, why don't we go and eat now? It's so crowded in here, I can't see a single free table.'

She was reluctant to go out into the cold again, especially as it had just begun to rain. The pub seemed so inviting: cheerfully warm – and *safe*. However, she followed him outside, hoping the restaurant wasn't too far. Instead of woolly leggings and fur-lined boots, she had put on sheer black tights and strappy shoes, in his honour, of course. A sleety rain was falling; cold pinpricks on her face and legs.

'Well, did you enjoy your party?' he asked as they turned the corner into the High Street.

'Yes,' she said dutifully; then, 'No, I didn't, Will, to be honest. I don't think it was quite my scene.'

'I loathe parties. All that superficial chit-chat, and no one saying anything they mean.'

He sounded terribly grumpy, hardly the romantic companion she'd expected. 'Oh, I have to say I usually enjoy them. In fact, that's how I met Nicky – at a party. It was actors, though, and publishers, not advertising people.'

Will skirted a puddle on the pavement. 'I rather envy actors – being able to take on new roles all the time. I get fed up with being me. I often think the best sort of holiday wouldn't be going somewhere different, but *being* someone different. And it would make us much more tolerant, especially if we could change sex and race as well. I mean, I'd like to know how it felt to be a West Indian matriarch with a dozen kids, or a Vietnamese peasant living in an entirely different culture. We're so imprisoned, don't you think, in our own narrow shred of experience.'

'But perhaps that's a sort of protection. We might not be able to cope if we experienced everything directly. Hold on a sec – my shoe's hurting.' She bent down to adjust it, balancing on one foot.

'Was your husband famous?' he asked suddenly.

'What?'

'Your husband. Didn't you say *he* was an actor?'

She nodded. She didn't want to talk about Gerry, not now. She was tense enough already, what with Laura being so upset and the long wait at HHA, and then Will complaining she was late, in spite of her heroic efforts not to be. 'No, he wasn't famous. He might have been, but . . . but he . . . he gave it up.'

'How awful for him.'

'Yes. It was. Except I don't think I quite realized at the time. I mean, what a wrench it must have been and . . .' Oh God! She could feel tears pricking at her eyelids. She couldn't cry – not here in Camden High Street in the rain. The scene with Simon had been bad enough.

'What made him decide? Or did he . . . ? Catherine, what's the matter?' Once he realized she was crying, he immediately stopped and pulled her towards him, clasping her so tightly she could barely breathe. Her face was pressed into the rough fabric of his jacket, her heart pounding from the shock of the encounter. She could smell damp wool, taste the tears salty on her lips. They were blocking the pavement, people bumping into them or muttering in annoyance. She pulled away, embarrassed, then saw to her astonishment that there were tears in his eyes, too.

'Will, what's wrong? What is it?'

He shook his head. 'Nothing.'

They stood motionless, in silence, she increasingly confused. They had only been together for five minutes, but they were no longer casual acquaintances, not after that embrace. Things were getting out of control. And why was he upset? Had something awful happened, some crisis he was trying to conceal? 'Look,' she said, 'if you'd rather we postponed this evening . . .'

'*No*,' he all but shouted. 'I wouldn't hear of it. I've been thinking of nothing but this dinner since Sunday night.'

She had no idea what to say. He seemed so vehement, and his mood changed so disconcertingly from surliness to passion.

He took her arm and they continued down the street. Every shop they passed flaunted a Valentine display – scarlet hearts, gold cherubs, bunches of pink and red balloons. She found it rather disturbing, as if the day itself was challenging them to move from friendship to romance. They must already seem like a couple, walking arm in arm, yet she knew next to nothing about this man. She wiped her wet face with her glove, shook droplets from her hair. The rain was getting heavier, soaking into her coat.

'I'm sorry,' he said. 'I meant to bring the car. But I'm afraid it

191

conked out this morning and I daren't take it near a garage in case they tell me it's a write-off.'

'Well, I suppose we could have gone in *my* car. But I have to park it miles away.' To save money, she didn't say, though even without the cost of parking, having a car in London at all was proving something of a trial. There was a constant risk from vandals, especially in lawless Camden Town. She had already lost a set of hub-caps and had her wing-mirror smashed. And according to Darren she was lucky that no one had nicked the wheels – so far.

Will steered her into a side street, then turned left again into a dark and narrow alley. 'We're almost there now, anyway,' he said.

The restaurant was so tiny it would have been easy to miss it altogether. And far from sporting hearts or cherubs, the decor was unashamedly plain: white plastered walls, tiled floor and bentwood chairs and tables. Again she felt a stab of disappointment. She hadn't expected the Ritz, but surely he could have found a more congenial place than this? The interior was murky, as if they were economizing on light bulbs, and the sole item of greenery – a bedraggled spider plant – was dying in its pot. But then he had wanted somewhere intimate, and that description wasn't wholly wrong in terms of sequestered semi-darkness.

'Will, how good to see you!' A swarthy man in white jacket and black trousers emerged from a back room and pumped Will by the hand. 'And welcome, *señora*. Can I take your coat? This weather . . . !' He rolled his eyes dramatically. 'But don't worry, you'll soon be warm in here.'

She handed him the dripping fur, wishing she had a towel to dry her hair and a pair of sheepskin slippers. Though it was true the restaurant was warm; indeed the air felt almost tropical after the brutal cold outside.

'This is Juan,' Will said, unbuttoning his coat. 'My favourite restaurant-owner north of Madrid! Juan, I'd like you to meet Catherine.'

Juan flashed her a gold-capped smile and bustled off with the coats. But her attention had already shifted to Will. He was utterly transformed. Beneath his shabby coat he was wearing the purple velvet waistcoat. And not just that – there was also a matching purple cravat and a cutaway jacket in an elegant shade of grey.

'You look terrific,' she said, delighted that he had bothered after all. 'The waistcoat's perfect on you.'

'You don't think I've overdone it?' he asked anxiously. 'I got the jacket at a car boot sale. The guy tried to tell me it was a Hungarian hussar's coat, though I have my doubts about that.'

'No, it's great – whatever it is – especially for a poet. You look quite Keatsian.'

His face lit up with pleasure. If he were deaf and dumb, she thought, he would be able to communicate by facial expression alone.

Juan had swept up again. 'I've reserved the best table,' he told them.

His grandiose air amused her. In fact, all the tables looked the same – small and somewhat rickety – and it seemed pointless to have reserved one when the place was practically empty. ·

'Drinks on the house,' he announced, still in his lordly tone. He ushered them to a table by the window, then vanished into the kitchen, returning with two glasses of amber-coloured liquid.

'What is it?' she whispered to Will.

'Try it and see.'

She took a tentative sip. It tasted warming, fiery, comforting – sweet and bitter at once. 'Mm, nice,' she said. 'But I still haven't a clue what it is.'

'Things are often better like that, don't you think? Unlabelled, undefined. Then you come to them with no preconceptions. Perhaps it's true of people, too. For instance, if you were described to me as a widow before I met you, I'd have imagined an old lady with a greying perm, not a gorgeous woman with that amazing hairstyle.'

She flushed, and not just at the compliment. It seemed a touch insensitive, the way he kept harking back to her widowhood. 'Have *you* been married?' she asked, deciding he could answer some questions, for a change.

'Yes.' He frowned. 'But it broke up eighteen months ago. Apparently my crime was being a poet.'

'That's a crime?'

'Oh God, yes! An unsuccessful poet, especially. It means you can't support a family in the style they feel entitled to.'

'So you've got children?'

'Only one. A boy.'

Juan appeared at that moment, bringing crudités and olives, a small dish of garlicky mushrooms and a bowl of dressing so thick it looked like cream. 'Now *señor, señora*, let me tell you the specialities this evening. I can recommend the red snapper with saffron sauce. Or there's roast breast of Barbary duck, served with *dauphinoise* potatoes and a compôte of aubergines . . .'

Catherine stared at him in astonishment. She had expected egg and chips.

'Or if the *señora* is vegetarian, we have fusilli with wild mushrooms, and a cornichon and caper salad.'

She had never heard of cornichons (if indeed they were plural), and continued to listen, intrigued, as Juan ran through the list of starters, all of which sounded equally sophisticated.

'They never bother with a menu here,' Will explained, as Juan returned to the kitchen. 'It beats me how they manage to keep going. The food's brilliant, but – as you see – the surroundings leave a lot to be desired. So, luckily for me, it never gets that crowded. Mind you, there's usually more people than this. I suppose because it's Valentine's Day everyone's gone to the trendier places. A lot of restaurants are doing special dinners tonight, but I hate that sort of schmaltz, don't you?'

She couldn't recall ever having attended a Valentine's dinner, but she nodded in agreement. Certainly the four other diners, who all looked fairly elderly, didn't appear to be celebrating romance. There were a couple of overweight balding men talking in a foreign language, and a grey-haired woman with, presumably, her husband (though she seemed more interested in some booklet she was reading).

'Well, what are you having to eat?' Will asked.

'Oh, the duck, I think.'

'Barbary duck. I wonder where it comes from. D'you think it's related to the Barbary ape? Except that's North African. Perhaps it just means wild – you know, like barbarian.'

'Okay, barbarian duck. It sounds even better!'

'And what to start with?'

'I'm not sure I can manage a starter.' She was actually very hungry, but worried about the cost. Without a menu, she had no idea of the prices and didn't want to lumber him with an enormous bill.

'Oh, you must. I'm having the smoked mussel salad. Do you fancy that? Or how about the leek and feta tart?'

'Yes, the tart sounds great, though I don't know how you remember all the names. He went so fast.'

'That's easy – I'm a glutton. I remember meals from years ago, even down to the details. Right, let's order.' He summoned Juan and after a brief three-way chat about the wine, he relaxed back in his chair. 'All settled,' he said, passing her the dish of mushrooms and taking a couple himself. 'Mm, they're delicious.' He licked his oily fingers. 'This place reminds me of those workers' caffs you get in Rome or Venice. You know, with sawdust on the floor and not a tourist in sight, but the most fantastic nosh.'

She *didn't* know. Nor did she like to confess that she had never been to Rome or Venice. Talk of foreign travel seemed to crop up with depressing frequency – at the market, in the flat, with Nicky and Darren's friends – and it embarrassed her to sit dumbly contributing nothing to the conversation. Travelling abroad was part of being civilized, part of normal life. Which meant *she* was a freakish philistine. She quickly changed the subject. 'How old's your son?' she asked.

'Seven.'

'And what's his name?'

'Sam.'

'Does he look like you?'

'No. He's the image of his mother.'

His tone had changed again – now terse and unforthcoming. However, he pulled a wallet out of his back trouser-pocket and showed her a photograph. 'That's him when he was five.'

She looked at the small boy: his hair straight, blond and, no, nothing like his father's; the eyes dark brown, not grey. 'He's gorgeous.'

'Yes. So's his mother, damn her. She went off with someone else.'

'Gosh, I'm terribly sorry.'

'Yeah. A director at ICI. She wasn't going to be caught out again, living on the breadline with some arty-farty poet who couldn't get his act together. They've just bought a place in Hampstead. Half a million pounds' worth. Sam adores it, of course. He's got his own television and computer and he's having riding lessons. It must seem rather a come-down when he visits Dad in his two-room flat.'

She was relieved to see Juan with the starters. Will brightened noticeably when he was presented with a plate of mussels and a bottle of white wine. Juan had also brought a basket of hot bread, its fragrant smell mingling with the spicy tang from the mussels.

'They do marvellous bread here,' Will enthused, offering her the basket. 'None of those ghastly rigor-mortis'd rolls full of air and nothing. This is bread you could sleep on, it's so soft and springy.' He broke off with a grimace. 'Hell! It's a good thing my father isn't here. He hates people raving about food. He thinks it's dreadfully bad manners. When I was little, mealtimes were more about good manners than eating. We had the usual footling rules of course: never put your elbows on the table, eat your crusts or you'll get them for breakfast, no pudding until you've finished your greens, etcetera, etcetera. I've rebelled in adult life. Pudding first, if you fancy it, and *lie* on the table if it helps you enjoy the meal.'

She laughed. 'My father was strict, too. Mind you, he was widowed very early on, so I suppose it's understandable. But I used to feel an awful pig if I was starving hungry and wanted to tuck in, and *he* was toying with half a slice of toast.'

'Well tuck in now. *I* won't call you a pig. But how sad for you to lose your mother. Were you very young?'

'Four and a half. I often think about her. But actually I remember almost nothing, so my mental picture is probably quite wrong. She's become a sort of phantom mother.'

'A phantom mother. I like that. Catherine, you do say interesting things.'

She sipped her wine to cover her confusion. Far from being interesting, she often felt her conversation bordered on the trite.

He took a second piece of bread and dipped it in the mussel sauce. 'No one important in my life has died, touch wood. I've been lucky in that respect. Or maybe it *isn't* lucky for a poet. I often think that poets and philosophers – and politicians too, come to that – should go through every human experience before they start pontificating. I mean, how can we be so arrogant as to think we have something important to say if we haven't been ill, or poor, or despairing, or bereaved, or . . .'

'Well, I've been all of those, Will, but I'm not sure I've got something important to say.'

'Oh but you have – you must. You just don't give yourself credit for it. I've noticed that about you, Catherine, you're modest, and that's rare, you know. And definitely appealing. Can I try a bit of your tart?'

She cut him off a chunk, amused by the way he jumped so abruptly from philosophy back to food. He ate the offering greedily, scooping up the crumbs.

'Here, have a mussel in return.' He speared one on his fork and held it to her lips. She swallowed, savouring the soft, moist, flabby fishiness. They were feeding each other like lovers, and she had to admit she found it rather exciting. She remembered Nicky saying that men who didn't like food were invariably lousy lovers, and wondered if the converse was true. But that was frightfully presumptuous – this could still be a one-off. Besides, alarm bells were already sounding in her head. He was divorced, after all, and his bitterness about it (and initial surly mood) didn't augur well for any continuing relationship. And yet he was undeniably attractive – not just his looks, but his energy, his ideas.

'I wrote you a poem this morning,' he said. 'Well, I had a bash, but it's nowhere near finished. You're rather a difficult subject.'

'Why's that?'

'Well, you're full of paradoxes – womanly and punky, spirited and bashful. Oh, and you're a most determined saleswoman, I might add. I'd never have bought this waistcoat without your powers of persuasion!'

'Is good?' asked Juan, gliding up to their table.

'Yes, very good,' they both said at once.

'*Bueno.* I bring you main course.'

'No rush,' said Will, picking up his glass. 'We've got all evening.'

She too sipped her wine, thinking back to the many occasions when Gerry had come home late from a sales trip, and the food she'd prepared hours earlier was spoiled. She would make cheese on toast or scrambled eggs instead, and while they ate he would still be tense and preoccupied, ploughing through urgent sales reports, or having to break off to take business calls. She had grown accustomed to truncated meals, or to eating on her own in the kitchen because he had rung to say he wouldn't be back at all. Then, more recently, there had been Manor Close – strained and over-formal meals where she often felt a little spare. So it would be a treat to have a long and leisurely dinner with a man encouraging her to dispense with the proprieties – eating garlicky mushrooms in her fingers, gorging on the bread. 'Can I see the poem when it's finished?' she asked, dolloping butter on a final knobbly crust.

'I'm not sure. Only if it's good enough. I'd hate you to judge me by a bad one.'

'But I wouldn't judge you, Will. I'd be flattered. No one's ever written me a poem.'

'All the more reason for it to be good, then. I'll work on it, don't worry. And I must add your splendid silver shirt.'

'It's Nicky's, actually.'

'So you wear each other's clothes?'

'It sounds awful put like that! And no, she doesn't borrow mine. It's one-way traffic, I'm afraid.'

Will fired a salvo of olives into his mouth – stoneless ones, she hoped, since in his eagerness to speak again he appeared to have swallowed them whole. 'I wore a suit of my father's once, for a wedding. A dark grey one he didn't want. And d'you know, it ruined the whole day for me. I'd somehow taken on his personality, as well as his clothes, and I just couldn't seem to relax. We've never been close, you see.' He stared at the window, suddenly dejected. 'I must have been a dreadful disappointment to him. He ran his own small printing business and he hoped I'd join him as a partner and eventually take it over. It's the same with my ex-wife – they both wanted a high-flier. Ah, here's the food. Good timing! It'll stop me whingeing about myself. A bad habit. I apologize.' He sniffed the food greedily as Juan unloaded the plates. 'What *is* a Barbary duck?' he asked him.

'Is French,' said Juan briefly, topping up their glasses.

'A French colonial duck, I take it.' Will scrutinized his own plate and the contents of the vegetable dishes. '*Bon appétit,*' he said, once they were alone again. 'Or *bueno appetito*, maybe, in deference to Juan. Now, I must stop talking and attend to important things.' He bent reverently over his plate, his face alert as he sampled the fish. She watched his features relax: evidently the food had passed some stringent test. He started eating with total concentration – no, devotion was the word. She cut a sliver of duck breast, copying his intensity; savouring the rich sweetness of the sauce, the hint of nutmeg in the potatoes, and the contrasting textures of crispy duck-skin and soft-fleshed aubergines.

She looked up from her plate for a moment, surprised to see that the restaurant was much fuller. She had been too involved with Will to notice people coming in. Also, another waiter had materialized, younger than Juan, but with the same stocky build and Mediterranean colouring. There was now a clatter of dishes, a buzz of conversation, interspersed with the noise of the rain spattering on the window. Will, however, was silent as he continued to eat with rapt absorption, only speaking again when he had demolished half his fish.

'*I* know which poem I'll show you,' he said, wiping his mouth with his napkin. 'One called "Truth", with thirteen lies in it. I wrote it after an argument with a friend about whether poetry is "true" or not. He kept trying to analyse what I meant by truth, but he was missing the point entirely. Then he changed tack and started banging on about how Plato banished poets from his ideal state on the grounds that they told lies. Of course, my father would agree with him. *He* sees imagination as highly suspect, because it tries to describe things which don't exist.' He helped himself to another three pats of butter, which he softened with his knife before smoothing them on to his bread. 'I love butter, don't you? In my opinion, anyone who champions margarine deserves to be hung, drawn and quartered. And the cheek of it – calling such a disgusting product Flora when she was the most delightful goddess. Are you a butter-eater, Catherine, or is this the end of a beautiful friendship?'

'No, I'm with you there,' she said, although she couldn't help thinking guiltily of Gerry. She had never bought him Flora, had always cooked with butter, and even . . .

'It's a modern-day neurosis, all this fuss about foods being unhealthy. It's replaced the fear of hell. We spend our whole life fretting about the death of the body instead of the death of the soul, as they did in medieval times. But going back to lies – I suppose people are hungry for them, and they can be very comforting, of course.'

'That's what Nicky says about advertising. But Darren thinks . . .'

'Don't you find it rather difficult,' Will interrupted, 'living with other people? I mean, when you've had your own home and been mistress of the house?'

She hesitated. It *was* difficult in some ways, as the tiff with Jo had proved. Yet mistress of the house sounded too imposing a title for her years as Gerry's wife. The house had been Gerry's business first and foremost, and though she'd organized the domestic side and been chief cook and bottle-washer, she'd had no sense of power. It seemed odd that she had submitted with such passivity, but she hadn't really been aware then how circumscribed her life was. 'Well, it's certainly very different,' she said, returning to Will's question. 'But in a way that's good for me. It makes me rethink everything – things I used to take for granted. And I like hearing all the various opinions. We argue, but it's stimulating.'

'*I* live on my own now,' Will said, picking a piece of carrot out of the dish. 'But it . . . it feels as if part of me's missing. Wow! Look at that gâteau.' The young waiter was serving dessert to the couple at the next table. 'There's more cream in it than anything else. Catherine, I do hope you're leaving room for pudding?'

She laid her hand on her stomach. 'Yes, just about,' she laughed.

'Good. D'you know, I'm reading Byron's letters at the moment, and he was a frightful prig about food. He was in love with an Italian opera-singer once – until he saw her eat. Her appetite appalled him, and he said all women should restrict themselves to a morsel of lobster and a soupçon of champagne. Now I'm the opposite. I could fall in love with a woman just *because* she eats.' He put his knife and fork down, and leaned forward to touch her hand. 'In fact, I could fall in love with *you*, Catherine.'

She looked down at the table to avoid the intensity of his gaze. How on earth could she respond to such a startling declaration? She busied herself with her bread, breaking a piece off and spreading it with butter. Behind her, the two old men were talking in their indecipherable language and a group of new arrivals were discussing what they'd have to eat. Yet she and Will were locked in their own silence as he gently increased the pressure on her hand. She glanced at him, hoping a moment's eye-contact and a brief, self-conscious smile would be answer enough.

He seemed embarrassed too, now, and came to her rescue by offering her a forkful of red snapper. 'You . . . you haven't tried my fish,' he said, sliding it between her lips.

She swallowed gratefully, giving him a slice of duck in return. At that moment someone called his name – a high-pitched female voice. She turned to see two girls who had just come in, their coats wet from the rain. They hurried across with a flurry of greetings; one kissing Will on the cheek, the other ruffling his hair.

'Will, how *are* you? We thought you might be here. You look great. Love the waistcoat!'

Will hastily finished his mouthful, then made the introductions: Miriam (foreign-looking, sultry, with lustrously black eyes) and Lee (blonde and pert and bubbly). They said a perfunctory hello to her before turning back to Will. She could make little of the ensuing conversation, but was struck by its intimate tone. This pair knew Will well – too well. Perhaps he had a whole string of girls and told them all he could fall in love with them. These two were certainly glamorous and young. And *rude*, she thought, to barge in on her tête-à-tête with Will without a word of apology.

She realized she was jealous, and despised herself for such pettiness, yet she couldn't really relax until they had finally departed to a table in the corner.

'Sorry for the invasion,' Will said. 'Miriam's a poet and Lee's a friend from way back.'

A *girl*friend, did he mean? And how long ago was 'way back'? Before his marriage? During it? Perhaps his wife had left not because he was a poor struggling poet, but a poor, promiscuous one. But as he seemed disinclined to volunteer more details, she returned to the (safer) subject of his work. 'Have you always been a poet?' she asked.

'Oh, no. That's probably why I talk about it so much – to convince myself I am one. After I left school, I felt I had to pacify my father by getting what he called a proper job – scores of "proper jobs", in fact. I never stuck them long, you see, much to his disgust. I tried to write in the evenings, but poetry needs leisure. You have to moon around a bit, *waste* time rather than use it, let things spring out and surprise you. But if you get tied into the system of being "productive" and "successful" – my father's favourite words – then the creative spark can simply fizzle out.' He speared a broccoli floret and devoured it in a bite. 'I've noticed how wonderfully inventive children can be because they have time to play and mess around. And – to return to my earlier point – they don't label everything as useless or worthwhile or whatever. They'll experiment with *bad* ideas and come up with something new.'

Like *I'*m doing with my life, she thought, jolted by the analogy.

'Jobs are a problem even now.' He pushed a piece of bread

round his plate to mop up the rich sauce. 'I'm becoming better known, thank goodness, so I'm being asked to do more readings and stuff, but that often clashes with my other work. I mean, if I did take a stall at the market, I might find I'm meant to be appearing at a festival or running a weekend workshop . . .' He broke off, frowning, and started fiddling with a button on his waistcoat. 'In fact, I was wondering if . . . This may sound a bit of a cheek, Catherine, but it's only a suggestion. And you did say your work with Greta was probably coming to an end. Well . . . how would you feel if we ran a stall together?' Before she could reply, he continued straight away. 'I had the idea on Sunday after you'd gone home, and the more I thought about it, the more sensible it seemed. You see, you need one person to do the buying – touring auctions and boot sales – while the other mans the stall. Of course, I was relying on having my car, but I'm still hoping to repair it once I've got the parts. But you say *you*'ve got a car, so maybe . . .' He stopped again, his fingers restless on the table.

She too was uncertain what to say. Was he simply using her, angling to borrow her car while his was off the road? No, surely not. If nothing else, he was generous, as he had demonstrated on Sunday and tonight. And he would be stimulating to work with – lively and exciting.

And moody and unpredictable, the voice of caution put in. And how often would he disappear for his festivals and workshops – or to look after his son, for that matter? Would it end up as *her* stall, but with him pocketing half the profits? 'I . . . I don't know much about antiques,' she demurred.

'But it wouldn't *be* antiques – more junk.'

'Well I don't know much about junk.'

'You'd learn. Like I have. Pick it up in no time.'

Yes, she thought, I probably would. Gerry used to say she had a good eye when they'd been looking for old furniture, whether a Victorian chaise-longue or office desks and chairs. But she and Gerry had been a partnership, in all senses, whereas she and Will – well, that was unknown territory. She looked out of the window: rain glinting in the halo of a street-lamp; shadowy dark beyond.

As if sensing her unease, he abandoned serious matters for food once more. 'Let's swap plates,' he said. 'You eat the rest of my fish and I'll finish your duck. If we do that with the puddings, too, we'll each have six courses.'

'Okay.' She hid a smile. This man could be difficult, but he would never be boring. She let him switch the plates and divide the remaining vegetables between them.

They ate in silence for a while, then he put his knife and fork down. 'Well?' he said. 'What do you think?'

'About swapping food?' she asked, deliberately obtuse. 'It's interesting. I can taste the fish and the duck at once now.'

'No, the market stall idea. Would you be willing to give it a try at least?'

'I . . . I'm not sure,' she said. 'I'll have to see.'

'When d'you think you'll decide?'

'Well, it depends on Greta, partly. She may need me for a while yet.'

'So you're really saying no.'

She shook her head in exasperation. 'I'm saying I'll have to *see*, Will.'

'Well, let's meet again tomorrow – I mean, even if you do decide against it. I'd love to see you anyway.'

She stole a glance at Lee and Miriam, who were chattering and laughing, apparently without a care in the world. How could she compete with them: their youth, their sheer high spirits? But did she *want* to compete? She knew from talking to Nicky and Jo how much aggravation relationships could bring, especially with men who . . .

'Just briefly, if you prefer. We could have coffee somewhere, or go for a walk, or . . .'

'I . . . I'm not sure when I'm free.'

'Well, *I'm* free all day, so I can make it any time you want – midnight, midday, three o'clock in the morning.'

'I'll phone you, Will, okay?' She must be very careful. This man was not only an unknown quantity, but dangerously persuasive.

16

'Okay, open the boot and let's get this lot in.' Will picked up the first of the cardboard boxes, grimacing at its weight. 'Christ, it's heavy! And we're already running out of space. Thank God we brought the roof-rack.'

'That's nearly full as well, though.' Catherine helped him manoeuvre the second box in beside the first. 'D'you think we'll need to make another trip?'

'I hope not. I don't fancy battling across London again. Mind you, it was worth it for a haul like this. We'll have masses to sell on the stall.'

'Too much!'

'You can never have too much. Anyway, we can leave some of it in boxes. People love poking around for themselves, especially if they think they're getting a bargain. We'll lump all the cheaper stuff together and mark it "Everything a pound". And there should be plenty more in the kitchen. Mrs Pearson was obviously a hoarder.'

Catherine picked up a stray bit of newspaper which had fallen out of a box. 'I'm surprised the auctioneers didn't clean the place out.'

'Yeah, so am I. They usually descend like vultures. I've even known them take the flowerpots out of a garden shed. But I wouldn't be surprised if Mags told them they could only have the bigger stuff – you know, so *we* could have the rest. She's always been generous like that.' He stowed the last of the boxes in the boot and slammed the lid down with a grunt of satisfaction. Wiping his dusty hands on his jeans, he went to sit on the front doorstep.

'We're lucky with every damned thing today! I mean, look at this weather. It's practically spring-like.'

Catherine gazed at the fields which stretched beyond the house – a collage of different shades and textures: bare earth newly ploughed, grey shadows on brown stubble, a green glaze of winter wheat. A puny but insistent sun was struggling through the clouds, glinting on a church spire in the distance. 'It's so wonderfully quiet and countrified here. I can't believe it's commuter-land.'

'Only just. And this house is miles from anywhere.'

'I like it, though, don't you?' She surveyed the weathered brick, the twisty chimneys and moss-furred roof: a house out of a storybook which you imagined full of dogs and children. In fact, Mrs Pearson had just died at the age of eighty-nine, alone, stone-deaf and childless.

'Yeah, I like the whole area. When I stayed with Aunt Mags as a boy it always seemed like paradise, especially compared with home. She'd let me go off all day with a picnic, and ride my bike after dark. Strange to think she's Dad's sister when they're so unlike each other. I remember she used to take my side when he threatened me with boarding school.' His face took on a defiant expression, as if he were confronting his father again. 'Actually, I suppose it's rather odd that I never met the Pearsons – they've lived here donkey's years. But then the old man was a bit of a recluse.'

'When did he die?' she asked. She liked it when he talked about his childhood. Although they'd seen a lot of each other in the last three weeks, he was still a stranger in many ways.

'Oh, six or seven years ago. I remember Mags saying she couldn't help admiring Mrs P – you know, for refusing to move into sheltered housing, or at least to a smaller place. Mind you, I doubt if she'd have managed without Mags. She went up there every day and cooked for her and everything.'

'And got her reward in the end,' said Catherine, pulling down the sleeves of her jersey. It was cold, despite the sun.

'Yeah – amazingly. I've never had *my* goodness rewarded.'

'Perhaps you haven't been good enough,' she laughed.

'Maybe not. Here' – he patted the stone step – 'come and sit beside me.'

She joined him, shivering. 'It's a bit nippy out here.'

'Mm. Nice, though. The air smells of . . .' He raised his head and sniffed, like a dog. 'I'm not sure what. Just clean, I suppose. My place reeks of curry. It should be called Tandoori Street.'

She wondered when she would see his flat. Secretly she felt hurt that he hadn't yet invited her. He had been to *her* place, met her house-mates, taken quite a shine to his tabby namesake. Was he hiding something in Tandoori Street – another woman, perhaps? Still, why spoil a nice day out. Just now she had him to herself and was determined to enjoy it. She stretched languidly in the sun, turning her face up to its grudging warmth. It felt like playing truant – escaping into the wilds of Berkshire on a humdrum Monday morning, when dutiful folk were toiling at their desks. And the countryside seemed to have chosen today to hatch from winter into spring. March was already a week old and had come in roaring like a lion, and although now it was more lamb-like, there was still a ferment in the air – green exploding out of brown; hedgerows full of rustling birds; streams swelling; pollen flying in the wind. Thanks to Will, she was seeing things with a poet's eye: the grey fur of pussy willow softening the stark blackness of the twigs; the sticky tautness of horse-chestnut buds, still furled but strained to bursting-point; the veined purple silk of crocuses.

'The sky looks busy,' Will said, shading his eyes with his hand. 'See those little cloudlets – they remind me of the pattern on my mother's lace doileys. Hey, imagine a cloud-arranger – some guy with various implements who's in charge of how the clouds look, and forks them up or rakes them smooth, or . . . no, *several* cloud-arrangers. A miserable sod who lays on dark grey rain-clouds, and his cheerful counterpart to whip up fluffy white ones like meringues. And an angry bastard for storm-clouds. Actually, I wouldn't mind a job like that myself. What power! – deciding on the weather, hurling things around the sky.'

'Oh, Will . . .'

'What?'

'You are funny.'

'I'm deadly serious. And it would look good on my cv.'

'You know, I've never had a cv. It makes me feel rather a failure.'

'Well, let's write you one now.'

'But what could I put? I haven't had any decent jobs to speak of.'

'Muse, most definitely. And superior chauffeuse. You're a

marvellous driver, Catherine, unlike me. And antiques-dealer, of course.'

'Hardly antiques,' she said, eyeing the old Hoover on the roof-rack, roped on top of a rusting metal foot-bath. 'Though if this is work, I have to say I like it.'

'Yeah. We're lucky. But don't think this is typical. I've often had completely wasted trips. I'd flog all the way to some boot-fair and find it wasn't worth the petrol. I blame the *Antiques Roadshow*. Everyone's clued up now, so you don't get priceless treasures lying around in the attic or handed over for jumble any more.'

'Oh, did you see it last week, Will? That marvellous old chap who paid twenty-five bob for a chest of drawers in a junk shop, then found it was Sheraton.' She broke off suddenly. 'Gosh! Look at that magpie with a huge great stick in its mouth. It must be building a nest.'

'One for sorrow,' he said frowning.

'No, there's its mate.' She pointed to a second bird: gleaming blue-black livery; long flamboyant tail. It was breeding time, budding time, yet still he hadn't kissed her. Two for joy.

'I'm going to make a cup of tea,' she said, 'before we freeze to death. And let's have it inside, okay?'

'Okay, though actually I'm boiling. It must be all that exertion.'

She turned to look at him; his face flushed, his shock of springy hair damp with perspiration. He seemed so alive, so vibrant, she could almost feel the blood pumping in his veins, watch his beard pushing through his chin. Why didn't he kiss her *now*, when they were so tantalizingly close? She was aware of his hip pressing into hers, his solidity and warmth, the smell of chocolate biscuits on his breath. Each time they went out together she hoped he would invite her back, or at least stop to kiss her in a doorway. But all he had done so far was squeeze her hand or put his arm around her. Today she was tempted to make some move herself: touch his face, stroke his hair, prompt him to go further. She must have been affected by the stir of spring all around – daffodils unsheathing, rooks jabbering and wheeling – she too primed for spring, and emerging from her drab chrysalis-case. Yet William, the poet, was unaware; sensitive to nature but not to her wild wings.

'Once we've had our tea,' he said, 'we must get back to work. No more lolling about.'

'You sound like your father,' she said, coming down to earth with a bang.

'God forbid! Though I must admit I feel sorry for the old bugger sometimes. He's seventy-two and still works a twelve-hour day.'

'And what does your poor mother do?'

'Oh, minister to his needs, listen to him ranting on about the youth of today. I'm afraid she's gloriously unreconstructed.'

'Why gloriously?'

'Well, don't all men secretly hanker for a good old-fashioned wife? The sort that bakes bread and warms your slippers by the fire?'

'Did *you* want a wife like that?'

He laughed. 'Well, actually, *I* was the one who made the bread, although I have to admit it was really for my benefit, rather than Vanessa's. She preferred Ryvita, can you believe. That's as bad as preferring Henry James to Dickens. And as for slippers, I don't remember either of us ever owning any. But I don't really want to talk about my marriage. *Or* Vanessa. And certainly not Henry James. I want to sit and drink my tea with the wondrous Catherine.'

She grinned foolishly. If only he were as generous with his kisses as his compliments. Wondrous was a new one. She'd been fantastic, brilliant, splendid, even scrumptious. 'All right, I'll go and put the kettle on,' she said.

She paused for a moment on her way through the hall; the sight of the denuded rooms reminding her of the sale of her own house – brash removal men heaving beds and wardrobes down the stairs. Yet, surprisingly, she could recall it without regret now, even feel relief at being free. Owning a large house meant an endless round of cleaning, gardening, decorating; tied you down with chains.

She walked into the kitchen. Mags had left the heater on and the room felt agreeably warm. Everything, including the heater, was obstinately old-fashioned: the iron range and square white sink, the slatted airer overhead, the kettle itself an ancient dented object with string wound round its handle. There were two lighter-coloured patches on the wooden floor where an oak table and a dresser had once stood. The auctioneers had taken those, but left a second cupboard and a collection of rather battered chairs – more treasures for the market.

She filled the kettle and put it on the hob. Mrs Pearson had obviously mistrusted electric gadgets. There was not even a toaster, let alone such refinements as a food-mixer or percolator.

Suddenly Will was behind her, pressing close and putting his arms round her waist. She felt her body tense with excitement. Surely *now* he would . . .

'Any biscuits left?' he asked, moving away to investigate the biscuit packet. 'Only crumbs,' he said disconsolately. 'We should have brought more food.' He scrunched up the empty wrapper and tossed it into the bin. 'Well, never mind. Let's make a start in here while we're waiting for the kettle.'

He started rummaging in the cupboard, holding things up to show her: two china jelly-moulds, a 1953 coronation mug, a pair of metal candlesticks and a badly chipped teapot in the shape of a cottage, complete with thatch and rambling roses. 'This stuff looks promising. It'll go a bomb with the tourists.'

'Is it actually worth anything?' she asked, stooping down to help him.

'No, not a lot. But it'll sell, and that's the main thing.' He rubbed the dust off a jelly-mould, examining the fine cracks in the glaze. 'If this was copper, we'd be laughing. Old copper jelly-moulds can fetch hundreds of pounds.'

'Well, we're doing pretty well as it is, getting all this stuff for nothing.'

'You bet! I told you, Catherine, you brought me luck. Right from the first.'

'I wonder if there's such a thing as luck, or whether it's just a matter of coincidence – or of Mags's kindness, in this case.'

'It's real, I'd say, but rare and precious. Like copper jelly-moulds. Or yaks.'

'*Are* yaks rare?'

'Red ones are.'

Their eyes met for an instant, and she looked away, confused. 'Sh . . . shall I use this teapot for the tea?'

'Why not? We'll christen it. *And* the coronation mug. I missed the coronation. I wasn't even a twinkle in my mother's eye. Strangely enough, my eldest brother was born that very day, though.'

'Well, *I* was on the scene, but I was only three.' It made her insecure talking about their respective ages. A six-year gap wasn't that enormous, but it seemed more acceptable somehow for the man to be the older. Was Will put off because she was in her forties – a mother-figure rather than a girlfriend? But then why should he say such complimentary things to her? Unless it was merely to keep her sweet because he needed her help on the stall. Yesterday – their first venture together – she had proved better at selling than he was. Working for Gerry had given her years of experience with customers, whereas Will was shy with strangers and took offence too easily if people were offhand. Yet if he did have a girlfriend (or even more than one – bubbly twenty-year-olds like Miriam and Lee), how on earth would he find time to see them, when he spent most days with her?

'Okay if I come in?'

She jumped at the tap on the door.

'Yes, of course,' said Will, lumbering to his feet as his aunt put her head round the door. 'You weren't long!'

'No – silly me. As soon as I got back I remembered I'd meant to ask you over for lunch. We're only having soup and salad, but you're welcome to join us. Bob said he'd love to see you.'

'No, we'd better not,' said Will. 'There's still loads to do here and I have to be back by five. Thanks for the offer, though. Look, why not stay and have a cup of tea now you're here? The kettle's just on the boil.'

'I never refuse a cup of tea.' Mags eased her bulky frame on to the largest of the chairs. 'Mind if I smoke?'

'I think I'd mind if you *didn't*.' Will found her an ashtray in the cupboard, an old metal one with CRAVEN 'A' printed in black letters round the rim. 'You've been smoking as long as I can remember, and you know how I hate change.'

'I was really asking Catherine,' Mags said. 'Though if she does object, I'm sunk! I can't drink tea without a ciggie.'

'No, of course I don't mind.' Catherine hunted for another mug, relieved that Will hadn't finished the whole pint of milk. She had taken an instant liking to Aunt Mags, although they had met only briefly that morning. At first sight she was a daunting figure, dressed in slacks and a man's shirt, her face devoid of make-up, her grey hair uncompromisingly straight. And her smoker's rasping voice descended sometimes to a croak, so that she sounded almost hoarse. But her manner was warm and friendly, and the kind blue eyes made up for any gruffness in her tone.

'Er, Auntie . . . ?'

'*Now* what?' Mags turned from Will to Catherine, raising her eyes to heaven. ' "Auntie" means he's after something!'

'Only the loan of your car,' said Will. 'And only for ten minutes. Just to nip down to the shop.'

'What's wrong with Catherine's?'

'Nothing, it's just that there's a load of stuff on the roof-rack and it's not properly secured. I'd hate it to fall off. Anyway, it's your fault for mentioning lunch. You've made me feel hungry and there's nothing to eat but biscuit crumbs.'

'Well, I offered you lentil soup.'

'Lentil – my favourite!'

'Want to change your mind?'

'No, better not. I'll just buy a pork pie or something and we can eat it while we work. Anything you want, Aunt? Chocolate, fags, the latest Mills & Boon?'

'Get away!'

They exchanged an affectionate smile, Catherine watching enviously. This woman knew Will better than almost anyone in his life; she had held him as a baby, fed him, probably bathed him. The pair were totally at ease with each other – no awkwardness, no mysteries. Mags had even got a kiss.

'I'll have my tea when I get back.' Will strode out of the kitchen, jingling the keys.

Catherine returned to the task in hand. The teapot was almost black inside, and the third mug she'd unearthed had a dead moth in the bottom. She washed both as thoroughly as no soap or hot water allowed, then hunted for another spoon. 'How do you like your tea, Mags? Weak? Strong? Milk? Sugar?'

'No milk or sugar, but strong. And I *mean* strong – you know, the spoon standing up in the cup.'

Catherine laughed. 'I'll do my best. What do you think of this teapot?' she asked, holding it up for inspection.

'It's a monstrosity. Whoever made *that* never lived in the country. Roses round the door, indeed!'

Catherine opened the packet of teabags, hoping Mags wasn't the type to insist on proper tealeaves. She made the tea and, in the absence of a table, balanced the tray on a chair. 'Look, I haven't even thanked you yet,' she said, pulling up another chair, 'for letting us have the pick of all this stuff. We're delighted, honestly.

But it does seem rather a cheek. I mean, are you sure there's nothing *you* want?'

'Good heavens no. Our house is like a tip already. Bob would keep his toenail-cuttings if I gave him half a chance. There just isn't room for anything else.'

'Yes, but you could sell it.'

'Oh, I can't be bothered with all that. And what would I do with the money, except buy more cigarettes and shorten the odds against dying of lung cancer. Besides, I expect Will told you I'm getting all the proceeds from the auction, and that's more than enough for me. Originally everything was going to the RSPCA, before Mrs Pearson changed her will. I must admit, I do feel rather guilty about depriving the poor animals.'

'But at least they get the house, I gather.'

'Well, not to live in, I hope! Though it must be worth a pretty penny, even in this run-down state.' She took a tentative sip of tea and nodded in approval. 'Let's neither of us feel guilty, my dear. I'll send a cheque to the RSPCA on behalf of us both, and we'll leave it at that, okay?'

'Well, that's really sweet of you. Thank you.'

'It's quite all right. You and Will are doing me a favour. It would have taken me an age to clear all those drawers and cupboards. Anyway, I'm very fond of Will.' She stubbed out her cigarette and took a gulp of tea. 'You're the new girlfriend, I take it?'

'N . . . no. We work together.'

'Well, you be nice to him. He deserves it.'

'Yes, I . . .'

'Have you met Vanessa?' Mags's voice took on a sharper tone.

'Er, no.'

'I could kill that bloody woman! Will had a breakdown when she left, and I'm not surprised. Oh, I admit I'm prejudiced, and I've only heard Will's side of things, but all the same, she does sound a scheming bitch – if you'll excuse my language.'

Catherine stared into her cup, feeling disloyal at hearing such confidences. Yet curious, as well. She longed to question Mags further, not only about Vanessa, but other women in Will's life. Mags's asking if she was the new girlfriend suggested there had been a previous one. 'Was he married long?' she enquired. Best to start with a fairly innocuous question.

'Oh, no. Barely six years.'

Six years. And his son was seven. Perhaps they'd got married chiefly for Sam's sake and then regretted it.

'In fact, we thought he'd never settle down. Bob and I used to worry. He seemed so restless – you know, always changing jobs, moving round the country.'

'And how did he meet Vanessa?' Catherine kept her voice low, in case he came in and overheard them. It still seemed rather traitorous talking about him behind his back.

'At some writing course he went on. She was one of the guest speakers, invited from the publishing side. Apparently she's a big noise at Penguin Books now – one of their top editors. She's older than Will, you see.'

Catherine drew in her breath. How much older? she burned to ask, but didn't want to sound too nosy. And how ironical that he had married an achiever, as if in deference to his father, rather than a mooner and a dreamer. Or perhaps there had been some baser motive – to advance his career as a poet, for example. She remembered Will telling her that Penguin were one of the few publishers who took poetry seriously (not that he'd mentioned Vanessa, of course).

'Any more tea in the pot?' Mags asked, lighting another cigarette. 'I mean, enough for Will if I have a second cup?'

'Who's taking my name in vain?' Will demanded, bursting into the kitchen with his arms full of packages. 'I've bought some hot cross buns.'

'Already?' Mags protested. 'Easter isn't for six weeks.'

'I'd eat them all year if I could. One for you, Mags?'

'No thanks. It'll spoil my lunch. Anyway I really must get back for Bob. I promised to give him a hand in the garden. See you later, alligators! You don't mind dropping the key in, do you? It's not out of your way.'

'Yes, 'course. And talking of keys . . .' Will fumbled in his pocket and gave Mags the car keys – and a kiss.

Two–nil, thought Catherine, keeping score. She stood beside him in the porch, waving Mags off. As the mud-spattered Astra rattled round the corner, he turned to go inside again. 'Right, food,' he said. 'Toasted buns with raspberry jam.'

'Wait!' Catherine grabbed his arm, astounded at her audacity. 'I . . . I want you to kiss me, Will.'

He looked at her in shock, his voice little more than a whisper. 'B . . . but I thought . . .'

The rooks filled the silence, mocking from the treetops. Her face was tilted up to his, vulnerable, expectant. She had made herself ridiculous. He would reject her, walk away.

There was a sudden sharp crack from the woods beyond the house – a gunshot. They both jumped at the explosion. The rooks scattered in alarm, caw-cawing in black turmoil overhead. Then, suddenly, almost violently, he took her in his arms and crushed his mouth against hers.

17

'And *then* what happened?' Nicky was wide-eyed.

'Nothing.'

'Oh come on, Catherine, something must have happened after a smacker like that!'

'We ate hot cross buns.'

'You're joking.'

'I'm not. Three each, with butter and raspberry jam. And he told me when he was little he used to think they were *cross* buns – you know, bad-tempered, like his father.'

Nicky laughed. 'But *after* the hot cross buns . . . ?'

'We went back to work – a bit shakily, I must confess – and finished the sorting and packing.'

'And then what?'

'We got in the car and I drove us back to London.'

'*And . . . ?*'

'And nothing. He had some appointment at five, so I dropped him off.'

'Where? At his flat?'

'No. The tube.'

'And he didn't say where he was going?'

'No.'

'But surely he kissed you again – if only when he said goodbye?'

'No.' Catherine's voice was noncommittal, but even three noes couldn't dilute her sense of triumph. Never mind a repeat – that one kiss had actually happened. Impassioned, violent, fierce. Then tender, gentle, slow. She knew Will better now – or at least the geography of his mouth: the taste and texture of his lips, the roughness of his chin, that incredible probing tongue. She was still on a high, as if he were continuing the kiss, electrifying her body, changing its basic chemistry.

'Maybe he's afraid of getting involved,' said Nicky, 'or going any further.'

'But why? I'm not that frightening, am I?'

'Of course not. But I suppose he might have some sort of problem – be impotent or something.'

Catherine didn't answer. She could feel Will's tongue running slowly round the inside of her lips, then pushing into her mouth, urgently, imperiously. Impotent was not the word she'd use.

Nicky rocked back in the wicker chair. 'I mean, it seems so odd that he hasn't asked you back.'

'I know. And I've dropped enough hints, that's for sure.'

'Perhaps the walls are terribly thin and he's got puritanical neighbours. Or he's hiding a mad wife in the cellar – you know, like Mr Rochester.'

'His wife – ex-wife – lives in Hampstead village.'

'Oh yes, you said. Well, perhaps it's just that he's into celibacy. It's dead trendy now, worse luck.'

Catherine disentangled herself from Will's arms, feeling guilty about her euphoria when Nicky was still so downcast over Jonathan. A less unselfish friend might well have been jealous, whereas Nicky had listened cheerfully to the passionate-kiss-in-Berkshire saga, even though she'd just come in after what she called a typical shitty Monday.

'Hey, *stop* that, William!' Catherine shooed the cat from the rug, where he was sitting contentedly, plucking at it with unsheathed claws.

'Is this rug new?' asked Nicky, stroking her stockinged foot across the pile.

Catherine nodded. 'One of Colin's rejects.'

'Really? It looks okay to me.'

'That's what *I* thought. But Colin's a bit of a perfectionist. He let me have it cheap.'

'Actually, the room looks great. You've worked wonders.'

'Well, I've probably gone a bit over the top. But since the walls were red to start with, I thought – what the hell – go for it!'

Secretly she was pleased with the results – the striking combination of mulberry red and damson purple. She had made a new bedspread and curtains from some old material Greta had turfed out. The wicker chair she'd found in a junk shop, and also a tarnished brass lamp which she had polished till it gleamed. And she'd arranged silk poppies in a vase and scoured the shops for posters. Fiona's naked man now shared the wall-space with several rivals: Wynton Marsalis, Salvador Dali, Humphrey Bogart and Roger Rabbit. This was the first time she'd had a completely free hand, with no one to please but herself, and the effect she'd tried to create was a counterblast to middle-class, middle-aged suburbia. She had even bought gaudy coloured soaps. Gerry had always used coal tar, for some reason, and she'd come to associate its medicinal smell with dull conformity. She glanced at his photograph, wondering what he'd think of the room. She liked the fact that he was smiling from the desk; the last face she saw as she turned off the lamp each night. *All* the family were here – Andrew and Antonia in a fancy silver frame, Kate scowling into the sun, Jack and Maureen out of focus. Although, Gerry apart, she had to say it was less of a strain living with their two-dimensional likenesses than living with them in the flesh.

'Listen, I've got an idea,' said Nicky. 'Why don't you invite Will here for a special meal? Stuff him with aphrodisiacs and make it madly romantic – lights low, soft music – and then, bingo, he'll sweep you upstairs!'

Catherine settled William on her lap. 'Well, even if he did, I think I'd be too embarrassed with everybody here. Anyway, it's not likely to be romantic with Jo washing her smalls in the sink and Darren crashing around. Oh lord!' she said. 'They're not in yet, are they? I'd hate them to have heard me.'

'No, Darren's doing a gig. And Jo's gone to see a friend. Anyway, they couldn't hear us three floors up. In fact, it's a pity Will wasn't free, then you could have asked him back this evening and had a bit of peace. But, you know, the other two are out again this Saturday. They're going down to Hampshire for the weekend to see their families. I heard them discussing train times. So why not invite Will then? And *I*'ll make sure I'm out as well.'

'Oh, Nicky, don't be silly. You don't have to . . .'

'That's all right. I was planning on going windsurfing anyway. The reservoir's quite fun, but I want to get out in the waves. I'll toddle off to Shoreham and leave you the run of the place. You can give Will a leisurely dinner, then shag till you're pop-eyed.'

Catherine ran her hand along William's back. Would she and

Will *ever* shag, she wondered, ever get that far? 'It sounds fantastic, Nicky, but I have my doubts, I'm afraid. I mean, even the leisurely meal may be a bit of a problem. I'm at the market all day Saturday, so there won't be much time for cooking. Mind you, I suppose we could eat late. Will's running a poetry workshop, so he won't be back till eightish, in any case.'

'Great – invite him for nine. And if you want to borrow my room after dinner, do feel free. He is quite a big chap after all, and this bed looks as if it was made for a dwarf.'

'I wouldn't dream of it, Nicky.'

'Why not? *I* shan't be there. Come to think of it, it's an awful waste of a double bed – no one ever using it.'

'Oh, Nicky, I am sorry about Jonathan.'

Nicky shrugged. 'Don't worry. It serves me right for aiming too high. A famous actor, for God's sake! Why ever should he stick around with me when he must have the pick of every luscious bimbo in the business? Mind you, he *was* quite civilized the few times we did go out. Which makes a pleasant change. Most blokes I meet turn out to be shits or creeps. Did I ever tell you about Craig?'

'No, I don't think so.'

'Christ, he was a bastard! Every time I saw him, he had to prove . . .'

Catherine tried to keep her mind on Craig, but it would keep returning to Will. The light was beginning to fade; a murky dusk pushing at the balcony window, blurring the view of Camden's chimneytops. She longed to stop night in its tracks; haul back the dazzling weather of the kiss; preserve the whole day as a trophy: gala day, red letter day. She even felt differently about Berkshire. A rather tame and stolid county had now become the most exciting place in England. Yet it was a crazy way to react. She wasn't in love with Will, for heaven's sake – on the contrary, she was all too aware of his faults. But that kiss had somehow impaired her powers of judgement.

She continued to stroke the cat, turning him into Will, ruffling his dark hair, running her hands down his back. She imagined him responding as William was doing, nuzzling his head against her body, purring rapturously.

'Well, finally, I'd had enough, so I decided to have it out with him. "Craig," I said. "I'm sorry, but I can't take all this crap."

And d'you know what he did, Catherine? He walked out – just like that. He wouldn't even discuss it. Which was typical, of course.'

Catherine made vague sympathetic noises, having missed most of what Nicky had said. And William's ecstatic purr only increased her sense of guilt – it seemed so tactless in the circumstances. 'It's, er, funny,' she said at last, in an attempt to break the awkward silence. 'We're always moaning about men, but when we were driving back this afternoon, Will was complaining about women.'

'Not *you*, I hope?'

'No, just generally. He thinks women today actually *want* men who behave like bastards, and run a mile from the caring sort, because they see them as weak.'

'But how on earth can he generalize like that?'

'Oh, he always does. About everything. It's part of his charm.'

'You must have got it bad, Catherine! Sweeping generalizations always piss me off. They're so arrogant.'

'Well, Will *is* arrogant in some ways. And frightfully unsure in others.'

'And I suppose that's part of his charm as well?'

Catherine grinned. 'Oh yes. Anyway, enough of Will. It must be a frightful bore for you. Tell me, how did Sunday go?'

'Sheer heaven!' Nicky stretched luxuriously. 'Give me windsurfing any day, rather than shits like Craig. And I much prefer that reservoir to the Ashford one. It's bigger, for one thing, so there's more room to blast about! And I'm definitely improving now I'm getting more time on the water. I can cope with almost any conditions, even the strongest winds. And the weather was damn near perfect. I stayed out a good three hours, and afterwards I felt like new – elated yet wonderfully relaxed.' She gave a sigh of frustration. 'But when I'm back at work, I'm for ever looking at the tree outside the office, trying to gauge the wind. And if there's a good old blow, it's all I can do to sit still. I want to jump straight in the car and drive over to the reservoir again, or down to the coast, even better. But I can't live solely for windsurfing.'

'Well, at least it's something you truly like. I envy you that, having one real passion.'

'You've got Will!'

'Don't speak too soon. Knowing my luck, he'll gobble the meal, then say he has to rush back for something.' She glanced at her watch. 'Oh hell,' she frowned. 'I promised to phone Kate.'

'Well, it's not too late, is it?'

'It'll be after midnight there by now. Mind you, she never seems to go to bed till some unearthly hour. Anyway, she's probably hanging around waiting for me to ring.'

'Well go on, then – quick! I'll watch the telly in my room and you can have the phone to yourself.'

'Thanks.' Catherine turfed the cat off her lap and hurtled down the stairs. At the bottom she noticed Will's stripy scarf draped across the banisters. He must have left it when he came in for coffee last night. She put it round her neck, holding one end against her face and inhaling his elusive smell; reliving the kiss again.

Stop it, she told herself. Kate would be appalled if she could see her once chaste mother mooning around like an animal on heat, forgetting Gerry in this obsession with a stranger. She went into the sitting-room and sat down by the phone. Even before Gerry's death she had sometimes feared Kate's scorn, for failing to espouse high ideals or campaign against human rights abuses, but being content to simply jog along, typing sales reports and pruning roses. Yet ironically, it was the children who had cramped her style: solemn Andrew and high-minded Kate. Without them, she might have run wild – had passionate affairs, sailed round the world in a catamaran, crossed the Gobi Desert on a camel. Or was she just deluding herself, blaming them for her own in-built unadventurousness?

She dialled the Gurgaon number, annoyed with herself for forgetting the call – Will's fault again, of course. There were the usual problems getting through – delays and interference – and then more delays while someone went to find Kate. She looked anxiously at her watch, tick-ticking away the pounds. These calls were a drain on her still sporadic income.

'Mum, hello! What happened?'

'Sorry, darling. I hope I haven't kept you up. I got a bit . . . delayed. I've been out all day, you see, and then I . . .'

'Are you all right, Mum?'

'Yes. Why?'

'You sound different.'

'What d'you mean?'

'Sort of high. Have you been drinking?'

'Of course not. But how are things with *you*?'

Kate launched into an account of her newest project: teaching a course on hygiene at the centre – elementary matters such as sweeping floors and keeping flies off food. Kate's work always sounded dauntingly primitive, and her living conditions positively medieval. The pig-loos, for example, which she had described in her first letter home: rough holes cut into planks, where you squatted over pig-pens, so the pigs could gobble up the faeces. Or the almost daily power cuts when you ate in the dark, feeling your food Braille-fashion and swatting at the mosquitoes. Yet Kate seemed happy there – far happier than in all-mod-cons Carshalton. She was even making good progress in Hindi, though that only seemed to cut her off still further from a mother who'd barely scraped an O-level in French.

She put in the odd remark, feeling ignorant, as always, about the complexities of Indian life, and even about the geography of the country when Kate mentioned unheard-of places with unpronounceable names.

'So that's me, Mum, for what it's worth. And what have you been up to?'

Catherine hesitated. Her own life seemed so trivial in comparison. 'Well, I'm, er, running my own stall now. At least, I share it with a . . . a friend. We're selling bric-à-brac and junky things.'

'You know, it amazes me, Mum, to think of you working in a market.'

'Thanks very much!'

'No, I'm not knocking it. I admire you. It must take real guts to do something like that. I mean, *before*, you always had Dad, sort of cushioning you and making the decisions. So after he . . . he died, I thought . . . well – to put it bluntly, I thought you'd go to pieces. But you've been absolutely great.'

Catherine twined the coils of the phone-flex round her fingers. She hadn't realized how important Kate's approval was; how absurdly much it meant. Those words of praise were her medal of honour.

'And listen, Mum, I . . . I want to say I'm sorry.'

'What for?'

'Well, I wasn't much help when I came home for the funeral, was I? In fact, I probably made things worse.'

'Don't be silly.'

'Look, let's be . . . *real*, for once, okay? You see . . . someone

221

died over here. Just a few days ago. You know Nasreen, who works at the centre – well, her husband had a stroke. They were devoted to each other and incredibly kind to me. I've been to their home quite a bit and they always shower me with food and drink, even though they're living on the breadline. The first time I went, Nasreen made me a rice pudding. It had just one raisin in it, rather like we'd put a sixpence in a Christmas pudding. Needless to say, they made sure I got the raisin. In fact, they pretended they weren't hungry and gave me half the pudding! And they always pile sugar in my tea. "The more sugar the more we love you," Venu used to say. And he was so interested in my life, Mum. He'd ask me about England and about you and Andrew and everything. But . . . but last Tuesday he just keeled over and . . . that was it.'

'Oh, I'm sorry, darling. How terrible. Did he . . . ?'

'Don't interrupt. Forgive me – I didn't mean to be rude, Mum. But I'm trying to make a point. Venu's death was a ghastly shock, of course it was, and quite dreadful for poor Nasreen. But what's important was that it made me think about what *you* must have been through. I suppose at the time I didn't want to think about your feelings. I was angry with you and . . .'

'Angry?'

'Mm. Oh, it probably wasn't your fault. I was angry about a lot of stuff then. It's different now – *I*'m different. You can't help changing when you live here. There's so much more to be angry about – poverty, disease, all the big issues – so you forget the personal crap.'

Catherine continued fiddling with the phone-lead. She hadn't even known that Kate was angry. Had she ever understood her – the new Kate or the old? Even as a child, her daughter had been a rebel, questioning everything, challenging authority, determined to experiment. Gerry had found it a terrible trial and had sometimes exploded in fury, while *she* would try to mediate, for the sake of a quiet life. Kate had probably despised their attempts to make her conform. Perhaps she had gone to India not, as they'd assumed, to see the world and salve her conscience, but to escape a restricting home. Only now could she sympathize, and only because she was experimenting with her own life, even rebelling in a sense, though in a smaller and more selfish way than Kate. *She* had become the teenager: rootless, restive, strapped for cash, in a tizz about a boyfriend.

'It's funny, though,' Kate was saying. 'When I first came out here, I used to get frightfully worked up about seeing tiny kids scrabbling around the rubbish tips for scraps of mouldy food, or beggars with no legs pushing themselves on skateboards. I wanted to change the whole system, sweep away the horrors, single-handed, if necessary. God, was I arrogant!' Kate gave a mocking laugh. 'But I'm much more accepting these days. The Indians have taught me that. However dirt-poor they are, they don't complain or even seem to want to change their lives. It's a sort of . . . spiritual thing, I suppose, and it's had a huge effect on me. I've learned to be calmer and more balanced, and now I'm content to do just small things, instead of taking on the world. Shit – I'm sorry, Mum, you don't want to hear all this.'

'But I *do*, darling. I love to know how you feel and what's happening in your life. It makes me feel much closer to you.'

'But this call's costing you a bomb.'

'Don't worry. If you were here, I'd be spending money on you in one way or another, so at least let me give you the odd phone call.'

'Well, thanks, Mum. But I've gone miles off the point. I was trying to . . . apologize. About the funeral.'

'But you have – you did. And actually, I want to apologize myself. I don't think I ever really understood how . . . how . . .' She made herself go on, determined to be 'real', as Kate had put it; to broach subjects previously out of bounds; even acknowledge she'd been in the wrong. Yes, the phone bill would be ruinous, but at last they were managing to communicate.

They talked for several minutes before there was a pause in the conversation. Then Kate blurted out almost sheepishly, 'Mum, I *miss* you.'

Catherine was taken by surprise, and also touched. In all the time Kate had been away, she had never admitted that before.

'I know I've just been going on about acceptance, but some days are really shitty. I mean, the chaos in the streets can suddenly seem menacing rather than picturesque, and for no reason at all. And the heat can be awfully wearing. It's just beginning to build up again. Mind you, I'm lucky to be in the north. It's thirty degrees in Madras. And the way the men *stare* – I suppose I should be used to it by now, but sometimes it feels like mental rape. It's then I wish you were nearer, or that I was still at home with Mummy!'

'Oh, darling . . .'

'But then other days you feel fantastically alive. The colours are so bright out here and everything's ripe and sort of bursting. All your senses are sharper and it's – well *real* again, you might say.' Kate broke off, tutting to herself. 'Sorry to keep using that word, but I'm into that stuff at the moment – trying to figure out what's fake and what's worthwhile.'

Me too, thought Catherine. Though ironically, as her daughter learned acceptance *she* was increasingly kicking against the pricks.

'You know, another thing I miss, Mum, is hot buttered toast and Marmite.' Kate had changed the subject disconcertingly. 'Sometimes I think I could kill for a jar of Marmite.'

Catherine laughed. 'Well, I'd better send you some right away. I don't want you had up for murder!'

'Oh, would you, Mum? That'd be great. I love getting things from home. But it's about time I shut up and let you get a word in. How are things? How's Camden?'

'Fine. Well, actually, there is . . . something I'm a bit worried about. I'm seeing another man.' The words were out before she could stop them. She hadn't intended to mention Will – not yet, at any rate. She cleared her throat, embarrassed. 'I . . . didn't know how to tell you. Or whether you'd mind, or . . .'

Silence.

'Kate?'

'Yeah?'

'You *do* mind.'

'No, I don't, Mum. Well, I suppose I might have done a year ago. It would be like a betrayal of Dad. But not now.'

'Honestly?'

'Yes, honestly. Who is he?'

'A poet. He's called Will. Oh, it may not come to anything. It's only early days.'

'A poet – I say!' Kate was evidently impressed. 'Well, I hope it does work out, for your sake. It's pretty lonely on your own. I know. When things broke up with Paul, I . . .'

Catherine felt another pang of guilt. She had no idea that things had broken up with Paul. He was still little more than a name. There were whole acres of Kate's life she knew next to nothing about. But at least they had made a start.

'Mum, I'll have to go now, I'm afraid. Someone's waiting for me.'

'At this hour?'

'Yeah. Anyway, I'm worried about your bank balance!'

'It doesn't matter, darling. It's been lovely to have a nice long chat, for once. And next time I win the lottery, we'll talk for a whole day.'

'Great!'

'I'll phone again in a couple of weeks, okay?'

'Yes, fine. And listen, Mum – good luck with Will. I mean that.'

Catherine walked slowly back upstairs. She could hear the newsreader's voice echoing from Nicky's room. Bad news, most likely – it invariably was. But *she* was still on a high. She closed the bedroom door and stood looking at Kate's photograph. She didn't even know what her hair was like these days, or what sort of clothes she wore, or how tanned she was from the sun. She would ask her to send a recent photo, and replace the old, sanctimonious Kate with a new, approving daughter.

She ran a finger down the freckled cheek, traced the line of the mouth. Kate was her namesake, yet they hardly knew each other. So many things seemed to have got in the way: her own jealousy, for one. At least she could admit it now – the fact she had envied Kate her freedom and opportunities, even her shortened name. 'Kate' sounded easy-going, jauntily young and casual, compared with the stilted formality of 'Catherine'. But things could change – were changing for them both.

She stretched out on the bed, tired after all the driving and this morning's early start. Will's scarf was still round her neck. She tied it tighter and imagined him holding her close; their limbs entwined; their tongues exploring. She *would* invite him for a romantic meal next Saturday. After all, today she had taken the initiative and he'd responded instantly, so why not a second time? But she wouldn't borrow Nicky's double bed. She wanted to bring him to her own room, make him part of her new independent life.

Wriggling to the edge of the bed, she pictured him lying next to her, both of them gloriously naked. She closed her eyes, wondering what he'd do first – kiss her breasts or . . .

There was a sudden stealthy movement beside her, and she felt a soft head nudge her chest. She opened her eyes and saw not

Will but William, who had managed to sneak up unawares and join her on the bed.

'Look, Puss,' she laughed, fondling his ears, 'I'm afraid you're going to have your nose put out of joint. I know we usually sleep together, but I'm hoping to change the arrangements.'

William purred in blissful ignorance. There won't be room for three, she thought. It'll be a squash just with Will and me. But that might add to the fun. And it's going to be fun, she told herself, running a slow hand across her breasts. Hadn't her own daughter wished her luck?

18

Catherine screwed up her eyes against the driving snow as she picked her way between the excretions from the market: discarded paper plates with sludges of glutinous rice, dented beer cans, a pool of congealing vomit. This was Camden Town at its worst – cold, dark, litter-strewn. Jaunty music thumped from one of the half-dismantled stalls, as if defying the bad weather. *She* had packed up early, lugged half a dozen heavy boxes upstairs to the storage room; stripped her stall to its skeleton: a bare trestle table and four iron poles. Though if she'd had a modicum of sense, she wouldn't have ventured out today at all. The arctic weather had kept most customers at home, and she was severely out of pocket on the rental of the stall. Worse than that: when her back was turned for a moment someone had stolen an old Bush Bakelite radio – part of Mrs Pearson's booty. On days like this she was tempted to give up altogether and find a nice safe job in a centrally heated office, with a monthly pay cheque (plus pension plan) and a leisurely hour for lunch.

She turned into the High Street, where shops were closing, stalls being taken down. Progress was slow – she had to skirt round stallholders heaving crates of records into vans, or trundling racks of clothes across the pavement. The relentless snow settled indiscriminately on jeans, sweatshirts, lurex tops; soaked into cardboard boxes; stung against her eyes. Yet just a few days ago she had been basking in spring sunshine.

Slowly she trudged on, past a grim-faced man standing outside his shop: black beard, black hair, mean features. Brad had told her that all these shops were owned by Iranian gun-runners who smuggled in drugs with leather goods. (Apparently the strong smell of the leather confused the sniffer dogs.) And there were also tales of laundered money, bribery and corruption, stabbings, fatal feuds. She would never understand the contradictions of the market, however long she worked here. Outwardly it was a small and close community, but behind the scenes – according to the rumours – lurked a ruthless mafia. It was a friendly London village, yet also an alien land; a place where you could make your fortune or land up destitute.

All at once, a sinister figure stepped out of the shadows and loomed in front of her – a man in a long khaki coat with a swastika on the sleeve, and a triangular scar gouged across one cheek. Briskly she crossed the road – she didn't want cut-price cocaine, or a flick-knife in the ribs. She quickened her pace, trying to keep her footing in the scum of slushy snow. Thank God she had done the shopping last night and didn't have to make a detour to the supermarket. The only thing she needed was a bar of Cadbury's flake to decorate her mousse. She went into the first newsagent's she came to, glad of a brief respite from the bitter cold outside. On impulse, she picked up a box of After Eights – Will loved chocolate in every shape and form. She had insisted he borrow her car for the day. Harrow wasn't far, but it was a pig of a journey by tube and she wanted him back in good time. He had accepted her offer of dinner with alacrity and, though nothing had been said on either side, she was sure he understood that she was inviting him for more than simply a meal.

In the 'teen romance' display, she noticed a magazine with a young couple on the cover, kissing in dreamy close-up. Will had kissed her again on Thursday, just as passionately as the first time – a foretaste of this evening, she hoped. He might even stay the night. After all, they were running the stall together tomorrow, so it was a practical idea. Or maybe they *wouldn't* go to the market, but stay in bed all weekend, wickedly indulgent.

She paid for the chocolate and braved the elements once more, warmed by thoughts of Will. She had spent a fortune on the dinner, but she wanted everything perfect – food, wine, atmosphere. She'd already done half the cooking and given the house a thorough clean last night. All that was left to do was the main course and the vegetables, and a final tidy-up.

By the time she reached Gosforth Road, her coat was drenched, her jeans soggy up to the knees, and even her supposedly waterproof boots appeared to have leaked. But she would soon be out of her wet clothes and into a hot bath, and then she'd change into her low-necked fifties dress (which she'd bought cheap from the stall next to theirs).

With snow-numbed fingers, she managed to insert the key in the lock. As she pushed the front door open, she was greeted by a blast of noise: music, voices, laughter. She stood stock-still in astonishment – the house was meant to be empty. True, Nicky had changed her plans on account of the bad weather, but instead she'd gone to stay with a friend. And Jo and Darren had left first thing to catch an early train to Brockenhurst.

She took a cautious step inside, alarmed to see strangers in the hall. Had she come to the wrong house? It certainly wasn't in the state she'd left it this morning. There were pools of beer on the carpet, an array of cans and bottles on the hall table, wet coats flung across the banisters or bundled in the corner. No one seemed to have noticed her come in, so she remained where she was, gazing at the scene with increasing resentment. A group of girls were giggling and shrieking like schoolkids; two couples writhing to the music, another pair smooching on the staircase and three scruffy-looking men were involved in some sort of drinking contest. She was tempted to slip straight out again, but where could she go? And what about Will? It was impossible to contact him – she had no telephone number; no details beyond Harrow.

Darren suddenly shambled out of the sitting-room, his normally pale face flushed, his hair coming loose from its ribbon. 'Cath!' he called, weaving his way through the scrum of people and kissing her extravagantly. 'What are *you* doing here? Aren't you meant to be in Shoreham with Nick?'

'Nicky's not in Shoreham.'

'Where is she then? Oh, never mind – come and join the party.'

'*Party?*' She was forced to shout above the music. 'What on earth's going on?'

'Well, it's not really a party, just a bunch of friends.'

She glanced from a bra-less girl in a transparent top to a long-haired man spreadeagled on the floor. 'But why aren't you in Hampshire?'

'The train was cancelled. It's absolute bloody chaos at Waterloo. And more snow's forecast, so they advised us not to travel.' He took a swig from the bottle he was holding and wiped his mouth on his hand. 'So we thought we'd come back and ask a few people round for lunch.'

'Isn't a quarter to seven a trifle late for lunch?'

Her sarcasm was wasted on Darren, who merely beamed at her benignly. '*Late* lunch. We told them to bring bottles, and it turned into a bit of a bash. Then more friends dropped in and . . .'

'Hi, Catherine!' Darren's girlfriend Sarah breezed up behind him and put her arms round his waist. 'How's things?'

Another girl rushed over, wearing a canary-yellow miniskirt and sunglasses, as if she'd just flown in from Miami. 'Darren, Sally wants you. She's looking for more wine.'

'Okay – coming. Cath, this is Bec.'

'Rebecca, if you don't mind.'

'Rebecca, if you don't mind,' Darren mimicked with a giggle. 'And you must meet Ann and Liz. And that's Rob with the moustache. He's a real laugh!'

Catherine could have murdered every one of them, but she said a terse hello, then followed Darren into the kitchen, aghast to see more drunken strangers, slumped against the worktop and lounging at the table; more empty bottles cluttering every surface; the sink piled with dirty plates. The air was thick with cigarette smoke and the floor she had polished last night was littered with fag-ends, crisps and bits of cheese. Suddenly she caught sight of her chocolate mousse – or rather its bowl. All that remained was a brown puddle at the bottom.

She wrenched open the fridge door. On the shelf stood a solitary can of Fosters, a carton of coleslaw, and a knob of garlic sausage. Yet this morning she had left it full – full of her expensive, romantic food. She could understand the cooked food disappearing, but the raw salmon steaks had vanished too, *and* the ingredients for the sauce.

'Where's Jo?' she asked, tight-lipped, but Darren was nowhere to be seen and she was addressing the empty air.

She squeezed her way into the sitting-room, to be assaulted almost physically by the music. The ornaments on top of the piano were juddering and shaking to the rhythm of thunderous drums. The rug was rolled back and the furniture pushed to the sides of the room, and people were dancing as if in a trance – eyes closed, heads thrown back. She peered through the smoke-filled gloom, and eventually spotted Jo lying on the floor beside a character with straggly ginger hair and a moustache.

'Jo?'

'Oh, hello, Catherine. Back already?'

'Listen, I'm expecting a friend for dinner tonight and . . .'

Jo sat up on one elbow. Her lipstick was smudged and there was a red wine stain on her shirt. 'It's okay, she can join us.'

'*He.*'

'Well he, then – whoever. Now can I get back to *my* friend?' She tittered inanely, then snuggled next to the man again, running her hand across his chest.

'Jo, I want to know what's happened to my food.'

'What food?'

'I left a lot of stuff in the fridge last night and it's gone.'

'Well, it's nothing to do with me. I haven't a clue where it is. Anyway, I thought you were in Shoreham.'

'Oh, for heaven's sake, I was never *going* to Shoreham! Listen Jo, I spent all last night shopping and cooking and . . .'

'Well, *I* didn't know. I wasn't here last night. Darren and I had dinner at Alfredo's.'

'I'm talking about *now*. Surely you must have realized it wasn't just any old food. It took me hours to make that mousse.'

'There's no need to shout. *I* didn't eat the bloody mousse – or anything else of yours.'

'Who did then?'

'God knows. We bought our own nosh – cheese and pâté and stuff – but it ran out ages ago, so I suppose people helped themselves. Look, I'm sorry, but I can't be responsible for everyone else. But at least there's plenty of booze left, so give your friend a drink and I'm sure he won't complain.'

'Jo, I invited him for a quiet dinner – just the two of us.'

'Are we talking about Will, by any chance?'

'Yes, we are.'

'Well, he won't mind, I'm sure. He didn't strike me as the type to . . .'

'But *I* mind. That food cost a bomb, I'll have you know. I can't believe the whole lot's gone.'

'Honestly, Catherine, you're being a bit precious, aren't you? We *share* this house, in case you've forgotten, which means we all muck in.'

'That's rich, I must say, coming from you. You never pay your whack.'

Jo sprang to her feet indignantly. 'Oh, you're having a go at *me* now, are you?'

'Look, cool it, you two.' The ginger-haired man sat up, rubbing the back of his neck and patently embarrassed.

'You keep out of this, Geoff. It's between me and Catherine, okay?' Jo turned on Catherine again, her voice rising in contempt. 'If you don't like it here, you know where you can go – back to bloody suburbia, where you belong.'

Catherine flinched as if she'd been struck. Blinded by a haze of tears, she stumbled into the hall.

Someone touched her arm. 'What's wrong?'

'N . . . nothing.'

'Don't cry. What on earth's been going on?' It was Sarah, more sober than the others and sounding genuinely concerned.

Catherine found herself pouring out the story, blaming first Jo, then the weather, then herself.

'Don't worry,' Sarah said. 'We're leaving soon, in any case. We're going to the Jazz Café. Courtney Pine's playing there tonight and Rebecca's a great friend of the guitarist. So when we've pushed off you can have your dinner in peace.'

Catherine wiped her eyes on her sleeve. 'Is everyone going?'

'Most of us, I think. But if anybody's left, why don't *you* have the kitchen and they can stay in the sitting-room? That's what we do in my flat – share and share alike.'

'But Sarah, the food's been eaten – the stuff I got for Will.'

'Well, nip out and buy some more. Something quick.'

She didn't like to mention the expense – or the snow, for that matter. If she made any more objections she *would* sound prissy and suburban. 'All right,' she said weakly, buttoning up her wet coat again.

'And while you're gone, I'll explain to Darren and get him to shoo people out of the kitchen.'

'Won't that cause trouble, though?'

Sarah shrugged. 'I shouldn't worry. The sitting-room's much nicer anyway.'

'But Jo may . . .'

'Look, leave Jo to me, okay? Go on – off you go!'

The cold cut like a knife as she stepped into the dark. She

shivered in the porch, still brooding on Jo's spiteful remark. Nicky had told her not to take things so seriously; that rows were inevitable in a shared house and soon blew over anyway. None the less, her instinct was to stay away; to avoid Jo this evening, at least. Wouldn't it be more sensible to write the meal off altogether and have dinner out instead? Except who would pay? – like Will, she was practically skint. The weekly rent took a hefty chunk of her income, and both the car insurance and car tax had come up for renewal last month. Also she was perilously near the limit on her credit card and didn't want to run up debts, as Will was already doing. *He* had the extra burden of child maintenance to pay, on top of everything else. Of course, they could buy a simple snack and eat it in his flat, but he hadn't yet invited her there and she didn't like to force the issue. Besides, he'd said how much he was looking forward to a home-cooked meal and what a rare treat it would be.

She wound her scarf round her neck and steeled herself to set off to the shops. There was still time to retrieve the situation. She must cook a meal, as promised – it would just have to be less ambitious. And with any luck, by the time she returned with a second batch of food, Jo and all the others would be gone.

'Oh, you're back,' Jo scowled, as she let herself in. 'I thought you'd taken Will to Acacia bloody Avenue!'

Catherine ignored the taunt and walked into the kitchen, relieved to find it empty. There *were* sounds from the sitting-room and the music was still pounding on, but less manically than earlier. The hordes had disappeared, thank God. The kitchen was in the same awful mess, but she could cope with that, if only Jo would leave her in peace.

'There – all yours. You've got Darren to thank for that. Frankly, I find it a bloody cheek that you expect to monopolize the kitchen.'

'Look, Jo, I . . . I'm sorry – honestly.' On the way to the shops her anger had subsided and she regretted her own harsh words. After all, Jo and Darren hadn't known she was expecting someone to dinner. And it *was* their house long before she had appeared on the scene. 'It was a misunderstanding all round,' she said, with an attempt at a smile. 'I mean, *I* had no idea that anyone would be here and *you* didn't know about Will.'

'Well, even so, I don't see why we should be turfed out of the kitchen. My friends are here too, remember, even if we *are* restricted to the sitting-room.'

'Look, don't be silly. You can come in here if you want.'

'Wow, that *is* kind – granting me permission to step into my own kitchen.'

'Jo, you know I didn't mean that.'

'Well, what did you mean?'

'I'm trying to apologize. I've said I'm sorry. I *am*. Can't we forget the whole thing now?'

'No, I don't think we bloody can. It's not just tonight, Catherine – it goes much deeper than that. You don't fit in, can't you see? It's a generation thing. Basically we don't *need* a nagging mum here. Everyone thinks you're a fucking pain. So I reckon it's time you pissed off elsewhere.' With that, she turned on her heel and slammed out.

Catherine stood appalled, the shock-waves from the door resounding in the silence. So she was a nagging mother whom everyone despised. And they couldn't wait for her to leave. Did that mean Nicky too? But she and Nicky were friends – weren't they? She took a shaky step towards the door. Perhaps she *should* return to Stoneleigh, rather than stay where she was a 'fucking pain'. She shuddered at the words, their vicious crudity. Yet the thought of Stoneleigh induced a wave of panic. She had become a different person and couldn't just slot back into her old restricted life.

She leaned against the table, trying to get a grip on herself. She couldn't go anywhere – Will was arriving shortly. Unless she took him to Manor Close . . . just this evening, as a stop-gap. No, that was out of the question, with Andrew and Antonia sitting there in judgement.

Shakily, she began to unpack the carrier bags. There was nothing for it – she would have to go ahead and cook him dinner *here*. Yet she no longer felt at ease. She had become an interloper, as if the kitchen itself was hostile, recoiling from her presence. Its usual comfortable clutter had mushroomed sickeningly: the draining board a sordid mess of burnt pans and greasy plates; fag-ends and other debris floating on a scummy pool in the sink. Mechanically she let the plug out and turned on the tap, but there was no hot water left. She filled the kettle, still haunted by thoughts of Nicky. All those long, confiding talks – hadn't they meant anything? It was so difficult to know people's innermost feelings, even so-called friends. All at once she felt a desperate longing for Gerry – the security and comfort of being bonded to a partner for life, joined by sacred vows.

She blinked the tears back, fighting for control. It was no good agonizing about the past. She must forget Gerry for the moment – *and* Jo – and try to salvage the evening. It would help if she kept busy, rather than standing around indulging in self-pity. There were pistachio nuts to be shelled, garlic to be chopped and fried, mushrooms to prepare; not to mention all the clearing up. She had decided on pasta for the main course – quick and cheap, and easy to spice up with an exotic sauce. Her lovingly made pâté had gone the same way as the chocolate mousse, so she had bought some pâté to replace it, a chunk marked down to half-price. Dessert was ice cream, shop-bought again, but another home-made sauce would add a personal touch.

The aggressive bass pounded monotonously through the sitting-room wall, so she switched on Radio 2, deliberately to cocoon herself in schmaltzy lyrics and cheery patter – a reassurance that the world was safe. To the saccharine crooning of Barry Manilow she swept the floor, sluiced the worktops, and thrust empty cans and bottles into a bin-liner, along with cheese rinds, crisp-packets and wine-sodden lumps of bread. Then she tackled the washing-up, soon realizing that a single kettleful of hot water was nowhere near enough. However, after half an hour's hard work, the kitchen was more or less presentable. The smell of cigarette smoke still lingered unpleasantly, but short of opening the windows and letting in the freezing air, there wasn't much she could do about it. She'd have to douse herself with scent and hope that would counteract it.

But first the cooking. She hunted in vain for an egg whisk to whip up the ice-cream sauce, eventually making do with a fork and elbow grease. The Gosforth Road kitchen was lamentably short of decent equipment. At Carshalton she'd had all manner of gadgets, from a pasta-making machine to an ingenious tool for producing radish roses. And of course Antonia had electric mixers – electric everything. But here she couldn't find so much as a cheese grater, let alone a garlic press.

Suddenly the doorbell rang. *Will* – an hour early! The blood rushed to her cheeks. She must look an absolute sight: eyes red, hair unwashed, clothes dishevelled and damp. So much for her plan to greet him wearing a sexy dress and Arpège, not smelling of garlic and looking like a bag-lady.

She dashed into the hall, hoping to sneak upstairs before he actually came in. But someone was already opening the front door. She froze, one foot on the bottom step, instinctively closing her eyes, as if, ostrich-like, she could become invisible.

'Christ! What fucking awful weather. It's enough to freeze your balls off.'

She opened her eyes to see a mane of reddish hair, shoulder-length, in dreadlocks. Scott – not Will – scattering expletives as he heaved off his old army coat.

'Catherine!' He caught sight of her and staggered over, decidedly the worse for wear. He was dressed in a checked shirt, several sizes too large for him, tattered jeans and his usual hulking Doc Martens.

She muttered a hello, torn between relief at not being caught by Will, unwashed and unprepared, and horror at seeing Scott. No hope of a romantic evening with *him* on the premises. He had dropped in several times since the ill-fated visit to Manor Close and seemed to consider himself one of the family, so how could she bar him from the kitchen? He was already halfway there, presumably in search of food – he was always ravenous. *Her* food was on the table, easy pickings. She rushed to its defence, ignoring the front door bell. It would only be more friends of Jo and Darren and, for all she cared, they could stay out in the cold.

She yanked the mixing bowl out of his reach before he could stick his grubby fingers into the sauce. 'Listen, Scott, I'm expecting someone for dinner tonight and we want to be on our own. So I'd appreciate it if you could make yourself scarce.'

'Okay, okay. Don't get your knickers in a twist.' He was already investigating the contents of the fridge. 'It's just that I haven't had a fucking thing to eat all day.'

'Well, you can't have that pâté. *Or* the cheese.' She thrust the carton of coleslaw and the piece of garlic sausage into his hands. 'There you are – that's your lot.'

He sniffed the sausage and pulled a face. 'Bloody hell, it doesn't half pong! Darren invited me to lunch, I'll have you know.'

She turned off Nat King Cole, who had just launched into 'Some Enchanted Evening'. 'Scott, it's ten past eight – *dinner*-time.'

'Well, better late than never.' He prised the lid off the coleslaw and began gouging out lumps with his fingers, spattering shreds of greasy cabbage on the floor.

'Catherine . . .' Jo's head appeared round the door. 'It's Will.'

Oh *no*, she thought, paralysed. Will was standing in the doorway, staring at her and Scott. He caught her eye and quickly changed his dismayed expression into an unconvincing smile. She smiled back weakly, untying the tea-towel she had been using as a make-shift apron. Will's elegant get-up – Hungarian hussar jacket and dashing red shirt – only made her more ashamed of her own unkempt appearance.

'Er, sorry I'm early,' he said, taking a step towards her. 'The weather's so appalling we finished at seven, to let people get off home.'

'I . . . I'm afraid I'm a bit behind,' she stammered. 'I haven't had time to change yet or . . .' The words stumbled to a halt. She sounded peevish and begrudging – hardly a gracious welcome.

'That's okay, I'll sit and have a drink.'

'Me too,' said Scott, speaking through a mouthful of coleslaw and giving Will a cool appraising stare. 'Hi, mate! Like the gear. Though if you'd *told* me it was fancy dress, I'd have come in my Roman toga.'

'Scott, I'm sorry' – Catherine glared at him – 'but if you've come to see Darren, he's gone to the Jazz Café.'

'Shit! What a bummer. He asks me round, then pisses off before I fucking get here.'

'And Jo's friends are in the sitting-room. So perhaps you'd . . .'

'Sure. Just give us that drink.'

It suddenly dawned on her that there *wasn't* any drink. The hordes had helped themselves to her wine along with everything else and she had completely forgotten to buy any more. She prayed Will had brought a bottle with him – he was concealing *some*thing behind his back.

'Will, this is Scott,' she said tersely, realizing she hadn't introduced them. 'He's just going.'

Far from going, Scott seemed overcome by an unusual attack of good manners and stuck out a mayonnaise-smeared hand. Will, whose right hand was still behind his back, looked increasingly embarrassed. Then, with a sudden impulsive movement, he thrust a bunch of flowers into her arms.

'Fucking hell!' said Scott. 'I thought you were going to give those to *me*. Red roses,' he drawled, poking a finger into the middle of the bunch. 'And they say romance is dead!'

Catherine ignored him and babbled her thanks to Will. Normally she would have been delighted to receive a sheaf of out-of-season roses, but Scott was ruining everything. Anyway, you couldn't *drink* red roses. And it was worryingly extravagant. She had lent Will £10 yesterday – he must have blown the lot on this bouquet.

'Well, if you two lovebirds can't offer me a drink, I'll try Jo.' Scott ambled out of the kitchen, closing the door with his customary kick.

Good riddance, Catherine muttered, putting the flowers on the table. Needless to say she couldn't find a vase and had to make do with two milk bottles. She struggled with the tall and thorny stems, pricking her fingers in the process. Her mind was elsewhere – on the problem of the wine. There might be some left in one of the bottles in the hall. She darted out to check, but every bottle was empty and she had no intention of confronting Jo again. She stood outside the sitting-room door, seething with anger at the sounds of drunken laughter from within. She had spent her hard-earned money on good French wine which had disappeared down a bunch of strangers' throats. Jo and Darren would never pay her back; it was just part of 'mucking in', as Jo put it.

She glanced uncertainly from the kitchen to the stairs. Should she return to Will or take the chance to nip up to her room and change? But if she disappeared, even for a moment, Scott might wander back and help himself to the food, and bang would go a *second* three-course dinner.

Reluctantly she trailed back to the kitchen, where Will was sitting at the table, looking tired and rather forlorn. He must be perplexed, to say the least, at finding this scene of chaos.

'Will, listen . . .' She sat beside him. 'I ought to explain. There's been a bit of a disaster . . .'

Instantly his features crumpled into an expression of tragic concern, as if she were about to announce a death. She burst out laughing at the sight of his shocked face. It *wasn't* a disaster – simply a chapter of accidents.

'Catherine, what on earth's the matter?' He sounded more concerned than ever.

She couldn't speak for laughing. 'I . . . I'm sorry,' she gasped, finally regaining her composure. 'Don't look so bereft! It's not as bad as all that – well, so long as you don't mind pasta and half a can of lager instead of a bottle of Muscadet and fresh salmon.' She explained briefly what had happened, concluding with a giggle, 'You see, you were supposed to find me reclining on the sofa in my finery, with the salmon gently poaching in the oven and the wine chilling in the fridge. Instead of which, the spaghetti's still in its packet, *I* look like the wreck of the *Hesperus* and I can't even offer you a drink.'

Will leapt to his feet. 'I'll go and buy some wine,' he said. 'Then you can change into your finery and we'll do the cooking together. I can just about manage spaghetti.'

'Oh Will, you are a darling. But I'm afraid I haven't much cash.'

'Don't worry – I'm pretty sure I can rustle up a fiver.'

She saw him to the door, then dashed back to the kitchen, hid the food on the top shelf of the cupboard and ran upstairs to change. There was no time for a bath or even a shower, just off with her wet clothes, a quick dab with a flannel, then into her best dress. While she was spraying herself with scent, William emerged from under the bed, where he had evidently taken refuge. He stretched and yawned, then sat gazing at her reproachfully.

'Oh, *William*! – how awful – I'd forgotten all about you. And I bet nobody's bothered to feed you. Come on, you can have your supper while I'm cooking ours.' She picked him up and took him down to the kitchen, determined to get the meal under way before Will reappeared.

Amazingly, no one disturbed her for a blessed twenty minutes. She even dared to put the pâté on the table, plus the Melba toast and celery sticks. The ice-cream sauce sat cooling in its bowl, while the pasta bubbled contentedly on the hob and its rich garlicky sauce simmered in a second pan. She was just washing the salad when the doorbell rang. She dried her hands and went to let Will in.

'Special offer at Oddbins,' he said, brandishing two bottles. 'Quite decent stuff. And it's already chilled.'

'Lovely,' she said, feeling in control at last. The meal was almost ready and they could sit down and relax. Even William was purring, replete after his supper and curled up on the windowsill.

'And you look really beautiful,' he whispered, kissing the top of her head.

She smiled. They were on course again – for excitement, for

romance. She ushered him back to the kitchen and placed the roses on the table as a centrepiece. 'They're gorgeous, Will. Thank you.'

His face registered its pleasure as he gently fingered one of the blooms, the same deep crimson as his shirt. 'Shall I open the wine?' he asked.

'Yes please.' She handed him a corkscrew and found two halfway decent glasses – fluted crystal, and barely chipped at all.

'To poetry and love,' he said, gazing into her eyes as they clinked glasses.

'To poetry and love.' It sounded awfully highfalutin' on her lips, but she was so relieved to be alone with him, she would drink to anything he liked. Alas, there was little chance of any actual love-making – not with Jo and Scott around – but at least they could set the mood, get closer in other ways. She put her glass down, frowning. Just the thought of Jo was painful; brought back that horrendous row. Would she have to move out? Find some grotty bedsit? Or could she somehow . . . ?

No, this wasn't the time to be dwelling on her problems. She was entertaining Will and must concentrate on him. She took a breath to calm herself, and then a long draught of wine. 'How was the workshop?' she asked, edging her chair companionably closer.

'Oh, fantastic! Sometimes you're stuck with a room full of half-wits and you wonder why you bother. But today they all seemed bright. One woman was quite outstanding. She'd written this thing about a bulb planted deep in the earth, groping upwards month by month, and finally breaking through in the spring. But it finds everything's raw and bleak – you know, snow on the ground, like today, and apparently no hope of light and warmth. Oh, I realize it sounds a bit corny, but it *wasn't*, the way she did it. She used very stark images and an extremely simple style. She almost had us in tears.'

Catherine hid a smile. Yes, she could well imagine him weeping for a snowdrop; even for a clod of earth.

He sipped his wine, cupping his hands round the glass. 'It reminded me of something I wrote myself when I was only twelve or so – a rather harrowing poem about a bird in a cage. Of course, I identified with the bird. I felt so trapped, you see, at home.' His face reflected his theme: brows drawn down, eyes troubled. 'I made the mistake of showing it to my form-master. He said it was affected and how could I be unhappy with all my advantages? It's funny, isn't it, the way we don't like to admit how deeply children can suffer. Though *you*'d know more about that than I do, with your mother dying so young.'

'Actually, I think at the time I felt I *shouldn't* be too upset. Death's not easy to grasp when you're four and a half. Besides, the grown-ups kept telling me how happy Mummy was, and how she'd gone to live in this wonderful place with somebody called Jesus. Anyway, for a long, long time, I expected her to come back. My father kept all her things around, so it seemed a fairly reasonable idea.'

'God, you poor kid!'

'No, honestly, it wasn't all that bad.' She picked up a celery stick and nibbled it reflectively. 'Of course, it was completely different with Gerry. We'd been together so long, you see, and he was so much part of my life. I mean, even now, it sometimes all comes surging back, or I remember ghastly little details for no reason. The day of the funeral, for instance, was rubbish-collection day, and the street was full of black dustbin bags piled up higgledy-piggledy. And it suddenly struck me: that's what *Gerry* is – just a bag of bones to be disposed of.' She shivered. 'Gosh, I'm sorry, Will. This isn't quite the conversation for a nice relaxed dinner.'

'No, but it's *real*, and you know how I hate small talk.'

Catherine crunched her celery, remembering Kate's same use of that word 'real' just a few days ago. In fact, now she came to think about it, Kate and Will were alike in certain ways – uncompromising, idealistic, moody, generous, and occasionally infuriating.

'That was the trouble with my wife. She had this habit of avoiding any . . .'

They both jumped at the crash of a door. Someone had slammed out of the sitting-room and was hurtling up to the bathroom, heavy boots punishing the stairs. They exchanged a glance of commiseration. The situation had bonded them, she realized with relief. It was them against the rest; they safe in their little haven while the barbarians rampaged outside.

'You were saying about your wife,' she prompted, raising her voice above the music from next door.

'Ah, yes. Vanessa. She . . . she never allowed people to be miserable. She felt it was bad form – bad manners, if you like. Every problem should be dealt with, and if there wasn't a solution, then you simply shut up about it. Otherwise you'd drive your friends away. Friends were very important to her – more important than *me*, I often thought. I imagine she must be in her element now, with all the entertaining she and Julian do, in their gracious house with the wine-cellar, and their well-bred Hampstead neighbours saying what they're meant to say instead of what they really feel.'

'But Will, lots of people live like that. My son and his wife, for example. I suppose it's a very English sort of thing.' She thought of Jo again – *she* had made no bones about saying exactly what she felt. Perhaps there was a virtue in dissembling, after all. Still, her instinct was to change the subject. Poetry was fine, but not death, divorce and ex-wives, whatever Will (or Kate) might say about such things being 'real'. 'Shall we eat?' she suggested, knowing food would raise his spirits.

Eagerly he drew up his chair. 'This looks good,' he said, eyeing the pâté with interest, 'even if it's Sainsbury's.'

'Well, not as good as mine, I hope! I'll make some for you another time.'

'Great! I'll hold you to that. Meanwhile . . .' He cut himself a slice, spread some on the Melba toast and took a slow, appreciative mouthful. 'Mm, delicious.' He ate in silence for a few moments, totally absorbed, then wiped his mouth on a napkin. 'How was *your* day, Catherine – before all the disasters here, I mean? Was the market busy?'

'No, the worst I've ever known it. All I sold was that toast-rack from the bargain-box. One good thing, though – Brad's going to make me some earrings, for free.'

'I don't know how you can stand that man. He gives me the creeps.'

'Only because you're a snob,' she smiled.

Will grunted. '*He*'s the snob. I mean, the way he calls me "the Posho" behind my back.'

'Well, you are "the Posho" compared with him – public school and . . .'

'Only day school.'

'Maybe, but still a cut above Hackney Comprehensive, or wherever poor Brad went. Oh, by the way, he's just discovered that Camden Lock is on a direct ley-line to Glastonbury. Which means it's a very special place, with healing properties – or so he says.'

'Well, there he may be right. In fact, the older I get, the more open I am to such things. I'm sure there are dozens of forces working on us which we simply don't understand – perhaps *can't* understand, with our limited brains and our determination that everything must be rational. I heard some scientist the other day saying that unless a thing could be proved, it wasn't interesting. I ask you! That rules out love, and prayer, and God, and ghosts, and . . .'

'Ghosts?' said Scott, barging in at that moment. 'Where?'

The cat jumped off the sill in alarm and shot through the door, recognizing a past tormentor.

'Scott,' said Catherine, tight-lipped. 'I particularly asked you to stay out of the kitchen.'

'Keep your hair on, mate! Jo said I could do myself some beans on toast.'

'Oh, did she?'

'Yeah.' He was peering into the saucepans on the hob. 'But spaghetti'll do fine.'

She darted over to protect their dinner. 'I'm sorry, Scott, there isn't enough. And there's no bread left for toast.'

He slouched back to the table and picked up a piece of Melba toast. 'What's this stuff then?'

'That's for the pâté.'

'Great! I love pâté.'

Disguising her fury, she gave him the last chunk, knowing Will would have happily finished it. 'There! And you can have the rest of that toast. But would you please take it into the other room.'

'Just a sec.' Scott pulled up a chair and squeezed between the two of them. 'I want to ask you something. About your son.'

'What about him?'

'He's a lawyer, isn't he?'

'No. His wife is – a solicitor.'

Scott giggled, spraying bits of pâté on to the tablecloth. 'A solicitor! That's hilarious. I thought it was *breaking* the law to solicit.'

'Scott, I've already told you, Will and I . . .'

'Hang on, I'm getting there. There's this mate of mine – needs help.'

'What sort of help?'

'Well, let's just say he's got a bit of previous, so the fuzz picked on him and banged him up for nothing. And I wondered if your son's wife – what's her name? Angela, Amelia, whatever – could do us a favour and bail him out.'

'No, I'm sorry, she doesn't do criminal work.'

'Criminal? Danny's not a fucking criminal! He wasn't even there when the others . . .'

Catherine flung an imploring look at Will. He rose to his feet, a solid figure compared with Scott's weedy frame.

'Scott, it was great to meet you, but Catherine and I have an important business matter to discuss. I suggest your friend rings the Citizens' Advice Bureau first thing Monday morning. Meanwhile . . .' He gripped Scott's shoulder and steered him firmly to the door.

'Sodding hell!' Scott tried in vain to shrug off the restraining arm. 'There's no need for the Gestapo tactics, mate.'

Will ejected Scott in silence, then leaned against the door, to stop him coming back in.

'Thanks.' Catherine gave a nervous smile. 'Do you think I dare dish up the spaghetti?'

'Yeah, go ahead. It's all quiet outside.'

'*Quiet?*' Again there came the sound of feet crashing up the stairs, followed by a long wail from a saxophone.

'Comparatively quiet. This is quite a memorable meal, you know – eating under siege.'

'Oh, Will, I'm sorry. Shall we . . . ?'

'No, it's rather fun. It certainly gets the adrenalin going.'

'I've had quite enough adrenalin for one evening, thank you very much. Listen, Will, one day when the weather's better, let's drive out to the country and have a picnic somewhere really peaceful, with no one to disturb us but the birds. I'll make you your pâté then.'

'Wonderful! Tell you what, we could go to Kintbury again and call on Mags for tea.'

'Mm,' she said, noncommittally. She had envisaged a rather different afternoon, lying naked on soft grass, not taking tea with Auntie Mags. The wine must have affected her already. She longed to undo his shirt, touch his warm bare skin. 'Aren't you going to sit down?' she asked. 'You can't eat doing guard duty!'

He went back to his seat, fondling her neck as he passed. Emboldened, she leaned over and kissed him on the lips, tasting wine and pâté. He responded instantly, seeking out her tongue, drawing her closer, one hand straying to her breast. Her body jolted alight, as if it were a match he'd struck; a match burning down to his fingers. The food was getting cold, but she didn't care – they were generating heat enough themselves. He was stroking her breasts through the flimsy dress, and in her mind she was already sliding out of it, lying naked in the countryside: soft grass beneath, hot sun above – *Will* above, passionate, insistent . . .

Suddenly the door opened. ''Scuse me,' said a ringing voice. 'Just looking for some beer.' A girl in a pin-striped trouser suit charged past them to the fridge.

Catherine pulled away from Will, blushing like a schoolgirl. 'There's only one can left,' she mumbled.

'That'll do. Thanks!'

The fridge door banged shut, the can of beer hissed open, and the girl swept out again. 'I . . . I think we'd better get on with dinner,' Catherine whispered, giving Will an embarrassed smile. 'Without any more diversions, I mean.'

Will nodded, keeping an eye on the door. 'Sorry, I got carried away.'

Me too, she thought, returning to the sink where she had left the pasta to drain. If they ever got as far as the coffee and After Eights, it would be a miracle. 'Do you mind lukewarm spaghetti, Will, or shall I heat it up again?'

'No, come on, let's eat.'

She dished up the spaghetti, amused to see Will's eyes following her every movement – just like William's rapt absorption when she opened a tin of rabbit chunks. 'Wow, that smells good!' he said.

'I've put in masses of garlic – in your honour.' She laughed. 'It'll probably frighten off the customers tomorrow. No one'll come within yards of us.'

'Don't remind me of tomorrow,' he groaned. 'Queueing for a stall at the crack of dawn.'

I'll wake you, she longed to say, *if only you'll stay the night here*. Scott and co must leave at some point, surely. There would still be Jo and Darren, of course, but once they'd gone to bed . . .

Will was busy winding a long strand of spaghetti round and round his fork. He guided it into his mouth, but one end came loose and dangled from his lip. Impulsively she scooped it up for him, as she would do for a child. He reacted not as child but as lover, trapping her hand against his mouth and using the very tip of his tongue to give tiny butterfly licks to her palm. It was so incredibly erotic, she shut her eyes to savour the sensation undistracted. His tongue began to trace circles – slow, tantalizing circles which rippled through her whole body.

'Oh, Will,' she said. 'That feels quite amazing. I just can't tell you how . . .'

'Quick – in here!' ordered a peremptory voice outside. The door opened and Rebecca staggered in, supported by another girl. The pair stumbled to the sink, where Rebecca was noisily and repeatedly sick, emitting harrowing moans between each bout.

Catherine sat transfixed in horror and disgust. She saw Will push his plate away and clap his hand to his mouth. With a sharp intake of breath, she kicked her chair back and strode into the sitting-room. 'Jo!' she said through clenched teeth. 'I've had just about enough. I mean, people throwing up when we're in the middle of eating. It's absolutely repulsive!'

Jo uncurled herself from the sofa. 'Oh, it's *my* fault is it, if Rebecca's not well?'

'Not well? She's blind drunk.'

'Oh, for fuck's sake, Catherine, get off your high horse. I haven't noticed *you* being particularly abstemious. Anyway, you *wanted* to stay in the kitchen. We can't even get a glass of water and then you have the cheek to turn on me.'

'There's water in the bathroom.'

'Sure! Flog upstairs every time we're thirsty.'

'Don't be stupid. You've got plenty to drink down here.' Catherine gestured at the array of cans and bottles. 'But that's the trouble, isn't it? – everybody's smashed.'

She broke off as Will appeared, still clutching his paper napkin. Other people crowded round, muttering or shouting, trying to intervene; the ginger-headed man tugging at Jo's arm.

Jo shook him off and turned on Will instead. 'Don't *you* join in,' she snapped. 'I've told Catherine once already – if she doesn't like it here, she can bugger off. And the same applies to you.'

'How dare you speak to me like that!' Will looked like thunder and seemed to be preparing for a fight – taking off his jacket, rolling up his sleeves.

'I'll do what I bloody well like.' Jo's voice was shrill with rage. 'This is my house, not yours, and I suggest you both get out of it before I . . . I . . .' She marched over to the stereo and turned the volume up. The music, already deafening, now crescendoed to the point of pain.

Cries of complaint intensified the mayhem. Catherine closed her eyes. The floor seemed to be shaking beneath her feet as guitars jangled and brass shrieked.

Will seized her arm. 'That's it!' he yelled. 'We're going.'

'Going? *Where?*' Her throat hurt from trying to shout above the din.

He led her through the hall and wrenched open the front door. A blast of icy air curdled with the feverish heat of the music.

He slammed the door, half-skidded on the icy step. 'To my place,' he said grimly.

19

They crawled in silence along Kentish Town Road, Catherine shivering in her wisp of a dress. The windscreen wipers struggled ineffectually against the onslaught of snow, which had blanketed the pavements and shrouded stationary cars; the usually garish colours reduced to stark black and white. She glanced anxiously at Will's grim face. Of course, driving in such treacherous conditions took a lot of concentration, but she wished he'd say *something*. Was he angry with her as well as with Jo? Perhaps he regretted ever coming to dinner in the first place. And he must be as cold as she was, in thin trousers and a shirt. He had left his jacket at Gosforth Road, and she wasn't sure she'd find the courage to go back and retrieve it. Her new life had just disintegrated before her eyes and, unlike Will, she couldn't simply slam the door on the problem.

They had turned left at the traffic lights and were nosing along a narrow street lined with seedy shops: a newsagent's, a launderette, a video rental shop. Will pulled up and yanked the brake on, and she rubbed the misted window for her first glimpse of Tandoori Street, as he called it. Yes, there was the Shahee Mahal, and a second Indian restaurant just a little farther along. Although he had switched off the engine he made no move to get out, but sat motionless, hands resting on the steering wheel.

'Is this it?' she asked nervously.

'Yeah. *Maison Victor.*'

'What?'

With a tilt of his head, he indicated a neon sign above a hairdresser's, glowing feebly pink. Half its letters were missing: MA S N V CT R. The window was plastered with head shots of impossibly glamorous models, whose sneering features seemed to express the utmost disdain for their surroundings. 'I live above the shop.'

'That must be useful,' she smiled, 'if you need a haircut in a hurry.'

Her attempt at humour fell flat. 'They don't do men,' he muttered. 'Anyway, I wouldn't go there if you paid me. I hate living in this dump.'

'Will, it doesn't matter where you live. I don't mind.'

'Well, I *do*. I'm ashamed of the place, if you really want to know. I'd rather you didn't see it.'

'But I'm not the sort of person to judge people by their houses.'

'House? You must be joking. It's two poky rooms. And they're both out of action at the moment.'

'How d'you mean?'

'Oh, forget it.' He banged his fist against the steering wheel. 'It's all Vanessa's fault. If she hadn't left me, I wouldn't be reduced to . . . to . . .'

She laid a hand on top of his and gave it a reassuring squeeze. In spite of his petulance, she felt enormous relief. So *this* was the reason he hadn't asked her to his flat. A little squalor was nothing compared with what she had anticipated. 'Will, you should have seen the tips *we* lived in when Gerry and I were young.'

'Yes, but I'm *not* young. That's the point. I'll be forty in a year and a bit, and what have I achieved? Damn all.'

'Oh, Will, that isn't true. You've got your poetry and your son and . . .'

'My son? I hardly see him. And no wonder. Why the hell should he want to come here?'

'Maybe because you're his father and he loves you?'

He stared out sullenly at the whirling snow. Was her remark too banal to deserve an answer? She had a sense of being trapped with him – trapped in his ill humour and also physically confined inside the car; its steamed-up windows enclosing her; a wall of cold and darkness looming just beyond.

'Catherine,' he said tersely.

'What?'

'I love you.' He leaned across and kissed her, a brief but ardent kiss, then he pulled the keys out of the ignition. 'Come on, let's go in. Before we turn to ice.'

She touched her lips. He *loved* her? 'D . . . don't feel you have to ask me in,' she said, feeling suddenly apprehensive. 'I can always go back to Stoneleigh for the night.'

'No!' It was a shout. 'I've wanted you to come here all along. It's just that – well, I couldn't bear you to see the place before I'd smartened it up. And now . . . Oh, shit! It's all gone wrong.' He stumbled out and opened her door.

'Lord, it's cold!' She gasped as her summery shoes sank into the snow.

Quick as a flash he picked her up and carried her across the pavement to a small side door to the right of the shop.

'Will, no. I'm too heavy – put me down!'

'Rubbish! You're light as a feather.' With some difficulty, he used his free hand to unlock the door. His other arm was clasped tightly round her body. Ignoring her protests, he carried her into a dingy hallway, pushing the door to with his foot. There was an overwhelming smell of hair lacquer (not the anticipated curry) – a sweet, cloying smell which reminded her of pear drops. But all sensations dwindled in the shock of being carried. Her arms were round his neck, *his* arms pressing – painfully – under her crooked-up knees, as he staggered slowly up the steep and ill-lit stairs. His face was flushed, his breathing laboured. Whatever he might say, she was hardly a featherweight and the stairs were awkward to negotiate. It was embarrassing in a way, yet she felt a sort of triumph; struck once again by his mercurial change of mood, this time from petulant child to forceful father. *She* was now the child – blushing and giggling in his arms.

He set her down gently on the landing. 'Well, which is it to be?' he said, recovering his breath. 'The empty room or the junk room? Or shall we do a grand tour? – which will take precisely two minutes.'

'Yes, a grand tour, please.'

'Okay, we'll start with the bathroom. It's the only room that's in its normal state.' He switched on more lights and led her along a passage. '*Voilà!* How d'you like the colour scheme?'

'I've seen worse!' The bath and basin were rose pink, while the roses on the wallpaper were green. The tiles round the bath featured cockleshells, not flowers – brown to match the lino. The limp nylon curtains were polka-dotted; the toilet-seat cover crocheted and mauve.

'Do you share the bathroom?' she asked, noticing a plastic duck sitting at one end of the bath.

'No, I'm lucky there. The guy upstairs has his own shower. He's away this week, thank God.'

'Why, is he a problem?' she asked, recalling her earlier fear that he might have awkward neighbours.

'Oh, I can't complain. He *is* a bit weird, but at least he keeps himself to himself.'

She perched on the edge of the bath and picked up the plastic duck. 'Is this Sam's?'

'No, mine. I like a bit of company in the bath.'

Was that a veiled hint, she wondered? Although they were on their own – no weird lodger or Monsieur Victor in residence – he had made no move to kiss her again. She tried to imagine the pair of them in that narrow rose-pink bath; their bodies wedged together, enticingly naked and soapy . . .

'Okay, now I'll show you the room you were meant to see in all its glory.' He ushered her in, to bare floorboards and stripped walls. There were several uneven patches of fresh plaster, which gave the room a two-tone effect. However, the general feeling was ghostly – an empty shell awaiting colour and solidity. The only things in evidence were a couple of tins of paint standing on some newspaper with a jam jar full of brushes, and an ancient wooden stepladder propped against the window.

'I haven't got round to painting it yet. In fact, I'd no idea what I was letting myself in for. The plaster was terribly old and crumbly, and when I started stripping the wallpaper, some of it came away. The mess was unbelievable. Grey dust everywhere – in my eyes and throat and hair, even in my shoes. And getting to the bathroom meant wading through piles of debris, which stirred up even more dust. I had to spring-clean the whole damned flat. And as for the re-plastering, well, suffice it to say I wouldn't wish it on my worst enemy. Still, painting will be a piece of cake in comparison. I bought the paint last week.' He held up one of the tins. 'What do you think of the colour? I chose it with you in mind, of course.'

'Fantastic!' she said, smiling at the strip of purple – their lucky purple: a dusky shade, somewhere between his waistcoat and her dress. She was tremendously touched, not just by his choice of colour, but by the whole labour of love in itself. 'Oh, Will, I feel quite humbled. Fancy going to all this trouble just for me.'

'What do you mean, just for you? You're worth it, for God's sake. I only wish it was finished, then we'd have somewhere to sit. I've moved the furniture in here' – he backed out and opened the second door – 'although it was pretty cram-full already. It's where I store the market stuff. And there's a ramshackle room downstairs. Well, it really belongs to the hairdresser's, but they let me use it as a workshop.'

She gazed at the hotchpotch of chairs, chests, wash-stands, up-ended drawers, overflowing boxes, hardly knowing what to say or where to look. Fascinating objects crowded every available surface: china chamber pots, old clocks, biscuit tins, bronze statuettes, a tide of books, old and new. His bed, a small divan, was jammed against one wall and a two-ring cooker stood forlornly on the floor amid the clutter.

'I usually keep the room I live in fairly shipshape. But *this* is the room I'm living in at present, and it seems to have got out of hand. It's your fault, Catherine,' he added, almost accusingly. 'I wouldn't have done this for just anyone.'

'I'm, er, flattered,' she said, wishing he could have sounded a little more gracious. Still, considering what he'd been through, she could understand his pique.

'Sit down.' He patted the divan and switched on an electric fire, moving it closer to her legs. 'I'm afraid I can't offer you a drink. Well, milkless tea – that's all. If you're hungry, I've got chocolate swiss rolls – the little individual ones. Or cornflakes, if you don't mind them dry. And I'm sure there's a tin of soup somewhere.'

'No, honestly, I'm fine, Will. That pâté was quite filling.'

'Do you mind if *I* have something? Eating calms me down and I'm still a bit shaky after that almighty row. Funnily enough, Jo reminds me of Vanessa. Oh, not to look at – they're quite different – but they do have a similar line in invective.'

She had no desire to recall Jo's invective; indeed, even now she wasn't entirely sure what had sparked off the whole ghastly business. When she and Jo first met, they seemed to get on fine. Distractedly she ran a hand through her hair, suddenly realizing she had no comb with her – no mirror, make-up, change of clothes. All her possessions were at Gosforth Road, which meant she would *have* to go back to collect them.

'And the way she swears, Catherine – fuck this and bloody that. Vanessa's just the same. I find it really offensive.' Will opened the lid of what looked like a blanket-chest, and after a bit of delving, eventually found the cornflakes. He shook some from the packet into his hand and scooped them up with his tongue, crunching noisily.

She watched, amused, hoping they'd take his mind off Vanessa. He seemed intensely bitter about his marriage, but there was little she could say to help without knowing more of the facts. Indeed, some of his previous remarks had made her wonder if he wallowed in his wretchedness deliberately, to induce guilt in his ex-wife. A different sort of man would have done something about the state of the flat *before* this – for his son's sake, if not his own – rather than continuing to live in squalor for so long. Or was that judging him too harshly, especially as he said he'd done it for her? For all she knew, *he* might be the one who felt guilty, and his squalid surroundings a form of self-punishment. But, whatever else, she had come to see that he needed frequent doses of approval, perhaps as an antidote to his father's constant criticism.

'I think you're jolly brave to tackle this at all,' she said, as he sat beside her on the divan.

'Well, you did your room, didn't you? In fact, that's what shamed me into doing mine. I realized you'd lost your home, too, but you damn well made the best of it.'

'Maybe so, but what you're doing here is in a different league. I didn't have to paint, let alone re-plaster. It was really just a matter of the furnishings, not all this upheaval. I really do admire you.'

'*Do* you, Catherine? Honestly?'

'Yes.' Her emphatic nod turned into a shiver.

'Oh, lord – you're cold still. That fire's pathetic, isn't it? I'll get you a sweater.' He rummaged through a pile of clothes: unironed shirts, baggy jerseys, a pair of jeans with holes in the knees. Had Vanessa once looked after him, she wondered – patched holes, sewn on buttons – or was she too busy with her career? He held out a shaggy grey jersey. 'This is the best I can do, I'm afraid.'

'It's fine.' She pulled it over her head. It smelled slightly damp and came down past her knees, covering her sexy dress completely. It struck her that there was a funny side to the evening – they had fled from one shambles, only to arrive in another.

Will returned to his cornflakes, now eating them from the packet. She remembered her ice cream and its elaborate chocolate sauce. Would Scott have demolished it already?

'Are you sure you don't want any?' Will asked. 'They're the kind with honey and nuts. I bought them for Sam, but he's never here to eat them.'

She shook her head. 'Is that him as a baby?' she asked, pointing to the photo by the bed.

'Mm.'

'He's gorgeous.'

'His hair's slightly darker now, but he was ash-blond as a toddler. I'll show you if you like.' He unearthed a photo album from one of the cardboard boxes and placed it open on her lap. After a brief glance at Sam, she studied the child's exquisite mother – haughty cheekbones, cascade of golden hair, full lips, even teeth. Then she scanned the rest of the page: Vanessa and Will, Sam and Will, Vanessa, Sam and Will – touching one another, involved with one another, smiling and relaxed. The photos prompted a mixture of emotions: a sense of exclusion, even jealousy; niggling resentment of Vanessa's beauty, and a genuine concern for Will. He had lost so much – not just his family, but a house and garden which looked, frankly, prosperous.

'D'you want to see *me* as a baby?' he said, hovering by her shoulder.

'Oh, yes!'

He turned to the first page of the album and jabbed his finger at a small black and white snapshot.

'That could be anyone,' she objected, trying to make out the amorphous bundle in the pram.

He laughed. 'Well, it was wintertime and I was muffled to the ears. Here's another, with my father.'

Intrigued, she peered at the man. He was formally dressed – overdressed for a garden – but looked totally inoffensive. He was sitting in a deck chair, holding his son awkwardly on his knee. So this was the no-nonsense paterfamilias Will had talked so much about. The eyes were hidden by owlish spectacles, but he was smiling shyly; his face kind and even vulnerable; more a shrinking violet than a martinet. How odd, she thought, that this fleeting moment should be caught by the blink of a camera; a mere detail in this man's busy life given solidity and permanence. Posing for his photo in the garden, it could never have occurred to him that, thirty-eight years later, a stranger would be gazing at him; a woman who had kissed his son.

She leafed on through the album, glimpsing other children, other men and women – siblings, cousins, relatives? Unknown places, peopled by blurred strangers. Again she felt a longing for Gerry – that reassuring sense of having lived with him so long that their once-separate worlds had merged; every face and backdrop comfortingly familiar. She paused at a photo of Will, aged twelve, solemn in his blazer and school cap. When *that* was taken, she was already married, with a baby on the way. She shut the book abruptly.

'Something wrong?'

She reached out to him, suddenly wanting to be held – not by the schoolboy but by the strong and solid man. He put his arms around her and she closed her eyes, as if to block out the sad memories. He began to stroke her hair, rhythmically and sooth-ingly, and she relaxed into the rhythm, the soft lapping of his hand. His fingers paused on the nape of her neck, then slid an inch or two beneath the jersey.

'Shall we take this off?' he whispered. 'You feel warm now.'

She nodded, enclosed for an instant in musty grey wool as he drew the sweater gently over her head.

'That's a beautiful dress.' He traced the curve of its neckline with the lightest pressure of his thumb; a tantalizing semi-circle from one shoulder to the other. She could feel the eddies way, way down, as if he had already unzipped the dress and was running slow, skilled hands across her thighs. She *wanted* that; wanted him to touch her naked skin.

She moved her head a little and gave him a series of tiny, teasing kisses, just feathering his lips. He responded greedily, deepening the kiss, using teeth and tongue. Oh God, she thought, go *on*!

As if she had spoken aloud, he began easing down her zip, gazing at her hungrily as he fondled her bare shoulders. She smiled at him, encouraging, and he held her so close, she could feel the entire length of his body pressed against her own.

Then, without warning, he let go of her and stumbled to the window. 'It's no good,' he muttered bitterly. 'It won't work.'

She stared at him in astonishment, watching him drum his fingers on the sill. Why was he so angry? What in God's name had she done? She yanked her dress back up, leaving his sweater crumpled on the floor. Why should she be subjected to these insulting switches of mood? 'I'm sorry, Will,' she said coldly, 'but perhaps it would be better if I left.'

'No,' he shouted. 'Don't go.'

'But what's wrong, for heaven's sake? I mean, you were all over me in Kintbury. And you said you loved me only a few minutes ago. Yet now I seem to disgust you.'

'Are you crazy? I *adore* you. That's the trouble. If I didn't care so much, I wouldn't be in such a state.'

Mollified, she joined him at the window, putting out a tentative hand. 'Will, you'll have to explain. I just don't understand.'

'I . . . I can't. It's humiliating.'

'But you said the same about your flat and . . .'

'That was different.'

'But Will, I'm *here* now. And I wasn't shocked, was I?'

'No, I suppose not.'

'Well, can't you trust me again?'

He shook his head. 'This is really shameful.'

Was he HIV positive? she thought with a stab of fear. Or was there something wrong with his body – some injury or scar? She had to know. '*I* might not find it shameful,' she said softly.

He turned away, moving among the boxes, as if too nervous to keep still. 'Listen, Catherine, last time I tried to make love – well, it . . . it was a total bloody disaster. I . . . never saw the girl again.' He jabbed his foot against a box, his voice rising in indignation. 'That's why I can't forgive Vanessa.'

'But why should . . . ?'

'No, please don't interrupt. This isn't easy, and I want you to understand. I lost my nerve, you see. That's all it was. I'm sure. Vanessa destroyed my confidence. Completely. She told me I was useless in bed. I *wasn't* useless. Not then. But now – well, I daren't even take the risk.' He picked up a wooden letter-rack, gripping it tightly in both hands. 'I keep telling myself she only said it out of spite. Or to shut me up, so she could win the argument. But that doesn't seem to help. She's passed judgement and it's set in steel. Well, it might have been okay – with *you*. I was just beginning to feel more hopeful.' Again he broke off, then turned to face her, banging down the letter-rack. 'But that appalling scene with Jo brought the whole thing back. You see, Vanessa and I were having a row like that when . . .'

'Oh, Will, people often say things they don't mean in the heat of an argument.' She squeezed his hand reassuringly. 'After all, the way you kiss me is anything but useless. I'd say you were an expert.'

He gazed at her a moment in mingled hope and disbelief. Then he lunged towards her and kissed her, violently.

'Will, you're hurting,' she protested, trying to pull away.

'There, you see. I'm doing it all wrong.' He let her go, his face abject. 'Just like Vanessa said.'

'It's not that, Will, it's . . .'

'Don't say it. I can't bear you judging me too.'

She let out an exasperated sigh. Whatever she said, he was bound to take it the wrong way. 'Excuse me,' she said, backing towards the door. 'I . . . I must go to the loo.' She needed an escape. There seemed to be a jinx on the evening and things might get worse still. If he *was* a disaster in bed, his confidence would be shot to pieces and she would feel guilty in turn. She suddenly remembered the evening with Simon: another traumatic occasion when she had taken refuge in a bathroom and sat in shivering isolation, feeling a total failure. Tonight was even worse, though. She cared about Will, as she'd never done for Simon; had let herself get close to him. And then there was the terrible set-to with Jo . . .

She looped back the nylon curtain and stared out at the dark, feeling almost homesick for her safe nun's cell at Stoneleigh: lights out at 10.30 and a regime of ordered peace; no moody, troublesome men; no vindictive house-mates. Andrew and Antonia might be rather stuffy, but at least they didn't indulge in histrionics.

She remained dithering at the window, trying to decide whether to cut her losses and go back to Manor Close. But it was still snowing hard and the roads would be treacherous. Besides, she hadn't the heart to abandon Will – nor the strength for the inevitable showdown.

She trailed back to the other room and stood miserably in the doorway.

'Oh, Catherine . . .' He approached her nervously, like a cringing dog expecting to be whipped. 'You look so tired and . . .'

'I *am* tired. It's been one hell of a day.'

'Look, lie down for a while. I won't say a word, I promise.'

She smiled, despite herself. The prospect of silence seemed unlikely in the extreme.

'Come on – over here.' He led her to the divan and pulled back the faded coverlet.

'You must be tired as well,' she said, too weary to protest.

'Shattered.'

She moved over to make room for him, but turned resolutely to the wall. This was to be strictly a rest, not an attempt to prove Vanessa right or wrong.

'I'll turn the light off, shall I, then perhaps you'll be able to sleep.'

She nodded. If she pretended to sleep, he might keep his promise. Real sleep was out of the question. Not only had she lost her home, but now, it seemed, Will too. How could they have any kind of relationship, given all his hang-ups? And that in turn jeopardized her work. It would be impossible to share a stall, with him feeling hurt and rejected. So she was back to square one: rootless, manless, jobless. She turned on to her back, aware of him lying rigid beside her, his black cloud of depression enveloping them both. Again her thoughts strayed to Andrew – his sheer uncomplicated sanity. She was lucky to have him. *And* Kate. It would be daylight in Gurgaon: strong colours, brilliant sunshine. Kate had wished her luck with Will, but her run of good luck had ended – that was clear enough. She stared up at the shadowy ceiling, shivering in the dark. Next time she phoned her daughter, there would be nothing to report except loneliness and failure.

'Good night,' she murmured to Will, realizing it was, in fact, the worst night she'd had in months.

20

'Oh, Will, I just can't tell you . . . That was absolutely . . .' It was difficult to speak. Her heart was thumping in her chest and her whole body seemed on fire. She eased her thigh from under his. His hot, damp skin felt wonderful against her own, but her leg was beginning to hurt.

'Are you okay?' he whispered.

She nodded, running her hand along the inside of his thigh. Excited, he began covering her with kisses: the last, delicious course of the meal; his lips nuzzling her throat, then moving slowly down across her breasts.

She lay marvelling at the silence; silence after uproar. He had been making an incredible noise; baying like an animal. And, after her initial sense of shock, she had found herself making the same wild, jungle noises, as if a different person had taken over her body – some abandoned, flagrant woman, spurred on by his cries.

He gave her a last teasing kiss, then sat up on one elbow. 'I think we ought to celebrate. There's no champagne, I'm afraid, but I *can* offer you a chocolate swiss roll and a bowl of mushroom soup.'

'At this hour?'

'What time is it?'

'Heaven knows.'

He fumbled for the bedside clock. She remembered watching its illuminated hands last night, moving almost imperceptibly: twenty past eleven, twenty-five past, half past . . .

'Good God!' He shook the clock in disbelief. 'It's quarter to five. Breakfast time, definitely.'

'Okay, but not the soup. Could I have tea instead?'

259

'Certainly, *madame*. It's on its way.' He leapt out of bed, as fresh as after eight solid hours' sleep, and switched on the bedside lamp.

She gazed, enchanted, at the weird shapes and looming shadows. This crazy cluttered room had become a sort of fairy palace where frogs turned into princes. 'Can I help?' she murmured.

'No, you're not to lift a finger.'

She watched him plug in the kettle, still fascinated by his naked body – the broad shoulders and muscly arms, the dark hair on his chest and stomach, even on his back. His penis looked so vulnerable compared with the way it had felt inside her: solid and substantial then, and every bit as dramatic as its owner. She smiled at the sight of their clothes entangled on the floor; his flamboyant red shirt straddled over her bra and pants, his trousers inside out, her dress sprawled languidly. They had thrown them off anyhow, not even bothering with a condom. She hadn't cared about the risks. There *were* no risks, she felt now, as she lay basking in the afterglow.

'I'm just going to wash the mugs,' Will said. 'Don't move.'

'I couldn't if I tried. You've worn me out!' As he picked his way towards the door, she could hardly bear to let him go, even for a minute. She wanted his body dovetailed back with hers: she pinioned underneath, or him kneeling behind, or standing at the foot of the bed with her spread-eagled on her stomach. There was no part of him she didn't like – not his rough chin (his stubble grew at an alarming pace at night); nor the darling strand of hair which refused to lie flat but curled obstinately over his forehead; nor even his horny toenails.

When he reappeared at the door it was as if the sun had come out again, dispelling the chilly gloom. She hugged her chest, aware that she was reacting like the heroine of some Mills & Boon romance. Though of course the surroundings would be rather different – a luxurious double bed, not a three-foot-six divan with broken springs. And he would be handing her a crystal dish of out-of-season strawberries, not a paint-stained carton of swiss rolls.

'Three each,' he said, counting like a child. 'But you can have all six if you want. I'd give you a diamond, Catherine, if I could – no, a diamond *mine*. With a bevy of slaves to work it for you.'

'That's politically incorrect,' she laughed. 'So someone would be bound to close it down.'

'Oh, I *am* incorrect, no question. I remember going to some arty-farty do where a woman actually objected to "Three Blind

Mice". She insisted they were "visually impaired". Which plays havoc with the scansion.' He sang, to demonstrate, grimacing at the rhythm. 'Three *visually impaired* mice, Three *visually impaired* mice . . .'

Grinning, she countered with, 'Three *blind* mice, Three *blind* mice . . .'

They continued singing; breaking down in giggles, only to start again. Will mimed the actions exuberantly, wielding a chocolate swiss roll in lieu of a carving knife.

They raised their voices, each trying to outsing the other:

'. . . *blind* mice . . .'

'. . . visually impaired . . .'

'. . . *blind* mice . . .'

'. . . visually impaired . . .'

'Oh lord!' she said, clapping a hand over her mouth. 'Your neighbours, Will! We've been making a hell of a din for hours.'

'Bugger the neighbours! They probably enjoyed it. Did *you?*' he asked, a hint of his old anxiety returning.

'Will, you know I did.'

'You might have been pretending.'

She coaxed him down on the bed and put her arms around him. 'Shall I tell you something, Will? I've never felt so . . . so *real* before as I did with you just now.' She deliberately echoed his word – and Kate's – though she was reluctant to explain it further, for fear of sounding disloyal to Gerry. But she realized now she had been inhibited for years, gradually slipping into a bourgeois role to fit her bourgeois setting. The tiger she'd been in her youth had dwindled into a domestic cat – a placid moggy who mustn't go wild in bed, in case she woke the children, or disturbed the next-door neighbours, or exhausted an already pressured husband.

'It's as if you've let me out of my cage,' she said simply.

'You didn't need much encouragement!' Will handed her the carton of swiss rolls. 'I'm starving, aren't you? I'll make the tea and then we can have a picnic.'

She helped herself, peeling back the silver foil. It might have been a diamond, so euphoric did she feel; every tiny sensation intensified as she bit into the glossy shell: the rich, dark smell of chocolate; the ooze of squishy cream; the caress of sponge soft against her tongue.

She finished two in succession, then lay back, sated, and not just from swiss rolls. How extraordinary that Vanessa should be so scathing about Will's performance. In fact, many things he'd told her seemed to be misleading: the tyrant father a shy myopic family man; the useless lover a stud. No, that was far too crude a word for the imaginative and tender poet who had gently woken her in the night because she was screaming in her sleep, and swiftly turned the nightmare into bliss. It was so different from the fiasco with Simon. She felt adored and cherished: her body accepted – stretch marks, appendicitis scar and all – as she accepted his. And as for any age difference, *she* was now the younger, the impassioned seventeen-year-old again. How dare Jo call her a dreary nagging mother! Not that she was worrying about Jo – not now, not after Will.

'Tea up.' He was approaching with the mugs, which he put carefully on the bedside table. 'Just look at you,' he said with mock severity. 'There's chocolate all down your front.'

'Where?' She squinted awkwardly at her chest, but he was already leaning down to scoop up the fragments with his tongue.

He licked his lips – just like his feline namesake, she thought, after a saucerful of milk. 'What luck,' he grinned, 'to meet a woman with chocolate breasts.'

'*And* a chocolate tummy,' she added, as he retrieved a last crumb from her navel.

'Oh, Catherine.' He gazed down at her. 'You look so exciting like that.'

'You too.' She reached out to touch his stiffening prick. Incredible that he could be hard again already. It had been years since Gerry could manage an encore. The comparison seemed terribly unfair, but this was more than just a sexual thing. Will was restoring her youth, stripping away the last dry husks of decorum and convention, and allowing the real Catherine to break free.

'Let's lie close,' he murmured, stretching out beside her. 'I want to just . . . just *bask* in you a moment.' His next words were swallowed up in a sudden gigantic yawn. 'Hell, I'm sorry. That took me by surprise.'

She laughed. 'I don't wonder you're tired, considering all that exercise! And did you get any sleep last night?'

He shook his head.

'You'll be like a zombie at the market tomorrow.'

Slowly he sat up and ran a hand through his wonderfully tousled hair. 'Catherine . . .'

'Mm?'

'We're not going to the market. I've just decided.'

'But what about . . . ?'

He kissed the rest of her sentence away. 'We can't get there – it's impossible. We're snowed up in the wilds of Scotland and there's absolutely no chance of a thaw. The weathermen are predicting another ice age, and it's on its way already, by the look of it. But *we*'re all right, curled up snug together. So' – he kissed her right breast – 'we can make love all day Sunday. And' – he kissed her left breast – 'the whole of Sunday night.' His fingers slipped between her legs. 'And all next week. In fact,' he whispered, positioning himself astride her and sliding gently in, 'we can make love for ever and ever.'

21

'Nicky, please be honest. It's better that I know. Do you find me . . . well – a pain, to put it bluntly? And would you rather I moved out?'

'Catherine, you're an *angel*! And there's no question of you moving out. Don't even think about it. Things have improved no end since you've been around.'

'Yes, but Jo . . .'

'Look' – Nicky pushed her cup away and folded her arms squarely on the table – 'Jo cocked up, okay? She admits she behaved appallingly badly. But what you need to understand is why.'

'I *do* understand. Because I'm a fusspot, and too old, and expect to have the place to myself and . . .'

'No – all wrong.'

'What is it then?'

Nicky lowered her voice and gave a wary glance to left and right, although there was no one actually sitting within earshot. 'Well, first of all, she's a tad jealous – about Will. She's the literary one, so she thinks *she* should be dating a poet. But that's a detail. The main reason she was in such a state on Saturday was that her period was late and she thought she was pregnant, by that Italian shit.'

'Pregnant? But she told us that was all over.'

'Well, yes, it only lasted ten days. But apparently he was in London for the Forsythe Prize. And she was so over the moon to see him again, she promptly fell into bed with him and of course the silly idiot let him do it without a Durex.'

Catherine felt herself blushing, knowing *she* had done the same. If you were smitten with a man, it was all too gloriously easy to take risks.

'Anyway, it was a false alarm, thank God.' Nicky waved away the waiter, who was approaching with more coffee. 'But she didn't know that till last night. On Saturday she was still fearing the worst and I'm afraid you caught the brunt of it.'

'Poor Jo! I'd no idea. And actually she did seem rather involved with *another* man on Saturday. Geoff, I think his name was. Ginger hair, funny little beard.'

'Oh, Geoff's just an old friend.' Nicky shrugged dismissively. 'She was probably only using him to drown her sorrows.'

'But, Nicky, between you and me, she seemed to be all over him.'

'Well, *I* don't know. Jo's a law unto herself when it comes to men – or to most things, for that matter. Anyway, as far as you're concerned, she feels guilty as all hell. So I suggest you get in there quick and heal the rift.'

'Oh I will, of course I will.' Catherine drained her coffee. It had gone cold and scummy, but it tasted like nectar, so great was her relief that she wasn't banished from Gosforth Road. She hadn't dared go back there without talking to Nicky first, so she had arranged to meet her straight from work this evening. Admittedly the intervening two days spent camping out in Will's flat had provided exquisite compensations.

Nicky was studying the menu. 'Now we've sorted that out, will you change your mind and have something to eat?'

'No, honestly, I'm fine.' She didn't like to admit that money was a problem. The Café Delancey wasn't cheap, though Nicky was paying for the coffee, thank heavens.

'We could just have something simple, like poached trout. *My* treat.'

'Poached trout's hardly simple. Anyway, you can't keep treating me, Nicky. It's not fair.'

'Yes, but neither is it fair that I'm paid vastly more than you. Go on – as a favour, to ease my pangs of conscience!'

Catherine laughed. 'Okay, it sounds delicious. But I insist on cooking you dinner in return.'

'It beats me how you can talk about cooking dinner, after what you've just been through.'

'Well, I'll do some ironing for you then.'

'We'll see. Anyway, let's choose the wine. And don't start telling me you'd rather have water, like you did last time we went out. I hate drinking on my own and we don't have to keep economizing. That's one of the few advantages of my job.'

'All right, I'd love some wine.' Catherine smiled her thanks. She and Will had been existing mainly on bread and peanut butter. He had ventured out just once to get supplies, but the dire state of their joint finances meant they couldn't run to luxuries like wine. The car alone had set them back a hundred pounds, and that on top of the tax and insurance. They were using it far more now, on buying trips for the stall, and it had needed two new tyres to get through its MOT. Still, peanut butter had never tasted so blissful, especially when eaten in bed, or licked off Will's warm fingers . . .

Leaving Nicky to discuss wines with the waiter, she did a few quick calculations in her head. Her period was due this Thursday, so the risk she had run was minimal. Still she would have to take precautions in the future. She tried to imagine being pregnant at forty-four, breaking the news to Andrew and Antonia that she was going to be a single parent and live on social security.

'What d'you think, Catherine – the Sancerre or the Saint Veran?'

'Oh, er . . . either would be fine.' She must stop mooning in an erotic dream and concentrate on Nicky. 'How was *your* weekend?' she asked.

'Fairly tame compared with yours, it seems! And of course, I was miffed about missing my windsurfing. Still, only another month and I'll be off to the Bitter End.'

'Where?'

'The Bitter End. Apparently the name's rather tongue in cheek, but they say it's *the* place to stay on Virgin Gorda.'

'Oh, your holiday – I see. You haven't mentioned it for so long, I'd forgotten all about it.'

'Well, I suppose it's conscience again. I feel like a bloated capitalist swanning off to the Caribbean while you slave all day at the market in the snow.'

'It'd better not be snowing in mid-April.'

'You never know, in England. It'll be a perfect eighty degrees out there. I just wish you could come with me.'

'But I'd never *see* you, Nicky. You'd be jumping the waves from dawn to dusk, or whatever it is you do.'

Nicky laughed. 'Dead right. But perhaps you and Will can get away at Easter, if only for a couple of days?'

'No chance. The market will be hectic then, so everyone tells me – hordes of foreign tourists pouring in. We'd be crazy to miss all those lovely gullible customers! Still, I may be going to Dorset a week or two *before* Easter. Keep your fingers crossed! Will's doing a reading at a festival in Sherborne and he says he can probably sneak me into his hotel.'

'There you are, you see. No wonder I feel guilty about having a whole luxurious lodge to myself – *and* right bang on the beach – when you're sleeping in the wardrobe or something.'

'Oh, I don't think it'll be as bad as that. Actually, Will says he's lucky to get any accommodation. He's had to sleep in the car before now, apparently. Some of these festivals are run on a shoestring.'

'Well at least Dorset's lovely country. I used to go windsurfing at Swanage.'

'I doubt if we'll see much of the country. Apart from his reading, he has to attend several other events. And then he insists on doing a tour of the local junk shops, not to mention the odd boot fair. The prices should be lower there than London.'

'All work and no play,' Nicky tutted, nibbling a grissini stick.

'*You* can talk!' Catherine laughed, knowing that if she and Will were sharing a bed there would be a great deal of play, even if they had to forfeit sleep. Last night they'd barely slept – again – too excited, too churned up. He had lain beside her in the dark, asking her every few minutes if she had managed to drop off yet, and after about her seventh 'no' he had suddenly got up, groped over to the bureau and returned with a slim notebook. He then proceeded to read her his 'Catherine' poem, clearing his throat nervously and stumbling over the lines, as if afraid it wasn't up to scratch. She couldn't judge it as a critic would – all she knew was that some passages were so sort of . . . raw they had sent shivers through her body. It was unlike any poem she'd heard: not conventionally romantic but wild, fierce, yearning, sad. She wanted to hear it a second time, but he had hardly finished reading when he began to write another poem, there and then, sitting on the bed stark naked and scribbling in the notebook. Hardly daring to breathe, she had watched his pencil flying over the page, sometimes stopping abruptly or crossing out so vehemently it all but ripped the paper, then starting again, full speed. She felt a certain awe in witnessing the creative process – and an immense pride that she had inspired it.

'Ah, here's the food,' said Nicky. 'I'm afraid I'll have to eat and run. I've got to work tonight, worse luck. Wayne's desperate for some ideas for a new shampoo commercial. And he wants them on his desk by ten o'clock tomorrow.'

'*I*'ve got an idea.' Catherine waited for the plates to be unloaded, then continued in an appropriately stagy voice, 'there's this guy, about thirty-eight – divorced, dark-haired, impulsive – decides to renovate his flat. He starts ripping off the wallpaper, but the plaster's old and crumbles away with the paper. There's dust all over the place, and all over *him*, especially his hair, which goes completely grey. But – wait for it! – one wash with your wonder shampoo and his girlfriend's jumping into the plaster-spattered bed with him, running her hands through his thick black curly hair . . .'

Nicky looked at her in amazement. 'That's not bad, you know. It might just work.'

'Glad to be of help. And I only charge a modest fee! Of course, I'd be happy to accept a post at HHA – Creative Director, say, on a hundred grand a year.'

'I'll have a word with the chairman,' Nicky laughed. 'Now come on, let's tuck in. We haven't got much time.'

Catherine attacked her fish as Will would, eagerly and sensuously, allowing each delicious mouthful to linger on her tongue. She took a piece of bread to mop up some of the sauce, imagining herself a soft slice of farmhouse loaf soaking up Will's juices. Already he had made her more imaginative – she had a gift for poetic imagery, he said, which ought to be encouraged.

Nicky was eating fast, deftly removing the trout from its bone. 'I am fond of this place, aren't you?'

'Mm,' said Catherine, feeling her crust and crumb dissolve in Will's hot mouth and slide into his bloodstream. Today she would have found even Fred's Caff enticing. But yes, she *was* fond of the place, although she didn't come here as often as the others – or only for a coffee. Even so, £1.60 was a bit steep for a cappuccino, compared with 30p for a mug of milky coffee on Rollo's market stall. Of course, you were paying for the decor: the elegant green china and marble table-tops, the posies of fresh flowers on every table, the Gallic singer crooning in the background. And there was always a bevy of attentive waiters, in black bow ties and long, white, French-style aprons. She watched one gliding past – a younger version of Will – and pictured him without his clothes:

the springy whorls of dark hair on his chest, running down to . . .

'How d'you like the fish, Catherine?'

'It's . . . wonderful.'

Nicky waved her fork at Catherine's plate. 'Well, you wouldn't think so! You've hardly touched it.'

Penitently she bolted down three mouthfuls in succession. It was hard to keep her mind off Will when he was only a mile away up the road. She could be there in fifteen minutes, back in his arms, his bed.

'Look, if you want to stay and eat in peace, Catherine, please do. I don't want to give you indigestion. I can settle up before I go and leave you to have some pudding. The cheesecake's really something here.'

'No, I'd rather come back with you, Nicky. I'm still a bit nervous about Jo, to tell the truth, so it would help if you were there, to sort of . . . smooth things over.'

'God, *she*'s the one who should be nervous. But don't worry, I'll do what I can – maybe make a bit of a joke of it. Leave it to Auntie Nicky.'

'She has got a point, you know.' Catherine was looking at the other tables. Every face seemed young – certainly there was no one over forty. 'Let's face it, Nicky, I *am* a different generation. Jo's almost the same age as Andrew, so it's not surprising she sees me as a dreary nagging mother.'

'Well, I know she's had a problem with her own mother, so that might be a factor, I suppose. But you're anything but dreary. And you never nag. Well, except about the cat – whether we've fed him when you're out.'

Catherine gave a gasp of horror. 'Oh my God! I'd forgotten all about him. He's probably dead of starvation by now. Quick, we must get back.'

'Honestly, Catherine, you dawdle over your food when I need to go home to work, but one mention of your precious cat and you can't get out of here fast enough!'

'But this is a matter of life and death, not a mere shampoo.'

'What do you mean, "a mere shampoo"? It'll be curtains for *me* if I don't come up with something by the morning.'

Catherine subsided in her seat. William could survive without her a few minutes longer. 'Okay, let me have another shot.' She put her fork down, frowning in concentration. 'Yes, I've got it!

There's this chap about thirty-eight – divorced, dark-haired, impulsive – who's giving a poetry reading. But hardly anyone turns up. And although he's rather dishy, he does look an awful mess – scruffy clothes, dirty unkempt hair. But he buys this purple waistcoat and washes his hair with your miracle shampoo, and the next time he performs he's an absolute sensation. Every member of the audience is totally and utterly hooked. And they begin to creep closer and closer, practically mobbing him on the platform and snipping off locks of his gorgeous black hair to keep as souvenirs.'

Nicky held up her glass in a salute. 'Catherine, you're a marvel! Forget the ironing – you can help me with the ad. You're obviously inspired tonight.'

Yes, she thought as she drained her wine. I *am* inspired. Hadn't Will just told her so?

Nicky asked for the bill and began juggling her impressive sheaf of credit cards. 'Right, I'll settle this. Then we'd better get going, okay?'

'Okay.'

They stepped out into a shining night no longer dark and raw. The three-quarters moon looked magical and a thaw was well under way; everything melting in a glorious ooze: roofs dripping, gutters running, pavements wet and gleaming. Catherine closed her eyes for a second: *she* was the snow and Will her sun. They were already in Dorset, in a sumptuous hotel room, and he was thawing her in the white heat of his passion.

22

'The bed's a bit small.' Will stood in the doorway, looking anxiously at the room. 'Not much bigger than mine.'

'I'm sure the springs are an improvement,' Catherine laughed. 'And just look at that wonderful view.' She took a step towards the window, where a great sweep of wooded hills stretched to the blue haze of the horizon.

Will locked the door, still frowning. 'I hoped it would be slightly grander than this. For *your* sake.'

'Don't worry, it's fine. And anyway, after your dire warnings about students' rooms with no wardrobes and no windows, this is an absolute palace.'

'Yes, I suppose I shouldn't complain. It's just that the Big Names are staying at the Eastbury.'

'Darling Will, do I detect a note of jealousy?'

'Not half!'

'But you couldn't smuggle me in as easily, with all those flunkeys standing around. *Here* they didn't even notice me skulking in the background.'

'Oh, you wouldn't have to skulk. I'd be rich and famous enough to book the bridal suite.'

'This *is* the bridal suite.'

'Quick, then' – he fumbled with the top button of her blouse – 'let's start the honeymoon!'

'No, wait a sec, I want to have a look round first. It's such a treat for me to stay in a hotel.'

'Really?' Will threw himself on the bed, bounce-testing the springs. 'I thought you and your husband would have travelled all over the place.'

'No,' she said briefly. 'Did you and Vanessa?'

'Oh God, yes! She was a real culture vulture – off to Florence or Athens at the drop of a hat.'

'But surely you didn't object?'

'Well, I loved the actual travelling – it was just the way she took control. *She* was paying, so *she* decided where we went and how long for and what we did when we got there. That's one of the things I love about you, Catherine – you're not bossy in the slightest.'

'Well, I intend to be now. I absolutely insist that we stay here for six months.'

'That suits me fine. I'll ring down straight away and extend the booking. And shall I order breakfast in bed?'

'We'll have every meal in bed. You can forget your poetry reading. All we're going to do is eat and make love.'

'So, what are we waiting for?'

'Oh Will, you're completely shameless!'

'D'you mind?' The anxious tone had crept back to his voice.

'No, I love it – you know that. But give me five minutes to get acclimatized, okay?' She opened the window and leaned on the sill, taking a deep breath. 'It's so nice to escape the smell of paint.'

'*And* the smell of perming solutions,' Will added, coming up behind her and putting his arms round her waist. 'I can't imagine why women spend such an inordinate amount of time and money dousing their hair in chemicals. They seem to flock to Victor in droves.'

'*I* used to go in for perms once.'

'Really? I can't imagine it.' He kissed the nape of her neck. 'I love your hair the way it is.'

'Brad's sister did it for me this time. She's rather good, don't you think? And she only charges a fraction of the going rate.'

Will grunted in assent. He was scrutinizing his watch. 'Right, your five minutes is up.'

'It's not. Get away! I want to fill my lungs with this marvellous air.' She inhaled luxuriously, gazing at the banks of trees shimmering in new leaf. It was only the first week of April, but already the country-side seemed lush – green frills on the hawthorn hedge, frail blossom on the blackthorn, and a wealth of early flowers. The clocks had gone forward last weekend, so the evenings were lighter and there was a sense of anticipation: the whole of spring ahead, with its dew-rinsed days and freshly lacquered colours, and after that the prospect of unstinting summer, lazy and voluptuous. She, too, was looking forward, as if she could begin to draw a line, at last, between mourning and renewal; enjoy her time with Will without pangs of grief or guilt.

She shut the window and went to explore the bathroom. 'Oh, look – a proper shower, and big white fluffy towels.' It was rare to find a dry towel at Gosforth Road (let alone a clean one), and Will's towels were a disgrace – discoloured and practically thread-bare, due to the ravages of the launderette.

She continued her tour of their tiny empire, delighting in this private country retreat, far removed from the clutter of Will's flat and the comings and goings at Gosforth Road. Every detail pleased her, even the misshapen wire hangers in the wardrobe, the limp pink hot water bottle and the hand-printed notice saying 'Thank you for not smoking'.

'I'd better unpack your clothes for tonight,' she said, opening the case. 'We don't want you looking creased.'

He shuddered. 'Don't remind me of tonight. I get nervous even thinking about it.'

'You'll be fine.' She had said the same to Gerry a million times. How odd she hadn't noticed before that the two men had things in common – their artistic bent, most obviously, their love of food and their enthusiasm for life, though Will lacked Gerry's easy social grace and was moodier altogether, downright unreasonable at times. Still, in the last week he'd been positively benign, partly due to *her*, she liked to think. Between them they had repainted the whole flat, and poems were pouring out of him – mostly Catherine poems, written in honour of his muse. Even their market stall was going better, now that they'd established a proper routine for buying and selling. True, trade was very volatile – one weekend they'd do brilliantly, the next barely cover the rental – but over the weeks she had gained in confidence and become much more skilful at setting up an eye-catching display. Will sometimes even wrote placards in verse, to draw attention to the day's best bargains.

She shook the creases from his waistcoat and hung it in the wardrobe, with his jacket. The rest of the unpacking could wait – well, except for her packet of Ovran, which she put proudly on the bedside table. Being on the pill gave her a real buzz, despite the doctor's warning that it was unsuitable for a woman of her age. How could *he* know that she was nowhere near the menopause? – on the contrary, she was just coming into her prime. Collecting her prescription from the chemist, she felt she was being given not merely a packet of pills, but another chance, a second stab at youth.

She opened the top drawer to put Will's shirt away. 'Oh, look,' she said. 'A hair dryer. Now that *is* grand.'

Will took it from her and switched it on.

'What are you doing?'

In reply, he unbuttoned her blouse and directed a jet of cool air between her breasts.

'Mm, that feels amazing.' Her breasts were exquisitely sensitive on account of the pill. She slipped out of her blouse and unhooked her lacy bra, gasping in shock when he suddenly changed the setting. 'No, Will, it's too hot. Put it back on cool. That was really exciting.'

He traced a slow figure of eight around her breasts, then let the nozzle play against her nipples, watching as they stiffened. She closed her eyes, shivering with pleasure. Recently she had noticed a change in her body: a sense of it being tuned and primed for love-making. Even when Will wasn't there, she would find herself touching her breasts or sliding a hand down inside her jeans. Or she might be doing something mundane like shopping and catch sight of her reflection, surprised to see she looked flushed and almost smug, as if she had just got up from his bed.

'Are you sure it's not too cold?' he asked. 'You're coming out in goose pimples.'

'No, it's wonderful! I'll show you – get undressed.'

They both threw off their clothes and she darted to the television and turned it on. 'I think we'd better drown the noise. You're meant to be on your own, remember.'

'Okay, as long as it's not *Neighbours*. That'll put me off my stroke.'

'Don't worry – it's too early for *Neighbours*.'

'What time *is* it? It would be awful if we were still having it off when I'm meant to be on the platform!'

'It's only half past three.'

'Oh great, we've got hours.' Will flung the bedspread back. 'Come and be ravished, my darling!'

'Coming.' She flicked through various channels, stopping at a ballroom scene: some ancient movie set in old Vienna with stately couples waltzing beneath glittering chandeliers. When he heard 'The Blue Danube', Will suddenly jumped up, clasped her in his arms and began waltzing her round the room. At first she tensed, clinging to him blindly as she recalled the last time she had danced – with Gerry. It had *killed* him, more or less. Since that day, she hadn't danced with anyone, out of loyalty, or superstitious dread.

Will sensed her change of mood. 'What's wrong, my love? Am I hurting?'

'N . . . no.'

'Want to stop?'

'*No.*' At some point in her life she would have to dance again; leave that terrifying memory behind. She moved stiffly, like an unco-ordinated robot, half stumbling, treading on Will's feet. She tried to let the music take over, sweep her along on its insistent lilting rhythm. Will was an energetic dancer, whisking her round the room, weaving in and out of the furniture, adding crazy spins and twirls. Each time they passed the television she caught a glimpse of black tail-coats, frothy gowns, until the boundaries began to blur and she couldn't tell whether she was dancing in a ballroom or a bedroom. The intoxicating melody seemed to buoy her up, drawing her away from death and loss to happiness and love. This music belonged to a world where there was nothing dark and menacing; only palmy days, romantic nights – she simply had to follow where it led. She abandoned herself to its sparkling mood, *and* to Will's firm hold. Her clumsiness was gone now. She moved in perfect time with him, responding to each change in tempo, slowing as the music slowed, speeding up at each blazing crescendo.

At a yearning passage from the violins, they slowed again dramatically, rocking back and forth. Their naked bodies were clamped together; warm skin against warm skin, flesh melting into flesh. She could feel his penis hard against her groin as they went whirling round the room once more, their breathing faster and more intense. The music soared towards a climax – brass thundering, strings pleading – driving them both on. They had *become* the rhythm, exhilarated, frenzied; Will's urgent body sweeping her into a final pirouette as the impassioned sound flooded over and over them.

He collapsed on to the bed and pulled her down on top of him, and suddenly he was coming, and she shouted, 'No, not yet, Will!'

and, miraculously, he went on, and then *she* was coming and the room exploded in a fanfare of triumphant brass and drum.

Catherine sat self-consciously in the middle of the front row, though everyone else seemed to be huddled at the back. Half turning in her seat, she counted surreptitiously. Eleven, twelve, thirteen . . . Not much better than the last count. It was already ten to eight, yet still that depressing array of empty chairs. Few people, evidently, were keen enough on contemporary poetry to traipse out to such an unfashionable venue – an annexe in the local comprehensive school, with a low polystyrene ceiling and unadorned brick walls. The metal chairs were numbingly hard, although most of the audience looked too young to care. She guessed many of them had been dragooned into attending as part of their English course. The older generation would probably be sitting in comfort in the gracious surroundings of Sherborne House, listening to Joanna Trollope, or watching *Samuel Pepys – A Life* at the attractive Powell Theatre. She felt aggrieved on Will's behalf. He deserved a bigger crowd than this. The few who had turned out didn't look exactly inspiring: a gaggle of chattering schoolgirls, a man sitting on his own and taking furtive bites from something in a brown paper bag, and a group of bored youths aiming paper darts at each other.

She watched in relief as two couples made their way in, oversixties this time, and smartly dressed in contrast to the slovenlylooking kids. She smiled at them encouragingly, as if she were the official welcoming committee. The organizer, Cecilia, was doing her bit too, shepherding people in and trying to persuade them to sit further forward. An intense, cadaverous woman, she had greeted Catherine effusively when Will first introduced them, and had come up several times since then to make sure she was all right. Will himself was being treated to drinks in the staffroom, along with the two other poets, Barry Roberts and Liam O'Connor.

She picked up the leaflet she had been handed at the door and studied the three photographs again. Liam was the star of the evening, already hailed by the pundits as the new Seamus Heaney, despite his tender age. He reminded her of childhood pictures of Gentle Jesus with a lamb – long fair hair, beatific smile – whereas Will looked mournfully romantic, a tortured soul suffering for his Art. And according to the brief biography printed in the leaflet, it *was* Art with a capital A. His first collection (which he'd dismissed as juvenilia, published by an unknown press and long since out of print) was here extravagantly praised as 'brilliant, haunting and ground-breaking'. She sat glorying in the adjectives, hardly bothering to read the rest of the leaflet. For her, Will was the star of the evening, not O'Connor.

Two minutes to go. Thank goodness the room was half full now, although the buzz of conversation only increased her apprehension. Suppose people talked while Will was performing, or fidgeted, or coughed? She fanned herself with the leaflet. God! If *she* was apprehensive, how must *he* be feeling? He had become more and more morose as they drove from the hotel to Hollymount; a different man entirely from this afternoon's exultant lover. He had told her several times that writing the poems was fine – it was reading them in public which unnerved him.

Eight o'clock. Exactly. Cecilia had disappeared, presumably to collect her charges, and a younger woman was rearranging the chairs on the platform and fussing with the water jug and glasses.

One minute past. The man beside her was also looking at his watch. Feet shuffled, people whispered, someone dropped a book on the floor. Then, just as she thought she'd burst with the tension, a small side door opened and the three poets trooped in, preceded by Cecilia. Will and Liam took their seats on one side of the platform, leaving Cecilia and Barry centre stage.

Catherine sat up straighter in her seat. Everybody but her was looking at Cecilia, who was saying a few words of introduction. Her eyes were on Will, sending him a silent message of support, although he was staring at the floor.

By now, Barry was in action, wooing the audience with his easy smile and attractive Somerset burr. His sweatshirt was a fierce fire-engine red, and his face was also ruddy, as if he were plugged into some private heat supply.

'I've just read a survey about people's greatest fears,' he said. 'And apparently fifty-four per cent of us are more frightened of performing in public than of mugging, burglary or death.'

Laughter from the audience. Catherine, though, remained anxious, wondering how Will could ever rival such an accomplished line in patter.

'So I hope you're feeling sorry for me. But then I feel sorry for *you*. I mean, do you realize what you're letting yourselves in for? According to a study by the Arts Council, most people regard poetry as – I quote – "out of touch, gloomy, irrelevant, effeminate, highbrow and elitist". And modern poetry's – wait for it – "completely inaccessible". Well, shall I leave *now?*'

Delighted roars of 'No!' The audience was totally won over. Barry had the confidence of a seasoned chat-show host, instinctively in tune with his fans.

'Well, you're a tolerant lot, I'm pleased to say. Even so, I'll start with a really short poem, in case some of you are still tempted to walk out.'

More laughter.

'It's called "Elephant", though it's actually about a tree.' He scratched his head, feigning bemusement. 'For reasons that quite elude me.'

Lord! Will's reading would seem hard work after such determined jollity. Not that she could make much sense of 'Elephant' – she was too on edge. And she missed most of the next, 'Chinese Take Away'. All it did was remind her that Will had eaten nothing since lunch – always a bad sign. He was sitting with his head bowed, as if awaiting execution. Liam, in comparison, was tranquillity personified: hands resting on his lap, palms uppermost; his expression almost smug.

> '. . . from glacial dreamscapes creaking
> to a raw Saharan noon
> visiting sleeping scorpions
> beside the . . .'

She must *concentrate*. Will might ask her opinion of the others' work and she wouldn't want to admit that, as far as Barry's was concerned, it had completely passed her by.

> 'Abruptly, I got up
> and walked the tightrope
> of the bedroom floor.
> She kissed me.
> I was scalded.
> Two into one won't go . . .'

A scalding kiss? This must be a love poem, though she hadn't caught the title. Perhaps they shouldn't have made love a second time. Will did look whacked, though *she* wasn't tired in the slightest. He enlivened her like a dash of bitters added to a drink. And that incredibly passionate kiss – starting almost lazily, with a mere brush of the lips, when she thought he was half asleep, then . . .

She jumped at the sound of applause. Wasn't Barry supposed to be on for twenty minutes? She consulted her watch, astonished to see it was nearly half past eight. She hadn't heard a single poem in its entirety. Still, too late to fret about that. Barry was already taking his bows, which meant it was Will's turn next. Cecilia bobbed to her feet and escorted him to the central chair, beaming as she introduced him to the audience.

Catherine smiled too, despite the churning in her stomach. He seemed so achingly alone as he cleared his throat and stood fumbling with his papers. At least he looked impressive in his purple waistcoat and grey and mauve cravat; his rebellious shock of hair giving him an aura of wildness and abandon. But the effect was lost as soon as he opened his mouth. He seemed to be hunting for words, as if they were rare truffles; his voice constrained and hesitant. And his cultured accent came over as rather superior, especially after Barry's matey tone.

He cleared his throat a second time, giving wary glances to right and left. Desperately she willed him to relax, directing all her mental energy at him. Then suddenly he caught her eye, and she held his gaze, encouraging him with every fibre of her being.

She was aware of a perceptible change, as if she had worked some sort of miracle. His stance became less rigid, his voice lost its strangled tone, and he stepped forward almost boldly. 'I've been writing a sequence of poems dedicated to someone I met earlier this year – a woman, needless to say.'

There was laughter, even a wolf-whistle. Heartened, he went on. 'Sometimes you're lucky enough to meet a person who has the knack of drawing poetry out of you, like treacle from a treacle well. Of course, there's always a risk with love poetry that it *can* be treacly – sentimental stuff that makes you cringe. But love is a dangerous force, in my opinion. Wells can drown you, don't forget, even treacle wells. The great love poets like John Donne and Robert Graves understand that perfectly, even if the greetings-card versifiers don't. Still, dangerous or no, I've decided this evening to restrict myself to love poems. What was it Shakespeare said about the lunatic, the lover and the poet?'

This time he joined in the laughter. Catherine sat silent, amazed at his professionalism. The confiding personal approach had won the audience over. There was now a stir of anticipation in the room as he unfolded his papers with a flourish.

'It all started with this purple waistcoat,' he said, looking down at his chest. 'Purple features rather strongly in this particular romance, though I hope that doesn't mean I've indulged in purple passages! But we'll come to the waistcoat later on. I want to begin at the end, so to speak, with something I wrote just a couple of hours ago. It's hot from the page, totally unrevised. I've never written a poem so fast before. Nor have I ever read one so soon after committing it to paper. As you can see from the scribbles' – he held it up to show them – 'it's not exactly a considered piece of work. But I hope that's actually its strength. I'll leave you to judge. I haven't thought of a title yet, but perhaps we'll call it . . .' – he caught her eye again, gave a hint of a smile – ' "The Purple Danube".'

'So you're the Catherine of Will Carter's poems!' The Head of English refilled her glass, flashing her a suggestive smile. 'Well, I'm honoured to meet you, I must say.'

Catherine blushed and took a hasty sip of wine.

'He's amazingly talented, isn't he? And the kids warmed to him straight away. Of course, his work *is* erotic and some might say too risqué for their tender ears, but then that's the way to get to them these days. There's not much mileage left in daffodils and celandines, I'm afraid. Ah, David!' A burly, bearded man had approached, his eyes steel-blue beneath dark unruly brows. 'So you managed to drop in after all. Excellent! Catherine, this is our headmaster, David Prescott. David, Catherine Jones.'

Catherine shook hands nervously, transported back to childhood fears in the presence of authority. Headmasters were an intimidating breed, although David's bushy beard and windburned face gave him more the air of a sea captain. He murmured a few pleasantries before moving on to greet a local bigwig, whose impeccable grey suit seemed somewhat out of place in the shabby surroundings of Hollymount staffroom. The furniture could well have come from one of Will's job lots: lumpy sofas, mismatched chairs, ancient saggy cupboards. Still, she supposed it was good community relations for the school to host this reception, and the room was gratifyingly full. Barry seemed to have brought his own private fan club, who were making serious inroads on the wine. And Will was barely visible amongst a throng of adolescent girls (poetry groupies, as he called them).

Barry spotted her and came over, putting an arm round her waist. 'Here, dig in,' he said, holding out a bowl of crisps. 'Not that we'll get very fat on these! I could do with a damned good nosh. And why the hell can't they lay on some fucking *beer*?'

She sidled out from his heavy arm. Of course, poets weren't exactly noted for their abstemiousness, but you could forgive them if they wrote sublimely well. Dylan Thomas (Will had told her) was paralytic at some of his performances. Barry, though, wasn't in that league, and anyway, she didn't like his boozy breath in her face. She cast about for an escape. Liam was deep in conversation with one of the sponsors of the festival and a woman from Southern Arts. She gave them a wide berth, feeling rather superfluous and also very much the novice. She didn't know anybody here and her acquaintance with poetry had hardly advanced beyond the school-syllabus *Golden Treasury* – apart from reading Will's, of course.

She gave Will a furtive glance, trying not to resent his adoring cluster of fans. She was reminded of Gerry's acting days; that same sense of being an outsider in his world; no more than an append-age, to minister and reassure. Even when Gerry had the business, *he* had been the boss; she the mere assistant.

She noticed an elderly female, also alone and looking somewhat lost. It would be a kindness to go and talk to her, not lurk in a corner feeling sorry for herself. Whatever else, she would be a safer bet than Barry, who was lurching over once more, wine slopping from his glass. Dodging out of his way, she squeezed through the crush of people to where the woman was standing.

After they had introduced themselves, the woman gave a smile of recognition. 'Ah, yes, someone's just pointed you out to me. I understand you inspired one of the poets here tonight.'

'Er, sort of . . .' Catherine murmured, still embarrassed to have her affair with Will broadcast to all and sundry, although she was pleased for his sake that his poems had been well received. She was so used to him disparaging his work, it was good to have it officially applauded. Not that she doubted his gifts. In fact, listening to him read just now, she had been struck again by the sheer verve and thrust of the words. It was the language not only of love but of sex – raw, wild, unfettered. Many of the poems sounded subtly different when she heard them recited in public, jolting her in unexpected ways. And as for 'The Purple Danube', it had come as a bit of a bombshell. True he had locked himself in the bathroom for the best part of an hour, but she had assumed he simply wanted a long soak.

'I'm afraid I missed the reading,' the silver-haired woman was saying. 'I've just come on from the Samuel Pepys.'

'Oh, was it good?' asked Catherine, glad to change the subject.

'First rate. I'm on the Sherborne Arts Committee and one of our ambitions is to encourage more drama in the . . .'

'Catherine!'

Will's voice. He was beckoning to her across the room. The groupies had gone and he was talking to a man in a black polo-neck. She extricated herself tactfully from the Sherborne Arts Committee and went over.

'Catherine, this is Leonard Upjohn,' he said. 'Liam's publisher. He runs the Scrivener Press.'

She put on a radiant smile. You had to be nice to anyone who ran a press. Not that Leonard looked particularly influential. His hair was a straggly grey, his corduroy trousers balding.

'I remember Will's first collection,' he said, proffering a hand. 'It was bloody good, but this new stuff's even better. In fact, I'm keen to see the full sequence of love poems. I understand there are more?'

'Oh yes,' she said. 'A lot more.'

'I can't promise anything, of course,' he said, turning back to Will. 'But how soon d'you think you could get them to me?'

'Say the, er, day after tomorrow?'

'Fine. Mind you, we'll probably sit on them for a while. You know how it is' – he laughed apologetically – 'we demand the stuff like yesterday, then keep you hanging around for six months, even for a decision.'

'That's fast, compared with my previous publisher,' Will put in feelingly.

'Well, I'm afraid the decision doesn't rest with me alone. If it was up to me I'd accept the poems on the spot, but I have to discuss it with my two editorial colleagues. And, as I'm sure you know, the money's pretty dismal in small-press poetry publishing.

Though just occasionally a book takes off. And in your case we could stress the erotic side, which always helps to sell copies. Even so, we could only manage our usual advance of a hundred pounds.'

Catherine stared at Leonard in horror. A *hundred?* There were over fifty poems – that was less than two pounds each. Nicky and Darren could earn a hundred pounds for half an inch of copy. And she knew for a fact that Nicky's trip to Virgin Gorda next week was costing in the region of three grand.

'That's okay,' said Will. 'The important thing is getting them in print. Money *is* a problem, but' – he shrugged – 'I'm resigned to that by now.'

Leonard crunched a cheese-ball thoughtfully. 'Have you considered applying to the Stanford Birt Foundation?'

Will looked blank. 'I've never heard of it.'

'It was only set up last year. Stanford Birt was a big property developer. He died in his late eighties, leaving a small fortune. His widow's much younger and writes poetry – or verse, I should say. It's very amateurish stuff. Still, to give her credit, she's established a fund to help struggling poets – five grants of seven thousand pounds each.'

'Seven thousand? Wow!'

'That's small beer to her, believe you me. But why not send for details? I mean, if *you* haven't heard of it, nor will many other people, which increases your chances. You'll have to get your skates on, though. The closing date for entries is April the tenth.'

'Next Friday,' Catherine calculated. 'And some of the poems still need typing, Will.'

'That's no problem. I'll stay up all night if necessary.'

'And you could phone for an application form, instead of writing. Hold on a minute . . .' Leonard rummaged in his shoulder bag and unearthed a battered Filofax from the jumble of poetry books. 'I've probably got the number in here.'

Will scrawled it in Biro on his wrist, while Catherine took the precaution of noting it in her diary.

'And now I must dash. I promised Liam I'd take him for a curry and it's already half past ten.'

As soon as he was out of earshot, Will hugged her in delight. 'Forget the grant – I haven't a hope in hell. But imagine being published by the Scrivener Press! God! I can't believe it.'

'Will, I'm sorry to be ignorant, but the name means nothing to me. Are they well known?'

'They're only small – tremendously prestigious, though. The fact that they're Liam's publishers says a lot in itself.' He took a handful of nuts. 'Of course, it may all fizzle out. I've had interest before, from other small presses, and nothing ever came of it except endless waffle and delays. But Leonard *did* seem keen, didn't he? It's a pity the money isn't better, but . . .'

'Yes, a hundred pounds! It's insulting.'

'Well, that's how it is. Poetry doesn't pay and you just have to accept that. The publishers are taking a risk as well. Sometimes they only shift a handful of copies. But what matters is getting my name known and being taken seriously. And, my darling' – he kissed her quite openly, unconcerned that people might see – 'if it does work out, I'll owe it all to you.'

'Will, don't be silly. *I* didn't write the poems.'

'No, but without you they wouldn't exist. Not these, anyway. You've brought me luck all along, and the luck's getting better and better. Look, tell you what – let's not bother with dinner . . .'

'Will, am I hearing you right?' she joked. 'Going without dinner? You must be seriously ill.'

'No, listen.' He lowered his voice. 'We'll buy some fish and chips and eat it in bed. Then, if things go according to plan' – he put his finger on her lips and slowly traced the outline of her mouth – 'who knows? I might be inspired to write another Catherine poem.'

23

'Wow, that tan – you look fantastic!' Catherine put the Sainsbury's bags down and gave Nicky a hug. 'They'll *hate* you at work! It's been horrendously cold and wet here.'

'Don't mention work. It's bad enough seeing you lugging all that shopping. I've been used to having lobster claws and tropical fruit dished up by willing slaves! Here, *I'*ll take those.' Nicky picked up the bags and led the way through to the kitchen.

'So when did you get back?' asked Catherine, unbuttoning her coat.

'This morning. I've been travelling all night. It's a hell of a trek – the first bit by motor launch.'

'Gosh, you must be shattered. But what was the place like?'

'Utter bliss. Didn't you get my card?'

'No, not a thing.'

'It'll probably turn up next month. That's what everything's like out there – totally laid back. Anyway, all I wrote was "This is heaven. Nicky." '

Catherine laughed. 'Let's have a cup of tea while you tell me all about it.'

'Yes, good idea. I'll make it. You look tired.' Nicky switched the kettle on. 'You're not usually this late, are you?'

'Well, it has been rather a long day, I must admit. We didn't pack up till half past six. I shouldn't complain though – we did incredibly well. This is the first day it hasn't rained for over a week, so there were masses of people around. But never mind that – I want to hear about *you.*' She settled William on her lap, looking expectantly at Nicky.

'I don't know where to start! It was like one of those cliché-ridden commercials, too idyllic to be true. Deserted beaches, pure white sand, turquoise sea – the lot. And the windsurfing was perfect. You get these steady trade winds blowing every day. I mean, some places, you can waste half your holiday hanging around in a dead flat calm. I was on the water most mornings the minute I'd swallowed my breakfast. And breakfast was a feast, by the way – fresh coconuts by the dozen, pancakes swimming in rum and maple syrup, mangoes, guavas, passion fruit, you name it.'

'Lord! Didn't you get indigestion, jumping about in the waves after *that* lot?'

'Well, I liked to stoke up for the day, and not have to bother with lunch. You can easily stay out till dusk, you see.'

'It sounds like hard work to me,' Catherine grinned, stroking William's ears.

'No way! And you should have seen me in the evenings, sprawled on a sun-lounger with a drink in my hand, indolence personified. Or occasionally we went island-hopping by yacht. And the islands are absolutely beautiful – some smaller than a tennis court with nothing on them except the odd pelican or palm tree. One of the smallest is called the Last Resort. It's so minute, there's only room for a bar. They do these marvellous cocktails called Pusser Pain-killers. A couple of those and you soon forget your aches and pains, I can tell you! Here' – she handed Catherine a mug of tea – 'this will have to do instead. I don't know how I'll ever come down to earth again. I was talking to Darren earlier and he was banging on about work. But I have to say HHA seems awfully sort of . . . alien at the moment.'

'Where *is* Darren?'

'He'll be back soon. He and Jo went to get a video. Actually, shall we take our tea upstairs? I want to have a word with you in private.'

'That sounds mysterious!'

Nicky gave nothing away. 'Your room or mine?'

'Mine. Then I can get out of these grotty clothes. But I'll just put this stuff away first. I don't want the peas to defrost.'

'I'll give you a hand,' said Nicky. 'It's time I started being practical. I haven't *seen* a shop for a fortnight, or not a food shop anyway. Just cutesy little boutiques selling shells and coral and native crafts and what-have-you.'

'Well, the break's obviously done you good. You look disgustingly healthy.'

Nicky smiled at her reflection in the window. 'Come on – down to work.'

As soon as they had disposed of the shopping, Catherine ran upstairs. She already felt revived – perhaps Nicky's euphoria was catching. Certainly it was good to have her back. Things with Jo could still be rather strained without Nicky to act as buffer. Humming to herself, she removed her grubby jeans and sweater and put on her Chinese kimono.

'*You* look exotic!' Nicky said, coming in with the tea.

'Two pounds fifty at a boot fair.'

'And you've got a new photo of Will, I see.' Nicky walked over to inspect it. 'Is that his son?'

'Mm.'

'Have you met him yet?'

Catherine shook her head. 'I keep dropping hints, but you know what Will's like. He always gets twitchy about taking the next step. First it was his flat, then the sex thing and now it's Sam.'

'I don't see what he's worried about. You are a mother, after all, and the boy looks harmless enough – positively angelic.'

'I think he's afraid it'll make things awkward between us. Though it could be Vanessa, I suppose. She does seem to lay down the law about where Sam goes and who he meets. I'm sure I'd never be acceptable – punky hair, working in a market . . .'

'Come off it. *Will* works there too.'

'Yes, I know, but she doesn't really approve.'

'Hey, talking of Will, what happened about his poems? Did you manage to get them off in time?'

'Only by the skin of our teeth. *I* typed them in the end because Will's so slow. It felt really odd sitting at the old Amstrad again. And the whole thing took for ever. He would keep messing around with them after I'd printed them all out, changing words or even adding lines. Just a sec – let me get my patchwork.' She took it from the sewing box and settled back with needle, template, scissors. 'You don't mind me doing this, do you? I'm making another quilt. I sold the first one to an American couple and they didn't even haggle over the price. I feel a bit guilty, actually. I'm sure they thought it was old, like the rest of the stuff on the stall.'

'They're still an absolute bargain,' Nicky said, 'when you think of the work that goes into them. It would drive me nuts, all that fiddly stitching.'

'I find it very soothing. But look, we're meant to be talking about *you*. Go on – fire away.'

Nicky, however, sat in edgy silence, picking at the braid on a cushion.

Catherine continued sewing for a while, but still Nicky didn't speak. 'It . . . it's nothing awful, is it?' she asked.

'Oh, no. Just complicated.'

'Ah, in that case, you've met a man!'

Nicky smiled, at last. 'How did you guess?'

'Let me guess again. He's married.'

'No, this time he's available. And not neurotic, or bisexual, or so old he's on a zimmer frame. In fact, he's exactly my age, good fun and very sporty.'

'Oh, Nicky, it sounds too good to be true.'

'It *is* too good to be true. First of all, you can forget romance. I just don't fancy him, unfortunately. He's great as a friend, and we've got loads of things in common, but . . .'

'But what? He fancies *you*, you mean?'

'Well, yes he does, and in the ordinary way, it wouldn't be a problem. I'd just say, "Sorry, Stewart, I'm afraid it's not going to work."' She broke off again, chewing her thumb. 'Oh, Catherine, I'm in such a muddle. I don't know what to do. You see, he's a windsurfing instructor – he works at the centre at the Bitter End. And he wants *me* to get a job out there as well.'

'A job?' Catherine dropped her scissors. 'But do they *have* advertising agencies in the Virgin Islands?'

'No, a job like his, teaching water sports.'

'You're not serious, are you?' She stared at Nicky, appalled.

'Well, at first I just laughed and told Stewart he was off his head. But the next day, I was sailing downwind to a group of tiny islands. It was a perfect morning, Catherine. The sun was glittering on the water and I could see the dark shadow of a coral reef underneath the surface, and palm trees swaying in the distance. And apart from the occasional dolphin and a few turtles bobbing on the waves, I had the sea to myself. And I began to think – imagine *living* here, away from all the pressures and the deadlines. Oh, I know I'd be working, not just swanning about on holiday. And it's bloody hard work in some ways, and long hours, Stewart said. In fact, he was so busy himself, some days I hardly saw him.' She grinned. 'Maybe just as well . . . But, you see, I'd be doing something I really love and that makes all the difference. I can't tell you what a stress it is to be for ever worrying about whether I'm clever enough or creative enough, and knowing there's always someone younger and brighter at HHA waiting to jump into my shoes. D'you know, as soon as we touched down at Heathrow, all the anxiety came rushing back. I mean, this new shampoo – it may sound frightfully trivial, but there's such a lot at stake. A five-hundred-thousand-pound campaign, which I personally could bugger up if the ideas don't materialize. And it's not just the job, it's everything that goes with it: feeling you always need to be slimmer, richer, smarter, more together – drive the right car, wear the right clothes, be seen in the right places. None of that matters out there.'

Catherine abandoned her patchwork, too shaken to speak. This wasn't just a flash in the pan – Nicky had given the matter serious thought. Yet, whatever the pressures at HHA, surely it was inconceivable that she would throw up her career for a glorified holiday job?

'Anyway,' Nicky continued, rocking back in her chair, 'Stewart took me along to see Eddie, his boss, and he seemed quite keen, believe it or not. They need another instructor, you see. An allrounder – water-skiing, sailing, all that sort of thing. Which I can do. Plus you have to get on well with people. According to Eddie, that's even more important than the technical stuff. My windsurfing's up to standard, though. I've done my level four, and so long as you can water-start and gybe any size board, that's all they really want.'

'Would it be . . . permanent?' Catherine asked. However shocked she was by Nicky's news, she couldn't just sit there like a dummy.

'A two-year contract initially, they said.'

'And what about the pay?'

'Lousy. That's one of the major drawbacks. Also, I'd have to share a room, which doesn't exactly thrill me. And then there's the business of Stewart. If I did go out there, it could be a bit dodgy. And I know my parents would be horrified . . .' Nicky ran a hand through her hair. 'I've been lying awake at night, going round and round in circles. I haven't told anyone else yet. And what the hell do I do about Darren? We've worked together so long, he's bound to take it badly. He was saying what a pain it was me being away just for two weeks, so if I resigned, he'd . . .'

The front door slammed downstairs. 'That'll be him now,' she added with a frown. 'Don't say anything, will you, Catherine? There's no point upsetting him, if I decide not to go in the end. Actually, I feel awful even telling *you*. I'd hate you to think I'd simply waltz off halfway round the world without a backward glance. But I need to discuss it with *some*one, and you're so good at this sort of thing. You always say what you mean.'

Do I, she thought wretchedly, staring out over the balcony at the hotchpotch of grey roofs.

'So come on – what d'you think? Am I crazy even to consider the idea?'

With deliberate precision, Catherine placed her thimble on each finger in turn. Of course it was a crazy idea. Nicky was her friend, her confidante, her ally in the house, and she was appalled at the thought of her vanishing to the ends of the earth. But that was totally selfish. It was Nicky who mattered, Nicky's future life. 'Have you tried making a list of the pros and cons?' she asked, hoping she sounded calmer than she felt.

'Scores of lists. But how can you balance things like status and good pay against freedom and excitement?'

Catherine opened her mouth to speak, then shut it again. Three months ago, *she* had been faced with a similar dilemma – not so much high status, but safety and security versus a new and risky life. And she had chosen freedom. So how could she advise Nicky to do the opposite?

'I'm so easily swayed, that's the problem.' Nicky sat hugging the cushion. 'Laura rang this afternoon, and she's in a really awful state again, trying to cope with the baby and the job. Ten minutes on the phone to her convinced me I ought to get out while I can. Imagine having to leave your kid when it's ill, just because some stupid client wants you to change a headline. I couldn't bear to be a mother and have that kind of pressure – if I ever *am* a mother! And that's another thing. I'm far more likely to meet a guy out there than here in London. The place is swarming with eligible men – mostly rich Americans, athletic types with year-round tans and yachts like bloody palaces. Oh, and a good sprinkling of movie stars and rock stars, to add a bit of spice. Though of course if Stewart was too clingy I might never get to speak to them.' Nicky crossed her legs and uncrossed them again. 'Then, later today, I came across my Barclaycard statement. And I thought God! How could I manage on the pittance I'd earn out there? My whole lifestyle would have to change. But I *want* it to change, don't I? And if I miss this chance, I might never get another. In windsurfing terms, I'm over the hill. Most of the instructors are in their early twenties. I'm surprised they even want me.'

'You'll just have to shed ten years.' Catherine forced a laugh. 'It's not that difficult. I've shed twenty, at least!'

'Catherine . . .' Nicky stared at her. '*You*'ve changed your life-style, haven't you? D'you know, it's only just beginning to register – what it must have meant. And *you* had no choice at all.'

'But Nicky, I did have a choice. I could still be in Stoneleigh, living a quiet suburban life. I was down there earlier this week, having dinner with Andrew and Antonia, and it seemed almost a foreign country. Andrew's my son, yet *I* was the one who felt like a child – a guilty teenager, keeping secrets from my parents. I haven't told them about Will, you see, but I was sure they could sort of smell him on me!'

'Why? D'you think they won't approve of him?'

'Oh, I don't know. They might feel I'm being disloyal to Gerry. But it isn't only that. I don't want me and Will to be seen as – well, a fixture, yet. I suppose I'm still sort of feeling my way in life – trying out various options before settling for any one thing. It's a pity *you* can't do that. Is there any chance they'd let you have a trial run?'

Nicky shook her head. 'Absolutely not. They pay my fare, you see, and arrange a work permit and everything. That's the trouble – it seems such a final decision. And I have to let them know by Monday week. Otherwise they'll take on someone else. And scores of young hopefuls will jump at it, I can tell you. They'd think I was out of my mind to turn it down. There's only one Bitter End. A job there is the *crème de la crème.*'

'But Monday week's ridiculously soon!'

'I know. I can't concentrate on anything. I'm sure they'll notice at work.'

'Let's hope they put it down to jet lag.'

Suddenly noticing her cold tea, Nicky drank it with a grimace. 'Oh Catherine, you are an angel to listen to all this. And to encourage me as well. I mean, my family would never understand. And some of my friends are bound to say, "Wow, go for it!"', assuming that's what I *want* to hear, though secretly they'll think I'm mad giving up a fat salary in London. They wouldn't bother to talk it through like this. At least you take me seriously.'

'Of course I do. But I must admit there's a nasty selfish bit of me that wants to put you off the idea, just because I'd miss you so much if you did go.'

'And I'd miss *you.* Terribly.'

'But you see, you do lose people, Nicky. It's part of life. You can't hold on to them, however much you'd like to. I remember when Kate went off to India, I had to stop myself from begging her not to go. It seemed such a long way and so dangerous and I felt I'd never see her again. I still feel that sometimes, especially when she has to renew her visa. Funnily enough, she renewed it again a fortnight ago. There was a tremendous amount of hassle, she said, and she had to keep going back and pleading, and grease even more palms than usual. But when she told me it had finally come through, I'm ashamed to say I felt disappointed, not glad for her. But that's just me being selfish again.' Catherine let out an impatient sigh. 'Actually, I respect her decision to stay on there and work. Right from the beginning, she knew what she wanted and went for it, regardless. And that's rare, you see, especially at her age. I just feel guilty that I didn't understand it at the time. I kept harping on about safety and security and getting a good job. And I completely missed the point.' She was seized by a great choking sob, and suddenly her shoulders were heaving and tears streaming down her cheeks.

Nicky stared at her in horror. She went over, took her hand. 'Don't *cry.*'

'I'm . . . sorry. I didn't mean to. I . . .'

'It's all right. You're upset about Kate. That's natural when she's so far away.'

'It's not just Kate. It's . . .' Her voice was racked by sobs. '. . . Gerry. He gave up his . . . his whole vision. He was born an actor – it was all he ever wanted to do. And he was bloody good. Everybody said so. But he became a businessman. Just a humdrum businessman – imagine. And that was partly *my* fault. God! He might not even be dead if we hadn't made the wrong decision.'

'Oh, *Catherine.*' Nicky put her arm round her shoulders. 'I'm sure that isn't true.'

She began to tremble uncontrollably. 'It . . . it's all coming back – I can't think why. I can see it in my mind, as if it's happening now. Him staggering. And falling. And the awful silence while we waited for the ambulance. It took so long to come. And when it did come, it seemed so sort of . . . loud. The wheels crunching on the drive. And the door slamming like a gunshot. And the men's voices, all so loud. They were *alive* you see, but . . .' She swallowed, caught her breath. 'And it was dreadful in the ambulance. He made this sort of choking sound. And he was dead. That was it. But I couldn't seem to take it in. I was saying fatuous things like "You're going to be all right, Gerry. They're going to save you, Gerry."'

'How *could* you take it in? You were in shock. I'm sure I'd have reacted the same way.'

'Nicky, I'm so sorry.' She bit her lip, clenched her fists, somehow managed to stop crying. 'This isn't helping you at all. It's *your* life we're meant to be talking about. But that's the point – it's desperately important for you to make the right decision.'

'Oh Catherine, my problems seem so trivial, compared with what you've been through.'

'Listen, Nicky' – at last her voice was more controlled and she spoke slowly and emphatically – 'Gerry only lived to be forty-nine and he spent fifteen of those years doing something he hated. And it happens to lots of other people. Maybe even Andrew and Antonia. Although I'm sure they think a good life means well-paid jobs and ideal homes and all the rest of it. But that's not living, is it? And it's because I'm fond of you that I feel we ought to talk . . .' She walked to the window, stood looking out at the darkness. 'I know it's an awful cliché, but there *are* no certainties. And nothing's really secure, however much you try and hang on to it. People change, or leave, or die. But you have to accept it somehow. And you *can* make a new life.' She touched the cold pane of glass, watching her blurred fingerprints mist away to nothing. 'Nicky, even if it takes all night, we must work out what's best for you. And that means not worrying too much about Darren, or your parents. Or *me*, for that matter.'

'Don't be silly. Of course I'm worried about you. I'm worried *now* in case I'm keeping you from Will. Aren't you seeing him tonight?'

'No, he's out.'

'How *are* things with Will? You haven't said.'

'Pretty good. Life's good altogether. So heaven knows what upset me like that. I thought I'd got over Gerry.'

'But Catherine, it must have been quite awful, him dying so traumatically. I don't suppose you ever really get over such a shock – not entirely, anyway. In fact, I remember you telling me you wouldn't even want to.'

'No. You're right – I did. I suppose it's a sort of tribute to him, keeping a core of sadness inside. But it does get better. Gradually. And of course it helps being so busy.'

'Yeah, you're getting worse than me these days! Christ knows how you fit it all in.'

'Oh, I've worked out a good system. That's business training for you! And I enjoy all the variety – auctions, boot fairs, market, sewing, even the odd poetry reading . . .'

'Catherine?' Nicky sat studying her fingernails.

'What?'

'If I did take the job, would you and Will be able to . . . you know, share a place or something? I mean, I hate the thought of going off and leaving you in the lurch. And I presume you wouldn't want to stay here with just Jo and Darren?'

Catherine hesitated. 'I . . . I'm sure we can work something out. And it would be great to spend every night with him.'

Not true. Fantastic as the sex was, she still wanted the option of sleeping on her own from time to time, or skipping supper and settling for a hunk of cheese (as she would probably do tonight). There was something important about having a kind of bolt hole, even if it was only one room in a rented house. In any case, Will's flat was too small for them both and although they'd given it a total face-lift, she didn't like Tandoori Street, or the ghastly hairdresser's with its constant smells and musak. Yet what *would* she do if Nicky went? She certainly couldn't afford a place of her own. It was bad enough shelling out the rent each week when she spent most of her time at Will's.

She folded her patchwork and put it back in its box. Her problems could wait – it was Nicky's that needed solving. 'Nicky, I've got an idea,' she said, sitting at the desk. 'Whenever Gerry was faced with a tough business decision, he would ask himself: what's the worst that could happen? He'd set out all the options in separate columns and take each one to its logical conclusion: if I did *this*, then what? For example, if you resigned from HHA and then the windsurfing didn't work out, would they consider taking you back? Or could you find a job with another agency? Or would it simply be the end of your career?'

'Oh, no, nothing as dramatic as that – though I doubt if HHA would want me back. But I'm bound to get something somewhere, even if it's only making tea in a third-rate agency.'

'Well, it helps, don't you think, just to know what's at stake? I think we ought to do it for every different factor – your pay, your parents, Darren, even Stewart. What a pity you don't fancy Stewart. Isn't it always the way?'

'Yeah. Sod's law! Still, it can't be helped. And I'm feeling better already, doing something positive.'

'Good. I'll get some paper and let's sit here at the desk. That'll make it more important. And it *is* important – very.'

Nicky drew up her chair. 'You really care, don't you, Catherine?' She nodded.

'And you *would* stay up all night, if need be, wouldn't you?'

'Yes.'

'You say yes as a matter of course, but you know lots of people wouldn't. Even so-called friends. Look, whatever happens, we mustn't lose touch. I'd absolutely hate that. In fact, I want you to promise me something. If I do decide to go, you'll come and visit me in my little cabin on the beach.'

Catherine doodled an N on the pad, then drew a Biro heart around it. 'Don't you worry – as soon as I've made my first million, I'll be out there like a shot. Just you try and stop me!'

24

'Will, are you in?' Catherine burst into the living-room, but found it empty. She tried the room next door. Also empty. 'Will?' she called again.

'I'm in the bath.'

'Oh good,' she said, opening the bathroom door, 'I thought you might be late back.'

'You're the one that's late, my love. Where've you been?'

'All over the place.' She kissed the top of his damp head. 'But listen, Nicky's *decided* – she's going.'

'God, how rotten for you, darling. I was rather afraid she'd go, all along.'

She sat on the edge of the bath. 'Well, actually she'd decided *not* to go and only changed her mind today. I've just been round to the house, and she and Darren are in a hell of a state, I can tell you. You see, someone was sacked from HHA this morning. He hit his partner, believe it or not – his partner at work, that is. Apparently they've been working late all week and he finally reached breaking point. He gave her a black eye. There was a tremendous kerfuffle – well, you can imagine, can't you? But Nicky said it was like a sort of trigger for her. She marched in to Wayne and said, "Okay, that's it. I'm leaving."' Catherine yanked off her sweater. She was hot from racing upstairs, and the bathroom was like a sauna.

'Thank Christ I don't work in an office. It sounds appalling. But I'm very sorry, for *you*.' He leaned over and squeezed her hand. 'You were dreading this, weren't you?'

'Mm.' She bit her lip. 'But you know, Nicky seemed so certain, all at once. She's been really weird this last week, but it's as if she's on a high now. So I'm pleased for her. At least, I'm trying to be pleased. She's got enough on her plate with Darren. He's terribly upset about her going, and also worried they'll use it as an excuse to give him the chop. Nicky's hoping he can work with Lynne, but . . .'

'Who's Lynne?'

'The girl who was hit. *She*'s lost her partner too, so it seems a fairly logical solution. Nicky said they do get on well, but of course it's up to Wayne to decide.'

'Lord! It's complicated. But what will *you* do – about staying at the house, I mean?'

She hesitated. For the last two hours she had been thinking of little else. Secretly she was hurt that Will hadn't asked her to move in with him – not so much as suggested it all week. Admittedly, she didn't like the flat, but it would have been nice to have the offer. 'Oh, I'll probably just sit it out for a while and see what happens. They'll have to get a replacement for Nicky, and a lot depends on what she's like.'

'Or *he*?'

'Yes, it could be a man. Jo said she'd prefer that.'

'Well *I* wouldn't.'

'Why not?'

'I'd be jealous.' He reached up and fondled her breast, dripping water on her blouse.

'Will, don't be silly. It would be someone in his twenties. He wouldn't be interested in me.'

'Don't you be so sure. Brad's in his twenties and I've noticed *him* eyeing you up.'

She said nothing. Brad was partly the reason she was late. He had suggested a drink in the Stag to celebrate another win on the horses. No one else was free, so it had been just the two of them. But the conversation was hardly erotic – mainly betting systems and Brad's views on the renovations at the Hackney Empire.

Will was busy soaping his feet. 'Talking of Brad, how was the market?'

'Remarkably good, you'll be pleased to hear. And I managed to sell those ghastly prints, at last. The woman was thrilled to bits. You'd have thought they were Picassos.'

He laughed. 'I don't know how you do it, Catherine. You could sell ice-cubes to the Eskimos. I'm useless at selling anything.'

'Of course you're not. I really missed you on the stall today. But how did the workshop go?'

'Not bad. A few duffers, as usual. But some bright ones too.'

She picked up the loofah. 'Want me to do your back?'

'Yes, please.'

She scrubbed vigorously – he liked it hard. 'Bridget sends her love, by the way. She's back from her travels, and bubbling over! It beats me how those market people get away so often. *And* to such exotic places. Bridget's always pleading poverty, yet it was Kashmir this year and Thailand last. And Greta's off to Mexico next week. We were chatting about it this morning and, you know, she's a bit of a philosopher on the quiet. She believes travelling's in our genes. She says man's been nomadic for so many hundreds of years, it can't help but affect us. Apparently we're *meant* to migrate, like the birds do.'

'But isn't there an equally strong impulse to put down roots, settle in one place?' Will gave a shudder of pleasure at the steady circling motion of the loofah.

'That's what *I* said, but Greta reckons the travelling urge is stronger. She thinks that's why there's so much aggression in the world – people are stuck behind desks in nasty crowded cities, so their natural instinct to explore turns sour.'

'Oh, that's just plain simplistic.'

'Maybe so, but it did make me think. And I mean, everyone seems to have travelled except me. Bridget just takes it for granted and pushes off somewhere new every year. She was telling me about this woman she met in Kashmir who'd been trekking with nomads across some Indian desert. Nomads again, you see! I felt green with envy, if you really want to know. It seemed such an amazing thing to do.' She gazed dreamily into the fug. 'The woman hired a camel and they slept out under the stars and cooked on a primus stove.'

'You'd hate it, darling. You complain enough about my Baby Belling.'

'Yes, but this isn't the desert.'

'Thank God. Deserts can be horrendously cold, especially at night. I can't see you sleeping under the stars when you're the one that hogs the blankets.'

'Will, I thought you were a romantic.'

'Not about deserts. Or camels, for that matter. They're notoriously bad-tempered beasts.'

'*Hers* wasn't. Bridget said she was devoted to it.'

'I see – you want to leave me for a camel, do you?'

'Yes!'

'Fair enough. If I get a grant from this Stanford Birt outfit, I'll give you half and you can hire one of the evil creatures and trek across all the deserts you can find.'

'Promise?'

'Promise.'

She jabbed him playfully. 'You're only saying that because you know you *won't* get a grant.'

'Of course. Do you think I'd want you to go gallivanting off with a bunch of randy nomads? No – jump in here instead. That's an order from the Chief Nomad!'

She gave him one last rub with the loofah. 'Will, I can't. I promised to ring Andrew and Antonia.'

'Ring them later.'

She glanced at her watch, in two minds. Then decisively she removed the watch – and her clothes.

He crooked his legs up to make room. His body was flushed from the heat, his penis already stiff and protruding through the pine-green foam. 'Right, I'm a rugged Mongolian tribesman, and you're a . . .'

They both jumped as the phone rang. 'Leave it,' Will said. 'They don't have phones in the desert. It's just a camel bell. Soap my prick, beautiful English virgin.'

She giggled. 'Where's the soap?'

'I lost it.'

They fished about in the water, grinning foolishly at each other, and she finally retrieved it, slimy soft. 'Lie back, Chief Nomad, and close your eyes . . .' She lathered her hands and moved them slowly up and back. But she could see him tensing, his brow creased in a frown.

'Hell! That bloody phone . . .'

'Ssh, darling.'

'Can't they take the hint and ring off?'

'Want me to get it?'

'No.' He guided her hands back to his penis. 'Unless it's Andrew,' he said suddenly. 'Perhaps he's ringing *you*?'

She shook her head. 'I didn't give him this number.'

'It's no good – I can't stand it. I'll have to answer the damn thing.' He clambered out of the bath, sloshing water everywhere. 'Don't move,' he said. 'Back in a sec.'

He wasn't. She could hear his voice echoing across the passage, getting louder and more annoyed. After a few minutes, she too got out, dried herself quickly and, with the towel swathed round her midriff, went into the living-room. Will was standing naked, dripping on the floor, shoulders hunched as he glowered into the receiver.

'Okay?' she mouthed.

He made a face. 'Vanessa,' he mouthed back.

She nodded and tactfully withdrew.

'All right,' she heard him say. 'Have it your own way. You always bloody do.'

She stood hovering in the doorway as he slammed the receiver down. 'What's happened?'

'That flaming woman! She's just gone and cancelled the arrangements for tomorrow. She says it's too late for Sam to be up and she doesn't want him watching violent films. Mind you, *she* thinks *Bambi*'s violent.'

'Oh, Will, what a shame. Perhaps you could take him out to supper instead?'

'No, she's kiboshed the whole thing. She said he's going out on Sunday, so he needs an early night tomorrow. Stupid bloody excuses! What she really means is she doesn't like him coming to this dump.'

'I'd hardly call it a dump, Will – not now anyway.' She glanced at the new striped curtains, the dusky purple walls, but no doubt Vanessa's critical eye would home in only on the lumpy chairs and sagging bed. She winced at the shriek of a siren in the street. That was another thing – the constant noise: traffic hooting, drunken brawls right outside the door, unattended shop-alarms wailing at all hours. Vanessa's Hampstead mansion looked on to the Heath, so Sam would be used to the sound of gentle birdsong, not police cars screeching past.

She went and sat beside Will on the bed, inwardly cursing Vanessa for making him so miserable.

'I'm sorry to go on, Catherine, but it sickens me the way she's giving Sam entirely the wrong values. He'll grow up the most frightful snob, judging people by where they live and how many cars they own. I want to show him the other side of life – all its other sides – but what chance do I get? Vanessa's so single-minded. In *her* scheme of things, everything has to have a point. But why? Dandelions don't have a point. Or house-mites. Or haikus. Or even deserts, for that matter.'

'Oh, Will, I'm sorry, honestly. I wish there was something I could do.'

'You do a lot, my love, just being here.' He pulled off her skimpy towel and ran his hands across her breasts. His skin was still damp from the bath and she clung to him greedily. She wanted to forget the problems – Vanessa, Nicky, Sam – and lose herself in his body.

'Is Stefan in?' she whispered.

'No.' He kissed her eyelids. 'I passed him on the stairs. He was going out as I came in.'

'So it won't matter about the noise?'

He kissed her again, in answer, then laid her gently back and pressed his head into her thatch. She loved the feel of his springy hair against her. It was one of their hors d'oeuvres, as he called them – preliminary indulgences before they got down to the main course. She closed her eyes, savouring the roughness of his hair, the subtle movements of his head.

'Oh God, Catherine, I *want* you,' he said, sitting up abruptly. 'Go and make that wretched phone call, then we can . . .'

'What phone call?'

'I thought you had to ring your son.'

'Damn! I'd forgotten.' She got up reluctantly. It seemed that both her son *and* his were conspiring to thwart their plans.

'Shall I go into the other room?' Will asked.

'No, but don't make a sound.' She picked up the receiver. 'They'd have a fit if they knew I was naked and alone with a strange man.'

'Strange?'

'Shush!' She was already dialling. 'Oh, Antonia, hello. It's Catherine. I just rang to see how you are.'

Will slid quietly off the bed and crept towards her. She raised a hand in warning, but he sneaked up right behind and pressed his naked body against hers. She tried to shake him off, suppressing a giggle. 'Yes, I'm fine. How's Andrew? . . . Good. And Jack and Maureen? . . . Oh, dear. Is it her arthritis again?'

She could feel Will's penis, exuberantly stiff, nudging between her buttocks. His hands were cupping her breasts, his lips nuzzling the nape of her neck. It was all she could do to talk coherently.

'Has she been to the doctor? . . . Acupuncture? Really? I wouldn't have thought . . .' He was kissing her right shoulder, fierce blue-laser kisses, followed by a slow swirl of his tongue. 'Oh, I see. The doctor suggested it. But wouldn't . . . ?'

He pushed her gently forward, and she stifled a gasp of shock as he slid defiantly in.

'What? Yes, I, er, am on my own. I just . . . dropped something. Sorry. So's Maureen going to try it then?'

He was moving now with tantalizing slowness, pushing in, drawing back, his hands still fondling her breasts. She pressed back against him, hard. Her voice was punctuated by his movements and must sound distinctly odd: jerky little gasps each time he thrust in. 'Yes, Antonia, I am a bit out of breath. I've been . . . running upstairs.' She used her free hand to stroke his thigh, but the angle was frustratingly wrong. 'Nicky tried acupuncture once, when she hurt her back windsurfing. She said it was quite good . . . Mm, of course I will. I'll phone them tomorrow . . . I'm in a bit of a rush at the moment, I'm afraid . . . Okay, just a quick word.' She used the pause to shift position, leaning forward across the table so that Will could thrust more deeply. '. . . Oh, hello, darling! How are you? I can't be long.' She had a peculiar feeling that Andrew could actually see her – see her stiffening nipples and the rapturous expression on her face. She tried to put on a different expression, one more suited to the mother of a twenty-six-year-old surveyor. But her lips were opening in frustrated kissing movements; her breasts pushing into Will's hands. She was so used to his wild animal noises, the silence seemed all wrong. She wanted him to roar and bellow; loved his sheer audacity. Who else would be so crazy as to *do* this during a phone call?

'. . . Er, nothing much. Just the usual. I've been at the market all day . . . Yes, it was, thanks.' How on earth could she concentrate? All her instincts urged her to let go, to respond to Will, move in time with him, yet she was forced to keep still, glued to the receiver.

'Oh, that's nice. Congratulations, darling. When do you start? Not till June – I see. Look, I'm sorry, Andrew, but I'm afraid I'll have to go now. I've got this urgent . . .'

She rang off, exploding with a howl of relief. Quickly he steered her to the end of the bed and, still behind, thrust in again as she sprawled forward on her stomach. At last they could give vent to their thwarted tiger noises, out-roar the traffic and the sirens.

No, they *weren't* sirens. She was no longer in Kentish Town, but lying on the starlit sand with her rugged Mongolian tribesman. And it was the camels she could hear bellowing and applauding as her breathless nomad lashed her towards an unstoppable climax and their final cries echoed across the steppes.

'So how *was* Andrew?' Will asked, scraping the last remnants of yogurt from the carton.

'Oh, he's all right. Maureen's not so good, though. Her arthritis is getting worse and she's finding it difficult to get about. I feel dreadfully guilty – I hardly ever see them now. But when I do, it's so dreary, and they want me to stay for hours. I know it sounds awful, but I sometimes wish I lived hundreds of miles away.'

Will sat staring into the empty yogurt pot. 'Catherine,' he said suddenly. 'I've just had an idea – one that might solve several problems at once.'

'Well?'

'I'm not sure if I can tell you. I'm frightened you'll say no.'

'Suppose I say yes?'

'I doubt if you will.'

'Well, give me the chance, at least.'

'No.' He took a gulp of tea. 'It would never work. Forget it.'

'Oh Will, you can't leave me in suspense like this.'

'Well, if I *do* tell you, will you promise not to shout me down till I've had a chance to explain?'

'When have I ever shouted you down?'

'I'm sorry, darling, that was unfair. It was how Vanessa would have reacted. Years of conditioning, I'm afraid.'

'Don't worry, I'll sit here quiet as a lamb.'

He ran a teasing hand across her thigh. 'You weren't very quiet just now. God, I love the way you let rip like that.'

'Don't change the subject. I want to hear your idea.'

He got up from the makeshift table and stood nervously by the window. 'Well' – he cleared his throat – 'you need a place to live, and actually I'd love you to move in here. But I wouldn't dream of suggesting it. This place *is* a dump. Oh, I know we've tarted it up, and I'm grateful for your help, but it's out of the question for two people. There's no kitchen, for one thing, and the other room's full of junk, and it's so noisy all the time.' He returned abruptly to his chair, gazing at her with mingled hope and wariness. 'But I thought if we moved to the country . . .'

'The *country*?'

'Ssh, wait. It just struck me that we could go up north, where you come from. Property's still a fair bit cheaper than in London. When I lived in Sacriston, you could rent a place for a song.'

She stared at him, astonished. She had only just established herself in London. Did she really want the upheaval of moving again, especially such a distance? Lord! She wasn't even sure if she was ready for such a commitment – to him or anyone. Besides, how could they afford to move? Will talked airily about renting places for a song, but she knew for a fact that property around Manchester was anything but cheap. Sacriston might be different, although she had her doubts. 'But, Will, what would we live on?'

'Well, if we weren't too far from a market town, we could run another stall. And you could sell your patchwork and maybe jams and stuff as well. And if I had more space, I could go in for furniture restoration on a bigger scale. There's money in that, I know. And I might even run writing workshops from home – make a feature of the country setting. And, given time, I'm sure we could come up with other things to do. The idea only came to me just now, when you said you wished you were hundreds of miles away. I suddenly thought, we don't *need* to be in London – we're just paying through the nose here, when we could be living somewhere cheaper . . . an old miner's cottage, maybe, or a converted barn or something.'

She avoided his eye. Converted barns were pricy – she had seen the Sunday supplements. What money they might earn from teaching poetry or selling jam would barely pay for an unconverted pigsty. Anyway, if they were near a market town, property *wouldn't* be so cheap.

Will licked a swirl of yogurt from the lid. 'We could work on the place together and make it really nice. And maybe Sam could spend his school holidays with us, or part of them, at least. He'd love the country.'

She could hardly take it in. Not just Will, but now his son. 'What would Vanessa say, though? She wouldn't let him, would she?'

'Well, strangely enough, I think she might. You see, even with all her money, the one thing she can't give him is the experience of living in the country. Oh, she's doing her best with riding lessons on Hampstead Heath, but that's a pretty poor substitute. Even Hampstead's full of traffic fumes and terribly congested, and she's out so much they can't have any pets. And she is aware of what he's missing because she grew up in the country herself. She used to have her own pony, and cats and dogs and hens and stuff. And when I think of the fantastic times *I* had at Auntie Mags's – bird-watching, fishing, collecting eggs warm from the hens . . .'

'So you *are* a romantic, Will!'

'You know I am. And I want life with *you* to be romantic. If you moved in here, how d'you think I'd feel, watching you struggle with those pathetic gas-rings and having to dish things up in the bathroom because we haven't got a sink. I *love* you, Catherine, and I can see you really blossoming in the country – growing vegetables, serving cream teas, lazing in a hammock watching the clouds . . .'

She bit back a retort. There'd be precious little time for lazing in hammocks after tending a vegetable garden, making patchwork to sell, and baking scones for the cream teas, to say nothing of renovating the house. And how would Andrew greet the news that she was setting up home with a penniless poet, hundreds of miles away?

'I knew you wouldn't want to go,' Will muttered dejectedly.

'Will, I haven't said that.'

'You haven't said anything, so you can't be exactly overjoyed.'

She took his hand. 'But I *am.* I'm very pleased that you want me with you at all.'

'Of course I do. Did you doubt it?'

She poured more tea, trying to choose her words with care. 'You're going a bit fast, darling. I need time to take it in. And as far as Sam's concerned, isn't it rather a big step to have him come and stay with us in Durham, or wherever, when I haven't even met him?'

'Yeah, you're right. You two ought to meet. But suppose you loathe him on sight?'

'Oh, Will, how could I loathe a seven-year-old?'

'Easily.'

'Is he *that* bad?'

'No. If anything, he's the other way. A bit too shy and quiet.

305

Vanessa blames me for that as well. She says he's inherited my genes.'

'But you're not shy and quiet.'

'Underneath, I am.'

'Shy, maybe, but not quiet.' She gave his hand an affectionate squeeze. 'Well, certainly not in bed.'

'Actually, it does worry me a bit,' Will said, kissing her fingers. 'Sam *is* too sensitive, and sometimes I find myself getting annoyed with him, just like my father did with me. It's awful, isn't it? – you vow you'll never make the same mistakes your parents made. But it's not that easy. Especially if the kid takes after you and you see your own faults coming out.'

'Oh, I know. That's how I felt with Kate. I was always rubbing her up the wrong way. And it's only recently I realized that *I* had a rebellious streak as well. But *she* was free to express it and I suppose I sort of resented that, subconsciously. I didn't have her opportunities . . .' She stopped short, startled by her own words. She *did* have opportunities now, yet she was reacting as she had to Kate: playing safe, being tediously practical, thinking of all the drawbacks instead of the advantages.

She stood by the window, staring out unseeingly. Compared with Nicky's venture, a move to the north was nothing. And maybe Will's idea could work. Even if it didn't, it wasn't the end of the world. She had little to lose these days – no bricks and mortar, no settled way of life. And there was no need for long-term commitment. It needn't be 'settling down' – more experimenting, playing almost. She could set her own conditions: six months' trial maybe and no hard feelings if either of them changed their mind. And not too much of the baking and suchlike, whatever Will's fantasies about unlimited cream teas. Of course, allocating the chores was an important aspect of living together, but the first requirement was a readiness to open her mind, to regard Will's plan as something positive – and possible. Given his normal wariness, it was surprising he'd even hatched such a plan, and indeed rather gratifying. And, ironically, she knew Kate would approve. Although still living on different continents, they had drawn closer in the last couple of months, as if Kate felt more of a bond with a rootless mother working on a market stall than one shoe-horned into affluent suburbia.

'Catherine, I haven't upset you, have I? I mean, just by suggesting it?'

'No. To tell the truth, I'm tempted.'

'Honestly?' He jumped up from his chair. 'Look, I could get in touch with Anthony tomorrow. He still lives in Durham and he'd know if there's anything going. Or if you'd rather go back to your roots, we could phone a few Manchester estate agents.'

'Hold on, my love! Don't you think we should work out some of the finances? We could make a list of the outgoings, to balance against any source of income we can think of.'

He laughed. 'You're so frighteningly efficient, darling. Let's leave that till the morning. I'd far rather curl up in bed with you and dream about country mansions.'

'Will, you're incorrigible! It's more likely to be a garden shed.'

'Okay, garden sheds.' He took her hand and pulled her up. 'Bedtime.'

'No, wait. There's one thing we ought to settle first. Sam. If you want us to make a home for him, then I must meet him, Will. Would Vanessa absolutely hate it if I came along next time you're due to see him?'

'She wouldn't need to know. In fact, she's going away in a fortnight to see an author in Geneva, and she wants me to have Sam on the Sunday. The nanny's off that day and Julian's got some golf thing. So we could take him out for lunch or something.'

'But he'd tell Vanessa, wouldn't he?'

'Who cares? You'd have met him by then. And for God's sake, Catherine, I don't need her permission to have another woman in my life. *She*'s remarried, and poor Sam has to live with the insufferable Julian, whether he likes it or not.'

'Ssh, don't get all upset again. Okay, let's take him out, and I'll just play it cool and be a casual friend of yours, until he gets more used to me. Where shall we go? The zoo? Oh yes, of course,' she smiled, 'to see the camels.'

'You and your blessed camels! Mind you, he'd adore it. He did a school project on zoos once, and hasn't been back since then. In fact, if I tell him it was your suggestion, he'll be your slave for life!'

25

'He's got an awful itch.' Sam watched the camel bobbing rhythmically up and down as it scratched its flank against the fence-post. Its back legs were splayed inelegantly, its raggedy tail swished.

'Perhaps he's been stung,' Will said, attempting to peer into the creature's eyes. 'He does look a bit uncomfortable.'

Catherine moved closer to the fence. 'No, I think he's trying to rub lumps of his coat off. It looks as if he's moulting.'

Sam turned to her, grave-faced. 'What's moulting?'

'Well, their shaggy coats are too hot for the summer, so they just sort of fall off, bit by bit. He's about halfway through the process now, which is why he looks so funny – bald on his back and neck, and still furry on his humps.'

'I wouldn't like *my* hair to fall off.'

'Oh, I think you'd look quite good bald!' Will spread his hands speculatively on top of Sam's fair head.

Sam wriggled away and stared unsmiling at his father. All Will's jokes had fallen flat so far. He's trying too hard, she thought. It was understandable, though. For her *and* Will, today was more than just a casual outing. There was such a lot at stake. Could she relate to Sam? Would she like him? More important, would he like *her*?

A second, paler camel emerged slowly from its sleeping quarters. 'Look, Sam,' she said, 'another one.'

'He's dirty.'

'Yes, he must have been rolling in the straw.' Catherine smiled at the animal's comical appearance, festooned with bits of grass and straw. His moult was slightly more advanced, and grey hairless patches alternated with a few shaggy tufts of off-white fur.

'He's a mess!' Sam sounded almost admiring. Presumably *he* was never allowed to be messy. His clothes seemed more appropriate for Sunday school than for a visit to the zoo. Unlike the other kids, casual in jeans and baseball caps, he was wearing a white short-sleeved shirt and neatly pressed blue chinos. Will, in contrast, looked frankly dishevelled, more the scruffy little boy than the sprucely conventional father. But Sam was causing heads to turn, in admiration of his striking good looks: eyes Bournville-dark beneath the thick blond hair; skin fragile-pale, translucent. She was proud to be taken for his mother, though nervous, too, at the responsibility. She kept thinking back to when Andrew was that age – the alarming sense of a child's absolute dependence on you. In some ways, Sam reminded her of Andrew: a naturally serious child, rather wary of the world. Sam, of course, had reason to be wary. His father had been supplanted by a stepfather (who had no experience of children) and was still bitter towards his mother. In any case, Sam probably saw more of his nanny than either of his parents.

'Hey, look!' Will pointed to a third camel, lumbering out to join the other two. With its unsteady gait and half-closed eyes it seemed unwell, or drugged. The back hump was completely bald, the front one thick and shaggy. Its flanks were patchy and unkempt, as if someone had thrown a moth-eaten fur coat over the poor creature. Yet it gazed haughtily down at the onlookers, oblivious of their comments.

'I think he's suffering from a hangover,' Will said, mimicking its expression.

'What's a hangover, Daddy?'

'I hope you'll never need to know, Sam.'

'It's when you drink too much,' Catherine explained. 'And the next morning you don't feel very well.'

'But why would camels drink too much? Miss Collins told us they hardly ever drink.'

'Yes, she's right. Daddy was only joking.' It seemed odd to refer to Will as Daddy, but 'your father' sounded pompous. Anyway, she liked the illusion of them being a normal family, and she knew it pleased Will too. In their stroll round the zoo they had seen a number of lone fathers, some looking glumly self-conscious as they tried to cope with fractious children. Will had eyed them with sympathy, then given her a quick smile. In the ordinary way he would have kissed her or squeezed her hand, but such tokens of affection were impossible with Sam there.

'Gosh, how odd,' said Will, squatting on his haunches and peering through the fence. 'They have bigger front feet than back.'

'*Why* do they?' asked Sam.

'I don't know. Perhaps it's for walking on the sand. See, Catherine?'

'Oh, yes.' She gazed at their broad two-toed feet. She had never been this close to a camel, and was fascinated by the details: the bulging eyelids and long-lashed amber eyes; the coarse cream whiskers protruding from velvet lips; the slit-like nostrils fringed with hairs. And their legs were surprisingly short, with bare bony knees and powerful thighs, still furry.

'That must be their keeper,' she told Sam, as a man in a green tee-shirt and dung-encrusted boots let himself into the pen. He was carrying a large bundle of twigs which he spread out on the ground in three roughly equal piles.

'What's he doing?'

'I think he's giving them their lunch,' said Catherine. 'Shall we ask him?'

Sam shrank back, clearly too shy to address a stranger. However, the question answered itself since all three camels began to munch enthusiastically, chomping through the dry brown twigs as if they were succulent bananas.

'What's that they're eating?' she called out to the keeper.

'Hawthorn twigs. They eat hay and vegetables, too, but hawthorn's their favourite.'

'You'd think it would scratch their mouths,' said Will. 'Look, Sam, see the way their jaws move from side to side.' Again he imitated the camels, making exaggerated chewing movements.

Sam blushed and looked at his feet, evidently not amused.

'They're also very partial to chocolate,' the keeper added.

'Chocolate?' Sam glanced up, intrigued.

'Like me,' said Will, jotting something on the back of his zoo-guide. 'In fact I can feel a camel poem coming on. I might even do a series: scratching camels, moulting camels, chewing camels, chocolate camels . . .'

'Oh, I see. I'm being ousted, am I, as the source of your inspiration?' Catherine forgot for a moment that she was meant to be a casual acquaintance, though luckily Sam hadn't heard.

'Oh no,' Will murmured, and their eyes met for a fraction of a second as they recalled this morning's lie-in. It was a rare treat on a Sunday, and as for taking the whole day off – the most lucrative day at the market – normally they wouldn't dream of doing so. But *this* Sunday was special, and if they were out of pocket, too bad.

'Is that one older than the others?' Will asked the keeper, pointing to the cream camel. 'He looks a bit doddery.'

'No, they're all quite young. That's just the way she moves. And they're all shes, by the way. We prefer to keep females. The males tend to be more cantankerous.'

'What's cantankerous?' Sam asked.

'*I* am,' Will replied, 'when I don't get my lunch. I'm beginning to feel peckish watching that lot tuck in. Aren't you two hungry?' He was already leafing through his booklet. 'There's a self-service caff, a picnic bar, pizzas, or fish and chips.'

Sam's face lit up. 'Oh, can we have fish and chips? I'm not allowed them at home.'

'Why not?' Will was instantly on the defensive.

'Mummy says they're bad for us.'

'Oh *does* she?'

'Ssh, Will,' Catherine whispered. 'Why don't we be diplomatic and just have a pizza or something?'

'Oh, pizzas would be just as bad. She's into this health kick at the moment. She read some article about children eating too much fat and then having heart attacks in their thirties. Actually, she'd probably approve of the hawthorn twigs – high in fibre, low in fat.'

'What are you two whispering about?' Sam sounded almost accusing.

Catherine flushed. She bent down to Sam's level and said confidingly, 'We're just deciding whether to have fish and chips.'

'Oh, *please*, Catherine!'

It was the first time he had used her name and she was ridiculously touched. He was gazing at her with his lustrous dark eyes and she felt a shock of recognition. *Will*'s eyes could plead like that. 'All right,' she said. 'Just this once.'

Her reward was a radiant smile which transformed his face completely; he seemed a happy, trusting child at last.

'Can I have double chips?'

'Don't push your luck, Sam,' Will said sternly.

'Tell you what,' said Catherine, daring to take Sam's hand. 'I'm not very keen on chips, so why don't you have mine?'

'The fish bar's only a few minutes away,' Will said, studying his map. 'Near the lions and tigers.' They had seen the big cats already and exchanged smiles over Sam's head. 'They're very quiet,' he'd said suggestively. 'For tigers.'

'This way,' he said now, steering them down a tree-lined path. 'It's nice to have some shade. It's getting really warm.'

'Mm.' Catherine stopped to take off her sweater and stuffed it in her bag. 'It must be almost in the seventies.' Squinting in the glare of the sun, she looked around at the lush green trees and shrubs. It was perfect mid-May weather and nature was burgeoning and budding with every shade of green, from the bright burnish of new ivy to the dark whorls of rhododendron leaves. And every colour, too: scarlet-jawed tulips, soft blue smoke of lilac, a confetti of pink blossom on the path. The place was all the more attractive because they were on holiday – playing truant, from work, from rules, even from Vanessa.

Will had spotted the sign. 'There it is,' he said. 'Why don't you run on, Sam, and save us a place in the queue?'

'Oh, yes!' He raced towards the fish bar – more a kiosk than a proper restaurant – where a long line of people waited at the serving hatch.

'Love you,' Will whispered as soon as Sam was out of earshot.

'Love you too.' She longed to kiss him there and then. There was something about the day – the late start, the warmth, the sense of freedom – that made her feel languorous yet aroused.

'Look, they do a special deal, Catherine –' Will was reading the metal sign swinging on its stand '– fish and chips with a choice of drink and a cake for three pounds ninety-five. Thank heavens. We're going through an awful lot of cash today.'

'Sam's very good, though, isn't he? He hasn't asked for anything.'

'Except your chips,' laughed Will.

'Oh, I'm sure I can spare him those. I'm getting fat as it is.'

'Not that I've noticed.' He patted her rump surreptitiously as they joined Sam in the queue. 'What drink d'you want, Sam?' he asked. 'There's Coke, Pepsi, Tizer, Seven-Up . . .'

'Can I *really* have those?' His eyes opened in wonder, as if his father was offering him something dangerous and depraved.

'You can have whatever you like.'

'Ooh, Pepsi, then.' He still sounded incredulous.

'Please,' corrected Will. 'And what for you, Catherine?'

'Let's see . . . I'd better have a Diet Coke.'

'Please,' corrected Sam.

They all laughed, which seemed to dispel any remaining tension.

'Why don't I wait in the queue,' Will suggested. 'And you and Sam go and grab a table.'

It was a tiny triumph that Sam went with her willingly, even slipping his hand into hers again. The tables – rustic picnic-style, with wooden benches attached – were surrounded by trees and flowerbeds and already very crowded.

'There's one.' Sam made a bee-line for it, and sat sideways along the bench with his legs stretched out.

'Clever boy! It's the only empty one.'

'Mummy says I've got good eyes.'

'Yes, you have.' He also had a beautiful voice, a younger version of Will's cultured intonation. When Will introduced him, he had struck her as rather charmingly old-fashioned, a far cry from the cocky streetwise kids who hung around the market.

'I'll sit this side and you and Daddy can sit the other side.'

'Okay,' she said. 'But you've got company, I see.' A group of starlings flurried and squawked beneath his feet, pecking at an abandoned meal.

Delightedly, he jumped off the bench and picked up the remains of some cake, which he held in his outstretched hand. Instantly half a dozen more birds descended, beaks jabbing greedily. 'It tickles,' he laughed.

'Careful they don't peck your fingers,' she warned, wondering what Vanessa would say if she could see her son crawling about under the table in search of further scraps; dirty marks on his once immaculate clothes.

'You'd better sit up now, Sam. The food will be here any minute.'

He knelt up rather than sat, suddenly noticing the two boys at the next table. They were roughly his age and both had their faces painted with flamboyant whiskers and black and yellow stripes. (They had passed the face-painting stall this morning, and had asked Sam if he'd like to be a clown or tiger or zebra for the day. He had refused the offer, out of shyness, she assumed.)

'Look, she said. 'There's another one – a cat.'

It was a little girl, this time, with green saucer eyes painted round her brown ones, black cheeks and long white whiskers. Sam studied her for a while before turning back to Catherine.

'Have *you* got a cat?' he asked.

'Yes. Actually, it's not really mine. I'm looking after it for someone.'

'I wish *I* had one. Mummy won't let me, though.'

'Oh, that's a shame. But I expect it's difficult in London.'

'Do *you* live in London?'

'Er, yes,' she said.

There was a brief and rather awkward silence, then he asked, 'What's your cat's name?'

'William.'

'That's my Daddy's name.'

'Yes. It's a nice name, isn't it?'

Another silence. 'My Daddy doesn't live with me now,' he said finally.

'Yes, I know, Sam.'

'I live with Mummy and Julian.'

She wondered how to respond, desperately grateful that Gerry hadn't died – or left – before her own children were grown-up.

'Julian bought me a computer.'

'Did he, Sam? That was nice.'

'And a bike.'

'Gosh, you lucky thing.'

'I fell off the bike and hurt my knee.' He rolled up his trouser-leg and showed her a large graze.

She felt absurdly moved. The graze was almost healed, yet it seemed to symbolize the fragility of things: knees, life, marriages, relationships. 'Shall I kiss it better?'

'Mm.'

Despite a gap of twenty-odd years, the drill instantly returned: lips just brushing the wound, a series of little kissing noises for added effect. Sam seemed satisfied, though he was still gazing at his knee.

'Mummy says it might leave a scar.'

'Well, only a tiny one. It looks as if it's healing pretty well.' She pulled his trouser-leg down and gave his leg a reassuring pat.

'Are you going to marry my Daddy?' he asked suddenly.

'Er, no, Sam. I . . . I'm just a friend of his.'

'Are you going to have a baby?'

'No!' she said, startled, wondering what on earth he might come out with next. Could Vanessa be pregnant, perhaps?

She was relieved to see Will approaching with a tray, which he proceeded to unload. Sam watched with rapt attention as each item was set before him: first his drink, which came in a stripy carton complete with matching straws, then his chocolate cake, and lastly his cardboard platter of fish and chips, topped with a miniature Union Jack. He removed the flag carefully and put it beside his plate. 'Where's the knives and forks?'

'There aren't any. You eat it in your fingers.'

He picked up a chip and bit into it uncertainly, as if expecting an instant reprimand. When none was forthcoming, he ate several more in quick succession. 'Can I eat this in my fingers too?' he asked, looking wonderingly at the fish.

'Yes, Sam. That's why they give you those little pieces,' Catherine said, 'so it's easier to manage.'

If anything, the pieces were *too* small – scrappy and unappetizing. And, taking her first bite, she wondered if they'd been served penguin food by mistake. It was coarse in texture, grey in colour, and tasted of nothing but the breadcrumbs it was fried in. And the chips were little better: soggy and none too hot. Sam, though, was in seventh heaven: fingers greasy, ketchup on his chin, a piece of fish in one hand, a clutch of chips in the other. He was wolfing his food, as if at any moment they might change their minds and insist on a knife and fork. But neither she nor Will said anything about manners, even when he made a slurping noise with his straw. She could see that this was Will's secret revenge on Vanessa and had no desire to spoil it. She passed Sam her chips, relieved to be rid of them. Will, however, was eating with the same gusto as Sam. Like father, like son, she thought, though actually they were strangely *un*alike in appearance, and not just in regard to clothes. Will's hair looked even darker and more unruly compared with Sam's smooth blond gleaming crop. And the boy seemed almost fragile against his father's chunky build: a delicate child who might have been brought by the fairies instead of sired by someone as solid as Will.

His appetite, however, was anything but delicate. He had finished her chips as well as his, and was now tucking in to his cake. 'It's got bits of chocolate in,' he said approvingly.

315

'Yes, it's called a chocolate muffin. The camels would like it, wouldn't they?'

He nodded. 'What's a muffin?'

'A mule,' said Will with a grin.

She was surprised he wasn't more serious with the child. He told *her* things with such passion – pointed out the poetic details of flowers, clouds, even maybugs, yet took this facetious tone with Sam. She suspected it was nerves – he was so keen to make a good impression, he felt he had to play the clown.

Sam took a last noisy slurp of his Pepsi, then said, a shade embarrassed, 'Daddy, I need a . . . wee.'

'Me too,' said Will. 'Do you think we dare leave Catherine on her own?'

'Oh, *she*'ll be all right.'

They couldn't help laughing at Sam's airy confidence. He was now on his feet and tugging at Will's hand.

'I'm too full to move.' Will groaned and patted his stomach.

'Come *on*, Daddy.'

Will got up reluctantly. 'See you later, alligator,' he said to Catherine, taking a bite of her cake.

'Oh, can we see the alligators?' Sam begged.

'In a while, crocodile, after our food's had time to settle.'

He and Sam departed to the gents, while Catherine sat nibbling her cake, enjoying the feel of the sun on her arms and vaguely aware of the symphony of noises – the twittering of birds, children's laughter, the distant lowing of some animal. She smiled at the woman on the next table, who was wiping ketchup off her daughter's dress. The child looked rather like Sam – blonde and beautiful. Now that she'd actually met Sam, she was more concerned about his reaction to their plans for moving north. They must be careful to include him at all stages; make it *his* home, too, somewhere he could come for holidays and perhaps have his own cat or dog. Will's first vague pipe-dreams about living in the country had begun to assume more practical shape. He had been right, to her surprise: there *were* cottages to be had at reasonable rents, at least in certain areas. The flat was awash in property details from every estate agent north of Watford. She couldn't see any particular problem about having Sam to stay. Of course, it was difficult to judge after only a few hours' acquaintance, but she was fairly sure she could manage. And as Will got used to the three of them being together, he was bound to be more relaxed.

She caught sight of them strolling back from the gents, Sam holding Will's hand and listening to him attentively. Once they reached the café, he darted up to her. 'Daddy says we can go and see the crocodiles.'

Will finished his Tizer and helped himself to the last knob of cake, Sam frowning in impatience.

'Hurry up, Daddy!'

'Wait a minute. We need to find the Reptile House.' Will brushed crumbs from his lip and scanned the map again. 'Ah, yes, got it. We turn left here, then it's straight down the main path. And we pass the elephants on the way, so if you're still peckish, Sam, you can have a jumbo-size snack.'

'It *can't* be real.' Catherine stared at the scaly body sitting absolutely motionless on the bank of its tropical pool. Its jaws gaped open, revealing a long pinkish tongue and two rows of uneven teeth. 'Look, there's a notice here saying they're going to move the croco-diles to Whipsnade. Perhaps they've gone already and that one's just a replica – you know, to show people what they look like.'

'Of course it's real,' said Will.

'But it wouldn't keep its mouth open so long. We've been here at least five minutes and it hasn't moved a muscle.'

'It's probably a way of keeping cool.'

'What do *you* think, Sam?' Catherine asked. 'Is it real or pretend?'

'Pretend,' Sam said confidently. 'It's a toy.'

With that, the creature blinked its eye and stretched its jaws still wider.

'Look, it moved! It moved!' Sam yelled. 'It *is* real.'

'It must have heard you,' said Catherine, 'and didn't like being called a toy.'

'It's smiling at us,' he remarked. She had noticed his preference for the quieter creatures – the gentle, passive slowcoaches. He had been fascinated by the fruit bats and the sloths; gazed enchanted at the turtles swimming lazily in their pool.

And standing watching them by that pool, she had remembered Nicky's description of the turtles in the Caribbean: corpulent old gentlemen, bobbing on the waves. In less than a month, Nicky would be back there; starting the new job on Virgin Gorda. Every time she thought of it, she was painfully aware of the gap it would leave in her own life.

'I'd like to see the tarantulas,' Will said, consulting the guide. 'It says here they have bird-eating spiders that are almost extinct in the wild.'

Sam's eyes widened in alarm. 'Are they as big as crocodiles?'

'Oh, no. They're small and furry – quite sweet really. They've got red knees.'

'Daddy, spiders haven't got *knees*.'

'Yes, they have.' Will showed Sam the caption to the picture. 'See? "Red-kneed Spider or Tarantula". Shall we go and find them?'

'I think it had better be our last port of call,' Catherine said. 'We've had a long day. Is it far?'

'Not too bad. Want me to carry you?'

'You can carry *me*,' said Sam.

'I don't know about that. You look awfully heavy to me.' Will made a pretence of picking him up, then sagged at the knees, tongue lolling.

'Don't be silly, Daddy.'

'All right, I'll behave.'

They trooped along to the Invertebrate House, which was claustrophobic and very dimly lit. Catherine felt growing apprehension as they moved from Millipedes to Robber Crabs, Hissing Cockroaches to Whip Scorpions. Any moment they would come upon the spiders. She had never lost her fear of them – a fear now compounded by memories of Gerry. Yet she had no wish to admit such weakness in front of Sam, and spoil his and Will's enjoyment. She hung back nervously as they approached each cage, and Will read out various names: Leaf-cutting Ant, Wart-biter Cricket, Assassin Bug. She was astonished at the sheer number of invertebrates. They had passed every species, it appeared, of insect, mollusc, worm, yet still no sign of a tarantula. Until suddenly Will exclaimed, 'Ah, here we are. Wow, look at the size of him!'

She stood paralysed, her eyes fixed on the monstrous thing, with its bulbous head and terrifying shaggy legs. At least it wasn't moving, although in her mind she could feel it advancing towards her, scuttling over her foot.

'Isn't he beautiful?' said Will. 'See his knees, Sam? They *are* red.'

'He's got lots of knees,' Sam said, impressed. 'Two on each leg.'

'And how many legs?'

'Six?' Sam guessed.

'No, eight,' said Will. 'That's sixteen knees in all.'

'More than me,' said Sam.

'And yours aren't red and furry.'

'No.' He looked back at the spider, pressing his nose to the glass. 'I wish *I* could have one.'

'Some people do keep them as pets, but I don't think Mummy would be too keen. You have to feed them live crickets.'

Sam looked puzzled. 'Crickets?'

'Insects. We saw some further back.'

'I thought they ate birds?' said Sam.

'Well, they are *called* bird-eating spiders, but in fact they very rarely eat birds – or so it says here.' Will was reading the details printed beside the cage. 'Though they do like the odd mouse or lizard as a treat. And apparently a big meal can last them a year. I'm glad *I*'m not a spider – imagine only eating once a year. Good God!' he exclaimed. 'The female lays over a thousand eggs, would you believe. And this one *is* female – Sharon's her name. Sorry, Sharon, for thinking you were a "he".' All at once he noticed Catherine's stricken face. 'What's wrong?'

'Nothing. It's just that . . . they make me think of Gerry. He loved spiders. Once he had to *be* one. At drama school. It was a sort of acting exercise.'

'Who's Gerry?' Sam asked, sharp-eared as ever.

'My, er, husband,' she said.

'Where is he?'

'He . . .'

'Did he go away?'

'Yes. Well, no . . .' Desperately, she looked at Will. Why on earth had she mentioned him?

'He died, Sam,' Will said gently.

She knew he believed in telling the truth to children, but the word sounded dreadfully harsh. Sam was staring at her fixedly, the tarantula forgotten. Several seconds passed. Will tried to show him a second spider, but he continued looking at *her*. 'Barney died,' he said at last.

'Barney?' A pet, perhaps?

'He was in my class.'

'Oh, a boy at school, you mean?'

He nodded.

'What happened to him, Sam?'

'He was run over by a car.'

Clumsily Will took his hand. 'That was a long time ago, Sam, wasn't it?'

He pulled away and seemed to be speaking only to her. 'We made him a card. We wrote our names and drawed pictures. I did a car. A red one.'

'Was it the car that ran him over?'

'Yes.'

Will did his best to distract him by suggesting a visit to the zoo-shop, but she could see Sam wanted to talk. He was scuffing his shoes on the floor and still looking at her anxiously.

'Do people go to heaven when they die?'

She hesitated. They had told her that when *she* was little and it had upset her even more. Why should her mother live somewhere else, without her? 'We're not sure, Sam, where they go.'

'Miss Collins said he went to see Baby Jesus.'

'Yes, maybe he . . .' She broke off. What right had she to tell him something Will regarded as myth? The whole issue of truth – or death – was so confusing for a seven-year-old.

'Robin says they put dead people in boxes.'

Will made an attempt to steer them towards the green light of the exit. 'Sam, why don't we go and see the otters? They're right next door.'

'It's okay, Will.' She put a hand on his arm. She knew how embarrassed people got about the subject, though she was surprised Will should be so edgy. No doubt he saw this episode as a blemish on a perfect day. But if the two boys had been close, perhaps Sam had never quite come to terms with Barney's death. This was a chance to let him talk about it, and at least she knew what not to say.

Suddenly she tensed. Out of the corner of her eye, she had detected a slight movement. The tarantula. Not scuttling, as she'd feared, but sidling across its cage in a ghastly furtive manner. Horrified, she looked away, tried to keep her eyes on Sam.

'Why do they?' he was asking.

'Why do they what, darling?'

'Put people in boxes.'

'Well, it's more comfortable like that. They're very *nice* boxes, with silky stuff inside, and flowers on top.'

'Flowers?'

'Yes.' It *was* grotesque. Flowers were for celebration, not for death.

'What sort of flowers?'

'Well, Gerry had roses.' Red roses for undying love. And she had bought a rose bush, later, to be planted in the crematorium garden. It had seemed better than a plaque. At least it was alive, and would bloom in red profusion every year.

'Did you cry when they put him in the box?'

'Yes.'

'Did you cry a lot?'

'Yes.'

'I cried when Barney died.'

'Mm, I'm sure you did. Was he a special friend?'

He looked at her a moment, then, without warning, two tears slid down his face. She crouched beside him, gingerly reaching out her arms, afraid he would want his father and not her. Will, however, was shifting from foot to foot, patently ill at ease. 'I expect you miss him, don't you, Sam?' she said.

Sam didn't answer, but more tears glistened on his lashes, threatening to spill over.

She put her arms round him and spoke as gently as she could. 'When people die, it's sometimes quite a while before we stop feeling sad. They've been part of our life, you see, and then, one day, they're just not there. And that's awful for us, isn't it? But you do make *new* friends, Sam.' Behind his head she could see the tarantula, right up against the glass now, as if about to burst out of its cage. Her natural instinct was to turn and flee, but Sam needed her as mother, so she must overcome the sick churning in her stomach. 'Have *you* got a new friend?' she asked, wiping his eyes with her handkerchief.

He nodded silently.

'That's nice. What's his name?'

'Robin.'

'And do you sit next to him at school?'

He shook his head, then unexpectedly pulled away, breaking the circle of her arms. 'Can we have a camel ride?' he asked.

She was so thrown by this change of tack, she could only stare at him, but Will came to the rescue. 'Of course, Sam. We'll go there now.' Hurriedly he began talking about camels and soon the two of them were deep in conversation.

She followed a few paces behind, unable to shake off thoughts of death with quite such speed. Indeed, Gerry seemed to be *here* with them, studying his beloved spiders. She could hear his voice; see his absorbed expression. In two weeks' time it would be his birthday and the rest of the family – Andrew and Antonia, Jack and Maureen – had suggested marking the occasion with a visit to the crematorium, as they'd done last year. Although she had agreed, secretly she dreaded the prospect of returning to that deodorized memorial-factory, which sold death at a profit. It wasn't the money she begrudged, but its association with grief and love.

'*Why* do they close their nostrils?' Sam was asking his father.

'Well, it protects them from the sand. Otherwise, on a windy day, it might blow into their noses.'

Thankfully Sam was preoccupied and appeared to have forgotten Barney's death. *She* still felt upset, and strangely exhausted all at once. And she was certainly more worried now about their proposed move to the north. Sam might well experience it as another loss in his life; a new source of rejection. After all, if he was still mourning Barney's death, there could *other* things distressing him – his parents' divorce for one. It would take time and patience on her part to persuade him to open up, but if he came for regular visits, he might gradually start to trust her and confide.

Will and Sam were striding on ahead and she found it quite an effort to keep up. It seemed miles to the Riding Lawn, especially in the heat, and her steps began to flag, as if the burden of being a stepmother was already weighing heavily. When they finally got there, she was dismayed at the length of the queue, but there was no way they could deprive Sam of his promised treat.

Will bought a ticket at the kiosk and they joined the line of parents and children. Two of the camels they'd seen earlier were lurching round the sand-strewn track with children on their backs. Sam observed them gravely, and as the queue shuffled slowly forwards, he began to take a closer interest in the details of the ride. He watched each child ahead of him clamber up the wooden steps, where a keeper swung him into the saddle. Then a second keeper led the camel on its circuit, after which the child was lifted down again and set gently back on the steps.

'I wonder which one you'll get, Sam – the brown or the white?'

Sam didn't appear to have heard his father, and just stood watching in silence. 'Is it scary?' he asked, at last.

'Oh, no. You sit between the two humps and you're very safe and snug.'

Sam looked unconvinced and began to drag his feet, in danger of being left behind as people overtook them in the queue.

'You'll enjoy it,' Will said, moving him firmly on. 'It's fun.'

Again, Sam was silent; his gaze fixed on the keeper as each child was helped on or off. Finally it was his turn.

'Right, off you go,' said Will. 'We'll wave as you go round.'

They both smiled encouragingly as the keeper led him up the steps. He reached the platform-top, looked back at them in panic for an instant, then came rushing down again, almost tripping in his haste.

'I don't *want* to go. I don't *want* a ride.'

'Don't be silly, Sam. You'll love it.'

She could see Will was getting exasperated, and gave him a warning frown. 'Don't force him, darling,' she whispered.

'But it's such a shame when we've queued so long and bought his ticket and everything.'

'Okay, *I*'ll go in his place.'

'Catherine, you can't!'

'I jolly well can!' Before he could stop her, she was climbing the steps. 'You don't mind adults, do you?' she asked the keeper.

'Not at all, ma'am,' he said, though not before a moment's hesitation. In the fifteen minutes they had been there, no one over ten had volunteered for a ride, let alone any over-forties. She realized people were gawping, not least Sam and Will, but as the camel set off round the track she was so taken with the marvellous swaying motion, she soon forgot her embarrassment. There was a sense of power about being so high up, no longer dwarfed by the trees. And she liked the firm feel of the hump pressing into her back, and the warm woolly fur beneath her hand, and the creak of the leather saddle. Even the smell of dung was strangely pleasing – an earthy smell which gave her more sense of the camel's living, breathing, eating, excreting existence. She wondered why the creatures were said to be bad-tempered; this one seemed docility itself. The only thing she resented was the stripling of a keeper leading her like a novice on a rein. But she could simply block him out, forget she was in a zoo at all, plodding round a cramped Riding Lawn, ringed with mums and dads.

No, this was her own camel – a mystic white one, who knew her voice and her touch, and she was crossing the Gobi Desert with the nomads. Bells from another camel-train tinkled faintly on the breeze, and the graceful fronds of date palms seemed to sway to the rhythm of the camel's tireless feet, the great rocking ship of its body. The light was blurring in a blue and golden haze; the world expanding with each step. Ordinary life had stopped. There was no time in the desert; no work save the task of crossing it; no problem children, or hateful crematorium visits; no rush, or noise, or hustle.

This is what I was *born* to do, she thought, with a jolt of surprise, as she gazed into the distance at the rippled sea of sand, stretching shining and unbroken to the horizon.

26

'Such a pity.' Maureen stood leaning on her stick, looking at the wreaths and bouquets laid out on the flagstones behind the chapel. 'All those lovely flowers dying in the heat.'

Andrew hovered solicitously beside her. 'Come and sit down, Grandma. There's a bench over there.'

'Just a moment, dear. I like reading the messages. Some of them break your heart. See that poem, Catherine, with the white chrysanthemums – isn't it beautiful?'

Catherine grunted noncommittally as she read the limping lines – the sort of ghastly sentiment you found on greetings cards. They should have called on Will for help. She couldn't seem to get him out of her mind. Even the once-white cushion of chrysanthemums, now semi-bald and withered, reminded her of the moulting camels at the zoo. And like that day, two weeks ago, this was another sunny Sunday when again she was playing truant from the market. But there the similarities ended.

She linked her arm through Maureen's, returning resolutely to the bosom of her family. In any case, Maureen needed support – physical as well as emotional. Her movements had become pathetically slow, and even with the stick she seemed unsteady on her feet.

'Look, Catherine dear, a cricket bat! Isn't it amazing what they can do with flowers these days?'

'Mm.' Catherine gave it a cursory glance. The bat-shape was sculpted in carnations, but like the cushion was long past its prime. Stupid bloody thing, she thought.

'I wish we'd done more for Gerry.' Maureen shook her head in distress. 'Our wreath wasn't as special as some of these. But at the time you're so numb, you can hardly think straight.'

Catherine steered her towards the next display of flowers. Yes, numb was the word. Frozen in grief, she had left the funeral arrangements to Andrew. Only later did she begin to resent his choice – this prissy, manicured Superstore of Death. She knew Gerry would have loathed it; ridiculed the pompous plaques set into the courtyard wall and ranged around the fountain. Jack was reading the inscriptions out to Antonia – more sentimental claptrap. The whole place was fake, though who was she to talk? She too was bogus, encased in a prim navy frock instead of her normal bohemian clothes. She had even put on a hat, though less for the sake of formality than to conceal her hair from Andrew. Neither he nor Maureen had become reconciled to its 'butchered' shape, let alone its colour, and saw it as a worrying symptom of her wayward life in London.

'Oh, look,' said Maureen, stooping to read another card. 'A little girl of five. How terrible! We did at least have our darling Gerry for nearly fifty years.'

Catherine murmured some response, wishing she didn't feel so irritable. But there was something about the sultry weather combined with the air of gilt-edged sanctity which made her want to scream. Little huddles of people were standing around in lugubrious silence or speaking in hushed tones. Only she was out of tune, restless and distracted.

Jack shuffled over, leaning on Antonia. 'Let's go and sit near Gerry for a while.'

The five of them trooped towards the Garden of Remembrance, at the halting pace necessitated by Jack's shortness of breath and Maureen's arthritic joints. With every step, thought Catherine, they were walking over the dead: trampling husbands, lovers, parents, children. Countless people's ashes had been scattered here; urns and caskets interred. Even the garden seats bristled with plaques. She had a sudden jarring vision of Gerry as a garden seat – her rumbustious husband reduced to a sedentary object, rooted for eternity in one confining space.

'What a shame the roses are still only in bud,' Maureen said as they finally reached the garden. 'They were further forward this time last year. I remember that glorious scent.'

'Well, we'll be here again on the anniversary.' Jack squeezed his wife's hand. 'They should be in full bloom by then.'

Oh God, thought Catherine, *I* shan't be here – I'll be living in Carlisle. But missing the anniversary was unthinkable. She would have to drive down from the north.

'I thought it would have been taller by now,' Jack observed, as they gathered in a group round Gerry's rosebush. 'And isn't that black-spot on the leaves?'

'I'd better talk to that nice man about it,' Maureen said, peering at a leaf. 'He was such a help last time.'

Catherine bit back a retort. The Memorial Consultant, as he liked to style himself, was a hardened salesman dressed in pious black. He had waxed lyrical over the range of urns, especially the most expensive: the 'Grosvenor' in inlaid mahogany, or the 'Aristocrat' in two-tone polished bronze. She had sensed his disdain when she ordered a mere rosebush, and purchased not in perpetuity – which here meant eighty years – only a measly five. After that, if she hadn't enough money to renew it, Gerry's rose would revert to someone else. Not even death was permanent: plaques were removed, plots reverted, unless you coughed up the appropriate sum every five, ten, fifteen years. Jack and Maureen had paid for Gerry to be entered in the Book of Remembrance in the Hall of Memory (hand-lettered script at £30 a line; emblem £69 extra). His entry ran to an emblem and six lines and, amazingly, cost no more for perpetuity.

'Let's sit down,' Maureen suggested, 'and have a quiet moment for Gerry.'

The nearest seat was copiously inscribed, sacred to the memory of an entire family: Simon, John, Eliza, Ann and Arthur Grayson. Catherine felt guilty sitting there – the Joneses encroaching on Grayson territory, when the going rate for garden seats was a cool two thousand pounds. She squeezed up to make room for Jack – the bench was built for four, not five. Five was such a difficult number: two loving couples and a hanger-on. She tried, and failed, to imagine Will beside her. He didn't belong in this part of her life – her former life, as she thought of it now. She glanced at the others, as if through his eyes. Andrew's face was respectfully composed as he observed the silence for his father; Jack looked close to tears; Maureen was crying openly and Antonia's head was bowed.

She fixed her gaze on the rosebush, trying to be equally dutiful. This time last year she too had wept, her grief still painfully raw.

Had she become hardened now, inured? The problem was, she had too much on her mind: Nicky's imminent departure, Fiona's unexpected return to Gosforth Road, and her own move to Carlisle with Will. She still hadn't told the family, dreading the protest that would inevitably ensue. In fact, it did seem callous now, turning her back on them all, even Gerry. *And* disloyal, to be going off with another man.

Angrily, she clamped her eyes shut. She mustn't think about it now. And if sorrow wouldn't come naturally, then she must have the decency to feign it. She put on a sombre expression and tried to concentrate her mind by repeating Gerry's name to herself.

'Gerry. Gerry. Gerry.' Irreverent birds were mimicking her; mocking with their exuberant song. A plane droned overhead, a baby wailed, the brutal sun scalded her bare arms. Her eyes refused to stay shut, but darted about, watching other families, seeing Grayson ghosts. The moment's silence had lasted aeons. She would go mad if it continued any longer – run amok, take an axe to the Memorial Consultant and hack him into pieces. She snatched off her hat, loosened her tight belt. She was hot and tense and sticky, ready to explode. Last night, too, was hot, lying under Will. Hot, but passionately noisy. The man upstairs had banged on the floor in annoyance, and they had paused guiltily, but only for an second. They *couldn't* stop – not then – not when she was almost, almost coming.

Horrified, she gripped the arm of the bench. What a monster she must be, reliving last night's sex in a crematorium, of all places. But her thoughts refused to be controlled. She could see Will's face in close-up as his open mouth sought hers; feel beads of sweat trickling down her naked, thrusting body. Her grip tightened on the wooden arm. It was *Will* she was holding; his tiger noises breaking through the clotted silence and roaring across the death-garden.

She sprang up from the bench. 'I'm sorry,' she blurted out. 'I, er, need the loo,' and before anyone could speak, she was running across the grass, back towards the main building. There were toilets there, she remembered, off the entrance-hall to the chapel. She must hide herself, her burning face. But as she reached the chapel door the blood drained from her cheeks. She recognized the place – ice-blue walls, heavy velvet curtains – though the chamber was eerily silent, without the ponderous organ or wailing, dirge-like hymns. Hardly knowing what she was doing, she crept up to the front pew and sat in her place for the funeral. *That* day had also been hot, but she deathly cold, as now, gooseflesh prickling her arms.

She stared at the wooden dais, half expecting to see Gerry's coffin there again. Never in her entire life had she felt such hatred for an object as she had for that repulsive coffin, not on account of its appearance, but because it reduced her husband to a few acquiescent bones. She had stumbled up from her seat and actually spoken out loud, saying, 'He *can't* be in there – he can't be,' until Andrew shushed her tactfully and persuaded her to sit down.

All at once, tears blinded her eyes; streamed unchecked down her cheeks. Tears for Gerry – not the Gerry under a rosebush or hand-lettered in a book, but her own beloved, private, beyond-price, longed-for husband.

'One of these for you, Grandma?'

'No thank you, Andrew dear.'

'Mother, you're not eating either.' Andrew passed her the plate of cream-filled brandysnaps.

Catherine took one reluctantly. So far, she had managed to force down half a cucumber sandwich. She kept thinking of Gerry's birthdays in the past: cheerful family get-togethers, with champagne flowing and lively music on the stereo. Jack would be dancing, Maureen chattering and laughing. Now both looked pitifully frail – shrunken almost, marooned in their armchairs. She took a small bite of brandysnap and smiled at her daughter-in-law. 'You've been busy,' she said.

'Oh, we did most of it yesterday.'

We. That enviable word. She and Will were not yet 'we' – there were still too many problems. But the move to Carlisle should help. If only she could break the news here and now; tell them flatly she was going and to hell with their approval.

'Delicious cake,' said Jack. Frail or no, at least his appetite was still good.

Maureen put her cup and saucer down. 'When you've finished your tea, Jack, I think we should be on our way. I'm only sorry to bother you again, Antonia. You've been ferrying us around all afternoon.'

'Don't be silly, it's no trouble.' Antonia stood up. 'I'll get the car keys.'

Catherine wished she could slip away herself, but she had agreed to stay the night at Stoneleigh. She didn't work at the market on Mondays, so Andrew and Antonia, knowing nothing about Will, assumed she had no special reason to go rushing back to London. Will was manning the stall alone today, and doubtless thinking of her, as she of him. He often said how easy it was to be distracted by lustful thoughts of his muse when he was meant to be running a workshop or selling bric-à-brac. She was flattered to have such power, enjoyed the self-esteem it gave her. One of the things which gradually faded after many years of marriage was that buzz of excitement sparked by a new man; that sense of being feverishly desired.

But such feelings were disloyal to Gerry, and she was about to wave his parents off. She stood at the front door, watching Antonia's spotless Renault disappear round the corner. Then she returned to the sitting-room and started clearing away the tea things.

'Leave that, Mother,' Andrew said. 'I want to have a . . .' The phone rang in the hall, cutting off his words. 'Excuse me a moment, will you?'

Left alone, she stood looking at the photos on the mantelpiece, including one of a large family group which showed Gerry's three brothers and their wives and the whole tribe of nieces and nephews. She had practically lost contact with them now, apart from the odd Christmas card or phone call. Not that she missed them particularly. When you married a man you accepted his relations too, without any choice in the matter. Frankly, she preferred her own crowd – that circle of new acquaintances so different from the Joneses: market traders, poets, Nicky's advertising friends, the jazz enthusiasts she'd met through Darren, and even the oddballs in the Camden shops. Certainly they had changed her outlook. The market people, especially, with their hand-to-mouth existence, had made her less security-minded, more willing to take risks. Why else would she agree to move three hundred miles away, to a cottage she hadn't even seen, in an unknown part of the country, with a man she'd known a scant four months?

She heard Andrew put the phone down in the hall. Wasn't this the perfect chance to tell him – on his own? Far easier than fending off *four* sets of objections. She needn't make the move sound final, but could present it as a temporary thing, even a sort of extended holiday. She could give a glowing description of the village, delightfully rural, yet only five miles from Carlisle. In actual fact, Thursby was nothing spectacular – just a church, a pub and a shop. But at least it would divert their attention from Will, who could be added as an afterthought.

She helped herself to a sandwich, swallowed it in a couple of bites, then took another, to fuel her courage.

'I'm glad to see you're eating, Mother.' Andrew walked in again, Filofax in hand. 'Shall I make another pot of tea?'

'No thanks, darling. Why don't we sit down and have a chat?'

'Yes, good idea.' Andrew pulled his chair closer to hers, though neither of them spoke. He, too, seemed nervous, fiddling with his pen.

Get *on* with it, she told herself. You can't be frightened of your own son, for heaven's sake. She took a deep breath. 'Andrew,' she said, at exactly the same moment as he said 'Mother . . .'

They both broke off with a laugh.

'You first,' said Andrew.

'No, you.'

'Well . . .' he cleared his throat. 'Antonia and I have some rather thrilling news. You . . . you're going to be a grandma!'

She stared at him, incredulous.

'Antonia's pregnant. It's just been confirmed.'

'Oh, Andrew, that's wonderful! Congratulations.'

He smiled proudly. 'You're the first person we've told.'

'Well, I'm really flattered.' Flabbergasted, actually.

'We were going to announce it over tea, but Grandma and Grandpa seemed so upset, we decided to tell them later. But we wanted *you* to know.'

'Yes, of course. I'm . . . I'm delighted. When's the baby due?'

'Not until early January. It seems ages, doesn't it?'

No, she thought, it seems incredibly soon. She had always assumed that Andrew and Antonia wouldn't start a family until they were in their early thirties and established in their careers. 'Is Antonia going to give up work?'

'Oh, no. Well, only for a couple of months after the birth. Actually . . .' Andrew looked embarrassed. 'We have a little plan to propose.'

'A plan?'

'Yes. We know you're upset about Nicky going away, and frankly, Mother, Antonia and I really worry about you living in that area. It's supposed to have the highest crime rate in London. And it's full of drug-dealers and heaven knows what else.'

She suppressed a smile, remembering Darren's recent party. There were easier ways of getting drugs than braving the pushers at Camden Lock. 'So you're trying to lure me back, are you?' she said, adopting a light-hearted tone.

'Well, not back *here*. I know that didn't really suit you. And of course, you want your independence. But Antonia was telling me the other day about one of the trusts she administers. It includes a cottage in Ewell village – only a tiny place, but it's got real character. The old lady who's been living there has just gone into a home, so Antonia has to find new tenants. And it suddenly occurred to us that it might be ideal for *you*.'

'For me?' Ewell wasn't a village, just a suburb with pretensions. She and Will were going to live in a *real* village, surrounded by wild hills, with sheep almost in the back garden.

'Well, it does seem a good idea. You'd be near us, you see, yet you'd have a place of your own. And I know you'd like it, Mother. It's awfully pretty and very well maintained.'

'In that case, I couldn't afford it.'

'No, the rent's kept deliberately low. Besides . . .' He gave a nervous cough. 'This may sound a bit of a cheek, Mother, but I know you haven't managed to find a proper job yet. And it can't be much fun working at the market such long hours and never having weekends off. So we thought . . . well, we wondered if . . . if you'd like to help with the baby, when it comes? We'd happily pay the rent *and* a bit of a salary. We could get a proper nanny, but Antonia's rather worried about employing a total stranger, in case she wasn't reliable. Of course, it may not appeal to you at all, but I remember you saying you were going to make some changes anyway once Nicky had left.'

'Yes,' she said tersely, 'that's true.'

'So what do you think?'

'Andrew, darling, I don't know *what* to think. I'm over the moon to hear about my grandchild, but . . .' She felt trapped in a web of deceit. If only she'd told them earlier about Will. How could she blurt it all out now?

332

'It's probably come as rather a shock. I was a little taken aback myself, to tell the truth. You see, we weren't planning on having a baby quite so soon, but' – he flushed – 'these things happen, don't they?'

She nodded, bereft of speech.

'And now that I'm used to the idea, I'm really pleased and proud. In fact, if it's a boy, we're going to call him Gerry.'

She swallowed. She couldn't go up north, not now – leave a precious grandchild, a child with Gerry's genes and name. But how could she live in a cutesy suburban cottage, tied to a newborn baby? And no way could she imagine Will fitting into the idyll.

'Actually, Antonia wants a girl and she wants to call her Lorna, with Catherine as a second name. Isn't that nice? She gets on so well with you – better than with her own mother, to be honest.'

Catherine smiled politely. Antonia's mother certainly wouldn't volunteer for the post of full-time grandma. Eleanor was a career woman and she and her husband Charles both had the sort of high-powered jobs which necessitated frequent trips abroad. When they weren't organizing conferences in some foreign capital they lived miles away, in Devon. And there was no question of Jack and Maureen helping – they were far too old and doddery. No, it was either *her* or some untried girl who might neglect a vulnerable baby. She felt deeply moved by the thought of this new life and of her son becoming a father. Yet she was also desperate to secure her *own* new life, which seemed to be dissolving in thin air. Will would have no patience with a baby – he found Sam difficult enough. And that was another thing – she had just started to get close to Sam and didn't want to let him down. Impressed by her bravado as the only grown-up to ride a camel, he now regarded her as someone rather special. Besides, they had told him about the cottage; promised him a cat.

She continued to sit in silence, her mind in turmoil as pride and pleasure struggled against anger and resentment. How dare Andrew talk so blithely about her independence, then shackle her to a cottage with his child? A *tied* cottage – that was the word. She would be tied in every way: tied to him and Antonia, tied to a wailing infant, tethered in suburbia once more. Yet *she* had also talked blithely about her former life. How could it be 'former' when Andrew was her son; the generations handing on a legacy of blood, and yes, of ties?

'Mother, I haven't upset you, have I?' He was looking at her anxiously.

'No. Of course not.'

'Perhaps I should have waited till Antonia got back. But she's a bit embarrassed, actually.'

'Embarrassed? Why?'

'Well . . . you know, about your helping with the baby. She was afraid you'd think we were just using you.'

Yes, it did seem exactly like that – Antonia was right. Yet she was shocked by the near-rage she felt. Rage undermined by guilt.

'And she felt you could speak more freely just to me. I mean, if you didn't like the idea, it would be easier to tell me, on my own.'

No, it wasn't easier. Rejecting the plan would still sound horribly selfish, regardless of whether Antonia was there. Best to say nothing at all. Today had been bad enough already, and to be faced with another bombshell after that dreadful experience in the chapel . . .

She stared queasily at the table full of food. The chocolate cake reminded her of Will again – and also of Sam and the camels at the zoo. Will would be devastated if she changed the plans at this late stage, when they had already paid the deposit on the cottage. And Sam would conclude that she didn't keep her promises.

Ignoring Andrew's bewildered look, she stacked the dirty plates and took them into the kitchen. If she was going to return to duty, she might as well start now. She put on Antonia's apron, a pink gingham affair with frills. It must look odd with her hair. Could grandmas have purple hair – or live-in lovers? And wouldn't tiger noises wake the baby?

Hardly aware of what she was doing, she whooshed half a bottle of Fairy Liquid into the washing-up bowl and watched helplessly as a mound of foam billowed up and up and up. Andrew had followed her and took the dish-mop firmly from her hand.

'I'll do this, Mother. You sit down.'

The considerate son and well-trained husband. Didn't she owe him something in return? 'It's okay, Andrew. We'll *both* do it. Here's a tea-towel. You dry.'

They had done only a couple of cups when they heard Antonia's key in the lock. Catherine wiped her hands and went to greet her daughter-in-law, who looked elegantly slim in her eau-de-nil two-piece. Difficult to believe that in a matter of months she would be wearing a maternity dress; that tiny waist ballooning out. And how would the immaculate house withstand the shock of a baby – champagne-coloured carpets spattered with bits of chewed-up rusk; dirty hand-prints on the walls?

'Congratulations, Antonia!' she said, giving her a kiss. 'Andrew's told me about the baby and I'm absolutely delighted.'

Antonia blushed and murmured her thanks. 'But you shouldn't be washing up. Take off that apron and let's have a drink to celebrate. There's some sparkling wine in the fridge.'

They returned to the sitting-room with bottle and glasses. As the wine was ceremonially poured, Gerry seemed to be watching from the mantelpiece. Catherine gazed at his photo, blinking back her tears. He would never see his grandchild – his namesake, maybe, or *hers*. If only he were still alive, she wouldn't have this conflict. They would be normal grandparents, living conveniently near. But she wouldn't be expected to be a full-time nanny; to be saddled with a role she didn't want.

Andrew and Antonia were looking at her eagerly, their glasses raised in a toast. *Her* glass was still on the table. She picked it up, surprised how heavy it felt. 'To the baby,' she said. 'May it bring us all great happiness.'

IV

27

'Listen to this, darling. It says here that crocodiles make deep grunting sounds during courtship. And they mate in a threshing frenzy.' He waved the book at her excitedly. '"The flanks may vibrate so violently that water is sprayed high into the air from either side." *That* should be worth a try!'

Catherine laughed. 'I thought you were writing a crocodile poem?'

'I was – till I got distracted by this book.'

'And you just told me not to disturb your concentration.'

'Grunts don't count. Apparently they mate in shallow water and . . .'

'The bath's got your dirty washing in it.'

'We can imagine the shallow water. "Copulation lasts approximately ten minutes."' He frowned. 'I don't think much of that, do you? Hang on – this sounds better: "Courtship starts with the two partners rubbing their muzzles against each other."' He got down on the floor and crawled on his belly towards her, making a succession of throaty grunts.

'Will, you're crazy!'

'Ssh. I'm a randy crocodile, stalking my mate.'

She grunted playfully in reply. 'But crocodiles don't wear clothes, you know.'

'Right, take them off and show me that luscious scaly skin of yours.'

She pulled her sundress over her head – in the sultry summer heat she had dispensed with any other clothes. It took Will longer to undress, but she helped him unbutton his shirt and unzip his trousers. Naked, they both lay on their stomachs on the carpet, rubbing muzzles – chins.

'Then the male mounts the female,' Will whispered, manoeuvring himself into position.

'Hey, Will, slow down a bit!'

'We've only got ten minutes.'

'No, you can be the exception that proves the rule – a considerate crocodile who takes time to please his mate.'

'Okay.' He grunted and snuffled comically, making little forays towards her, only to retreat again. But all at once there was an uproar outside: a siren wailed, a car screeched to a halt.

'Oh, no,' she groaned. 'Not another raid.'

'Ignore it.' Will kissed her on the mouth.

She returned the kiss half-heartedly, but then wriggled out from under him. Love-making (crocodile-style or any other fashion) wasn't easy with that din. The windows were wide open and the familiar noises seemed amplified in the heat: slamming doors, pounding feet, interspersed by shouts and scuffles and the crack of splintering wood. 'I'm sorry, Will, I just can't function with all that drama going on. It's worse than *The Bill*!'

'For heaven's sake ignore it,' he repeated.

Angrily, she sat up. 'Stop ordering me about, Will. First you tell me not to speak because the Great Poet is at work, and now . . .'

Will sprang to his feet. 'What do you mean, "the Great Poet"?'

'Don't be silly, it was only a joke.'

'I don't find that sort of sarcasm funny in the slightest. What's wrong with you today?'

'I'm tired, if you must know.' She snatched her dress from the floor and yanked it back over her head. 'This is the first Friday we've taken off in weeks, and I thought we were supposed to spend the day in the park, soaking up the sun. Instead of which I've been stuck indoors, slaving since the crack of dawn.'

'I've been working too, haven't I?'

'You've been writing poems.'

'And I suppose that isn't work?'

'Look, writing's something you *want* to do. I've been cooking and cleaning all day and I'm sick of it.'

'You don't have to cook and clean.'

'Someone's got to do it, and anyway you keep complaining you're hungry.'

'There's always takeaways.'

'They're expensive, Will. You know how tight money is.'

'Okay, bread and cheese then.'

'But you *don't* buy bread and cheese. On the rare occasions you do the shopping, you get things we can't afford.'

'Oh, I see you're really having a go at me – I hardly ever do the shopping, and when I do, I'm wasteful. I sit around on my arse all day. I order you about . . .'

'Will, you're overreacting.'

'*And* I overreact.'

She lowered her voice, ashamed to realize they were both shouting. 'Yes, you do. And it gets incredibly wearing.'

He sank on to the bed without another word. He looked so utterly dejected, she felt a surge of remorse. It wasn't all his fault – certainly not the lean time they were having at the market. Trade was bad in general at the moment. And he was right – she did choose to cook, and often gloried in his extravagant praise for her meals. She went over and put her hand on his shoulder. 'Let's not quarrel, darling.'

'No, I'm sorry.' He drew her down beside him on the bed and kissed her eyelids softly.

'D'you think crocodiles have rows?' she whispered.

'God, I hope not. They'd probably tear each other limb from limb.'

She gave a shudder and pressed closer. 'Listen, my randy crocodile, let's start again – okay? The noise has stopped.' As far as it ever did stop. The police car had left as mysteriously as it had come, but there was still the incessant roar of traffic and a workman in the street was using an electric drill.

Will was sitting with his head bowed. His erection had dwindled to nothing and she knew he was still haunted by past failures – not with her, with his previous girlfriend. She tried to stroke him stiff, without success.

'It's no good,' he said irritably. 'I've lost it now.'

'It doesn't matter, darling.'

'It does. I can't bear letting you down.' He thumped his fist on the bed. 'We should have moved north. I hate this bloody racket all the time. At least we'd have had some peace and quiet in the country.'

'Oh Will, don't start that again. You know how awful I feel about it. But I keep telling you, I didn't have much option.'

'Of course you did. You just let your family bully you.'

'I did not, Will. It was *my* choice. I didn't want to be so far away from my grandchild.'

'You could always visit. Cumbria's not exactly another planet.'

'Have you any idea what the petrol would cost? Even if I only drove down every couple of months, we still couldn't afford it. Anyway, we'd need a better car. Mine's on its last legs, in spite of all we spend on it. I mean, another eighty pounds last week for a camshaft belt, and the new battery the week before.'

'It gets frightfully boring, you know, the way you keep banging on about money.'

She flounced up from the bed. 'You've got a nerve, I must say. *Your* car's still off the road and you happily use mine. Okay, I don't mind, but you could at least put some petrol in it occasionally.'

'I pay for other things, don't I?'

'Yes – extravagant things we don't need.'

'God, I've never known you be so bitter, Catherine. Why not ring your darling son and say you *will* move into his bijou cottage after all.'

Stung, she stood gripping the windowsill, looking down at the street. Black dustbin bags were clustered against the graffiti-daubed brick wall. Several windows were smashed; two shops boarded up. Perhaps she should have accepted Andrew's offer and escaped from this depressing squalor. 'I gave the cottage up for you,' she said tersely, keeping her back to him.

'You did not. You gave it up because you didn't want to be a full-time grandma.'

He was right. She had tried to take a stand with Andrew and Antonia, not to let things happen by default, as had been the case so often in the past. Whatever decision she arrived at, though, she was bound to upset someone. In the end she had compromised, declining the role of full-time nanny, yet also refusing to go north with Will, thereby upsetting everyone. She had tried to make it up to Will by suggesting they look for a new flat together – not, alas, in Cumbria, but in a more attractive part of London. They were still looking. The whole point of moving north was that property was cheaper. Nothing was cheap in London, not even Tandoori Street.

She glanced over her shoulder at Will. He was putting his clothes back on, his movements brusque and angry. 'I think I'll go out,' she said. 'I don't want to spend all evening quarrelling.'

'Nor do I. I love you, Catherine, can't you see? That's why it hurts when you always put your family first.'

'But Will, I put *us* first.'

'Oh, really? That's news to me. We're *surrounded* by your family.' He glanced in annoyance at her collection of photos from Gosforth Road. 'Even Gerry, for God's sake. How do you think I feel waking up to your brilliant actor-husband every day?'

'Will, he's dead,' she said softly.

'Okay, I'm sorry. I shouldn't have mentioned it. But it's not only him, it's the others. You just don't seem able to cut the umbilical cord. And certainly Andrew can't. Shit!' His shoelace had snapped and he flung the broken lace across the room. 'It's becoming pretty clear to me that your wimp of a son can't manage without his Mummy. So perhaps you'd better go back there and let him bloody keep you in the style you're accustomed to.'

She grabbed her bag and marched to the door. She wouldn't stand for him attacking Andrew, *or* swearing.

'Oh, running out on me, are you?'

There was a note of panic in his voice, but she had no intention of crawling back. She was tired of his insecurities and the petulance he'd shown since their country idyll had foundered. Okay, it *was* her fault, but she couldn't grovel for ever.

She hurtled down the stairs and into the street; kept running in case he tried to follow. But as she turned into Kentish Town Road, her steps faltered to a stop. Walking out was a fine dramatic gesture, but where did she actually go? Restaurants, theatres, cinemas all cost money. It was already quarter to eight, so no point searching out friends in the market – they'd have shut up shop two hours ago. Some of them, including Brad, would be drinking in the Stag, but the relationship between her and Brad had become rather awkward recently, after an unpleasant scene with Will. That was another thing – Will was so possessive. Just because Brad made her jewellery it didn't mean they were having an affair.

She walked aimlessly along, envious of the couples strolling arm in arm and the cheerful groups of people spilling out of the pubs on to the pavement, chattering and laughing as they downed their pints of beer. It was a perfect summer's evening, less hot than earlier, but still sunny with a cloudless sky – weather for romance, not rancour. And the fact that it was Friday made it worse. London seemed to pity you if you were alone on fun night, party night.

While she waited at a crossroads for the traffic lights to change, she noticed the sign pointing to Kentish Town sports centre. Rosie's son went swimming there on Fridays – a children's life-saving class which finished at 7.30. With any luck they'd still be around. Rosie was just the person to talk to. Working at the market together they'd become firm friends; snatching a coffee when customers permitted, and sometimes meeting afterwards for a natter and a drink. Rosie was a good listener and invariably sympathetic when it came to problems with men. In fact, they'd been chatting only yesterday about the unfair sex in general and Will in particular.

Quickening her pace, she reached the sports centre in a matter of minutes, relieved to see that there was still a swarm of parents and children outside. It should be easy enough to spot Stephen – his ginger hair was a beacon in any crowd – but there was no sign of him or Rosie. She went inside and checked the foyer: more kids, more milling parents – but not, unfortunately, the pair she was looking for.

Stephen was rather a slowcoach, so perhaps he was still getting dressed. She'd give them a while longer. Better to hang around here than wander the streets on her own. Ten minutes passed. Fifteen. More people were flocking in for the water aerobics session advertised on the board – energetic types with impressive-looking kitbags slung across their shoulders, who made her feel sluggish and superfluous. She leaned against the wall, watching a blond boy of about Sam's age getting a drink from the machine. The last day Sam had spent with them had not been a success. He was bitterly disappointed that the promised country cottage, complete with his longed-for cat, had failed to materialize after all. The ensuing sulks and tears had only increased her guilt, though guilt had turned to resentment when Will left her to look after him practically all day, insisting that if inspiration struck, any poet worth the name must catch it on the wing, regardless of such considerations as visiting sons or resident women. Well – she shrugged – at least she wasn't a full-time single parent, like Rosie.

She mooched out to the street again. Rosie and Stephen must have left ages ago and were probably sitting down to supper by now. Of course, she could call in and see them – it was only a short bus-ride away – but Rosie's mother was often there and would want to talk about her ailments. She dithered for a moment, then set off for the Lock, in the hope of meeting someone else she knew. A bit of lively company would stop her brooding on the Thursby cottage. Apart from being a lost opportunity, it meant they had lost the three-hundred-pound deposit and the month's rent paid in advance. No wonder they were skint. And she wasn't even sure that she had made the right decision. If only she and Will could afford a place in Kent or Sussex, somewhere within easy reach of Stoneleigh, yet still in the country . . . But properties cost a fortune in that well-heeled commuter belt.

She kicked out at a beer can on the pavement, suddenly furious with Gerry. If he hadn't been so feckless, she would be sixty thousand pounds better off. She had prided herself on accepting the loss – working in the market, you came to regard a lack of security as a simple fact of life – but tonight's row about money had reopened the wound. How dare he chuck sixty grand away on some precarious fringe theatre, and deceive her into the bargain?

Angrily she strode into Chalk Farm Road and crossed the road to the Lock. The market manager, Frank, was standing by the bridge – just the person she *didn't* want to see. They had crossed swords last week because she and Will had fallen behind with the rent. Frank had been quite stroppy about it, despite the fact it was the first time it had happened.

Preoccupied with avoiding him, she nearly bumped into Roy, strolling along in his familiar sequinned cap and floral leggings.

'Hi, Plum. How're you doin'?'

'Oh, hi. I'm . . . fine.'

Roy ran a food stall in West Yard, selling veggie burgers, Celestial Tea and home-made carrot cake. 'Fancy a drink?' he asked. 'I'm just going over the road.'

She glanced wistfully across at the pub. Will could hardly be jealous of Roy, who was unashamedly gay, but it would be hypocritical to spend money on drinks after nagging Will about extravagance. 'I'm sorry, Roy, but I can't just now.'

'Ta-ra then, sweetheart. You look great, by the way. I like the tan!'

'Thanks.' She felt a little better, even without the drink. People here were so friendly and accepting. It *was* a sort of family, whose members helped and supported each other. And after all, if Gerry had left her comfortably off she would still be cloistered in suburbia, ignorant of this way of life, or even disapproving of it. Anyway, there was no point digging up the past – what was done was done.

Her way was blocked by a novice juggler practising on the pavement – all fingers and thumbs and fumbled catches – and she couldn't help but smile. His chest was bare, and emblazoned with a lurid tattoo of an eagle with a sun in its beak. His feet were also bare, and dirty, and his hair was a minor masterpiece in electric blue and green. A crowd of tourists stood watching him – giggly Japanese girls; overweight Americans armed with camcorders. She squeezed past, only to find more people laughing at a wild-eyed preacher, who was urging his audience to accept the Lord into their hearts while refreshing himself from a gin bottle. The whole place seemed alive; gangs of rumbustious kids on their way to gigs or clubs; seasoned locals watching the world go by; a boy in baggy harem-pants busking with a guitar.

Her feet moved in time to the music as she crossed the cobblestones to the stalls, reduced now to gaunt scaffolding frames. Only in the last few weeks had business slackened off, despite the hordes of tourists. Before that, she and Will had been doing remarkably well, though you never knew with the market whether you were in for a bonanza or a slump. But if things failed to improve, well, perhaps it was time to look for another line of work. The market crowd were infinitely adaptable, working to live, not living to work, and always willing to move on. Bina was in Brighton selling tie-dyed tee-shirts, Colin had landed a job on a canal boat and Spiff was working as a barman down the road. And considering the fact that she and Will had come up with dozens of ideas for earning a living in a tiny place like Thursby, surely they could do the same in a city of seven million people.

She walked back to Camden High Street, only realizing after she'd passed the tube that she was heading in the direction of Gosforth Road. Force of habit, no doubt. Although actually it might be fun to call in – catch up with Darren's news, renew her brief acquaintance with Fiona. She began walking faster, her spirits rising as she reached number ten and found the door ajar. At least somebody was in.

'Hi!' she called. 'Anyone around?'

346

It was Jo who came to the door, not bothering to smile. 'Come in,' she said grudgingly.

'Are you sure I'm not disturbing you?' Catherine hovered on the step. 'I really came to see how Darren was. Has he accepted that new job at Saatchis?'

'Yeah,' said Jo. 'But he's out.'

'Oh, I see. Well . . . do say congratulations, won't you?' She was about to back away – it was clear she wasn't wanted – when Fiona appeared in the hall.

'I thought it was you, Catherine. I've been meaning to ring you for ages. I still owe you money for the vet.'

'Oh, that's okay. You paid most of it.'

'No, I haven't and I feel terribly guilty. Look, if you've got a minute, why don't we sort it out now?'

Catherine stepped into the hall, ignoring Jo's frown. She liked Fiona, the little she had seen of her, and she just couldn't leave without saying hello to William. He was sitting at the bottom of the stairs and she went over to make a fuss of him, fondling his ears the way he'd always enjoyed. But he just stared blankly with passionless green eyes, as if she were a stranger. His indifference was extraordinary, not to mention hurtful. Could a cat forget you in less than three weeks, when for months you'd been the most important person in his life?

'Oh, dear, I'm interrupting your supper,' she said, trailing after Jo and Fiona into the kitchen. The table was laid with knives and forks.

'It's only a snack,' Fiona grinned. 'And why not join us? It'll probably stretch to three.'

'No, honestly, I've eaten, thanks.' Not true. But the brown congealing substance in the saucepan (chilli? curry? lentils?) looked as if it would barely stretch to two. 'And don't let it get cold.'

'It's cold already,' Jo muttered. 'I turned it off half an hour ago, but the bloody phone keeps ringing.'

'Never mind. We can heat it up again.' Fiona turned on the gas. 'And in the meantime I'll sort things out with Catherine. Give me a moment and I'll see if I can find the bills.'

She disappeared upstairs, while Jo sat at the table, hacking slices off a loaf of bread. The silence felt uncomfortable. Catherine perched on the edge of a chair, remembering cosy suppers with Nicky: giggling, chatting, exchanging confidences. Although she would never admit it to Will, she did miss the old regime at times. 'Have you heard from Nicky?' she asked, to be polite.

'Yes, Darren had a card. She's having a whale of a time by the sounds of it.'

Catherine smiled. 'I know. I had a letter last week. Seven pages. All about coral reefs and steel bands and snorkelling and what-have-you.'

'Isn't she doing any work?'

'I suppose she must be, but heaven knows when!'

'Fuck,' Jo muttered, as the phone rang. She picked it up. 'It's for you, Fiona,' she yelled. Two seconds later the doorbell rang as well. She grouched off to answer it, Catherine straining to hear the voices in the hall. Perhaps it would be somebody she knew.

But two unfamiliar girls walked in, evidently good friends of Jo's since she promptly got them drinks from the fridge and produced packets of crisps and nuts.

'Judith and Helen,' she said, indicating the newcomers with a cursory nod and offering no further information. 'This is Catherine. She used to live here.'

'Used to' was the operative word, Catherine thought. Now she didn't merit so much as a salted peanut. She exchanged a few brief pleasantries with the girls, wishing Fiona would hurry up. But she was still on the phone in the sitting-room. And as for William, he was curled up on the windowsill with a supercilious expression, ignoring her completely.

Jo and her friends were soon deep in discussion about some hated female editor at *Elite*, until they were interrupted by pounding feet on the stairs. A man burst into the kitchen. Well, more a boy – he looked barely out of his teens.

'Finished!' he said, waving a sheaf of typed papers aloft. 'Thank God. Now I can get absolutely rat-arsed.'

'Here's something to be going on with,' Jo grinned, passing him a six-pack. 'This is Pete,' she said to Catherine, her offhand tone returning.

Catherine recognized the name. Pete was the friend of Darren's who had taken over Nicky's room. A week after his arrival, Fiona had decided to come back, which was fine so long as *she* went north with Will. But when she subsequently changed her plans, there was no place for her at Gosforth Road. No place in any sense, she thought, looking at the four heads round the table.

The average age in the house now couldn't be much more than twenty-three. And judging by the present talk (the relative merits of various types of Ecstasy and how they compared with speed), she was completely out of it. She felt more at ease with Fiona – and they could at least talk cats – but the phone call seemed no nearer a conclusion. Her voice could be heard in sporadic bursts from the other room, punctuated by occasional yelps of laughter.

Having waited vainly for a gap in the conversation, Catherine finally stood up. 'I don't want to be rude,' she said, 'but I'm afraid I must get off. I'm in a bit of a rush. Jo, could you tell Fiona not to worry about the vet thing? We can sort it out later on the phone.'

'Yeah, sure.' Jo was plainly relieved to see the back of her. And no wonder. Why should they want some boring middle-aged woman hanging round all evening? This chapter in her life was over – even her beloved cat seemed to regard her as an intruder.

She trudged back the way she'd come. It was still light, still sunny, the velvet air warm on her bare arms. Today was the last day of June; the evening long and languorous, as if defying the sun to set. Even the dreary, treeless street looked glittering and gilded beneath an unwaveringly blue sky.

She straightened her shoulders and took a few deep breaths, the beauty of the evening acting like a tranquillizer. There was nothing to be gained by being negative and self-pitying. Gosforth Road had been fun while it lasted, but she had never intended staying permanently. After all, Will had called her a 'work in progress', which meant there were bound to be changes and revisions. And Will *did* have many good points – he was a brilliant poet, a fantastic lover. She would go back and make her peace with him, and perhaps they could resume their crocodile roles; not tear each other limb from limb, but rub muzzles in the bath.

She found a note on the table, scribbled on a dirty scrap of paper and propped against a beer can. *Vanessa rang – last straw. Going out to drown my sorrows. Back by midnight. Maybe.*

She kicked her shoes off with a clatter. *She* had refused Roy's offer of a drink, yet Will had gone out boozing without a second thought. And his continual rows with Vanessa were beginning to wear her down. Now that she'd actually met her, it was impossible to see her as the villainous ex-wife. A little cold, perhaps, but basically a decent person.

349

She re-read the note stonily. No 'darling', no 'love, Will'; just a bald statement and that rude and taunting 'maybe'. She sank into a chair, tired after so much traipsing about. Not only that – she was tired emotionally. Giving up the Thursby cottage had cost her sleepless nights, especially as she was the one who'd done most of the spadework in finding it. And now she was lumbered again with the job of looking for a new London flat. Will left it all to her – *he* had important poems to write.

She crumpled up the note and closed her eyes, trying to make her mind a blank. Too much had happened in too short a space of time – Andrew's bombshell about the baby; Nicky's departure to the Virgin Islands; her own move from Gosforth Road. Was it any wonder she felt exhausted? And moving in with Will had needed a lot of adjustment on both sides. She missed her independence; a room of her own where she could retreat undisturbed, not answerable to anyone. And Andrew's attitude hadn't helped. When she'd finally plucked up the courage to tell him about Will, he had listened in shocked silence, like a Victorian paterfamilias reacting to the news of his daughter's elopement with a ne'er-do-well. Another man was bad enough; a divorced and impecunious poet even worse.

That was another thing – the poetry. Will insisted it came first. Of course, if the Scrivener Press wanted more poems before deciding whether to publish, he had little option but to sit down and produce them. But it meant *she* was landed with a greater burden of work, both in the flat and at the market.

Her fingers were tapping impatiently on the chair-arm. She ought to take advantage of Will's absence and have an early night, but she knew she wouldn't sleep. His 'maybe' still rankled. Damned cheek!

Suddenly decisive, she put her shoes back on and marched downstairs, giving the door a satisfying slam. If Will had gone out drinking, so would she. Brad was often in the Stag till closing time on Fridays and even if he had left, no matter – she would go on to the Hawley Arms and find Roy; spin the evening out, be back by midnight.

Maybe.

28

Dusk was falling at last as she crossed the road from the flat and turned into the main road; the dazzling scarlet sunset reduced to a few streaks of pink.

Seeing a bus approaching, she sprinted to catch it – she'd had enough of walking today and the wretched car was parked miles away, as usual. Months ago Nicky had advised her to get a permit, but permits cost eighty-odd pounds a year.

She alighted three stops later and strolled the last stretch to the Stag. Although the sky was now a slatey grey and the street lamps had come on, the evening retained its sultry warmth and many drinkers were still lounging outside. One of them she recognized as Paula, who sold hand-made shoes in West Yard. 'Is Brad around?' she asked her.

'Yeah, he's inside.' Paula gestured with her cigarette. 'But he's off to some do, he said.'

'Damn,' Catherine muttered, pushing her way into a blast of noise and smoke. She spotted him by the window and eventually managed to reach him through the crush of bodies.

'Hi, Brad – it's me!'

At first he eyed her warily, looking over her shoulder for Will but, reassured she was on her own, he jumped up and gave her an exuberant kiss. 'Plum, sweet'eart, we was just talkin' about you. What 'appened to you today? Playin' truant, was you?'

'Er, yes.'

'And where's our friend the Posho?'

'He, er, had to go out so I . . . I thought I'd join you for a drink.'

'You can join me for a *party*, darlin'. I'm just this minute leavin'.'

This is Mervyn, by the way. A mate of mine from way back. 'E's promised me a lift in 'is van.'

Catherine smiled a greeting then looked enquiringly at Brad. 'Where's the party?'

'Holloway Road,' Mervyn interjected. 'And it's not a party, it's a bloody rave. I wouldn't touch it with a bargepole if I was you.'

'A *rave?*' Catherine had to shout. An Irish fiddler had just launched into a riotous jig.

'Raves are dead and buried, mate,' Brad said morosely. 'The Criminal Justice Bill knocked 'em on the bleedin' 'ead.'

'Rubbish!' Mervyn said. 'Chrissie went to one last week. It was held in this sodding great warehouse, just like the good old days.'

'Yeah, but that's the point, innit? *I'*m goin' to an ordinary club, not a soddin' great ware'ouse.'

'Ordinary?' Mervyn's tone was scathing. 'I wouldn't call Club Vamp ordinary. Anyway, if you want a lift, look sharp. I'm leaving now, okay?'

'Come on, darlin',' Brad said, putting his arm round Catherine's waist. 'Seein' as the Posho's out, *I'*ll give you a good time.'

'No, honestly, Brad, I can't.'

'Why not? It's Friday night, innit? We gotta do *some*thin'. And I reckon you need a bit of cheerin' up.'

She hesitated. 'But I'm not dressed for a party.'

Brad laughed. 'This is one you *un*dress for. Anyway, I don't know what you're on about. You look bleedin' ravishin' to me.'

She couldn't help but smile. *He* was wearing tartan trews with heavy hobnailed boots and a sort of string-mesh waistcoat thing over a tee-shirt with a skull on it. In spite of his clothes and his shaven head (not to mention the scar on his face), she no longer found his appearance menacing. He had become someone she was comfortable with, and his easy-going temperament was frankly a relief after Will's infernal touchiness. All the same, she ought to say no. A drink in the Stag was one thing, but a rave, for heaven's sake!

'And you can meet some of me mates,' he said, the silver rings on his fingers glinting as he ground his fag-end into extinction in the ashtray. 'I know you'll 'it it off with Noreen. She's artistic, too.'

She liked the way he praised her: ravishing, artistic. Will had told her she was boring and unreasonable.

'And Bill's a great bloke. I've known 'im since we were kids.'

'Okay,' she said suddenly. 'I'll come.' An hour or two wouldn't hurt and she could always leave if she didn't like it.

Amid a raucous chorus of farewells (and a few lewd winks and comments), Brad steered her out of the pub, Mervyn bringing up the rear. She was bundled unceremoniously into the back of his ancient van, where she shared the space with some fishing tackle and half a dismembered wardrobe. After a bumpy but mercifully brief journey they shuddered to a stop outside a faceless building in the Holloway Road.

'God, look at that queue,' Mervyn snorted, winding down the window. 'You won't be in before midnight.'

'No sweat. I gotta guest pass.' Brad held up a card.

'But what about me?' Catherine glanced in dismay at the queue, which stretched a good two hundred yards and seemed to be composed exclusively of under-twenty-fives in ultra-weird or ultra-casual gear – certainly no one else the wrong side of forty wearing a Laura Ashley sundress.

'Don't you worry, darlin'. You're me girl for the evenin'.'

'Well, all right,' she murmured doubtfully, wondering what Will would have said to that – or to the posse of bouncers: all very large, very black and very intimidating, positioned at the entrance.

Brad sailed up to the nearest one, undaunted. 'Friend of MC Skin-Up,' he announced, brandishing his pass. 'And me girlfriend.'

To Catherine's surprise they were neither thrown into the street nor told to join the queue, but waved on to a second guard, still more muscular than the first. He frisked them and searched their bags, though whether for bombs or drugs she didn't know. Some party! They were standing in a bleak entrance hall with peeling paint and a concrete floor.

'Up 'ere,' said Brad, indicating a flight of narrow stairs. 'Unless you want a pee first?'

'Er, no,' she said. 'I'm fine.' If she took refuge in the toilet she might never dare emerge again. This was definitely not her scene. She could already hear music, which became more deafening and aggressive with each step they went up. 'Brad,' she said, pulling at his sleeve, 'I'm not too sure about this.'

'Oh come on, babe, you ain't seen it yet. And you'll 'ave a great time, I know you will.' He took her arm and led her into a cavern-ous low-ceilinged hall, seething with bodies. All her senses were assaulted simultaneously: strobe lights flashed and stabbed in a kaleidoscope of colour, and the music was sheer pain, battering like machine-gun fire. Never in her life had she been subjected to such a relentless volume of sound, nor so savage a beat. It was as if her body had been wired up to the sound system; the decibels pounding through her very organs, making her pulse and heart-beat race. Clouds of smoke poured from some unseen source, choking the air and swathing the dancers in a ghostly pall: surreal figures, writhing and jerking, and deaf to all but the iron-willed music. Their bodies were spangled with light – tiny explosions of pink, blue, purple, silver – programmed to the same insistent beat. The whites especially glowed in eerie brilliance under the ultra-violet light – teeth, clothes, the whites of eyes jolting out alarmingly, so that when Brad turned to smile at her, his face resembled the leering skull on his tee-shirt.

She stood in shock, cowering by the door. Brad was saying something, but his voice was completely inaudible and her own feeble protests were swept away like feathers in a hurricane. She pulled him back out of the doorway, until she could just about make herself heard. 'Brad,' she shouted, 'I'm afraid this isn't quite my thing. Why don't *you* stay and I'll . . . ?'

He spread his hands in exaggerated horror. 'Sweet'eart, you can't do this to me! Anyway we gotta find MC Skin-Up.'

'Who?'

'Well, Alan to you and me. 'E's me best mate's cousin, and 'e's compèrin' tonight.'

'Where is he then?' She was still forced to shout, her throat aching from the strain. Also, they were blocking the entrance – a gaggle of teenagers in crop-tops and Doc Martens were trying to push past.

''E'll be backstage at the moment and I want a word before 'e starts. Get a move on, darlin', or we'll miss 'im.'

'But won't he mind me coming too?'

''Course not. It's dead casual 'ere, mate. Not like some places, where they charge you an arm and a leg. That's why Alan set it up. 'E couldn't stand all them poncy dress codes and stupid rules about drugs. This is alternative, see, and you get the anti-road crowd, anarchists, New-Agers . . .'

She nodded, although it struck her as odd that somewhere 'dead casual' should need so many bouncers. And she felt still more out of her element. She might have moved a million miles from staid suburbia, but no way was she an anarchist, let alone a raver.

But Brad had seized her arm again and began to shoulder his way through the dancers towards the stage at the far end. She clung to him like a nervous child as they penetrated deeper into the flailing mass of bodies. Some people were dancing with glasses or bottles in their hands, others with lighted cigarettes which they waved around in hazardous arcs. Suppose there was a fire – how would they all get out? There seemed to be only one exit and it was now a frighteningly long way behind. And there were hundreds more people waiting in the queue outside. This hall would never hold them all.

She tried to focus on the stage to stop herself panicking, though it appeared anything but solid; shifting and dissolving in the strobes. Two surly-looking DJs manned a battery of machines – huge black boxes bristling with dials and wires. Even in Darren's world, the music involved recognizable instruments; here all was alien, just a towering wall of sound.

A third man suddenly bounded on to the stage. His top half was conventional enough – black leather jerkin, cropped dark hair – but he appeared to be wearing a skirt, and a skirt so short it was more like a pelmet. Below it stretched bare hairy legs, shod incongruously in black parachute boots. He leapt around the stage, shouting encouragement to the crowd through a microphone. They cheered and applauded in response, but Brad threw up his hands theatrically. 'Missed the bugger!' he groaned.

She, frankly, was relieved. What in God's name did you say to a man in a micro-skirt?

MC Skin-Up continued to cavort and shout, but it was impossible to make out any words. The microphone distorted his voice, which anyway was swamped by the manic roar of the music – still more overwhelming now that she was closer to its source. The technicians had shoved their wires deep into her body, so that she herself was a throbbing, booming amplifier.

Brad bellowed into her ear, 'Come on, Plum, let's dance!'

She looked dubiously at the dancers. How could she rival their rapt absorption or manic energy? They must have different ears from her, different shockproofed bodies. Some seemed lost in their own private trance – no contact with a partner, no recognition of another human being. Many were half-naked: males stripped to the waist; females wearing bra-tops and minuscule shorts. The heat *was* intense, of course. A few were sweating so profusely their clothes were saturated, their faces flushed and gleaming. One woman had a tattoo on her thigh: a glittering web of interlocking roundels. And there was a black girl in a fluorescent silver wig, the contrast between her face and hair accentuated by the ultraviolet light.

'What's up, Plum? You okay?'

To make himself heard, Brad was standing so close she could see the puckered edges of his scar; feel his warm breath on her face. There was something rather disturbing about such intimacy: the feeling of brushing skin with him, and his intense blue-laser gaze which seemed to pierce right through her body. She stepped back a little and made a half-hearted move to dance.

Responding gleefully, Brad flung himself into action in a frenzied variation of the twist. She envied him his lack of inhibition. For her, dancing still evoked grim memories of Gerry's death. Besides, the music was so painfully aggressive, she found it impossible to let herself go. The atmosphere reminded her of scenes of war on television: sudden flares blinding in the darkness, gut-wrenching clouds of smoke, hails of bullets coming at her. Her head was throbbing, her body shot to pieces in the never-ending bombardment. Even the movements of the other dancers seemed threatening; wild and out of control. And Brad was lost to her already, roistering in his own euphoric world.

Panicky, she grabbed his arm. 'Brad, I'm sorry, but I need a drink,' she mouthed, miming the action of lifting a glass to her mouth. What she really needed was an excuse to get out.

Brad took some seconds coming back to earth. Then he nodded serenely and pointed to the bar, running the length of one wall. 'No problem, sweet'eart. I'll get you a beer.'

She surveyed the bar in horror: not only were a scrum of drinkers already queuing three deep, it was in the direct line of fire from the sound-attack. 'Is there another bar?' she shouted. 'Somewhere quieter?'

Brad had the grace to look disappointed rather than disgruntled, and began the long trek back through the lurching swaying figures. She clung to his hand and when at last they reached the door, she almost fell through it in her eagerness to escape. They continued down the first flight of stairs, pausing on the landing once they could actually speak again.

''Ow d'you like it, Plum? Fantastic, eh?'

She didn't want to sound ungrateful, or – worse – thoroughly neurotic. 'I'm probably just tired,' she murmured.

'You need some 'elp, me darlin'.' Brad beckoned her into a dark alcove on the landing and, with a wary look to left and right, took a paper hanky out of his pocket, folded neatly into a square. 'One of these'll get you goin',' he whispered.

'What are they?'

'Ssh.' With another furtive glance all round, he unwrapped the paper to reveal four small white tablets. Briefly she glimpsed the outline of a bird on them before he closed his hand again and slipped one into her palm. She was intrigued, despite herself. She had never seen an Ecstasy tablet, even after four months at Gosforth Road. Jo and Darren smoked joints, but as far as she knew took nothing stronger.

'Go on, darlin', swallow it. They give you loads of energy.'

'No, honestly, Brad. You know I don't do drugs.'

Before, they'd had to shout; now they were whispering like conspirators, standing in a huddle with their backs turned to the staircase.

'Believe me, Plum, these are absolutely 'armless. Far safer than booze or smack. They just make you feel blissed out. Get one of these down you and you'll love the 'ole fuckin' world.'

'No, Brad, thanks all the same.' Jo and her friends had been talking about Ecstasy at Gosforth Road this evening. *Was* it only this evening? Already it seemed years away. They had mentioned Doves (which these presumably were) and also other innocuous names like Dolphins, Strawberries, and Swallows.

'But it'll keep you dancin' all night, sweet.'

'I can't *stay* all night. In fact I really should be going soon.'

'Bloody 'ell! Can't you enjoy yourself for once, darlin'? The Posho's out, ain't he? And the party's 'ardly started yet. Me mates probably won't show up till after midnight.'

'Well, I certainly can't stay till then.' She heard the edge to her voice and for an instant was tempted to wrest the other three pills from him and swallow the whole damned lot. It would be great to feel happy and relaxed; to have the energy to dance all night. The last few weeks she had been feeling just the opposite: tired and irritable. She uncurled her fingers and took a quick glance at the pill. It looked innocent enough, just an aspirin with a bird of peace.

357

'Listen, Plum, you gotta drink loads of water with E, else you get dehydrated.'

'I'd prefer a stiff drink, to be honest.'

'Booze and E don't mix, darlin'. We'll get some water at the bar.'

She slipped the pill into the pocket of her dress. 'Brad, if it's all the same to you, I'll stick with booze, okay?'

'Come on, then. It's downstairs and on the right.'

She led the way and found herself not in a bar but a second murky hall, smaller than the one upstairs. Again the music was deafening, but it had a slightly less oppressive beat. She had no idea what type of music it was. She had learned something about jazz from Darren, but this sounded just a barbarous cacophony. She gazed at the walls, which were swathed in midnight-blue material painted with silver stars. The ceiling was similarly draped, making it claustrophobically low. Here there was only one DJ and the stage was smaller altogether, but the same maniacal strobes assaulted the gloom with a blitz of blue and gold. In fact, the room seemed in the throes of an epileptic fit: floor rippling, walls in spasm, no solid planes at all. She picked her way between the dancers – amorphous shapes stippled with bursts of coloured light – her eyes fixed on the exit-sign. Its small green arrow was the only unwavering point in the room, the only light which wasn't flashing.

She stumbled through the doorway, but still couldn't see a bar. They were now in a third room, where clusters of people were slumped on the floor in sepulchral darkness. The tips of cigarettes glowed red, but faces remained in shadow and some bodies lay alarmingly still, as if only semi-conscious. Although the music was much softer here, again the room was pulsing and throbbing. She was beginning to feel that the whole thing was a nightmare and that she was trapped in some hideous labyrinth and becoming more and more enmeshed as she searched for a way out.

But then Brad caught up with her and hustled her down a dingy passage and finally into the bar. Not that it afforded much relief; the jolting contrast between light and dark was every bit as fierce. And there were the same disconcerting flashes of white erupting from the gloom, as teeth glowed in disembodied smiles. Her own teeth must be gleaming in that spooky fashion, and her hair, no doubt, had turned a lurid shade.

Brad introduced her to some people he knew: a girl in red

hot-pants whose face was painted to match in crimson zigzags; a bare-chested man sporting two elaborate nipple-rings, and someone of indeterminate sex whose short frizzy hair was tied in half-inch bobbles with strips of fluorescent ribbon. Considering their appearance, their names were surprisingly conventional: Annie, Martin and Pat respectively.

'What d'you fancy, Plum?' Brad asked, pushing his way to the bar.

'*I'll* get these,' she protested.

'No, it's my shout. Anyway, I've just had a win on the dogs.'

'Again? Gosh, you *are* on a run of luck!'

'Yeah, like I told you, Plum – stick around with me and you'll be a winner too. Come on, what'll it be?'

She hesitated. Most people were drinking beer or mineral water, but it would take more than a measly Perrier to help her loosen up. Yet asking for gin or vodka would only emphasize the gulf between her and the others – a yawning gulf in age, style, everything.

'How about a Harlem Mugger?' Brad suggested.

Again she paused. She had never heard of it, but it sounded dangerous in the extreme.

'Or a Tropicana? Nice and fruity!' He gave her a suggestive wink.

'Okay,' she said nervously, although when it arrived it looked and tasted like apple juice. 'Cheers, Brad,' she said, taking another large sip.

'Cheers! To peace and love.'

'Peace and love,' she echoed, trying to keep her mind off Will. There would be little chance of either if he knew where she was and who with.

They went to find Annie, Pat and Martin, who were now sitting at a table beneath a psychedelic mandala painted on the wall.

'Martin's a nuclear physicist,' Brad announced, indicating the naked chest.

She smiled uncertainly, wondering if Brad was pulling her leg.

'And Pat lives in a squat in Brighton.'

'Oh, I see . . .' Pat's gender was still unclear, as he (she?) had given only the odd grunt. The clothes weren't much help either – baggy trousers and a voluminous blouson thing.

'Plum's new to this scene,' Brad explained, offering round a packet of cigarettes. She was relieved he'd called her Plum – it felt safer than Catherine, more anonymous.

'It's great, isn't it?' said Annie. 'We get a very friendly crowd here. Everyone's accepted – any type, any age. Even a few grannies.'

'Really?' Catherine hadn't noticed anyone who could conceivably qualify. And the word granny prompted an instant surge of guilt. Andrew would be appalled if he knew his mother was risking arrest (or worse) for possessing Class A drugs.

'It's important, don't you think, to have a sense of community?' Annie inhaled deeply and blew out a spurt of smoke. 'We tend to be shut up during the day in our own little world, but at a place like this, you feel you're one big family.'

'So do you come mainly for the company? Or the dancing? Or . . . ?' Catherine's voice tailed off. It sounded as lame as 'Do you come here often?'

'Both,' said Annie. 'The dancing,' Martin put in, simultaneously. 'Once you get going, you feel it's – like – religious. You're part of the spiritual energy.'

'Yeah,' Pat agreed. (Patrick rather than Patricia, judging by the deep voice.) 'The music takes you over rather than you dancing to the music. You just flow into it and it takes you on a journey.'

'When you dance, it's like you're expressing yourself in a universal language,' Martin continued, warming to the theme. 'It puts you in touch with your tribal roots. I've spent some time with shamans in Dakota, and it's the same sort of thing – that incredible sense of union with God, Nature, Spirit – call it what you like.'

Perhaps he *was* a nuclear physicist, Catherine thought. He was certainly articulate, although his high-flown description of dancing bore no relation to her own (admittedly brief) experience. *She* had felt disconnected, even threatened.

'You can actually feel reborn,' Pat said, taking a swig from his bottle of water. 'The music and the dancing gets you out of your head and into the moment. You lose your sense of self and you're one with everybody else. It's the most blissful feeling ever.'

Did bliss mean Ecstasy, she wondered? Surely they couldn't be that euphoric without drugs. She put her hand in her pocket and fingered the tiny pill. Of course she couldn't take it – not a grandmother-to-be – however tempted she might be. Instead she gulped her drink, surprised to see Brad so quiet. Perhaps E could make you meditative as well as energetic.

Just then a girl in tight gold leather trousers rushed over to their table. 'Hi, Brad,' she said, kissing the top of his head. 'How's tricks?'

'Soddin' 'ell!' He sprang to his feet. 'Where've you *been*, Louise? I ain't seen you in months.'

'Oh, all over the place,' she laughed. 'And right now I'm going to get a drink. Want one?'

'Ta. One of these.' He waved the empty plastic bottle. 'Plum, this is Louise.'

Catherine smiled shyly, hoping she would remember all the names.

'Want another?' Louise asked, pointing to Catherine's glass.

'No, let *me* get these,' said Catherine, resolving to buy them all a drink, then leave. More than one round would be terribly expensive, and anyway it must be getting late.

'Thanks, Plum, I'll have a Bailey's.'

Fortunately the other three were drinking mineral water, though even that cost over two pounds a bottle. She pushed her way to the bar, suddenly feeling ravenous – she hadn't eaten since lunchtime. But there was no food to be seen, not even packets of crisps.

She ordered the drinks, including a second Tropicana for herself. 'What *is* this stuff?' she asked the barman as he poured the yellowy liquid into a glass.

'Dynamite!' he grinned. 'They're all the rage, these fruity things. You have to watch them, though. This one's as strong as gin.'

So much for harmless apple juice. Still, it was too late to change her mind, and when she returned to the table and saw the intimidating new arrivals, she was glad of a bit of Dutch courage. Jonas was at least six foot six and had a lethal-looking dagger at his waist – plastic, she realized with relief, after a moment's panic. His girlfriend Kerry wore a studded leather dog-collar buckled round her neck, and a tee-shirt saying SEX VICTIM. The third member of the trio, Keith, said he was an accountant – not quite the occupation she'd have expected, in view of his dreadlocks and heavy silver ankle chain.

The only free chair was next to Jonas and his dagger, so she sat down rather warily. Not that he took much notice of her – he was too busy rummaging in his bag. She watched hungrily as he pulled out a Flora margarine carton. Perhaps it was the custom here to bring your own provisions or make sandwiches. He opened the carton and handed it round, and everyone helped themselves to what looked like squares of chocolate fudge.

'What is it?' she whispered to Brad.

''ash cake. Go on, 'ave a piece. It'll loosen you up.'

She blushed. He had spoken rather loudly and everyone was looking at her. 'Ash cake?' she repeated.

'*Hash*,' Jonas grinned, pushing the carton towards her. 'My own recipe – home-grown skunk and real Belgian chocolate. I can guarantee it's good.'

She had a sudden vision of Antonia passing round a plate of sponge fingers and assuring her guests they were made with the purest ingredients. However, she was reluctant to accept. She had tried smoking a joint with Darren once and hadn't got beyond the first few puffs.

Jonas looked a little hurt and Brad tutted in annoyance. 'Plum, don't be so bleedin' toffee-nosed. It won't *bite* you!'

Chastened, she took refuge in her drink. If even Brad despaired of her, perhaps Will had been right and she *was* boring and unreasonable. She listened to their persuasive arguments: hash was safer than fags and booze, and was certain to be legalized within the next few years. Yet she could also hear Andrew's voice droning in her head, pulling her the other way: responsible people didn't do drugs (or live in squats on the dole, squandering taxpayers' hard-earned money on dubious places like this). It occurred to her that even Will disapproved of drugs; not on moral grounds like Andrew, but because they fogged the mind. God! Suppose he was home already. He'd be wondering where on earth she was; maybe think she'd had an accident.

'Go on,' Jonas urged, still holding out the box. 'One little piece won't hurt.'

She took a chunk and quickly stuffed it in her mouth. She was starving hungry and at least it was a form of food – in fact rather agreeably squidgy in texture and with a strong chocolatey taste; not bitter as she'd feared. She finished it with a mouthful of drink, then helped herself to a second piece.

'Great!' said Jonas, while Louise squeezed her hand and Pat chinked glasses with her. She had become the centre of attention, with smiles of approval all round. Annie was right: there *was* a feeling of community, almost of family – a more tolerant family than her own. She no longer felt a stranger from a different generation, or was aware of any gulf. She belonged here; she was welcome. It was like the market again: people from every walk of life rubbing shoulders with each other. At Andrew and Antonia's parties, everyone was stamped from the same narrow mould, as if vetted by some quality control system. But to hell with virtuous Andrew and Antonia! She was beginning to feel quite amazingly relaxed and she was damned if she'd let them spoil things.

She closed her eyes, free-falling into the deep blue ocean of sound. She *was* the sound; the rhythm pounding through her body, thrilling down to her fingers and toes. All her life she'd been encased in a tight corset, a second skin of duty, guilt and fear, but now it was peeling off and she was emerging free and naked. She was beautiful, enchanting. She could feel the blood pumping into her skin, making it glow and tingle; could even feel her hair growing, pushing through her scalp in a burst of purple joy.

Brad was beautiful too, his eyes a magical blue; the fiery point of his cigarette astounding in its brilliance. He smiled at her and her face opened in response; every pore and particle opening to him freely. She was pouring out like bubbles in champagne, frothing up, fizzing over, to the wild pulsating rhythm of the music. The sound built up and up, never reaching a climax, but plunging on tireless and unstoppable, always stronger, louder, wilder. She too was tireless – floating, flying, falling all at once. She had died to her old semi-life and been rapturously reborn, and now jolts of pleasure were surging through her bloodstream – molten scarlet pleasure, bewitching blue, raw gold. And other, still more dazzling colours glittered on her tongue; exploded in slow waves behind her eyeballs.

She was surrounded by her friends, new friends she loved profoundly: Annie, Martin, Jonas, Noreen, Bill. Their faces kept retreating and advancing, their bodies were only spinning shapes, but she was gloriously at one with them, united in the electrifying music.

She floated towards Noreen and Louise, who were no longer dancing but embracing. They hugged her too, warm skin against warm skin; long rippling hair brushing her bare shoulders. The flowers on Noreen's headband opened as she watched; the leaves a frenzied green, the petals hot wet crimson mouths.

Then another mouth was kissing her – Annie's soft lips on her cheek – an exquisitely intense sensation, quivering down her spine, making her whole body smile. And behind Annie an unknown face was gazing at her – the face of a dark god.

'May I hold you?' he whispered, his eyes black pools enticing her into their depths. She nodded and he drew her close, his bare arms encircling her. Never before had skin felt so entrancing: ingenious fingers gliding down her back; velvet graze of stubble tantalizing her cheek. She was blooming in his love like some exotic flower, and she loved him too, infinitely.

But now the music was calling them – urgent and impassioned, leaping from one crescendo to the next. Obedient, they began dancing face to face. The blue sheen of his shirt was a summer sky condensed; his teeth hot snow; his hair tumultuously black. Other bodies weaved around them; other faces loomed and smiled. She loved them all with unbounded love. There *were* no strangers here. This was her new family and she cherished every one of them. All hate and fear had vanished, all barriers dissolved, as body merged with body, soul with soul. She was a child again, untrammelled; the still centre of a whirling storm; the pulsing lighthouse on an ocean.

Suddenly the ocean parted as a vast tidal wave began gathering speed and she was swept along in a rush of power and energy, rolling over and over and over in the exhilarating, brilliant, endless *now*.

29

She crouched on the pavement, clutching her thin dress round her knees. Her teeth were chattering with cold, yet her head burned and she was drenched with sweat. She had been calling out for help, but no one heard. There were only drunks in the Holloway Road.

She licked her lips. Thirst gnawed her throat, a physical pain. She would gladly have lapped from a puddle, but the gutter was dusty-dry. She groped her hand along it and encountered an empty can. Desperate for a few dregs of liquid – beer, Coke, anything – she tried to pick it up. But her fingers wouldn't obey her and closed on empty air.

Tears slid down her face again. Crying hurt. Her eyes grated in their sockets as if they'd been taken out and rolled in grit, then shoved roughly back in place. She watched the tears make damp spots on her dress. It was dark in the street but a lamp-post cast an eerie glow, and cars flashed past occasionally, tearing up the shadows, their headlights blinding and then gone.

Footsteps were approaching – lurching, coming closer. A man in a ragged overcoat drew level with her; stopped. Swarthy skin, black hair. She couldn't understand what he was saying, though he seemed to be waiting for an answer. She tried to make her voice work, but her tongue lay like a dead thing in her mouth. None the less, she was glad he was there. It made her feel less lonely.

Moments passed. She could hear her teeth still chattering in the silence. Then another car sped by, uniting them in a split second's roar and glare.

Darkness again. Silence. The man muttered to himself, then

stooped towards her, his face within inches of hers. His lips were blotched with sores; his teeth mottled and uneven. He seemed to be speaking with no sound, and she all but retched at the reek of beer and piss. She too must smell repulsive: her body stale with sweat; vomit on her dress.

He was holding out his hand to her: a dirty hand with broken nails and bits of frayed sticking-plaster on the fingers. But it might help her to stand up. She couldn't do it on her own. She reached out her own hand and made miraculous shaky contact. And somehow she was stumbling to her feet and they were clinging to each other, her dress crushed against the rough fabric of his coat. She felt tears sting her eyes again. She loved this man – her protector and her brother; all that remained of her family. But he too was abandoning her, staggering off again, his shadow limping behind him.

He tottered into an alleyway and the tall buildings closed in round him, swallowing up his traces.

She was utterly alone.

30

Catherine jolted awake. For endless hours sleep had been a rollercoaster, plunging her into nightmare, then shuddering back up a slow, uneasy incline, only to crash down again into terrifying panic. But every time she woke, there had been a point of light in the darkness, a reassuring presence, a soft voice.

It was speaking now, close to her ear. Was she all right? Would she like some water?

An arm helped her sit up, held a glass to her lips. Her throat felt bruised and raw. Swallowing was painful.

The voice asked again how she was feeling.

'Cold,' she whispered. 'Cold.'

'I'll fetch another blanket.'

'No! Don't go.' She couldn't bear to be alone again. She clutched the arm. She couldn't see the rest of the person. Everything was blurred – everything but her blazing thirst.

'It's all right. I'm here. I'm with you. Can you get back to sleep, d'you think?'

The questions were so difficult. Had she been asleep? Did you sleep in the street? She shook her head. More pain.

The arm was spreading something over her, something warm and comforting. Then it began to stroke her hair. The rollercoaster subsided.

She closed her eyes, sank down.

31

Lying back against the pillows, she watched the shifting patterns of sunlight on the carpet. The window was wide open and it seemed a minor miracle that she could look into the light without her eyes hurting. She could even hold a glass and drink. She savoured the cool refreshing sharpness of the grapefruit juice. One took so much for granted: being able to swallow without a feeling of obstruction, or eat without throwing up.

She refilled the glass from the carton Will had left by the bed, together with other things he'd thought of: fruit, yogurt, Marmite and Ryvita, his treasured childhood copy of *The Wind in the Willows* and a pile of paperbacks. His devotion had amazed her. Instead of greeting her with fury and recrimination when she limped in at dawn on Saturday, he had put her to bed and nursed her like a baby, refusing to leave her side until this morning. He hadn't even made a scene about her going off with Brad – who, apparently, had called round in the early hours, desperate for news of her.

Deeply ashamed of having worried them so much, she sat staring into her glass. Both had feared the worst, and indeed, considering the state she was in and the dangers of the street, she was lucky to have got home in one piece. (Though quite *how* she'd got home she couldn't remember at all.)

Slowly she swung her legs out of bed and drifted to the window, leaning on the windowsill and looking out at the scene below. She found its very ordinariness reassuring: litter-strewn pavements, graffitied walls, people trudging past with cartons of milk and armloads of Sunday papers; a couple of rollerblading tearaways zigzagging perilously down the middle of the road. From this perspective, Friday night seemed a hallucination, out of focus and frighteningly extreme in both its highs and lows. This morning she had discovered that the Ecstasy tablet was no longer in the pocket of her dress. Of course, it could have fallen out, but . . .

Frantically, she gulped more juice, as if, even at this remove, it would flush out whatever it was she had swallowed. She still couldn't quite believe that a middle-aged woman who never touched drugs and was wary even of aspirin had taken hash on top of alcohol, and probably E as well. How else could she have danced so long, with such spontaneous rapturous energy?

She wandered out to the bathroom. She would have a bath and wash her hair – wash away the whole outlandish experience and get back to normality. Not that it was normal to be lying in bed at well past noon on a Sunday. Will had left hours ago, without a murmur of complaint, although she knew he hated running the stall on his own.

In the bathroom she found more proof of his devotion. The bath and basin were gleaming, the towels neatly folded on the rail; he had even washed the floor.

She ran a bath and a few minutes later was lying in pine-scented foam, feeling very nearly content. Although the aftermath of Friday had been horrendous, there were positive aspects too: the rare and unforgettable sensation of ecstasy (whether drug-induced or not) and the healing of the breach with Will. This morning he had admitted that imagining her mugged or raped (or worse) had brought home to him how shockingly he had taken her for granted. He had resolved from this day on to do his share of the cooking and cleaning; he would even tackle the repairs on the car. She smiled to herself, unable to quite believe in this new paragon. Still, he had made an impressive start and she had apologized in her turn for putting him through so much over the last two days.

After a luxurious half-hour soak she went back to the other room and slipped one of his old shirts on. She had promised not to move from the flat or do anything too arduous, so there was little point in getting dressed. She picked up *The Wind in the Willows* and sat with it at his desk. Even the desk was unnaturally tidy, cleared of everything save his crocodile poem. She read the poem slowly, awed by the startling use of language: the way he made you see and feel and almost *taste* the crocodile; undercutting the sadness with little barbs of humour. She realized she had taken him for granted as much as he had her. A man of such talent couldn't be judged by ordinary standards. She must try to be more tolerant, less nit-picking. And above all, they must find a nicer flat. Then they could start again – rethink everything: work, money, shopping, chores. It was still possible to build a life together, if they were both prepared to make concessions.

Looking up, she happened to catch Gerry's eye. Behind him smiled Andrew and Antonia; Jack and Maureen on the shelf above; Kate in splendid isolation on the mantelpiece. It *was* a bit insensitive to have all the family photos on display. No wonder Will had made that remark about waking up to her brilliant actor-husband every morning.

Impulsively she collected them up and shoved them into a drawer. All except Gerry. It would be callous to consign him to oblivion – the man she had loved and lived with over half her life. While she was still debating what to do with him, the phone rang. It was probably Will – he had said he'd ring at lunchtime to see how she was. It suddenly occurred to her that he might have heard compromising rumours. Gossip spread like wildfire in the market and several people had seen her leave the Stag with Brad. And Brad himself was bound to have regaled his friends with an account of her night on the tiles.

'Er, hello,' she said, defensively.

'Oh, Mum, you're in! Thank goodness. I thought you'd be at the market. I've just this minute got back from the hospital and . . .'

'Hospital?' Catherine gripped the receiver. 'What's happened?'

'Don't worry. I'm okay. It was this cyclist – he crashed into the Jeep. Shivan was driving me to Palwai to pick up an old typewriter, and this crazy guy just shot out of a side street right in front of us. We took him straight to hospital, but we had to wait for ages and I . . . I was sure he was going to die. He just lay there, sort of horribly still. And well . . . I kept thinking about Dad. It brought it all back again – I mean, first Venu's death, then this. Well actually he didn't die. It was only concussion and he's going to be all right, they said. But it made me feel how . . . how fragile we are. One minute everything's fine, then out of the blue – bang! – that's it. And I suddenly thought, suppose something had happened to *you*. I might not have heard all this way away, but you could be lying in a pool of blood, or . . . Oh, I know it's stupid and I'm probably just in shock or something, but I had to ring and find out if you're okay.'

'Yes,' she lied convincingly, 'I'm perfectly all right. Look, let me ring you back and we'll have a proper chat.'

'But it's so expensive for you, Mum. Our phone calls seem to get longer and longer and it's always your bill.'

'Don't worry about that. Just give me a couple of minutes.' She closed the window against the noise, trying not to think about how horribly close to reality Kate's picture of her had been. It was true – anything could happen.

She got through again without too much delay and the line was mercifully clear.

'Mum, how do you *deal* with death? Shit – that's a really naff question, isn't it?'

An impossible question, she thought. She and Will discussed it sometimes, but Will's contention that poets could keep people alive (as Shakespeare had with the Dark Lady of the Sonnets, or Thomas Hardy with his first wife) was little compensation for the personal pain.

'I mean, I ought to have got over Dad. It's coming up for two years now.'

'Two years isn't long, darling. And someone else dying is bound to be a reminder.'

'Well, at least the guy *didn't* die.'

'No, fortunately. But accidents like that are always terribly upsetting, and you're probably still in shock. I think you should take it easy, Kate. Promise me you'll stay in today and not do anything too arduous.' Will's exact words to her. She wished she had his poetic gift, so she could say something profound and inspiring about death. She was stuck with fatuous clichés: time heals, scars fade. Yet Kate seemed to find them comforting.

'Oh, Mum, I'm so glad you're there. And forgive me going on like this. It must be much worse for you, with the anniversary coming up and everything.'

'No, I'm fine. Really. And you know, having a grandchild to look forward to does help. Of course, it can't make up for Daddy's death, but in a way the baby's part of him – it's sort of saying, life goes on.'

'Yeah, I see what you mean. But I hope they're not still expecting you to drop everything and devote your life to the sprog.'

Catherine flushed. When she'd mentioned Andrew's proposition, Kate had been outraged at the idea. Even as children, brother and sister had rarely seen eye to eye, and Kate made no bones about her feelings towards Antonia. She affected to despise both marriage and motherhood, though Catherine sometimes wondered if it was simply a façade, hiding loneliness, even jealousy.

'No, they're going to get a nanny.' She felt guilty saying it. But apart from her unwillingness to take on bottle-feeds and nappies, she was hardly grandmother material now – not since Friday night. 'What about you, though? How's work?'

'Frantic!' All at once, Kate laughed. 'Oh, Mum, I must tell you – your Marmite arrived last week. It took nearly four months to get here, would you believe. It'd been opened and stuck up again with government-issue tape. They must have thought it was a suspicious package. Actually, it did look a bit like a bomb. It's the biggest jar I've ever seen. Thanks – it'll last me ages. I had some this morning for breakfast.'

'So did I, funnily enough. Though perhaps I should say lunch. It was getting on for midday before I surfaced properly. I'm being a real slob today.'

'Yes, why aren't you at the market? I thought Sunday was your best day?'

'I, er, had a bit of a hangover.'

'Mum, you shameless thing! Were you living it up with your gorgeous poet last night?'

'Well, no. Actually, I . . . I went to a rave.' What was she saying? The last thing Kate needed on top of a near-fatal accident was an account of her mother's lunacy. But, somehow, she was pouring it all out – not the lows, the high.

There was a worrying silence the other end. 'Kate, are you still there?'

'Yes, 'course.'

'I haven't shocked you, have I?'

'No. I'm just trying to imagine you at a rave.'

She flushed. 'Well, I never intended going, I assure you. I just landed up at this extraordinary club without realizing what I was in for.'

'It's okay, you don't have to apologize. Actually, I think you're rather brave. Most people your age wouldn't dream of going to a thing like that.'

'No, they're far too sensible.'

'It's not being sensible, it's fear. Fear of new experiences.'

'Well, it was certainly an experience! In fact, I can't stop thinking about it. It was so intense. And liberating. My worries just seemed to float away, as if I was dancing them out of my mind. And I don't think it was the drink or drugs, necessarily, more the . . .'

'Drugs? Christ, Mum, you didn't *take* anything, did you?'

'Not really.' She was blushing like a guilty adolescent. Only a few years ago, she and Gerry had been giving dire parental warnings to Andrew and Kate. Now the roles were reversed. 'It was just a sort of . . . aberration. Tomorrow I'll be back to reality. Whatever reality is. I'm not sure I know any more.' She broke off. One part of her – the conventional mother – knew she should play down the whole thing, or, better, change the subject. Yet the other, curious, adventurous part yearned to discuss it in engrossing detail. She hadn't had much chance with Will – he'd been too concerned about the state of her health. 'It's funny, Kate, while I was dancing, *that* seemed more real than anything. And it felt so . . . so absolutely right. As if that was how we were born to be. Free and loving and open. And sort of connected to everyone else, however different we might all be in ordinary life.'

'Gosh, Mum, you sound just like Paul! It's a spiritual thing, you see, that feeling of connectedness. Paul's into Zen, and he used to say you can even feel a bond with sticks and stones and clouds and stuff.'

'Well I envy him, I must say, if he feels that all the time. I'm afraid I came down to earth with a crash and now I'm just thoroughly ashamed.'

'Ashamed? I don't see why.'

'Well, *you* obviously disapprove, and . . .'

'I *don't*, Mum. I was just surprised, that's all. It's so long since I've seen you I'm probably remembering you all wrong.'

Catherine tried to think back to the person she had been when Kate left for India. Three years ago. Three centuries.

'Anyway, it shows how open-minded you are. It pisses me off when middle-aged people assume they know it all and there's nothing new to get their heads round. When I was in Goa, there were all these old hippies – older than Dad, some of them – who were still searching for the truth. There was no way they were going to sell out, and I have to say I admired them – envied them too, I suppose. I know Andrew would think they were a load of drug-crazed layabouts, and, okay, they did sit around a lot of the time smoking pot and meditating. But what's wrong with that? At least they're trying to work out what we're here for, which I bet Andrew never does. I got talking to one of them, who was into this thing about how drugs can bring you closer to God. He'd travelled all over the world and lived with primitive tribes who use magic mushrooms or cactus or whatever to get in touch with – oh, I know it sounds a bit naff, but the supernatural, the sacred, all that stuff.'

'Yes, some of the people at the rave were like that. I must admit I thought it was a bit airy-fairy until I experienced it myself. But once I started dancing I felt this sense of – well, communion, I suppose you'd call it. As if we were all part of a religious rite. And it seemed sort of . . . holy to love the world and everyone in it. There weren't any of the usual prejudices or divisions. Actually, it was more than dancing – it was like . . . discovering a truth. It reminded me of that bit in the Bible – perfect love casteth out fear.'

'God, Mum, you sound as if you're *still* high!'

She grinned. 'Don't worry, I'll be back to normal soon enough. I'm going on a junk-shop tour tomorrow to stock up for the stall, and I'll need my wits about me then, to spot the best bargains.'

'Heavens, Mum, I've just noticed the time. Your phone bill's going to be astronomical. *That*'ll sober you up when it arrives!'

Catherine laughed. In spite of the expense, she felt she could talk endlessly about the new astounding world she had glimpsed, and was reluctant to ring off. Poor Kate – she had phoned for reassurance and got a mother in full flood. 'I'm sorry, darling. I went off at rather a tangent. We were talking about that poor cyclist. I only hope I haven't added to the shock.'

'No, I feel loads better, to tell the truth. It's helped take my mind off death. Oh, and by the way, I'm afraid I won't be able to phone you on Dad's actual anniversary. We're going on a camping trip that week.'

'That's okay.'

'But I expect you'll be with Andrew, won't you?'

'Yes.'

'Are you going to the crematorium?'

'Well that's the plan, but I'm not awfully keen, to be honest. I hate the place. And I have a horrible feeling Daddy doesn't like it either. It's funny, I'm sitting here with his photo on my lap. I was just trying to decide what to do with it when you rang.'

'Why, don't you want it?'

'It's not that. We're . . . just a bit short of space.'

'Well, you can always bung him in a Jiffy-bag and send him to me. I've only got a few snapshots of him and they're getting terribly faded.'

'Good idea. I'll put it in the post first thing in the morning. Let's hope it doesn't take four months again.'

'Thanks, Mum. Listen, before I say goodbye, how's Grandma?'

'Not quite so stiff, thank heavens. The new pills seem to be helping.' Now they *were* back to reality: crematoria, arthritis.

'Well, give her my love, won't you. I take it she and Grandpa are going to the crematorium as well?'

'Yes, all the tribe. I suppose it'll become an annual pilgrimage. Poor Daddy. I wish now that I'd scattered his ashes on stage at some theatre or other.'

'Hey, that's a thought. Why not *go* to the theatre? For his anniversary.'

'What do you mean? What theatre?'

'Any one you like. Well, no – try and choose somewhere connected with Dad. Book seats for the seventeenth and *celebrate* his life instead of mourning him.'

'Oh, I couldn't, darling. The others would be horrified.'

'Stuff the others. Go on your own. And make it a comedy, or at least something fairly light. I'm sure Dad would rather you spent the day laughing, not mooning around some morbid graveyard.'

Catherine smiled. The idea was crazy – typical of Kate, though. 'Oh, darling, I do love you. But you're right – I must ring off.' She dreaded to think what the call had cost. The last phone bill had been bad enough. 'And don't forget, take it easy for the rest of the day. No more tearing about on those dangerous roads.'

'And don't *you* forget, either, Mum, book that theatre ticket. And make it the front stalls – really go to town for once. I'll be with you in spirit and give you a wave from my tent. 'Bye. Good luck!'

Catherine put the phone down, feeling almost light-headed again. Perhaps she *would* go to the theatre, crazy idea or no. It would do her good to spend Gerry's second anniversary laughing instead of crying. She picked up his photo. He was laughing too, as if he approved of the proposal. She smiled back at him, surprised to realize how much less painful it was to look at his picture. Time did heal.

As she hunted for a Jiffy-bag for the photo, she decided to enclose a copy of Will's poem on death. It expressed things better than she could, and would also give Kate an idea of his work. Then she'd do nothing else all afternoon except lie on the bed and luxuriate, if not in ecstasy, then peace – peace with Will and Kate and God and all the world.

32

Catherine pushed the heavy glass doors and walked in with a frisson of excitement. It was so long since she'd been here, she had forgotten how fond she was of the place. More than just a theatre, it seemed a treasure-house full of entertainments. She stopped in the foyer to listen to a duet on flute and grand piano; the pianist an intense Byronic-looking fellow whose slender hands caressed the keys sensuously; the flautist a willowy girl in a waft of flower-sprigged silk. Their sprightly music followed her as she strolled across the foyer and up the stairs. After the free recital below, she found a free exhibition on the first floor: moody black and white photographs of writers of the twenties.

While she stood admiring them, a man brushed her arm and apologized, holding her eye for longer than was necessary. Already she had attracted other glances, perhaps due to her clingy hot-pink dress, bought in Gerry's honour – second-hand, of course, but striking, none the less.

The clock said quarter to one – time to eat before the show began. The Terrace Café was one floor above and overlooked the river. It wasn't cheap, but Kate had sent her a cheque, clipped to a scribbled note: 'Mum, this is for the 17th. I'll be thinking of you all day.' The amount was considerably more than her daughter could afford and the gesture had touched her deeply.

A waiter met her at the entrance to the café. 'Just one, madam?' he asked.

She nodded. 'Just one', maybe, but she didn't feel alone – not when Kate was with her in spirit.

'I'll sit outside if I may,' she said, noticing several picnic-style tables already occupied. It was perfect weather for eating on the terrace: the warm sun tempered by a skittish breeze. Besides, she wanted to look down at the spot where she and Gerry had sat twenty years ago. The National Theatre was new then, and famously controversial, and they had come from the north to see it for themselves, booking seats for a matinée. They had travelled by coach on a day-return – an unaccustomed break from work and children. Six months later they were back, this time to see a friend of Gerry's playing Lucilius in *Julius Caesar*. A minor role, admittedly, but a tremendous achievement for Christopher. 'Your turn next,' she had said to Gerry, but in less than two years he was tethered to a desk, selling cut-price office furniture.

The waiter seated her at an outside table and she looked eagerly over the balcony to the riverside below. Yes, there was the wooden bench – or one very similar. She could almost see herself and Gerry sitting side by side, munching their cheese sandwiches and drinking coffee from a flask. The whole trip was done on a shoe-string: picnic lunch and seats up in the gods – but it had been a marvellous day. Travelling back on the coach, Gerry, elated by the performance, had poured out his hopes for the future; the parts he aimed to play; his refusal to give up even when those aims were thwarted. It was autumn then, the leaves on the plane trees beginning to fade and fall. Today they were luxuriantly green and rippling in the breeze. Beyond them lay the Thames, the colour of weak tea; above, a confidently blue sky and clouds like great white dollops of meringue. Motor launches were chugging past; red buses rumbling over the bridge; a lone seagull swooping low across the water.

As the waiter returned she hurriedly scanned the menu for something Gerry would like – in other words, something rich and fattening. She sensed him here with her: an almost palpable presence; his voice animated as he waxed lyrical over sauces and desserts.

'I'll have the pasta in brandy cream sauce,' she said, 'and half a bottle of Sauvignon.' Sometimes in their hard-up youth, they had shared a single glass of wine between them, but today she refused to feel guilty, either about splashing out, or about her family, *or* Will. They all disapproved of what she was doing, but she had decided to please herself – and Gerry.

The people at the other tables were nearly all elderly, doubtless attracted by the special-offer matinée seats. Among the ranks of conventional grey perms, her own cropped head must stand out like a purple thistle in a field of shrivelled grass. How sad that Gerry would never make it to old age – although she couldn't imagine *his* hair being anything but wildly black. Suddenly a siren wailed and she saw an ambulance speeding across the bridge. At once, she was back inside it, clutching Gerry's cold hand. Had he been in pain at the moment of his death? Or terrified? Did he even know she was there? She had gone over it and over it in her mind, desperate to interpret his last choking sounds as some sort of message to her, a final word of love, perhaps. The harsh truth was, she would never know.

'Your pasta, madam.'

She started, wrenched herself back to the present.

The waiter set down her bottle of wine and plate of sizzling pasta thatched with melted cheese and garnished with radicchio and roasted red and yellow peppers. 'Enjoy,' he said as he poured her wine.

Yes, she thought, she *would* enjoy. But first, a toast. 'To Kate,' she murmured, picking up her glass. After all, it was her daughter who had saved her from that grisly crematorium.

The attendant took her ticket. 'Aisle two,' he said. 'Right down the front.'

She smiled to herself. Following Kate's advice, she had booked a seat in the front stalls, the very first row, in fact. Ironically, they were the cheapest seats in the house, so close to the stage they could give you a crick in the neck. But *she* had no objection. She liked the fact she could reach out and touch the stage. Also, she was sitting at the end of the row, which meant that the orchestra, too, were only a few feet away, positioned on raked seating above her, on the right. It gave her a sense of involvement, of belonging with the performers rather than the audience. Once you'd been married to an actor, you could never again sit through a play as a dispassionate observer. Not only were you conscious of the sheer hard graft that went into the production, but you actually got high on the players' adrenalin or sweated blood with them.

The orchestra started tuning up. She had a marvellous view of them: the portly clarinettist perspiring in his pink-striped shirt, the frail foreign-looking man dwarfed by his double bass. She had never seen *A Little Night Music* – she and Gerry rarely went to musicals – but it had been a matter of elimination. Of the three matinées at the National today, one was fully booked and the second some depressing thing about the conquest of the Incas, lasting four and three-quarter hours. *This* show boasted such adjectives as 'sophisticated', 'sumptuous' and 'bitter-sweet', and although it might be hype, she would still far rather be here than contemplating a mournful rosebush.

The auditorium was filling and the murmur of conversation gradually increased in volume. An elderly couple settled themselves on her left, armed with programmes and a box of chocolates. They proceeded to read out snippets to each other, interspersed with comments on the relative merits of cream centres or nuts. The orchestra, still tuning, sounded like a multi-headed animal, bleating, growling, braying by turns, until suddenly the pianist raised his hand for silence, the house lights dimmed and the cast trooped on to the stage. Their costumes were, yes, sumptuous, and as they moved right down to the front she could see the intricate details of their make-up: elongated eyebrows, blue-mascara'd lashes, lipstick in cupid's bows. Her palms were damp with nerves. She was back in her youth in her usual front-row seat, alert to every nuance of Gerry's performance so that she could discuss it with him later; watching his every gesture and expression. But nerves gave way to excitement as the actors glided into a strange surrealistic waltz, continually changing partners, recoupling, pirouetting. The bewitching music soared and swirled, and she knew with absolute certainty that this was where she was *meant* to be today.

The curtain calls were a feat of bravura in themselves: first the whole cast circling on a slowly revolving stage, then re-forming in two rows, then in pairs, then singly; the applause swelling with each variation. And even after the house lights had come up, the orchestra continued playing a reprise of the main themes and were applauded in their turn.

As the last clapping died away she remained motionless in her seat, not wanting to break the spell. People squeezed and jostled past, but only when the theatre was almost empty did *she* get up, and then reluctantly. She was on a high, too exhilarated to return tamely to the flat.

She lingered in the foyer, drinking in the atmosphere, wishing she could afford to see more shows – toss aside her sewing, desert

380

the market stall and enjoy a week of shameless indulgence. But no way could she spend more money – rather, she had to *earn* more, to make up for today. Just at present, though, she would continue with the illusion that she was a lady of leisure, like most of the women in the musical, whose main purpose in life seemed to be to titivate their hair and fall in love.

She sauntered out of the main doors and walked towards the river. It was still a golden afternoon, the plane trees flecked with sunlight, the dark shadows of their dappled trunks criss-crossing the path. Skateboarders rattled by, lovers strolled arm in arm, children guzzled ice-cream cornets – everyone enjoying themselves. She stood by the railing and looked out at the water, its surface in constant shimmering motion, as if too excited to lie still. Across the river the skyline was a mishmash of architectural styles, from slender spires in sculpted stone to steel and concrete tower blocks. And here and there grey scaffolding and orange cranes signalled the embryo skyscrapers of the Millennium.

She gazed at the scene, trying to regain that intensity of feeling she had experienced at the rave – a heightened perception of the present moment, the perfect astounding 'now'. Today it wasn't so difficult, released as she was from the demands of work and the distraction of other people. But during the past couple of weeks she had been, frankly, just too busy for any emotional or spiritual highs. Will's resolve to turn over a new leaf had lasted all of three days. An urgent phone call from the Scrivener Press had sent him scurrying back to his desk: there wasn't time for domestic trivia when Leonard Upjohn demanded still more poems.

She watched a pigeon scavenging in the brown sludge at the river's edge, pecking contentedly at every find; its very absorption in its task a demonstration of how to be. She shouldn't even be thinking of Will – just luxuriating in this rare day off. Yet Will's bad grace in agreeing to man the stall alone today had left her with a sour taste of resentment. He could write affecting poems about death in the abstract, but seemed unable to accept her need to mark the anniversary of one death in particular. And while he pursued his career as poet, she was marking time, fitting in with *his* needs rather than satisfying her own.

She found herself humming one of the songs from the show, snatches of the words echoing in her head:

> *Later,*
> *When is later?*
> *How can I wait around for later?*

Exactly what she was doing – postponing decisions, making no real effort to find another flat; merely working through the jobs each day, only to start again the next. Living in the 'now' was one thing, but not at the expense of her happiness and future.

> *Though I've been born, I've never been.*
> *How can I wait around for later?*
> *I'll be ninety on my death-bed.*

Or maybe forty-nine on her death-bed – like Gerry, who had never fulfilled his ambitions. If she kept waiting around for later she would never fulfil hers either. But it was so difficult without money, and if she took the line of least resistance and returned to an office job, it would leave her with still less freedom.

On an impulse she turned and walked towards Gerry's bench. Someone was already sitting there: a bespectacled young man, dressed entirely in black. He was engrossed in a book and didn't so much as look up when she sat at the other end of the bench. *She* had no desire to read – it was enough simply to be for a while. Escaping from her duties today had made her realize how tired she was. Six months ago she had deliberately tried to change her life; now she wondered if she had merely exchanged one set of constraints for another. The rave had made her question things more deeply: fulfilment, freedom, 'reality' – her own and other people's.

She jumped as a hooter brayed from the far bank. It was a motor launch, setting off from the quay, slicing a white furrow through the water. She watched until it vanished under the bridge, the choppy backwash gradually subsiding. It was like the process of mourning: the initial shock of grief cutting swift and deep, then continuing to churn, until little by little the ripples dwindled and the surface almost regained its lapping calm. Today, she realized, was a turning-point. In some way she couldn't quite explain she had finally come to terms with Gerry's loss. Of course it would always leave a scar, but she felt she had laid his ghost to rest. She hoped fervently that it would happen for Kate, too. Their last letters had crossed and, strangely, both of them had written on similar lines, expanding on their long phone call and the subjects of truth and death.

She put her hands on her lap, palms uppermost, as if letting Gerry go; releasing him from the confines of that anonymous crematorium. Let him rest here instead, she thought – in death, if not in life – beside the theatre he loved.

She gave a long, deep sigh – his final requiem.

The man looked up from his book. 'You English?' he asked abruptly.

'Er, yes.'

'Me Romanian.'

'Oh . . . I see. Hello.'

'Sergiu. My name.'

She nodded, hoping he would resume his reading.

'*Your* name?' he asked, taking off his glasses to reveal lustrously dark eyes.

'Catherine.'

'Catherine.' He mispronounced it. 'You like drink with me?'

'I'm afraid I've got to get home.'

'You married lady?'

She shook her head.

'So we have drink together?'

'Well, no, I . . .'

'You not *like* me, Catherine?'

She couldn't help but smile. No doubt he was perfectly charming, but there was Will to be considered. True, Will had been magnanimous about the rave and Brad, but she could just imagine his reaction if she arrived home late after going off with some unknown young Romanian. Sergiu was keen, no question – scribbling something on a piece of paper, which he thrust into her hand.

'We make date. Tomorrow.'

She glanced at the scrap of paper: an indecipherable name, followed by a string of numbers.

'You telephone me, Catherine. Please.'

'We'll see. But now I have to go.'

She gave him a brief smile and walked purposefully away. It was flattering to be chatted up (especially by someone little more than thirty), although actually she was quite happy on her own. Not once had she felt lonely today, or envious of married couples – an achievement she wouldn't have thought possible even as little as two months ago.

She strolled on along the riverside walk, suddenly aware that she was walking not towards the tube but away from it. She ought to be getting back, though. Having evaded the crematorium visit, she had promised to phone Jack and Maureen, and Andrew and Antonia, as soon as she was in. And Will would hardly welcome an evening on his own after running the stall all day. Yet she was tempted *not* to return; to prolong her freedom like some rebellious adolescent playing truant. The show must have affected her more deeply than she'd realized. Billed as a musical romance, it was spiked with regret and disenchantment, even bitterness. She hummed one of the tunes: a song about ordinary mothers. She could remember only the first line – '*Ordinary mothers lead ordinary lives*' – but after that came a long list of their duties: sweeping, cooking, keeping house. Well, she refused to be an ordinary mother any more, *or* an ordinary daughter-in-law, or an ordinary partner to Will. But what *was* she going to be? That was much more difficult.

She stood leaning on the railing again, gazing out over the river. There was a general air of busyness and purpose: boats with destinations, barges pulling strings of tugs; trains rattling over Hungerford Bridge; traffic on the Embankment nosing determinedly along. All at once, a flicker of movement caught her eye. A silver speedboat was just coming into sight, on its way down-river. Seconds later, it streaked past her with a glittering plume of spray. She watched it enviously, longing to join it in its headlong rush towards the open sea.

33

Catherine sat on the floor, surrounded by tools, spare plugs and broken bits of Hoover. The wretched thing had proved beyond her powers of repair, so she lugged its still smoking corpse outside and went to fetch the broom. With things so hectic all last week she hadn't had a chance to catch up with the housework, and she wanted the place nice for Sam.

The broom had a wobbly handle and the stiff bristles left marks on the carpet, so she finally resorted to a dustpan and brush to pick up the worst of the crumbs (Will *would* eat while walking around, without a plate). And there was a pile of washing-up waiting in the bathroom basin. One of the flats they'd looked at had a really splendid kitchen, complete with microwave and dishwasher. Needless to say the rent was astronomical. Another one they'd seen was actually affordable, but it was so close to a railway line, the whole building vibrated each time a train went by.

There was enough noise here, for heaven's sake. Closing the window to shut out the worst of Maison Victor's muzak, she spotted the postman outside. She went down to get the letters, pleased to see an airmail envelope with Nicky's writing on it.

Upstairs again, she put the kettle on. The housework could wait – she would read Nicky's news over a cup of coffee. Not that there was much news other than windsurfing and more windsurfing, but she laughed at the PS: 'Don't forget you promised to visit. Just let me know when your launch arrives and I'll windsurf out to meet you!'

She put the letter back in its envelope and sat looking at the stamps. One showed a hump-backed whale frolicking in turquoise water; the other a palm-fringed bay with tropical birds. How ironi-

cal it was that having given Nicky all that good advice about freedom and self-discovery, she had heeded none of it herself.

Capable, pliable . . .
Women, women . . .
Undemanding and reliable,
Knowing their place . . .

That damned musical – she couldn't get it out of her head. She
had borrowed the cassette from the library and been playing it,
off and on, the last three weeks.

Women, women . . .
Very nearly indispensable . . .

Well, today she *was* indispensable, at least as far as Sam was
concerned. Vanessa and Julian were abroad, and Lisa, their nanny,
had phoned to say that her father had been suddenly taken ill and
that she had to catch the midday train to visit him in hospital. Will
couldn't change his plans – he was on his way to Norwich to meet
Leonard Upjohn from the Scrivener Press – so *she* had stepped
into the breach. It was petty to feel resentful; after all, this could
be Will's big break. He had already written most of the new poems,
and once he'd finished the rest she would have the time and energy
to look for more lucrative work. The market seemed to be going
from bad to worse, and if they couldn't make a living in August, with
perfect weather and a glut of tourists, they might as well give up.

She put Nicky's letter in a drawer and went to tackle the
washing-up, working quickly through the pile. She hadn't that
much time. Will had taken the car, and although Hampstead was
only a couple of stops on the tube, there was a long walk the other
end. She could do the shopping after she'd collected Sam – he
seemed to regard a slog round a crowded supermarket as a fantastical excursion.

Three-quarters of an hour later, she was walking along South
End Road, admiring the view of the Heath. It was a world away
from Kentish Town, with gracious homes, tree-lined streets and an
air of almost rural calm. She had never been to Vanessa's before,
and arriving at the Georgian house (wisteria-covered, double-
fronted), she could understand Will's bitterness. It *was* hard for

an impoverished poet to be saddled with child maintenance while Vanessa and Julian lived in such lavish style.

The nanny, too, was a perfect adjunct to her surroundings: a peach-complexioned girl in a well-cut dress, whose vowels were pure Roedean.

'Oh, do come in, Mrs Jones. Sam's all ready. It's sweet of you to help out at such short notice.'

'Don't mention it. I'm just glad I was free.' She was riveted by the grandeur of the hall: the array of abstract paintings, the antique settle and expensive-looking carriage clock.

'Well, I've managed to arrange a substitute, thank goodness – a friend of mine, Michelle. She's looked after Sam before, so I'm sure Vanessa won't mind. I haven't been able to get hold of them yet, but they're bound to phone Sam this evening, so Michelle can explain what's happened. Unfortunately she can't get here till five, so I wondered if you'd be kind enough to stay till then?'

'Of course. It's no trouble at all.'

'I'm so grateful, honestly. I just don't know how to thank you.' She turned and called upstairs. 'Sam! Catherine's here.'

Catherine eyed Lisa's elegant back. What a pity she already had a job – she would have made the ideal nanny for Antonia: well-dressed, well-spoken, well-mannered. Antonia had been on her conscience recently. She'd not seen her in the last month or so, and when they spoke on the phone and the conversation inevitably turned to the pregnancy, it made her uneasy about how little she had done to help. True she was working flat out at the market and doing her best to help Will, but *he* wasn't suffering from morning sickness.

All of a sudden Sam came rocketing downstairs and hid behind Lisa's back.

'Hello, Sam,' Catherine said encouragingly.

He refused to meet her eye. 'I want my Daddy,' he whimpered.

Catherine put out her hand to him. 'Well, he's going to ring later and you can talk to him on the phone. That'll be nice, won't it?'

He ignored the hand and pulled at Lisa's skirt. 'Why can't *you* stay?'

'I've told you, darling. *My* Daddy's ill and I have to go and see him.'

Poor kid, thought Catherine. He must have a pretty dim view

of fathers – absent, ill, away. 'Listen, Sam,' she said. 'I thought we might have chips for lunch. And ice cream with toffee sauce. Shall we go and buy them together?'

A flicker of interest crossed his face. 'Can we have chips at the zoo?'

After a quick mental calculation – thirteen pounds to get in, plus another seven or eight for lunch – she realized the zoo was out of the question. 'I'll cook them for you at home, then we can have lots and lots. And after that we could go and look at the pet shop.'

'Will you buy me a cat?'

She could see today was going to be difficult. 'No, I'm sorry, Sam. I've told you – we can't have a cat in London.'

'*You* had one.'

'Look, Lisa's got to catch a train, so we really should be going. There are fantastic things in that pet shop, you know – all sorts of different snakes. And beautiful green lizards. And salamanders. And tree frogs. And Chinese water dragons . . .'

They had admired the water dragons, bought a tiny (toy) cat, eaten a disgustingly large pile of chips, polished off the ice cream and home-made toffee sauce. And it was still only half past two.

'Why hasn't Daddy phoned?' asked Sam, pushing his empty dish away.

'He's rather busy today, darling. And it's probably hard for him to get to a phone.'

'He *promised.*'

'Yes, well, give him a bit longer and I'm sure he will phone.'

Sam got down from the table and started prowling around the room, finally stopping at the bed. 'Is that where you sleep?' he asked.

She nodded.

'And where does my Daddy sleep?'

'Er . . . in the other room.'

'Why don't we ever *go* in the other room?'

'It's full of furniture and stuff.'

'Why does Daddy sleep there then?'

'Look Sam, I've just had an idea. Let's go for a bus ride. We could sit on top at the very front and go all the way to Alexandra Park and back.'

His face lit up. 'Oh, yes!'

She knew that buses were an exotic treat for children chauffeured everywhere since infancy. 'And we'll play the red and blue car game.'

'What's that?'

'Well, *you* look out for red cars and *I* look out for blue. And we get a point for each one we see. The person with most points wins a prize.'

'What's the prize?'

'Wait and see.'

'A cat!'

'No.'

'A camel?'

'No. Smaller than that.'

'A flea?'

She laughed. 'I told you – wait and see.'

He looked at her reflectively. 'Did you like that camel ride at the zoo?'

'Oh, yes.'

'Can *I* have one next time?'

'Of course.' It was just a little matter of an extra twenty quid or so. The thought needled her into a sudden decision – she *was* going to take a proper job, dreary office or no. It was ridiculous to be so strapped for cash that she couldn't afford the zoo. 'Come on, Sam, let's get that crust from the bread bin, then we can feed the ducks in the park.'

'Oh, great!'

Thank heavens he was easily pleased. She could just about run to a bit of stale bread and the bus fare to Alexandra Park. As for the prize, it would have to be conjured out of thin air.

She stood scouring the chip pan, wondering what to cook for Will. Leonard Upjohn had mentioned lunch out, but knowing the financial straits of small presses, that probably meant a ham roll in a pub. She was surprised Will wasn't back yet, *and* that he hadn't phoned. Of course he might well have tried earlier, when they were out on their long bus-ride. Fortunately Sam appeared to have forgotten about his father and had only brought the subject up again when she handed him over to Michelle. That was nearly three hours ago.

She finished washing the pan and took it back to the living-room. Perhaps spaghetti bolognese would do – fairly cheap and filling and it wouldn't spoil if Will was held up in traffic. It was such a pain having only two gas rings to cook on. You needed an oven for so many things, especially the cheaper cuts of meat.

She cleared a space amidst the clutter on the table and set about chopping some onions. Outside, the light was fading, the sky a dull grey-blue. August was half over and next month would be autumn; the evenings drawing in. Why did everything take so long? – finding flats, getting poetry published, even handing over nervous boys to new nannies. She had hated leaving Sam: he seemed wary of Michelle and had kept begging *her* to stay.

She heated some oil to brown the onions, turning the gas low as the phone rang. She hoped it wasn't Will ringing to say the car had broken down. Recently it had been making ominous noises again, despite all they'd spent on it.

'Hello,' she said apprehensively. 'Oh, Anthony, how are you?' Anthony Foster was an unsuccessful poet who had given up writing to run festivals. He was organizing a 'Versathon' in Shropshire in October and wondered if Will might be free.

'I'll get him to ring you,' she said, scribbling the details on a pad. Will was more in demand these days and although she was pleased for him (and grateful for the fees), there was still a niggling resentment. It was as if she had returned to the era when Gerry was an actor and she the supportive wife, looking after the children and the house, keeping his meals warm when he was late home. Will and Gerry were the 'stars' – the talented, temperamental ones who must be cosseted and cared for. It made no difference that neither of them had actually achieved their ambitions – they were still the ones *with* ambitions, and she the nobody. At Will's last reading she had watched people queue to talk to him after the performance, flirtatious females *touching* him, for God's sake, and offering to buy him drinks, while she sat in the corner nursing an empty glass.

> *Men are stupid, men are vain,*
> *Love's disgusting, love's insane,*
> *Love's a dirty business . . .*

She marched over to the cassette player and wrenched the tape out with a clatter. She would take it back to the library first thing in the morning. Those stupid songs were only making her bitter. Love *wasn't* a dirty business, but a matter of mutual support. As soon as Will was less pressured, she knew he would help her in his turn. He seemed genuinely sorry at being unable to do his share, but, as he pointed out, he had waited years for this break and it would be folly to risk his whole future for the sake of a few more weeks. She agreed – the height of folly. She must simply be patient a while longer and try to do things with good grace. For instance, she could surprise him this evening with a nice chocolatey pudding, or make a . . .

'Catherine!'

She rushed to meet him, relieved to see him in one piece and in fact looking remarkably cheerful. 'Will, at last! I was beginning to get worried. I mean, you said you'd phone . . .'

'I *did* phone, but there was no reply. And then I got hopelessly lost in the wilds of Norfolk. I wasn't concentrating and must have taken the wrong turning.'

'Well, thank goodness you're all right.'

'I'm more than all right.' He swept into the room, tossing his jacket on to a chair. 'I'm over the moon! They're definitely going ahead, darling. *And* with a bigger collection than the one they originally planned.'

'Oh, Will, congratulations!'

'No, wait, it's even better. My book won't come out till the autumn of next year, but they're also going to include me in an anthology – well, just a mini one. You see, what they do each year is publish a sort of taster for the new poets they're promoting – usually just three or four. That comes out in the spring and of course it'll help sell my main collection. Or at least arouse some interest.'

'Gosh, darling, that's fantastic! If only we had some champagne.'

'Hm, I'm afraid we can't run to champagne. I *shall* be getting two payments instead of just the one, but it's still not exactly a fortune.'

'Well let's drink you a toast in beer. I can probably rustle up a couple of cans.'

He took her in his arms and kissed her on the lips. 'Catherine, you're the one who deserves a toast. You've been wonderful these last few weeks. I couldn't have done any of it without you. Quite apart from the fact you inspired the poems. They loved the zoo ones, by the way, *and* the courting crocodiles . . . Oh, I didn't tell you, I met the publicity girl – well actually she's more of a general factotum. She's only about twenty-five, but she's really on the ball. And gorgeous into the bargain. Anyway, she's got some great ideas about promoting my collection.'

Catherine hunted in the cupboard for the beer, wishing there were slightly fewer gorgeous young girls on the poetry circuit. She opened the cans and held hers aloft. 'To "Burnt Crocodiles",' she said with a smile. 'Did they like the title?'

'Loved it. In fact, I could do no wrong today. Leonard even bought me a slap-up lunch.'

'Oh good. I wasn't sure how hungry you'd be. I'm making spaghetti bolognese, but I haven't got very far with it, so if you'd prefer a sandwich . . .'

'No, spaghetti would be great. With lashings of lovely garlic.'

'Okay.'

'Oh, and Catherine darling, I haven't thanked you for looking after Sam. I rang him at Hampstead on the way back and . . .'

'Honestly, Will, couldn't you have rung *me*, at the same time?'

'I did try, my love, but you were engaged. And I didn't want to hang around and make myself even later. Anyway, Sam seemed on top form. He said you'd cooked him millions of chips and bought him a cat and . . .'

'A *toy* cat.'

'And you'd been on a bus to see Alexander someone.'

'Alexandra Park.'

'Oh, that was it. And he won a prize.'

'Only a measly sherbet dab.'

'He was thrilled with it. You know, you're a brilliant mother, Catherine. Far better than Vanessa.'

'Ssh, Will, don't say that.'

'It's true. You're good at everything – cooking, sewing, running stalls, inspiring poems, entertaining my rotten friends, making garlic sauces . . .'

She grinned. 'Okay, I can take a hint.' She broke off three cloves of garlic and began removing their papery skin. Will made it all worth while. Whatever his failings, he was always more than generous with his praises. And once he'd finished his work and they were undressed for bed, he would lavish his undivided attention on every curve and hollow of her body. That made up for everything; made her feel cherished and special.

She interrupted her garlic-chopping to squeeze his hand affectionately. 'By the way,' she said, 'I've put your letters on the side there. They looked a rather dreary lot. *I* had one from Nicky.'

'How is she?'

'Great. Working every hour God sends and loving it, apparently.'

Will ripped open the first envelope and made a face. 'Phone bill,' he muttered. 'Bloody hell! – it's enormous.' He waved the second letter in the air. 'Would I like to buy a case of château-bottled claret at only ninety-nine pounds? Well, I'd *like* to but . . .' He threw it in the bin. 'Now, what's this? Oh, the invite to Malcolm's launch, lucky dog. Faber are doing him proud – party at the Café Royal.' He opened the last envelope and pulled out a sheet of paper. Something else fell out – a smaller, folded slip of paper which fluttered to the ground. He ignored it while he read the letter. 'Oh, my *God*!' he exclaimed.

Catherine looked up from the chopping board. 'What is it?'

He was staring at the letter and appeared not to have heard.

'What *is* it, Will?' she repeated.

He picked up the piece of paper from the floor and studied it without a word.

She prised the letter from his hand and scanned the half-dozen lines. 'Oh *Will*,' she said, 'I can't believe it.'

Still silent, he handed her the piece of paper. It was a cheque – a cheque made out to Mr William Carter. For the sum of seven thousand pounds.

She looked incredulously at the row of noughts, then at Will's dazed face, then back again at the cheque. 'Will, this is wonderful . . . amazing! I'd forgotten you'd even applied for it. And you said you hadn't a hope in hell, remember?'

'Well, that shows what a modest chap I am.' He began to laugh, kissed her, hugged her, whirled her round, still laughing. 'Seven grand!' he yelled. 'I still can't take it in. When you think how many other people must have put in for that grant – why me, for heaven's sake?'

'Because you're a brilliant writer, darling. And Leonard Upjohn obviously thinks so too.'

'Oh, Catherine, our luck really *has* changed. I thought today was pretty good already, but now this . . .' He covered her in kisses, then kissed the cheque as well. 'We can trade the car in. We can get a better flat. We can even pay the phone bill.' He waved it at her triumphantly. 'And we can afford some time off from the market to look for other jobs. I'll be less busy anyway – Leonard only wants a couple more poems, and the way I feel at the moment they'll probably write themselves!'

All at once he shoved the letters on the bureau and gripped her hand tightly, painfully almost. 'Catherine – my darling, precious Catherine, will you marry me?'

She stared at him, astounded. She knew he was wary of commitment, terrified of marriage.

'I couldn't ask you before. My life was such a shambles. But this seems a sort of . . . sign that today's a new beginning. I love you darling, and I want you to be part of it.' He gazed at her intently, his body rigid with tension, his fingers interlocked with hers. It suddenly occurred to her that her hand must smell of garlic: an acrid, inappropriate smell.

'For God's sake, Catherine, *say* something. Tell me – will you marry me?'

It was impossible to speak. Proposals of marriage happened in romantic novels to dewy-eyed young girls. She was overwhelmed. Dumbfounded. To be wanted with such passion . . .

She opened her mouth to reply, but someone else's words jangled in her head.

> *Ordinary mothers, like ordinary wives,*
> *Fry the eggs and dry the sheets and . . .*

She tried to ignore the insidious words, but they continued to creep in:

> *Every day a little sting*
> *In the heart and in the head . . .*

But what relevance had the song for *her*? The woman who'd sung it in the musical had been shackled to a pompous, vain philanderer, whereas Will was sensitive and talented and faithful. Today *could* be a new start. They had the money to move and a chance to get off the treadmill, if only for long enough to rethink where and how to live. Marriage to a poet would actually be exciting; to be part of his success and perhaps a permanent inspiration to him. And she would have a husband who adored her.

Impulsively she pulled on an old sweater, grabbed her purse and rushed to the door. 'I'm going to buy some champagne,' she called as she clattered down the stairs. 'To celebrate!'

34

'Oh Will, don't stop, don't *stop*!'

The climax was like a jacuzzi deep inside her: bubbling, rippling, churning. And – God! – she was coming again, he still thrusting into her, their tiger noises roaring through the room.

'Oh Will! Oh yes! I love you.' She collapsed back breathless on the bed. 'That was the best ever. *Ever,*' she repeated. Then, suddenly, great choking sobs shuddered through her body and she turned to face the wall.

He lay in silence beside her. There was nothing more to say. It had all been said when she returned – without the champagne.

He passed her his handkerchief, already wet. His hopeless weeping had been far worse than the storm of protest, the impassioned arguments. And the silence now was unbearable; his mood of hurt and rejection like a dark pall on the room.

Slowly she sat up, appalled by his expression, its utter desolation. 'I . . . I'm sorry, Will. I feel terrible. But it's not really to do with *you*. It's *me*. I need more . . .'

'It's okay. I'm not a fool.' He suddenly got up and strode across the room.

Oh God, she thought, he's walking out. It's past midnight. What if he does something stupid? 'Will, let me try and explain. I want you to understand.'

'I *do* understand.' He trailed back to the bed, head bowed. 'And it's because I do that I want you to have this.' He pushed something into her hand.

She looked at the cheque, bewildered. 'Will, what are you talking about?'

'It's yours. Take it.'

She laughed, a nervous laugh. He must be out of his mind. 'Will, that was given to you so you can continue your work as a poet.'

He shrugged. 'I can continue it anyway. And you need a grant as well.'

'But I'm not a poet,' she said with a frown. He was behaving very strangely.

'You're a work in progress, Catherine. And you have to find out where you're going and assume some sort of final shape. This could help, maybe.' He thrust the cheque back into her hand. 'I've only realized recently, from various things you've said, that I've been spoiled, compared with you. *I* took foreign holidays for granted. I mean, even as a child I thought it perfectly normal for my parents to take me abroad at least once a year. By the time I was a teenager I'd been to all the major cities – Paris, Venice, Munich, Rome, you name it. But you've never had a chance to see those places. I hope it doesn't sound patronizing – or horribly pretentious – but I want to sort of . . . *give* them to you. Or at least the air fare to a few of them.'

'Oh, Will, it doesn't sound pretentious. I love you for the thought, but I wouldn't dream of taking your money.'

'Listen . . .' Tears slid down his cheeks again. Angrily he brushed them away. 'I'm losing you and I can't bear it. My childish side wants to scream and shout and *make* you stay. But my adult side wants you to see the things which are a sort of poetry in themselves. The funny little gardens on top of some of the old walls in Venice, with plants cascading down to the canals. The fabulous stained glass at Chartres. The flea-ridden cats in the Roman Forum sunning themselves on bits of ancient temple. All those things are part of me. And thousands more. You deserve to have your *own* memories, to nourish you when you're home again and maybe feeling low.'

Silently she put her arms round him. So often she had complained about his almost reckless extravagance, but this was its up-side – a wonderfully reckless generosity. She had thought him self-absorbed and obsessed with his work, yet here he was, offering her another sort of poetry. Taking his money was out of the question, but she was deeply touched by the fact he cared so much about her life – even her life without him. 'Will, thank you for even suggesting it, but I couldn't possibly accept. It would be like stealing from the Stanford Birt Foundation. I'd be paralysed with guilt.'

'But I want you to have it, Catherine. Poems have to be finished, and you're an important work – an epic.' He dragged himself to his feet and stood with his back to her, fists clenched. 'Oh God, I feel like shit. I can't stand the thought that you won't be here any more.'

'Nor can I.'

He swung round, his face imploring. 'Will you change your mind?'

She hesitated. True love was rare and precious. Why refuse it and face life on her own? More than that – Will was irreplaceable: a brilliant poet, a skilful lover. She must be crazy to turn him down. They *could* make a life together, even a happy life. But it would be on his terms – she knew that. Marriage to an actor or writer meant a supportive role for the wife; the 'art' invariably came first. Anyway, it wasn't a matter of weighing pros and cons – that would be insulting to Will. It was something more fundamental. She had to listen to her own inner voice; that voice she had so often ignored in the past, heeding only what *other* people wanted.

Will was still gazing at her, his expression growing more desolate in the long uneasy silence. 'Well?' he prompted softly.

She shook her head, hearing the insistent words of the song.

> *Later, when is later?*
> *How can I wait around for later?*

'Will, I'm sorry, but I can't.'

He let out a sound, part groan, part sigh. 'Okay,' he said. 'I won't ask again. And as for the money, let's compromise – half each.'

'Will, *no.* You need it far more than me. I can get an office job.'

'Absolutely not. You must go off and see the world.'

'Well, look, give me just a tiny bit and I'll go to Paris on Eurostar. That would be wonderful: Notre Dame, the Seine – all the things I've read about.'

'Well, Paris'll do for a start, but you've got to go further afield. Hire your camel and cross the Gobi Desert.'

She forced a smile. 'Are you trying to get rid of me, packing me off to the ends of the earth?'

He kissed her fiercely on the lips. 'God forbid. I'd come with you if it weren't for Sam. Actually, it did occur to me that we could have gone to live abroad instead of Carlisle. But it wouldn't have been fair on him.'

Catherine said nothing. She too had thought about Sam as she stood in Oddbins looking blankly at the bottles of champagne. Having grown so close to the boy, she felt terrible about hurting him by simply disappearing from his life. Yet the duties of a step-mother weighed heavy, and not just duties but anxieties. If she accepted Will's proposal, it would mean taking on a big responsibility. She had seen enough of Sam to know he needed tremendous reserves of love and patience.

She turned her attention back to Will. 'You must keep the money, darling. Apart from anything else, think of how it'll help with Sam.'

'I'm sorry, I've made up my mind. We'll split it fifty-fifty and that's the end of the matter. Christ Almighty!' he burst out, 'there wouldn't *be* a grant without you. *Or* a second collection. Listen, Catherine, just occasionally someone comes along who has that gift – and God! it's rare – of inspiring poems out of . . . out of . . .' He shook his head, impatient at not finding the words. 'What you've got to understand is that I've never worked as well as this before. Or as fast. It's as if you've got a direct line to my unconscious, or my creativity, or whatever you like to call it. You *produced* the poems, so it's right that you should share in the reward. And anyway, I'm not giving it to you for nothing. I want you to continue to be my muse, long-distance, even if you won't marry me. I can't pretend to be happy about it . . .' His voice became unsteady again. 'But I'll still write everything *for* you and because of you, even if they're poems of despair.'

'Oh Will, you're making me cry again.'

'We've got to cry. This is awful for us both. But whatever happens I don't want it to be like the break-up with Vanessa, full of spite and anger.'

'No,' she said, running her hand tenderly down his cheek. 'I love you, Will, and I always shall. And I'm honoured to be your muse.'

'So you'll accept your half of the money?'

'Will, I can't. I really can't. Besides, what would people say?'

'What do you mean, "people"? No one else need know.'

'But my family . . . Andrew knows how tight things are.'

'Well, tell them you won the lottery. Yes, that's it. *I* got a grant – amount unspecified – and *you* won three and a half grand this Saturday. It's no great shakes, you know. Last week's prize was seven million, for heaven's sake.'

'Oh, Will, I don't know what to say.'

'Don't say anything. Otherwise I'll bawl my bloody head off.' He slumped back on the bed, looking utterly wretched. 'Oh, Catherine, I'd rather have you than the biggest lottery prize in the whole world.'

She lay beside him, smoothing his defiant shock of hair. 'Will . . .'

'Mm?'

'I wish I could make things better.'

'You can. You *can*. All you have to say is . . .'

She kissed his lips to silence him. He returned the kiss half-heartedly.

'Give me a real kiss, Will. To seal our pact.'

'What pact?'

She heard the faintest note of hope in his voice and loathed herself for crushing it. 'That I'll be your muse – long-distance.'

He kissed her eyelids, so gently she could barely feel his mouth.

'And that we'll always love each other,' she continued in a whisper, 'wherever we land up.'

This time he used his tongue to force her lips apart, deepening the kiss still further, as if trying to devour her. In spite of her misery and exhaustion, she could feel herself responding. She was opening to him, everywhere, yet crying at the same time, tears streaming down her cheeks, and his.

Grief seemed simply a part of it – part of their frenzied, final love-making, and as they came, together, he let out a howl of pure despair.

V

35

Catherine ploughed up the five flights of stairs and arrived breathless at the top. Jubilee Court didn't have a lift, but at the rent she was paying she could hardly complain. Anyway, she loved the flat – her own place at last, until Brad's friend came back in April. After that, who could say?

She let herself in, to be greeted by the rock stars on the walls – a collage of sax-players, singers, drummers and guitarists in various dramatic poses, covering practically every inch of wall space. At first she'd been put off by them, but now she found their presence reassuring, almost a substitute family.

She put the shopping on the table and opened all the windows. It was a sultry day with no breath of air, the trees parched and dusty in the drought. She looked across the rooftops shimmering in the heat haze. It was like her old room at Gosforth Road – that sense of being exhilaratingly high up, with London laid out below. She was getting to know the area – shops, streets, restaurants, bus routes – and Brad had introduced her to some of the locals. Yesterday she had got talking to Chiaka, a six-foot-six Nigerian who lived on the third floor. That too had been reassuring. If ever she needed help, Chiaka looked a match for any troublemaker.

The answerphone was flashing – three messages in all: Rosie saying she was on her way and should arrive soon after twelve; Maeve phoning from the north to say thanks for the long letter and when the hell were they going to meet; and her new friend Gill suggesting a meal out together on Saturday evening. It still took some getting used to, all the calls being for her. After thirty-odd years of taking messages for other people – Gerry chiefly, but then Andrew, Nicky, Darren, Will – she now had a phone-number all to herself. And investing in an answerphone was a bonus – in fact she wasn't sure how she had ever managed without one.

Resetting it, she thought back to the day she'd moved in: the pain of leaving Will, the wrench of disentangling their possessions, and that first solitary night, lying sleepless in the dark and starting at every noise. It reminded her of the desolate time following Gerry's death. Never, apart from then, had she lived on her own without someone else to fill the empty silence, and at first she wondered how she'd cope. Yet here she was, only three weeks later, positively exulting in her independence.

She took the shopping into the kitchen, which was little bigger than a galley, but well-equipped and airy, with a window facing south. She surveyed the room with approval: no one else's clutter around; no burnt saucepans in the sink; no jars with the lids left off. She loved the sense of being in charge; putting her stamp on everything. And there was a marvellous freedom in no longer being answerable to anyone – no one else's schedules to have to consider; no one else's extravagance (or debts) to imperil the state of her finances.

And no need to cook, she thought as she opened the various packets and cartons and put them in the fridge. Old habits died hard, though, and it did seem rather remiss to ask Rosie for Sunday lunch then give her shop-bought snacks. Obviously she needed more practice in simple indolence, so, having transferred the pre-washed salads to a bowl, she poured herself a glass of Coke and took it into the other room, where she stretched out on the sofa. She sat in delicious idleness, reflecting on her achievement. It might not seem that big a deal – thousands of people lived on their own without congratulating themselves – but for her it was a milestone. After a lifetime of dependence, she was proving once and for all that she could be self-sufficient and actually enjoy it.

The buzzer intruded on her thoughts. Rosie – early, but who cared? They had nothing to do all day but laze around.

She ran downstairs to let her in. 'Hi, Rosie. Good to see you. Where's Stephen?'

'I left him with Mum. It's so seldom I take a day off, I wanted to make the most of it. Anyway, we can't talk with him around.'

'Oh dear. I've got in a stock of ice cream for him.'

'Don't worry, I'll eat it. I love ice cream, especially on a day like this. I've brought some wine. It should be fairly cold still.'

'Rosie, I told you not to bring anything!'

'And a house-warming present. Here.' She handed Catherine a bottle and a large knobbly gift-wrapped package.

'Gosh, thanks. I'll open it upstairs. I hope you're fit, by the way. It's five flights up. But worth it when you get there.'

'Yeah, the view's fantastic,' Rosie agreed, as they stood together at the window. She turned back to the sitting-room. 'The decor's a bit weird, though.'

'Mm. I gather Dinger's a bit weird himself.'

'*What*'s his name?'

'Dinger. He's gone to Thailand to buy cheap silver jewellery, and then he's travelling all round India. You're not really meant to sub-let, but Brad says he's fixed it, whatever that's supposed to mean. The rent's incredibly cheap, so I'm not enquiring too closely. A lot of the properties round here are owned by some housing trust. That's one of the advantages of living in Hackney – perks for us proles. It makes Andrew apoplectic. He says the council's worse than loony left, it's out and out Trotskyist.'

Rosie laughed. 'Has he been here yet?' she asked, as she wandered around on a mini tour of inspection, peering at the books on the shelves, picking up ornaments and photographs.

'No. And I can't say I'm looking forward to it. He thought Camden Town was bad enough, but this is beyond the pale. He's quite convinced I'm in danger of my life every time I put my nose outside the door.' She smiled in defiant satisfaction at having moved to an area so at variance with Stoneleigh. Although, to be fair, it was nothing like the hell-hole Andrew assumed. There was Victoria Park, for instance – a green oasis, with venerable old plane trees and a boating lake complete with ducks and swans – and the canal, and Hackney Marshes. And behind the soulless estates and ugly high-rise flats were quaint narrow streets with an almost villagey feel to them. In fact, despite its dubious reputation, the whole district appeared to be thriving. New businesses were springing up, even in the shabbier parts, and there were dozens of rejuvenated buildings – galleries and workshop units and artists' studios and the like. There seemed to be hoardings all over the place announcing RENOVATION and REDEVELOPMENT, so her own personal redevelopment fitted in well.

'Come and see the bedroom,' she said, opening the door

gingerly (one of its hinges was coming loose). 'There's only room for the bed, but it's quite something.'

'Wow!' Rosie gazed at the old-fashioned monster with its massive headboard and gargantuan slab of mattress. 'You'd get three or four in there, I'd say.' She looked at Catherine anxiously. 'You must miss Will.'

'I do.' For all her triumph in managing to cope on her own, there were still days when she couldn't think of Will without a feeling of utter wretchedness. And the nights were worse. Although the bed was exceptionally wide – especially compared with Will's tiny single one – she hadn't yet broken the habit of sleeping on the very edge and would wake up in the morning practically falling over the side.

She was aware of the sudden silence. 'We're trying not to see each other,' she said despondently. 'It makes things a bit less painful.'

'Well, you know my views on men.'

'I certainly do!' Catherine led the way back into the sitting-room. 'But what about Stephen? *He*'s a male, in case you hadn't noticed. And he won't stay ten for ever.'

'Oh, Steve's all right. I'm relying on him to keep me in my old age, then I'll forgive him anything. Hey, d'you mind if I smoke? I'm gasping.'

''Course not. Here's an ashtray. And I want to see what's in here.' She unwrapped Rosie's present: a yellow wooden vase with six purple wooden tulips sprouting from the top. 'Oh, Rosie, it's gorgeous. Flowers that won't die – how clever! Thank you, you're an angel.' She put it on the mantelpiece and gave Rosie a hug. Then she picked up the bottle of wine. 'Chardonnay – perfect. Let's get it opened right away. There's a corkscrew in the kitchen.'

Rosie followed, goggling at the dandelion-yellow walls. 'I say! Terrific colour scheme. You practically need sunglasses! Bit of a squash, though, isn't it? There's barely room to swing a cat in here.'

'Talking of cats, I'm thinking of getting one.'

'Won't it be rather dodgy, five floors up?'

'Mm, that's the problem. It would mean litter trays, I suppose. D'you know, there's a woman down the road who takes her cat for walks on a lead, just like a dog. You get all sorts of weird and wonderful people here.' Having poured two generous glasses of wine, she steered Rosie back to the other room. 'Make yourself comfortable,' she said, patting the sofa.

'It's okay, thanks, I'll sit here.' Rosie settled herself on one of the squidgy scarlet floor-cushions. 'Well,' she raised her glass, 'here's to your new life, complete with perambulating cat.'

'Hold on, I haven't got one yet – a new life, I mean. Let's drink to being slobs, instead. It still feels very odd, you know, not being at the market after all those Sundays getting up at the crack of dawn.'

'Well, it's odder for me, I can tell you. I haven't missed a Sunday in two years.'

'I'm honoured, Rosie! I only hope I'm worth it.'

'Definitely. Anyway, I needed a break. The summer's been hell – so hot and . . .'

'You've done pretty well, though, haven't you?'

'Mm, can't complain.' Rosie took a drag of her cigarette. 'And certainly this is the first time I've been able to afford to pay someone else to run the stall. Mind you, I can't help worrying. Sue *is* reliable, but she's never done it on her own before. I suppose I'm just not used to delegating. When I first started, I had to work flat out simply to cover the rent of the stall. And look at me now – employing slave labour so I can swan around all day!' She raised her glass. 'To slobs. Long may it last.'

'Not *too* long,' said Catherine. 'It's funny, I was dying to have more time to myself, but now I'm quite keen to find a job. I'm not sure I'm cut out to be a lady of leisure.'

'Come off it, Plum. Your feet have hardly touched the ground, what with moving flats and everything. Anyway, what sort of job do you want?'

'I wish I knew. Colin suggested working as a courier. This friend of his has been taking rich Americans round the markets and antique shops, and she says it's money for jam. But they expect you to look smart. Purple hair's definitely not on. I suppose I could dye it back to mouse and buy a suit with shoulder-pads . . .'

Rosie surveyed her critically. 'I can't see it, somehow.'

'Nor can I. But I want to keep my options open. In fact, you know the Circus Space?'

Rosie shook her head.

'It's in Coronet Street. Half a mile down the road. Well, there's a job going there, believe it or not.'

'Heavens! A lion-tamer or something?'

Catherine laughed. 'No, admin – receptionist cum secretary, but it would be rather intriguing, don't you think? People come from all over the world, apparently, to train as trapeze artists and clowns and what-have-you. I spent a couple of hours there and the place really gives you a buzz. They even do evening classes in knife-throwing – just the thing for bored housewives!'

'Perhaps I should enrol,' grinned Rosie.

'Me too. I wonder if they let you work there *and* attend the classes?' Catherine kicked off her sandals and wriggled her bare toes. 'Anyway, there are more conventional jobs around as well. I mean, Arthur told me the other day he could do with some help in the antique shop and asked if I was interested. I'd quite like it, actually, especially the chance of travelling abroad. He goes to France every month or so, to buy stuff from the big antiques fairs, and he said I could go with him sometimes.'

'I thought you were going to France anyway. Paris, wasn't it?'

'Yes.' Catherine hesitated. She had mentioned Paris, but not Venice or Rome. Rosie would wonder why she was suddenly so flush. 'I didn't tell you, Rosie, but Will gave me some . . . some money.'

'Will? I thought he was skint. And why on earth should he give you money when you've chucked him?'

Again she paused. It did seem extraordinary and she hadn't told a soul about it yet. But Rosie had always been open with her, and girlfriends were important, particularly now. She explained about the grant, wishing it wasn't still so difficult to talk about Will dispassionately.

'Bloody hell!' said Rosie. 'That's decent of him.'

'Especially for a man, I suppose you mean!'

'Yeah, too right. Both Jim and Pete pissed off without leaving me a penny, and we were married, for God's sake.'

'Will's not like that. He's amazingly generous. D'you know, the day after he got the cheque, he gave twenty pounds to some home-less kid begging in the street.' She recalled the scene: Will flinging smoked salmon and asparagus into the supermarket trolley as if there were no tomorrow; then sweeping out of the shop and showering largesse on every down-and-out they passed. 'Of course, knowing Will, he'll go through the money in a matter of months and then he'll be broke again. Apparently he was like that as a child. His brother used to save his pocket money in a piggy-bank, but Will always spent his as soon as he was given it.'

'Plum?'

'Yes?'

'You don't regret breaking up with him, do you?'

Catherine took her time answering. Some things she did regret. 'The first week was utter hell,' she confessed. 'I felt sort of . . . raw, and kept wondering if I'd made a terrible mistake. But it's gradually getting better, and I'm pretty certain now that marriage wouldn't have worked. I've come to see that I repeat the same pattern, maybe unconsciously. I suppose basically I need to be needed. It makes me feel important if I'm the strong supportive one, like I was with Gerry, or even with my father, as a child. I had to help him survive without my mother.' She remembered how vital it had seemed to be dutiful and uncomplaining, otherwise he too might disappear. 'Well, I *say* I was the strong one, but actually it wasn't strength at all. It was more a form of weakness, though I've only just realized that. I was so dependent, first on my father, then on Gerry, that I was willing to be whatever they wanted, simply to maintain the status quo. Was it like that for you?'

Rosie flicked the ash from her cigarette. 'Well, certainly not while I was married – either time. And even when my mother died, Dad coped remarkably well. He remarried within a year, *and* he had another woman on the side.'

'But that must have been ghastly, especially as you were so young.'

Rosie shrugged. 'At least he didn't need *me* to buck him up. But go on about Will.'

'Well, I don't know what to say. I mean, I'm tremendously glad I met him and in many ways it was a wonderful relationship. But there were quite a lot of problems and I was also beginning to worry about Sam. I felt I should either become a fixture in his life – someone he could depend on – or I should get the hell out before he came to regard me as a substitute mother. He's been hurt enough as it is.' She frowned into her glass. 'I still worry about him, to tell the truth. Will complains that he doesn't see enough of him, but when he *is* around he gets impatient and resents the interruption to his work. I know *you* have to cope without any help from Stephen's father, but I think I'd be too selfish for that.'

'Come off it, Plum, Sam's not your child. Other people's kids can be hell.'

'Actually I'm very fond of him. I just hope to God I haven't hurt him as much as I've hurt Will.'

'I'm sure he'll survive. He's got a mother of his own, for heaven's sake.'

Catherine topped up the wine. 'I know, but Vanessa seems terribly wrapped up in her career, so I suppose I could have been a help – for both of them, I mean. But I have this gut feeling that before I shack up with any man or take on any child, I need to convince myself that I can be someone in my own right. It's not that easy, alas. But I'm determined to be independent for a while. Independent of everyone – men, children, in-laws . . .'

'Good for you. I'll drink to that. Well, no, actually . . .' Rosie put her glass on the side. 'Before I drink any more, I'd better have a pee.'

'The bathroom's just along here.' Catherine got up to show her. 'No, not that one.'

Rosie had opened the wrong door and was peering into the tiny second bedroom, where a suitcase lay open on the bed. 'Oh, you've started packing already. When are you off?'

'Friday. I can't wait.'

'So I see. How frighteningly efficient! *I* never pack till the last minute.'

'Yes, but you're a seasoned traveller – I'm a novice. You probably won't believe this, Rosie, but I've never even owned a passport before. I'm usually too embarrassed to admit it, but' – her voice tailed off apologetically – 'it just never sort of . . . happened.'

'Don't worry, you'll enjoy it all the more.'

She nodded. 'Mm, I'm sure that's true. I was so thrilled to get my passport, I practically had it framed and hung it on the wall! And I'm getting a real kick out of all the preparations. I've bought loads of things for the trip – walking shoes, suntan lotion, a rather fetching straw hat. I even had to buy the case.' She gazed fondly at the large conker-coloured suitcase, with its luggage labels and security strap. Beside it sat a matching flight-bag, also partly packed, with paperbacks, the tickets, and of course her brand new passport.

'Well, you're certainly going to be busy.' Rosie was flicking through the guidebooks on the bed. She picked up one on Italy. 'Why this?'

'I . . . haven't told you yet, but I'm going to Venice as well. And Rome.'

'You're a dark horse!' Rosie tossed her the book and squeezed past out of the room. 'Won't be a sec,' she said, opening the adjoining door. 'Then I want to hear all about it.'

'Okay, we'll talk over lunch. Well, lunch sounds a bit too grand – it's only cold, I'm afraid.'

'Cold's fine on a day like today. It's absolutely sweltering out there.'

'It does seem rather a waste of a kitchen, though. I haven't used the oven once yet.'

'Give it time. You will.'

Maybe, thought Catherine, as Rosie disappeared into the bathroom. Or maybe not. It was up to her entirely. She could give her friends picnic food, or fish and chips from the shop. And she was no longer tied to mealtimes. She could raid the fridge when she felt like it or take a bowl of cereal to bed. It was like being a student – carefree, undomesticated. Living on your own involved not only far less cooking, but less washing, ironing, cleaning. As Rosie often said, most men needed 'carers'. There was also a certain relief in not being subject to someone else's moods. Even Will's *good* moods had been exhausting sometimes, and he automatically assumed that if he was up, so must she be, and if he was down, she ditto.

She arranged the food on plates, crammed them on a tray and took it into the sitting-room, where she found Rosie by the bookshelf, examining Dinger's fossil collection.

'Sorry.' Rosie put down a murky-coloured stone. 'I should have offered to help.'

'There's no need – it's all bought stuff. Mind you, I could have got you something more exotic. The shops round here sell things like calves' feet and pigs' tails.'

Rosie shuddered. 'Spare me!'

'It's all right, you're quite safe. Even the quiche is vegetarian. And I've brought some iced mineral water, to cool us down a bit. Lord, I do hope it's not as hot as this in gay Paree.'

'I do envy you, you know. I haven't been to Paris in years.'

'Why don't you come with me, then? No, I'm serious. You could meet me there just for two or three days if you can't manage the whole trip.'

'And what do I do with Stephen?'

'Leave him with your mother again. Oh go on, Rosie – you'd be doing me a favour. I'd love to have your company. And you can get to France dirt cheap these days.'

Rosie sipped her wine reflectively. 'I must admit I'm tempted. We could do the tourist bit during the day and spend the evenings in pavement cafés – maybe pick up a couple of Frenchmen.'

'I thought you didn't *like* men!'

'Oh, holiday romances are fine.'

'How many have you had, for heaven's sake?'

'Dozens,' said Rosie airily. 'They're the only sort of relationship I do have. You get the best of the blokes without the disadvantages and it's all over in two weeks.'

Catherine nibbled a piece of quiche. She was still a babe in arms compared with Rosie, or compared with Jo and Nicky, for that matter. 'Well, come to Venice too, Rosie, and you can have a fling with a gondoliero – or several gondolieros, come to that. I've got a whole ten days in Venice.'

'Hm. Lucky for some! Why didn't you tell me before?'

Catherine flushed. 'I don't know. I suppose I felt, well . . . guilty.'

'Hell, you're *allowed* to travel, you know, especially as you've missed out on it in the past. I've been to Venice four times and I don't feel the slightest twinge of guilt. And you'll adore it, Plum, I know you will. The last time I went was in January two years ago and it poured with rain and the pavements were flooded, and there I was clumping around in these huge great borrowed wellies, but it was still quite magical.'

'That's what Will says. In fact he's given me a list of so many things to do and see, I certainly won't have time for any flings myself.'

'Talking of flings, I suppose you know Colin's got his eye on you.'

'You're joking.'

'No, honestly. He asked if I thought he stood any chance.'

'Really? What did you say?'

'I told him to ask you himself.' Rosie paused to crunch a celery stick. 'And then there's Brad.'

'What d'you mean?'

'I'm sure he fancies you.'

'Don't be silly, Rosie. He's years younger than me.'

'Makes no difference. Why do you think he went to so much trouble getting you this place? Because it's only half a mile from *his* – that's why.'

Catherine looked at Rosie dubiously. She still found it hard to believe that other men found her sexually attractive. Yet since the break with Will, Brad had certainly been attentive – not just finding her the flat, but offering to help with the move and anything else she might need.

'Well, don't say I didn't warn you, Plum. Next thing you know he'll probably turn up on the doorstep in the middle of the night, offering to share that big bed of yours!'

'Gosh, I hope not. I *am* fond of him, but not in that way.' She scooped up a few pastry crumbs, trying to work out what she felt for Brad. It was true there was something between them, if not sexual, then intimate. The rave had bonded them, even its down side, when Brad had been so worried about her. And she had to admit that she had offered no resistance when he'd hugged her more closely than usual the other day. But it wasn't only Brad. She was feeling sort of charged in general, and sometimes found herself eyeing total strangers with a mixture of lust and curiosity. Even talking to Chiaka, she had been disturbingly aware of his body, defined by tight blue jeans and a navel-skimming tee-shirt. Such feelings seemed disloyal to Will, yet in a way they were a tribute to him. He had reawakened her from a state of tepid celibacy, leaving her open to more experience. After all, far from Rosie's dozens of affairs, her total for a lifetime amounted to only three (and the disastrous one-night stand with the television agent didn't really count). Just comparing Will and Simon, though, underlined how different sex could be with different people; if you weren't lucky enough to meet the right partner, you might spend your whole life paddling in the shallows and never risk the challenge of the deep end.

'Funnily enough,' she said, cutting another slice of quiche, 'Brad did make me a proposition, but not quite the sort you had in mind!'

'Really?' Rosie looked intrigued. 'Tell me more.'

'Well, he thinks we ought to go into business together – set up a jewellery workshop or something. Apparently Hackney's on a winner at the moment. The Council's been given masses of lottery money and a big government grant to regenerate the area. So they're falling over themselves offering people special incentives and start-up schemes and what-have-you. And Brad reckons we ought to jump in quick.'

'That's not a bad idea. I wouldn't mind setting up in business myself. I'd love my own toyshop. And actually it wouldn't be half as stressful as running a stall. At least I'd have a roof over my head.'

'The only thing is, you have to live in Hackney.'

'Well, I'll come into partnership with you and Brad. Hey, listen – how about a toyshop on the ground floor, a café above, and a jewellery workshop in the basement? I'll make the toys and you make the nosh.'

Catherine raised her eyes to heaven. 'And just when I've vowed never to cook again!'

'No, seriously, it might work. If they're pumping all that money into the area, the trick is to get in there before everybody else. It's like Camden before the boom. Of course, we'd probably need to put up a bit of capital ourselves . . .'

That wouldn't be a problem, Catherine thought. She *had* some capital for the first time in her life, and Rosie wasn't exactly broke. If the idea of cooking didn't appeal, she could always make children's clothes to sell. Having worked for Greta, she knew plenty of places to go for cheap material. Rosie would make an excellent business partner: reliable, hard-working and one of the few success stories in the market. And what Brad might lack in management or accounting skills, he made up for in enthusiasm and a remarkable ability to sell. In fact, *she* could take over the admin side and turn her years as Gerry's assistant to good use. 'Rosie, you may be on to something,' she said, offering her more quiche. 'When Brad first mentioned the idea, I must confess I rather dismissed it, but it could be a real money-spinner.'

'But what about your circus school? A shop's a bit tame compared with knife-throwers and clowns!'

She laughed. There seemed to be a wealth of options all of a sudden. It had been quite a wrench giving up the market stall, despite dwindling trade and long working hours, and she had feared she might not find another job. (Also, she missed the market 'family', though of course many of the stall-holders were good friends now.) But in just the last fortnight, several opportunities had come up and she was in the enviable position of being able to pick and choose. However, she would only plump for something she felt positive was right. Perhaps she'd revisit the Circus Space, and also have another talk with Arthur about helping in the antique shop. And she would certainly make enquiries about start-up grants in Hackney. Any job she took, though, must leave her space for other projects – evening classes, theatres, more trips abroad. 'Listen, Rosie, I'll phone the Council first thing in the morning and get them to send some bumph. Then we can see exactly what . . .'

She was interrupted by the phone. 'Excuse me,' she murmured, picking up the receiver. 'Oh, hello, darling. How are you?' She turned to Rosie. 'It's Andrew,' she mouthed, making a comic face. Rosie raised her eyebrows in sympathy, while Catherine braced herself for a diatribe on the insalubrious elements in Hackney. It was funny how in their different ways both Kate and Andrew worried about her safety, as if *they* were the anxious parents, she the wayward child.

But Andrew's words hit her like a bombshell.

'*What?*' she said, gripping the edge of the table. 'Oh my God, how awful.' She was no longer aware of Rosie; no longer aware of anything save Andrew's shaky voice. 'Yes, of course I'll come. I'll leave at once. Hold on – try not to panic.'

36

She thrust a five-pound note into the taxi-driver's hand and was almost at the hospital entrance by the time he'd fumbled for the change. The automatic doors slid open with infuriating slowness. She darted through them and up to the reception desk. 'Lonsdale Ward?' she asked.

'Second floor. Turn right out of the lift.'

The lift was crowded with hot and sweaty bodies. Outside it must be almost ninety, though there had been occasional rumbles of thunder, threatening the end of the heat wave. And inside seemed just as oppressive as she ran along the windowless corridor, only slowing as she approached the nurse on duty at the desk. What if Antonia had already lost the baby? How would she face her? What could she say? She took a deep breath before speaking to the nurse.

'I've come to see Mrs Antonia Jones. She was admitted a couple of hours ago, from Casualty.'

The nurse looked at her suspiciously; her glance travelling from the purple hair to the multicoloured dungarees.

'I'm her mother-in-law,' Catherine persisted. 'Could I see her, please?'

The nurse's expression remained chilly. 'I've only just come on, so I'm not sure where they've put her. I'll have to go and find out.'

Catherine stood fidgeting impatiently. She detested hospitals. Some poor wretch behind her was lying on a trolley-bed, seemingly forgotten or abandoned. And a woman sat hunched in a wheelchair whimpering to herself; her left leg was bandaged from knee to ankle, the bare pink toes looking strangely vulnerable. Further down, the door of a ward stood open, revealing rows of beds, rows of ailing patients – perhaps Antonia among them. A siren wailed outside: more horrors, more emergencies.

She watched the nurse chatting to another in the office, as if they were enjoying a good gossip rather than discussing Antonia's whereabouts. 'For God's sake get a move on,' she muttered through clenched teeth. Since Andrew's phone call, everything seemed to have happened in slow motion. Rosie had driven her to Waterloo, but every traffic light was stuck at red. Then she'd had to wait ages for a train, and when at last it lumbered on its way, there were interminable stops between stations, as if the engine was suffering from heat-exhaustion and needed frequent rests.

The nurse took her time returning to the desk, and then paused to check a pile of folders before finally sitting down. 'Yes, that's all right.' She gave Catherine a brief nod. 'Third door on the left. She's in a room on her own.'

Oh God, thought Catherine, that's a bad sign – she *must* have lost the baby. She dithered for a moment, suddenly reluctant to go in. Having cursed the delays, she herself was now moving in slow motion, raising her hand like a dead weight to tap on Antonia's door, only to let it fall again. She glanced at her dungarees, heartlessly bright in these clinical surroundings. She should have changed, but she had rushed straight out without thinking.

She caught the nurse's eye, watching from the desk. If she dallied any longer, she would be regarded with new suspicion. She smoothed her hair, tapped lightly at the door.

'Come in.' Antonia sounded weak. She lay propped against a pile of pillows, the snaking tube of a drip attached to the back of her hand. The hospital gown looked starkly white against her ashen face; her usually neat hair hanging in limp strands around her shoulders. The covers were drawn up to her chest, so it was impossible to tell whether the bulge was still there or not. The room itself was bleak: no pictures on the ice-blue walls; one poky window looking out over the car park.

Catherine went up to the bed and kissed her on the cheek. 'How are you, darling?'

Antonia's only response was a mute shake of her head.

Catherine dared not ask about the baby. 'Where's Andrew?' she asked instead, sitting on the bedside chair.

'He's gone to see if he can find someone who knows what's going on. They haven't told us anything.'

'Oh Antonia, how awful. Is there anything *I* can do?'

'There's nothing anyone can do except hang around. And we've been doing that all day. We waited hours in Casualty and they couldn't have cared less that I was about to lose the baby.'

And *have* you lost it? Catherine longed to ask, but all she did was squeeze Antonia's hand. They sat in silence for a while, Catherine gazing at the drip and its intrusive paraphernalia. Had Antonia lost a lot of blood? Andrew had mentioned pain and bleeding on the phone, but had supplied no further details.

She was relieved to see him a few minutes later, although he too looked pale and dishevelled as he burst angrily into the room.

'It's absolutely disgraceful. There's not a doctor to be seen. Even the one in Casualty could hardly speak any English, and now *he*'s disappeared.'

'Let *me* try,' Catherine offered, getting up. 'And why don't you come with me, Andrew? Two of us might make more impact.' Alone with him, she could find out what had happened. 'Will you be all right, Antonia? We shouldn't be too long.'

Antonia nodded wanly.

'Try and rest, darling.' Andrew laid a protective hand on her shoulder before following Catherine out of the room. 'Actually, I don't know what we can do, Mother. I can't seem to get any sense out of anyone at all. I've never known such inefficiency.'

Catherine returned with him to the desk, but in place of the previous nurse sat a young Asian girl who knew nothing whatsoever about Antonia and was already being besieged by a group of other visitors.

'I *told* you,' Andrew fumed. 'The whole situation's a farce. God, am I going to raise a stink!'

Catherine steered him away from the desk to a quieter part of the corridor. 'Andrew,' she said softly, 'the baby . . . ? Has Antonia . . . ?'

'It's touch and go, as far as I can gather. The doctor thinks she's in danger of miscarrying. At least that's what he seemed to be saying. It would help if they taught these doctors the rudiments of English before they let them loose in Casualty.'

'Five months is late to miscarry. Do they know what brought it on?'

'I doubt if they'd tell us if they did know. The policy here seems to be say nothing and do nothing. But Antonia *has* been over-working, and yesterday we had people to dinner – my boss and his wife and two other colleagues. And you know what a perfectionist she is. She was on her feet all day and I couldn't help because I had a rush job on.'

'What, on a Saturday?'

'Yes. Work's been hectic the last few weeks. In fact, this couldn't have happened at a worse time. Anyway, I said I'd do the clearing up, and made her promise to stay in bed this morning. But then Grandma rang first thing to say she and Grandpa had both gone down with 'flu and were feeling absolutely dreadful. I drove straight over, and, as I should have guessed, Antonia *didn't* stay in bed. She was moving the table back in place when she had this crippling pain and then the bleeding started. I wasn't even there. She didn't want to go to Casualty on her own, so she waited for me to get home. Needless to say, the delay didn't help.'

Catherine stared down at the floor, consumed with guilt. If she had been on hand, all this might never have happened. It was like a judgement on her for being selfish and undutiful; neglecting not only Andrew and Antonia but Jack and Maureen too. She remembered her own two miscarriages all those years ago. On both occasions, Maureen had dropped everything to take charge while she recovered, and had never uttered a word of complaint about having to travel up north and put her own life on hold. Jack and Maureen had always been a tower of strength, helping out with loans or looking after the children. And now she had turned her back on them, ignoring the fact that they were getting older and frailer and might need her in their turn.

Andrew ran a distracted finger round the collar of his shirt. 'I'm worried about Grandpa as well. I had to dash off and leave him and his temperature's quite high.'

'I'll go over there straight away,' said Catherine, 'while you stay with Antonia. But do phone me, won't you, the minute you have any news.'

'Of course.' He gave a half-hearted smile. 'There is one bit of news, Mother, though I'm not sure if it makes things worse or better. The doctor in Casualty gave Antonia a scan and though he didn't have the courtesy to let us know the result, the nurse up here told us it's . . . it's a boy.'

'A boy! Oh, darling . . .'

'Gerry,' Andrew murmured. 'If he lives.'

She hugged him, close to tears. Suddenly Antonia's bulge was a person, an individual with a name. No one could ever replace *her* Gerry, but this baby would have his genes, even his looks, perhaps. Yet for all her joy in his existence and her determination that he survive, other, more ignoble thoughts were stampeding through her mind. How could she go on holiday when she was needed here – for months, maybe, if the pregnancy continued to give cause for concern? Rome was flattened to a ruin; Paris dwindling to a mirage; Venice submerged beneath its own canals. Of course that was being ridiculously melodramatic. A holiday was nothing compared with a child's life.

Andrew had pulled away, patently embarrassed at being hugged by his mother in a public corridor.

'Look, before I go,' she told him, 'I'll just say goodbye to Antonia.'

She returned to the room and stood shamefaced by the bed, Antonia's desolate expression increasing her guilt. She had talked so loftily to Kate about this baby being a symbol of life, a way of coping with Gerry's death, yet she hadn't lifted a finger to help Antonia. Easy to criticize Will for being self-centred, but wasn't she as bad, thinking she had no one to please but herself? And when – if – the baby was born, she had breezily consigned it to the care of a nanny. The example of Nicky's friend Laura should have been warning enough. Nannies let you down, threatened to leave if you were kept late at the office. Did she really want Antonia to become another Laura – an emotional wreck, too tired to enjoy her life or child or marriage?

She took Antonia's hand. 'I'm going over to Walton,' she said. 'To be with Jack, while Andrew stays here with you.'

Antonia nodded. 'Fine.'

'And Andrew's promised to phone if . . .'

Again Antonia nodded. She and Andrew were clearly expecting her to go. But she didn't go. She just stood there like a dummy, paralysed by the conflict in her mind. If she put the baby first, it wouldn't be simply a matter of giving up her holiday (plus the hefty deposit she'd paid on it) – the new flat would have to go as well, and the new jobs she might have taken, the new men she might have met. Evening classes, theatres, even the chance of owning a cat, were fading into oblivion. Yet they were mere blips in the grand scheme of things, and only proved how self-indulgent she'd become.

Andrew was looking at her anxiously and she realized that her fists were clenched, as if she were about to do battle with an enemy. No, only with herself, that part of her which still clung so tenaciously to her selfish plans and dreams. It would be intolerable to land back where she had started, to become a drudge again, a stay-at-home, her horizons bounded by a privet hedge.

'Well, goodbye,' she said – second time. She was tempted for an instant to make it a real goodbye; to dash not to Walton but back to the Hackney flat, and barricade the door.

'Mother, are you all right?'

'Yes, of course,' she snapped – a last flicker of rebellion. Then she leaned against the wall and closed her eyes, trying to rid her mind of all the seductive images: the Seine, St Mark's, St Peter's, Chartres. And London too: Jubilee Court, the Circus Space, Brad and Rosie in their newly-opened shop. The suitcase was emptying – out went guidebooks, passport, airline tickets, and in went dowdy clothes, ball and chain.

No, she wasn't bitter. Not really. And she had made her decision at last. Her mind was mercifully blank now, as the last strains of laughter and music from the Parisian pavement cafés subsided into Andrew's nervous cough.

She fixed her eyes on him, somehow managing to keep her voice steady. 'Andrew,' she said, 'I've decided to move back to Stoneleigh – if you'll have me, that is. Then I'll be on hand to help.' She swallowed, forced a smile. 'I want to look after Antonia and . . . and Gerry.'

37

Catherine dawdled along the aisle once more, wondering what to buy. Andrew and Antonia were out for dinner tonight, so there was nothing she actually needed. But supermarkets had become a sort of refuge, a way of killing time. She deliberately went to different ones – Sainsbury's in Cheam on one day, the Sutton Safeway another. And she could while away a good couple of hours in the huge New Malden Tesco with its acres of displays: every conceivable type of food, toiletries and housewares, flowers and stationery. Already she had three birth congratulations cards and an impressive collection of birthday cards for the next five years at least.

She stopped at the fresh meat counter. There was always tomorrow's meal, of course. It would be fun to cook something adventurous or wickedly rich, but Antonia was becoming even more faddy as her pregnancy advanced. Beef was *verboten*, needless to say. Indeed all red meat was suspect; cheese indigestible, sauces too high in cholesterol, puddings brimming with sugar. They didn't actually need her to cook – they could just as easily have existed on cottage cheese and salad. In fact they didn't need her, full stop. There was practically no housework with both of them out all day, and the small general stores in Stoneleigh had a perfectly good delivery service.

She put a free-range chicken in the trolley, then took it out again. How would she fill the yawning void of tomorrow if she did Tuesday's shopping now? Monday was the worst day, with four more days limping in its wake, when all serious worthwhile people were at work. A few of them had stopped off here to stock up on lunch-time sandwiches, or buy fruit and yoghurt to eat later in the office. She herself wasn't usually out so early, but after dropping

Andrew and Antonia at the station she had decided to drive all the way to Dorking, to delay returning to an empty house.

She trudged into the next aisle, passing the baby foods. No need to buy anything *here* yet. The baby wasn't officially due until 5 January – still fourteen weeks to go. Both mother and foetus were doing extremely well. The crisis last month had proved to be a false alarm, blown out of all proportion by a lack of communication. Apparently Antonia had been admitted only as a precaution, but no one had explained that until the following day when she'd been discharged with instructions to take it easy and report any further trouble. There *was* no further trouble, and after a fortnight's convalescence she had returned to the office, leaving the 'nanny' in situ.

Catherine dropped a plastic rattle into the trolley. Perhaps it would fill the echoing silence of Manor Close, which seemed more of a morgue than ever. Unfortunately the Ewell cottage had been snapped up by someone else, and Andrew and Antonia simply assumed she was happy to live with them. After all, she had given up her market job and ended things with Will before Antonia was rushed to hospital, so in their opinion she was clearly at a loose end.

Angrily she abandoned her trolley – rattle, chocolate bar and all – and darted to the exit. She had no one to blame but herself if she spent her days mooning around indulging in self-pity. If she didn't have enough to do until the baby came, then it was time she found herself some useful work – voluntary work, if necessary.

She strode to the car park, relieved to see Antonia's car unscathed. She had a secret fear of one day finding a scratch on its immaculate white paintwork. Her own car she had left with Will – a small return for his generosity. She thought of him often these days, wondering what he was doing and whether he missed his muse. She missed *him*, to tell the truth. And London. These suburban streets seemed so dreary compared with Camden Town or Hackney. If only she hadn't given up her Hackney flat. She had upset Brad in the process and quarrelled with Rosie, who accused her of selling out to suburbia. Yet she also had to contend with Andrew's frequent warnings about the perils of the inner city. She felt she was losing her own judgement, or maybe simply losing heart, on account of all the recent changes and upheavals.

It was only half past nine when she arrived back at Manor Close;

the whole day still stretching ahead. She removed a scrap of paper from the inside of the car. Although Antonia's Renault was far superior to her own elderly Allegro, she hated the dependency – having to keep it so unnaturally clean and tidy; having to ask whenever she wanted to borrow it.

She slammed the front door and picked up the post from the mat – a pile of stuff for Andrew and Antonia, including two Christmas catalogues. Christmas in September was depressing at the best of times, but this year she could hardly bear to think that far ahead. December seemed so distant, yet the mornings were already colder and darker, the evenings drawing in, and the first jars of mincemeat had gone on sale in Sainsbury's. Jack and Maureen would be there on Christmas Day, of course, but now she saw them anyway, several times a week. And Antonia's parents were coming up from Devon, so the tiny house would be bursting at the seams. She tried to imagine Antonia nine months pregnant. The prospect ought to thrill her, but all she could see was three complacent couples round the Christmas table and one rebellious single – a square peg in a round hole.

Sorting the post into the two customary piles – Andrew's and Antonia's – she pounced on a flimsy airmail envelope. A letter for *her*, from Nicky. She brightened instantly and took it into the sitting-room, kicking off her shoes and curling up on the sofa in a way she would never do with Antonia around.

Catherine, how awful! I was horrified to hear your news. Is Antonia okay now? And when are you going back to London?

She raced through the next two paragraphs to get to Nicky's own news: she had met another man, a Canadian called Dominic, who was single and available, not to mention charming and attentive – in fact, similar to Stewart who had originally lured her out there, but with one important difference: she actually fancied him.

She returned the letter to its envelope, stifling a twinge of jealousy. Would *she* ever meet another man? It seemed increasingly unlikely when the only people she talked to these days were checkout girls or the milkman. If only she could ring Nicky and have a proper chat. But apart from the prohibitive cost of the call, Nicky would be busy, like everybody else. Surely she could find something to occupy herself, even if it was only knitting for the baby – blue bootees or a shawl.

'Fuck blue bootees,' she said out loud. She had to talk to *someone*, renew her links with the real world. Rosie should be in – she worked at home on Mondays, making toys for the stall. She dialled the number, but the phone shrilled on, unanswered. Just as well, perhaps. Things were still tense between them; Rosie thought her a fool for caving in to her family.

Next she tried Gill at the office, but was told she was in a meeting. Well, what did she expect? People in the real world had engagements on a Monday morning, commitments all the week.

She replaced the receiver and stood in the hall, wondering who else to phone. Maeve was away in Greece and Brad had gone to Brighton to buy gemstones – and was annoyed with her in any case, like Rosie.

She decided to write a letter instead – an instant reply to Nicky – and then she'd go out and post it. Big deal: a trip to the pillar box, all of two hundred yards.

She helped herself to a piece of Andrew's paper and sat chewing her pen, unable to compose so much as the opening sentence. Nicky was puzzled about her breaking up with Will and assumed she was going back to London, so there was a great deal to explain. She wrote a few rambling sentences, only to cross them out again. She wanted to make her arguments coherent, but they sounded feeble, contradictory. Anyway letters were so long-winded; no substitute for talking face to face.

Abandoning the messy sheet of paper, she drifted upstairs to the baby's room and stood gazing at the cot, which her efficient daughter-in-law had bought already. It was wicked to feel resentful about the baby, instead of giving thanks each day that it was so exuberantly alive, kicking in the womb, its heartbeat loud and clear according to the midwife. She touched the tinkling mobile suspended from the ceiling. It had arrived yesterday from Kate – the work of an Indian woman at the centre: crudely coloured, roughly made, and out of keeping really with the rest of the cutesy room.

On impulse she ran downstairs again. *Kate* might be in if she phoned – it was about half past two in Delhi.

After the usual delays, an Indian woman answered and offered to take a message.

'Thanks,' said Catherine. 'Would you please ask her to phone her mother at Stoneleigh? It's important,' she added, hardly knowing why. 'Tell her it doesn't matter how late she rings – any time at all, so long as she reaches me.'

Why was she making it sound so urgent? Kate would probably think that Antonia *had* lost the baby this time. But the woman had rung off already.

With a sudden decisive movement, Catherine seized the phone book and started riffling through its pages in search of a local charity. She would say she had only three months free, but hoped that was better than nothing. It would certainly be better for *her* than mooching around making pointless phone calls. Even if she only sorted jumble in a charity shop, at least it would get her out of the house.

'Oxfam here I come,' she said, grinning for the first time in a week.

She giggled to herself. How shocking that the new Lady Bountiful, who had already landed a job typing letters for a human-rights charity, was sprawled on the sofa in a state of inebriation. Well, hardly inebriation – this was only her second sherry – but it did feel reprehensible at four o'clock in the afternoon. Even more depraved: she was deep in a pornographic magazine. She had actually gone out in search of a knitting pattern – yes, blue bootees after all – then wandered into the newsagent's to buy *Woman's Journal*. She couldn't find a copy, and looking for a substitute had discovered *Women Only*. Intrigued, she had taken it home. Having gawped at a succession of full-frontal naked men, she was now reading the 'true' stories – women like her, on their own at home, seduced by Adonis-like window-cleaners or masterful plumbers. Samantha from Southend (conveniently dressed in her négligée) had just opened the door to a double-glazing salesman. Mesmerized, Catherine took another sip of sherry. Double-glazing salesmen didn't call at Manor Close and even if they did, she doubted if they were in the habit of romping on the bed stark naked within minutes of their arrival. Blast! The phone was ringing, competing with Samantha's orgasmic yelps. Reluctantly she went to answer it. The last two calls had been for Antonia – friends who thought she was still off sick.

'Mum?' said a familiar voice.

'Oh, Kate. I . . .'

'Is everything okay? Vatsala said it was urgent, but I've only just got back.'

'Everything's fine,' Catherine murmured, feeling guilty at leaving a panicky message, then forgetting all about it whilst she slavered over naked men.

'Vatsala said you sounded awfully worried.'

'I'm sorry, darling, I *was* a bit het up, but it was just me being stupid.' Poor Kate. She had better things to do with her evenings than reassure a neurotic mother. 'Put it down to PMT. My period's due any moment.'

'So's mine. How odd.'

It seemed a touching bond between them that, although separated by thousands of miles, their menstrual cycles were synchronized. 'Do you still get those awful period pains?'

'Yes, worse luck. Remember when you used to rub my tummy? Oh Mum, I miss you.'

'And I miss you. D'you realize, we haven't seen each other since the funeral. That's over two years.' Suddenly she startled herself by bursting into tears.

'Mum, whatever's wrong? What is it?'

She wiped her eyes. 'I . . . I don't know. I'm sorry. I didn't mean to cry. It's just that I feel so . . . stranded here.'

'I'm not surprised. Frankly, I think Antonia's got a frightful cheek expecting you to drop everything.'

'Oh, she doesn't expect it. I offered.'

'But *why*, when things were working out so well? You don't realize just how far you've come since Dad died. I really admired you, getting that flat and everything, and coping on your own. I mean, never mind Antonia – surely Andrew ought to understand you've got your own life to lead. *I* have to manage without you. Why the hell can't he?'

Catherine fiddled with the phone lead, surprised by her daughter's words. She had often wondered if Kate had used her trip to India as a means of escaping home and parents. Yet now she sounded almost homesick.

'I felt really lousy last week. There's this tummy bug going round the centre, and I was lying on my bed in the heat wishing you weren't so far away.'

'Oh, Kate . . .' Catherine was close to tears again. 'Look, let me ring you back. You can't afford these calls.' She put the phone down and went into the cloakroom, splashing her face with cold water. She hardly knew why she was crying, except all last week, once Antonia had returned to work, she had felt waves of sort of

. . . emptiness, as if she were living in a shadow-world, isolated from other people. She tore off a length of toilet paper and wiped her eyes again. Secretly she was gratified that Kate was on her side. If only they weren't restricted to these brief expensive phone calls.

She returned to the hall and dialled the Delhi number, but for some reason it failed to connect. She was almost grateful for the delay, which gave her longer to pull herself together. It wasn't fair to unload her troubles on Kate, who obviously had enough to contend with: PMT and a tummy bug, on top of her gruelling job.

At last she got through; Kate's voice clear and sharp for once.

'Mum, what happened? You were ages. Is everything all right?'

'Yes.'

'Well, you don't seem very sure. Last time we talked – I mean before all the hoo-ha with Antonia – you were like a different person. Even though you'd just chucked Will, you sounded as if you were coping okay. And you were so chuffed about the flat and . . .'

'Yes, I know, darling, but things . . . changed.'

'Mum, all that happened was that Antonia had a bit of a glitch with her pregnancy and, as far as I can gather, Andrew went doo-lally and hit the panic-button. But if she's back at work now, she must be perfectly all right. So why on earth are you still stuck at Stoneleigh waiting on her hand and foot?'

'I'm *not*, Kate. She . . .'

'And what about that holiday you booked? You were really look-ing forward to it. Well, what's to stop you rebooking it?'

'I . . . I'm not sure. I suppose I'm worried that Antonia might have another glitch, as you put it.'

'Tough luck. She'll have to manage, like everybody else. Shit! You ought to see the women here – washerwomen and sweepers and what-have-you. *They* haven't got doting mothers who'll drop everything and help them out, not even if they're dying. And they have to work right up till the day of the birth. Too bad if they're tired, or ill. There's no such thing as maternity leave.' Kate's voice had risen indignantly, but now she gave a snorting laugh. 'Anyway, why the hell are we banging on about babies? Antonia's isn't due for over three months, and if you hang around till it's born you'll *never* get away. Once she comes to rely on you, I can't see her letting go.'

'Look, I don't like criticizing Antonia. It's not her . . .'

'Mum, listen – you were dying to see Paris and Venice. Well, go and see them, okay? You've never really had a chance before to do the things you wanted.'

She nodded in silent agreement. Will had said the same. And Nicky. Though she was surprised that Kate had noticed. Somehow, as a mother, you expected your children to remain blinkered to your own needs. And that *was* true of Andrew, at least in certain ways. She hadn't dared to tell him about Will's money – he was bound to disapprove of her accepting it. But Kate knew all about it, and understood perfectly well why Will had offered it. How odd, and yet how heartening, that her daughter and her ex-lover should both want her to expand her horizons, to strike out on her own.

'In fact, why stop at France and Italy when you've got the whole world to choose from? Now think about it, Mum – is there anywhere else you'd like to go?'

All at once her eye fell on Nicky's letter, which was sitting on the table beside her own unfinished one. 'Well, yes,' she stammered, 'the Virgin Islands. I did promise Nicky I'd visit her one day – only as a joke, of course, but . . .'

'Well, now you can. Go on, phone her and tell her you're coming.'

'Oh Kate, I couldn't possibly. It's so *far*. The fare would be astronomical.'

'Mum, you've got the money, for heaven's sake. That's why Will gave it to you.'

'But it wouldn't work in any case. She's always terribly busy.'

'She must get *some* time off.'

'Yes, I suppose so. But I feel I should go to a more cultured sort of place, not laze around on a tropical beach drinking rum.'

'Mum, you're impossible! Can't you just enjoy yourself for once? You know, if I was there now, I'd jolly well march you to the nearest travel agent and stand over you while you paid the deposit.'

'Oh darling, I wish you *were* here.'

'Well, promise me one thing anyway – that you'll go out today and book a ticket to somewhere. Then phone me back and tell me what you've decided.'

'Kate, it's nearly five. They'll all be shut. I'll go later, when . . .' She broke off, no longer hearing her daughter's voice, but the words from *A Little Night Music* – words she'd all but forgotten in the last three joyless weeks.

429

Later
When is 'later'?
How can I wait around for later?

Gerry had died without achieving his ambitions; her mother had died at the age of twenty-five, and even her father had opted for an arid death-in-life. Hadn't she resolved to change the pattern?

Confused, she tried to listen to Kate, but her daughter's words only reinforced the song.

'Of course they won't be shut, Mum. Stop making excuses and get yourself round there this instant! And in exactly two hours' time I'll be waiting by the phone. And I warn you, if you don't ring me, I'll ring you.'

'Oh Kate, I . . .'

'Ssh. No more arguments. Off you go.'

Catherine put the phone down in a daze. Kate was right. There was absolutely nothing to stop her rebooking a holiday. In fact she could hardly believe she'd been so stupid as not to think of it herself. She had become a noble martyr, upholding her commitment to a baby who wasn't even born yet. This way she could still honour the commitment, yet salvage something for herself.

She grabbed her jacket and the car keys, glancing at the stamps on Nicky's letter: one of them a prickly cactus bursting into flower. It was a crazy idea to go so far to visit Nicky, but she had to admit she *felt* crazy. And it would be a tremendous relief to discuss the whole dilemma with someone who understood. Nicky was less extreme than Rosie and was bound to sympathize. And she was the only person who knew Will well enough to make sense of what had happened. Apart from the chance to talk, it would be great to meet Dominic, and see some of the places Nicky described in her letters: roller-coaster mountains plunging down to the sea; sunsets straight out of *South Pacific*. She might even have a go at windsurfing . . .

Stuffing the letter in her pocket, she scooted out of the front door. At least she could enquire about the fare and if it turned out to be astronomical, well, as Kate had said, there were other exotic places.

As she started the car and pulled out of the drive, another song from the musical burst into her head.

There's a lot I'll have missed
But I'll not have been dead when I die!

'No, I certainly shan't,' she yelled, swinging out of the cul-de-sac and leaving Manor Close behind. 'Look out, world – here I come!'

VI

38

Churning with excitement, Catherine followed the others along a mysterious grey walkway. The floor sloped down, then turned a corner and before she knew it, two smiling stewardesses were welcoming her on board. Surely this couldn't be the plane? It seemed no more than a continuation of the claustrophobic passageway and looked impossibly small inside, considering it was a jumbo jet. But as she passed the stewardesses she saw rows of seats stretching into the distance. This *was* the plane – the first plane she had ever been on in her life.

She inched her way down the aisle, smiling like a child at anyone and everyone. Those other bored-looking passengers must be old hands at flying – *she* could hardly contain herself; her heart beating so loudly she was sure the whole plane could hear it.

Still grinning foolishly, she found row thirty-seven. Her seat was next to the window and the two adjacent ones were already occupied. She was pleased to see her neighbours looked congenial – an arty man dressed in black, with an interestingly weathered face, and a cosy plumpish woman in the aisle seat.

'Bit of a squash, I'm afraid,' said the man as she squeezed apologetically past his knees. She nodded, hoping he wouldn't be too chatty – not yet, anyhow. She wanted to savour every moment of this new experience. She put her bag under the seat, as she'd seen other people do. The zips would barely fasten, so much was crammed into its various compartments – presents from all and sundry, including Rosie, Brad and Will; eau de cologne from Maureen, a zoom compact camera from Andrew, and a supply of fresh fruit from Antonia to supplement the 'wickedly unhealthy' airline catering.

The drive to the airport had been something of a strain. Andrew and Antonia had made valiant efforts at light-hearted conversation – to disguise their dismay at what she was doing – but frankly she'd been relieved to see them go. There was a glorious sense of freedom in being on her own, as if she had shed a heavy burden. She didn't envy the couples around her, and certainly not the parents trying to cope with squabbling children. A harassed pair across the aisle were distributing colouring-books and crayons to their brood of little girls. She almost wished she had some crayons herself, something to calm her down.

She delved into the pocket in front of her knees and found a glossy magazine complete with route-maps, a pair of headphones and a mini sponge-bag containing an eye mask and a child-sized toothbrush with a miniature tube of toothpaste. Overhead a bank of tiny televisions was suspended from the ceiling. How intriguing it all was! And there were even . . .

'Ladies and gentlemen, would you please ensure that your seat-belts are fastened and that your seat is in the upright position.'

The announcement made her jump. They must be about to take off. But no – the disembodied voice went on to inform them that a safety demonstration would be shown on video and would they please give it their full attention. She gazed up at the screen, but could hardly take it in: all those gruesome details about emergency exits and oxygen supplies. Not that she was frightened, only exhilarated still. Once the drill was over, they were each served with a drink – a small plastic carton of orange juice with a peel-off lid – and a tiny packet of nuts. She was fascinated by the minute size of everything, as if they were children on a picnic and this was some marvellous game, not real life at all.

Before opening her juice, she took out Will's letter, now smudged and rather dog-eared. He still loved her, he still cared – cared enough to let her go and to rejoice in her adventure. The last sentence she knew by heart: 'Remember you're a work in progress, and this way you'll achieve your final form.'

He had also written her a poem. A love poem. A loss poem. He would never publish it, he'd said – it was hers alone to keep or chuck away. She read it once again, smiling at the reference to the camels; elated by the fact that, as his muse, she could still inspire such powerful words.

'Good morning, ladies and gentlemen . . .' A different voice was speaking now: a well-modulated female voice. 'Welcome aboard Air India 112 to Delhi. Our flying time today is . . .'

Delhi! She all but hugged herself in delight every time she heard that word. It had crackled over the tannoy in the departure lounge, flickered on the television monitors, and was printed on her ticket and her luggage labels, yet she still couldn't quite believe that she was actually on her way there. The proof was all around, though – the buzz of unknown languages, the many dark-skinned passengers: Sikhs in turbans, stewardesses resplendent in dazzling blue and orange saris (not the drably formal uniform she'd expected). In fact, with the sitar music floating in the background and the faint smell of curry wafting from the kitchens, it would be easy to imagine she was in India already. The safety drill had been given in both Hindi and English, and now an Indian travelogue was showing on the screen. A picture of the Taj Mahal suddenly jolted her back to the Stoneleigh travel agent's. She had been standing at the counter, poring over brochures of the Virgin Islands, when she'd happened to look up and see – yes, the Taj Mahal: a large poster in vivid colours, with COME TO INDIA! in red letters underneath.

'I'm sorry,' she had blurted out, 'but I've changed my mind. I want to go to India instead.'

If the man was confused, he didn't show it. After a few brief phone calls, he found her a special deal: a return ticket to Delhi for well under five hundred pounds. She had almost lost her nerve and bolted home – after all, she hadn't even consulted Kate or asked her permission to visit. Yet the man said he was closing in ten minutes and advised her not to leave it till the morning, in case the ticket was snapped up by someone else.

Again she had looked at the poster: COME TO INDIA! And it had seemed as if she was hearing Kate's own voice, assuring her it would be all right – the rebel daughter reunited with her rebel mother. And when she had made the promised phone call two hours later, Kate was over the moon, though incredulous at first. 'Stop kidding, Mum, and tell me the truth. You're going to see Nicky, aren't you?'

'No, I'm coming to see *you*. And then I'm going on a camel trek.' She had no intention of outstaying her welcome. Any hint of that and she would set off somewhere else. In any case, she wanted to see as much of the country as possible, Rajasthan especially, with its miles and miles of desert. Whatever else she missed out on, it wouldn't be the camel trek – she owed that to herself, and Will. Of course she could only travel as long as her money lasted, but Kate had told her that trains were cheap, buses cheaper, and that you could live on a shoestring if you didn't mind a sleeping-bag and a diet of dhal and chapatis. It might even be possible to find a job teaching English somewhere, which would pay for bed and board.

'When do we take off?' she asked a stewardess, as if she couldn't wait to exchange the clichéd illustrations in the brochures for the living, breathing reality.

'In about twenty minutes, madam.'

Why so long, she wondered. She had assumed the plane would depart as soon as everyone was on board, as trains and buses did.

'Impatient to get going?' the man beside her smiled.

She returned his smile. 'Yes, I am a bit.' Impatient to see Kate, who would be meeting her at Delhi airport a mere nine hours from now. That too seemed incredible.

'We're bound to be delayed. We always are.' The man passed her his *Independent*. 'Do look at this, if you want. It'll help to pass the time.'

'Thanks,' she said politely, noticing the day and date at the top. Could it really be Monday – no-nonsense back-to-work day? There ought to be a *new* day, a glittering, gold-star day for occasions such as this: Departure Day, Delhi Day, Reunion With Daughter Day.

She made a pretence of reading, though the words remained a blur and the front-page picture of Downing Street seemed to be overlaid with dromedaries and date palms. It was odd to have the time to sit flicking through a paper. The last couple of weeks she had been rushing from pillar to post getting her visa and immunisations, and saying goodbye to all her friends. And then there'd been the packing – deciding what to take for so many unknown situations and such a range of temperatures, yet needing to travel as light as possible. She glanced down at her Levis, amused to think how startled Kate would be to see her staid mother clad in blue jeans, with newly purpled hair.

A baby was crying in the bank of seats behind. The colicky wail provoked a surge of guilt, which she hastily suppressed. She might be back in time for her grandchild's birth, but there again she might not. She had no definite plans – that was the whole point of the trip. Christmas, too, she'd left open. Christmas at Stoneleigh was still a possibility, though Kate had urged her to stay on and share the celebrations at the centre – apparently quite an experience in itself. Or she might spend Christmas with friends as yet unknown, or in places only unpronounceable names on a map. Or even in the desert with the nomads.

'Ladies and gentlemen, we are about to proceed to the runway for take-off, so will you kindly ensure that your seat-belts are fastened.'

She gripped the buckle; fear and elation curdling in her stomach. There was a general air of expectancy as books were temporarily abandoned and people sat up straighter or craned their necks to look out of the windows. She too peered out as the plane began to move – barely perceptibly at first. It turned slowly to the left and all she could see was grey tarmac dotted with trucks and the hulks of other planes. Then it turned again and an expanse of scrub came into view, and a no-man's-land of storage sheds and withered yellow grass. The plane was still crawling along in a desultory fashion, as if in two minds about whether to leave. And then it came abruptly to a stop. She glanced round in alarm. Was something wrong? Please God, not a terrorist. Yet no one else seemed concerned, and anyway wouldn't . . . ?

Without warning there was a surge of noise and the plane lurched forward and began careering along the runway at terrifying speed. Everything juddered and rattled and she clutched the arms of her seat, convinced that they were about to crash. Then suddenly the bumping stopped, the ground fell away dramatically, and the plane leapt into the air like a magnificent new species of bird – the lumbering grey dinosaur transformed. She swivelled in her seat, bubbling with excitement – they were *flying*, actually flying. Her neighbours, though, appeared totally unmoved: the man already deep in a book and the woman in the aisle seat all but dozing off.

Amazed at their indifference, she turned back to the window, exulting as the plane climbed higher. She could feel herself ascending with it, escaping from her cul-de-sac; leaving the tedium of ordinary life far behind her, far below. Soon they were rising above the clouds and she was looking out at a vast white foamy duvet streaked with blue and amethyst. She watched, entranced; the sky stretching to infinity, boundless and eternal. There was a burst of blinding light as the sun blazed through the window. She was forced to shade her eyes; even so, she could feel its brilliance searing into her hand. And all at once she knew with utter conviction that she would not – must not – achieve a final shape. She must stay fluid like the sky, constantly changing and adapting, not settling into a wife-shape, a parent-shape, a grandma-shape, but remain for ever a work in progress. There would be uncertainties, false turnings, but they were a valuable part of the process, as Will had shown her in his work. She could go in any direction, respond to intuition, gain enlightenment from mistakes. Like a poet, she would be open to inspiration and willing to explore, to subvert the rules if need be.

Already she felt lighter, released from inflexible duties and the cage of convention. She continued to gaze out at the sky; the Midas-like sun turning everything to gold. *This* was the 'now', the ecstatic present moment she had barely grasped before, the art of living in full flower without the straitjacket of past or future. What she had failed to understand was that the 'now' was as real as grief and loss, and perhaps the only means of transcending them.

'Gerry,' she whispered, aware of his enduring presence – her beloved husband somewhere in that infinite sky, smiling in encouragement as she broke her last remaining chains and soared fearlessly away.